D0279619

THE LAST VIKING

Also by Berwick Coates:

The Last Conquest

THE LAST VIKING

BERWICK COATES

**SIMON &
SCHUSTER**

London · New York · Sydney · Toronto · New Delhi

A CBS COMPANY

First published in Great Britain by Simon & Schuster UK Ltd, 2014
A CBS COMPANY
Copyright © Berwick Coates 2014

13 5 7 9 10 8 6 4 2

Simon & Schuster UK Ltd
1st Floor
222 Gray's Inn Road
London WC1X 8HB

www.simonandschuster.co.uk

Simon & Schuster Australia, Sydney
Simon & Schuster India, New Delhi

A CIP catalogue record for this book is available from the British Library

HB ISBN: 978-1-47111-198-3
EBOOK ISBN: 978-1-47111-201-0

This book is a work of fiction. Names,
characters, places and incidents are either a product of
the author's imagination or are used fictitiously.

Typeset by Hewer Text UK Ltd, Edinburgh
Printed and bound in Great Britain by CPI Group (UK) Ltd, Croydon, CR0 4YY

To the many people I have taught over the years.

Education is a two-way business. Without their realising it,
they have taught me too.
For that I thank them. There is a tiny bit of each of them in
what I write.

List of characters

English-speaking characters

Harold Godwinson, King Harold II of England, January–
    October 1066
Gyrth Godwinson, Earl of Anglia, his brother
Leofwine, Earl of Kent, his brother
Stigand, Archbishop of Canterbury
Aldred, Archbishop of York
Gytha, Harold's mother
King Edward the Confessor
Edith, widow of King Edward the Confessor, Harold's
    sister
Edith (the 'Swan-Neck'), Harold's mistress
Mildred, widow of Llewellyn ap Gruffydd, later Harold's
    Queen, called herself 'Gwen'
Morcar, the new Earl of Northumbria, after the banishment of
    Tostig (q.v.)
Edwin, Earl of Mercia, brother of Morcar and Mildred
Wulfstan, Bishop of Worcester
Edric, Reeve (nowadays 'Mayor') of Scarborough
Coelwen, Edric's daughter
Thora, Coelwen's maid
Gunnar Palsson, a businessman of Scarborough
Vendel, Gunnar's son

Bernard of Lorraine, canon of Waltham Abbey, head of
 Harold's intelligence service
Brother Conrad, a novice of Waltham Abbey
Brother Eustace, an agent of Bernard's
The Prior of an abbey near Scarborough
Wilfrid and Oswy, two housecarls in Harold's entourage
Owen and Llew, two Welsh archers
Alfred, a young fyrdman (in the simplest terms, a part-time
 soldier)
Other fyrdmen, unnamed
Two sea captains in Harold's spy fleet
A sergeant in Harold's army

English non-speaking characters

The Witan of London and York, the King's councils of advisers
 – the men of 'wit'
The children of Harold and his mistress Edith
Wulfnoth, Harold's youngest brother, a hostage at the court of
 William of Normandy
Sweyn, Harold's older brother, died mysteriously on pilgrimage

Norwegian-speaking characters

Ellisif, Queen of Norway, daughter of Prince Jaroslav of Kiev
Maria, daughter of Ellisif and Harald Sigurdsson (q.v.)
Tostig, renegade brother of King Harold, an ally of Hardrada
Sigurd, an adventurer
Magnus, a refugee from a blood feud, who joins Sigurd's band
Finn, Lars, Ketil 'Splitnose', Ivar, Tore, Haldor and Hakon, all
 members of Sigurd's band
Jarl Thorfinn ('the Mighty'), ruler of the Orkney and Shetland
 Islands, a vassal of Hardrada
Rolf of Bergen, one of Hardrada's longship captains

Norwegian and other foreign non-speaking characters

Harald Sigurdsson (Hardrada), King of Norway
Aud, his second ('handfast') wife
An axeman, who defends the bridge at Stamford
Judith, wife of Tostig
Baldwin, Count of Flanders, brother of Judith and father of
    Matilda of Normandy
Paul, son of Thorfinn of Orkney
Olaf, son of Hardrada
Malcolm, King of Scotland
Ragnar, a Viking feud enemy of Sigurd
Sigrid, sister of Magnus
Sweyn, King of Denmark
William, Duke of Normandy – 'the Bastard'
Matilda, his wife
William Fitzosbern, William's chief adviser
Lanfranc, Abbot of Caen, another adviser of William's
Pope Alexander II

Chapter One

When Magnus woke, he was already choking. How could it have happened so fast? How could he have slept so long before the smoke brought him to his senses? As he threw aside the bed covers, he knocked over an empty pot.

That told him – the drinking. He did not remember going to bed, but he certainly remembered the drinking beforehand. Now the thickness in his throat and lungs was as bad as the hammering in his head. The one made it as hard to breathe as the other made it hard to think.

As he struggled to an upright position, he glanced instinctively at the remains of the fire in the hearth. No – no threat there. Swaying on his feet, he stooped and peered.

Now it was the noise that told him. Up above his head. The smoke billowed away his view, but he could hear the roaring and crackling. The dread of any thatch roofed hall – which meant almost every hall in creation. The greater dread of the night: if it was bad indoors, what would it be like outside? What threats awaited?

He tried pathetically to wave away the worst of the smoke before his face, but his eyes told him little; it was his ears that gave him the news. First, the roaring, which he had already noticed. Then the padding of rapid feet, throwing up yet more confusion from the rushes on the floor. The voices – the shouting, the panting, the bellowing of men trying to make some

1

kind of order, any kind of order, out of a rushing sea of pain and ignorance; the wailing, the screaming of every mother in bafflement and dread; the crying and whimpering of young panic.

Then, through the confusion, he began to make out another sound – from outside. There were people out there. And they were not there to help. Screams of agony reached him. So – it was the typical treachery: a knife in the throat of the sentry; burning brands tossed up onto the roof; ambushes round the door; and a hideous choice for the inmates, who were not going to be baffled for long.

It was burn or bleed.

Magnus took in the situation the instant his head began to clear and his brain began to work. It had been a mere matter of time before things came to a head like this. The only surprise was that it had happened so quickly. They had only just finished celebrating their own recent triumph in the escalating feud that had run on for nearly two years: early, perhaps even unwitting, offences to etiquette; later calculated insults; challenges, contests, brawls; rick burnings, assaults on cattle – the usual things. Then the squalid death in ambush, the reprisal, the counter-reprisal. Gradually growing. And now this. The last play of all.

Magnus knew all about family feuds: he had been born into them and he had grown up with them. Every instinct told him that this attack had been badly planned. Because of that, every instinct also told him that this was Ragnar's work. It reeked of haste and rage. Ragnar's father would have watched and waited. But he was getting old. Ragnar had lost patience, and had taken the matter into his own hands. The old man had not been able to stop him.

So the attack had come on the heels of the previous incident. Far too quickly. Little planning. Ragnar's temper – his bristling black beard and his blazing eyes had taken over. A hundred things could go wrong in the dark. It gave Magnus and his clan just one chance.

All this passed through Magnus's beating head in barely a blink of an eye. As he raced to the back of the hall, he sensed other figures doing the same. It was too thick to recognise individual faces or figures, but he recognised voices. They too had made the same rapid decision.

A dozen hands tore at the hangings that masked the rear door. A dozen more snatched weapons off the walls.

Suddenly Magnus stopped. He had heard another sound. Sigrid. He would know his sister's voice anywhere, even, as now, in mortal terror. For all he knew, in pain, too. It was coming from above.

He rushed back to a ladder. As he climbed to the women's loft, the smoke became thicker. His eyes ran. Pieces of burning beams fell past him. The noise became infernal. Sigrid's voice lashed him into further effort. Flaming straw fell all over him. Panting and grimacing with anguish and near-blindness, he bellowed Sigrid's name.

Two bodies lay before him. He turned them over violently, looked in their faces, and almost threw them back into their previous position. One jagged scream reached him from the deepest part of the loft.

He tore a skirt from one of the bodies, wrapped it round his hands, and wrenched flame-licked timber out of his way.

There she was. But there would be no more screams. He knew he would have dreams about the death mask of her face.

After only a moment to shake his head and think, he rushed back to the ladder and scrambled down. As he did so, more noises came to him – from outside. So the hidden rear door had taken the attackers by surprise. In a hell of flames and fury, the defenders hurled themselves on the murderers of their wives and families. It did not matter whether it was the flames or the steel that had killed; the crime was the same. The attackers, caught unawares and thoroughly unnerved, swung and hacked in random desperation. Any survivors of those terrible minutes would have had to confess later that they had not always seen the person they were cutting down.

Magnus, pausing in the doorway, and gasping in some air that was at least slightly thinner than the poison clouding his throat, surprised himself with how clearly he was thinking.

Everything he had held dear was gone. What was there for him now? One thing and one thing alone – revenge. That meant staying alive. There was no point in searching out the culprit in that pitch-night, yelling throng a few paces away. How could he know who he was killing? No. He wanted more than that. Certainty – face-to-face certainty. He wanted the leader of the raid. He wanted the author of the outrage. He wanted that black bastard Ragnar. And he wanted Ragnar to be certain who it was who was going to kill him.

He had no idea how many attackers there were, but there were certainly too many. He needed time and leisure, and better odds, for what he had in mind. But not now. Later. The need now was to get away.

It was a fairly safe guess that they were all too involved in the continuing slaughter to notice any change in the throng. And now he could turn the smoke into an ally.

A few paces in the opposite direction was the well. As men bawled and bled and fell, a shadowy figure slipped over the low wall, let down the bucket, and fastened the rope to the pulley. It would be a cold vigil down there, but any attacker who survived would be most unlikely to pull up a bucket of water to douse a fire that he had deliberately started. Besides, the fire had by now taken complete control; no surviving defender would even begin to look for water; a hundred buckets, a thousand, were going to be no use now.

Whatever his chances, he now had no choice but to wait. And hope.

*   *   *

Earl Harold of Wessex looked at each of his brothers in turn.

'So Tostig will have to go?'

'Yes,' said Gyrth. Leofwine nodded.

Harold beckoned a clerk towards him. 'I shall convey our – our recommendations to the King.'

Suddenly the door opened, and the Lady Gytha swept in. All three sons rose. Gytha seated herself in front of the fire, and beckoned to a scurrying maid to arrange her skirts. The sons sat down again. For a moment nobody spoke. Gytha at last broke the silence. 'Well?'

Harold braced himself. 'Mother, Tostig will have to go.'

'Why?' A challenging stare. She was not making it easy.

Harold sighed briefly. 'You know perfectly well why. Tostig has been impossible. He has put his earldom in revolt. Half Northumbria is up in arms.'

'And the other half? What is wrong with that?'

Harold glanced briefly at his brothers before replying. 'He has abused his authority.'

'He is a good leader of men,' said Gytha. 'You said so yourself. You depended on him in the Welsh campaign.'

Their mother was patching up an argument, and they all knew it. Harold tried again.

'Tostig is a good soldier and a good leader of men *in action*. But he is a bad ruler. He does not give his subjects justice.'

Gytha folded her hands across her stomach. Always a bad sign. 'Nonsense. You have been plotting against him. You and –' she gestured towards Gyrth and Leofwine '– and your *loving* brothers.'

It was always the same. Gytha was lashing out because her precious Tostig had been slighted. All sound sense went out of the window. It had always been the same: all Tostig ever had to do was shake his blond curly locks, flash his charming smile, make a flattering joke, and his mother, and his sister Edith, were clay in his hands.

'Plotting,' repeated Gytha, as if the mere repetition added force to her argument.

'Mother, that is not fair,' said Gyrth. 'I am Earl of East Anglia. Leofwine is Earl of Kent. Harold is Earl of Wessex. What time do we have to plot against anybody? We hardly see each other from one month to the next.'

'And Tostig is Earl of Northumbria,' added Leofwine. 'We wanted Tostig to succeed. Four brothers between them holding nearly all England. It would have been beyond Father's wildest dreams.'

Gytha looked at Harold. 'You are condoning a rebellion. And you have always said the rebellion is the greatest threat to the peace of any country.'

'True,' said Harold. 'But God makes it clear that a ruler has responsibilities. A ruler swears an oath – to bring peace and justice to his subjects. And this Tostig has not done. By the Rood, mother, he has had ten years to do it. He has failed. He is the one upsetting his country, not his people. Certainly not us. We must have peace.'

'So you are getting rid of him.'

'We are recommending this course of action to the King.'

Gytha leaned back to emphasise her scorn. 'Rubbish. Edward will do exactly what you tell him. He is so ill now that he barely knows the time of day.'

'We shall do what is best for England – all England,' said Harold, though even as he said it he felt rather pious.

Gytha scorched him with another glance. 'All England. You mean *your* England.'

'*Our* England,' corrected Harold. 'The kingdom of the English. If we are divided, we shall not be short of enemies to take advantage of it.'

Gytha's attitude changed from disdain to sarcasm. 'And banishing Tostig will of course strengthen England against all its enemies.'

'Tostig will be replaced,' said Harold patiently.

'Oh?' said Gytha. 'And who are you . . . recommending to take his place?'

Harold refused to be drawn. 'Morcar,' he said. 'Earl Edwin's brother.'

Gytha raised a sardonic eyebrow. 'That, I am sure, will be a great improvement. Has he begun to shave yet?'

'He is nineteen,' said Harold evenly. 'And he has learned a great deal at Edwin's side in Mercia.'

'Then I am sure he will be an enormous improvement. We need have no further worries about the future of "our" England. Come, girl.'

Gytha nearly upset the kneeling servant as she stood up. All three sons once again rose as she left.

As the door was shut by a sentry, Gyrth looked at Harold. 'We have not heard the last of that.'

Harold nodded wryly. 'We shall not have heard the last of Tostig, either.'

Leofwine smiled. 'I wish I could be there when he is told. What do you think he will do?'

'Swear revenge, I should imagine. That would be Tostig's style.'

Gyrth corrected him. 'He will go to Flanders and cry on Judith's shoulder first.'

'Only for a while. No wife, however devoted, will put up with Tostig's tears for long.'

'Then what?' said Leofwine.

'Then, brother,' said Harold, 'we brace ourselves for whatever Tostig gets up to. One thing is sure: he will be thinking far more about Northumbria than he has been doing for the last ten years. Now that he has lost it.'

The early Norwegian night made the snow colder. It also obscured the hut, nearly surrounded as it was by the tall pines. Magnus almost walked past it. His near-exhaustion clouded his vision. In daylight, or with his full faculties, he would easily have noticed the tracks turning off the main trail towards it.

Grunting with the effort as he turned from the trail, he heaved his leaden limbs around, and began to wade through the deeper snow. As he approached, his nose caught the smell of woodsmoke. Then he noticed the shutter, from which shafts of light shot into the shadows outside. Such was the gloom that they glowed brighter than they really were.

As Magnus hammered on the door, the noise of voices inside stopped at once. Then there was a rustle of movement, followed by metallic noises. Weapons were being drawn.

A beam was lifted, and the door opened. A tall figure stood framed in the light from a handful of candles on a rough table behind him.

'Well?'

'Shelter, if only for a few hours,' said Magnus.

The figure did not move or speak.

'Please,' said Magnus. He was swaying with fatigue.

Somebody got up from the table and laid aside a dagger. Magnus vaguely heard somebody say, 'Catch him.'

When he opened his eyes, he felt as if he had been asleep for a week. He felt a glow of warmth, turned his head, and saw rough-hewn logs crackling near his nose.

Crying in anguish, he recoiled in horror, and found himself on his feet. The sheepskins in which he had been wrapped still dangled from his shoulders.

The tall man from the doorway got up from the table and looked him up and down.

'Ah, you are with us, then?'

Magnus, still not in full control, gazed at him in incomprehension.

The man gestured towards the hearth. 'Too hot for you?'

Magnus pulled himself together. 'What? No. No. I have been recently in – in a fire.'

The tall man nodded. 'Still scorched, eh?'

'Something like that.'

The tall man beckoned him to the table. 'I am Sigurd, son of Bjorn. Who are you?'

Magnus, after a moment of hesitation, slid off the sheepskins, and sat down. 'I am Magnus, son of Vidkun, from Halland.'

There was a stir of interest from those round the table.

'You are a long way from home,' said Sigurd.

'I am on a quest,' said Magnus. 'I have no home.'

'Nonsense,' said Sigurd. 'Everybody starts somewhere.'

'My home was burned. I am on a quest.'

Sigurd leaned back and nodded. 'Ah. The scorch marks. The family feud, eh?'

Another murmur rippled round the table.

Sigurd pushed a platter towards him. 'Are you strong enough now to eat?'

Magnus began to wolf some cold meat and cheese. As he chewed he eyed his companions. They all looked the same – young, tough, able-bodied and very rough round the edges.

Sigurd in turn looked at Magnus, and formed the same impression – young, tough, able-bodied and extremely rough round the edges. A likely recruit. He read the recruit's thoughts.

'Yes, I agree. We look almost as untidy as you do. But we are warm and well fed.'

Magnus nodded, still chewing.

'But you could be too, if you wish,' said Sigurd.

Magnus read Sigurd's thoughts this time. 'You mean, join your gang?'

Sigurd laughed. 'Come now, dear boy, do we look as scruffy as that? But yes, that is what I do mean. Let me introduce some of our – er – our company. Hakon, Haldor, Finn, Lars.' He gestured up and down the table. 'That one with the split nose is Ketil. That is what we call him – Splitnose.'

There was a rumble of laughter. Magnus nodded to everyone.

'What do you do?' he asked.

'We should like to know what we do too,' said Finn. 'We have not moved for five days.'

'For a start,' said Sigurd, 'you can get outside and have a scout round. It is high time.'

Finn scowled, but obeyed. When he had gone, Sigurd turned back to Magnus.

'I am working on that,' said Sigurd. 'Our company is not big enough yet for what I have in mind. I need more men. What about it?'

Magnus summed up the situation for himself. This man Sigurd was building. Building a – he was right in a way – a company. A knot of beefy young men who could be turned to many kinds of venture, wherever there might be profit or advantage of one kind or another. In a country like Norway, where the King's writ did not run universally, there was plenty of scope for such bands. Not outlaws exactly. But groups of adventurers who had an eye to the main chance – sentry work, labouring in boatyards, escort duty, mercenary soldiering, frontier guard, debt collecting – anything where not many questions were asked so long as the goods were delivered. Their success usually depended on the wits and the luck of the man who led them. And Sigurd's attitude suggested that he did indeed have the wits and the luck.

With the Norwegian winter well on its course, he would have his work cut out to hold them together, because the work was harder now to come by. But he looked superbly confident in his own ability to do so. Magnus felt drawn towards him. First things, however, came first.

'Well?' said Sigurd.

Magnus took a cup offered by Hakon, he thought it was, and nodded in thanks.

'Thank you, but no. I am grateful to you for probably saving my life, but I am not in a position to show I am grateful. Not yet.'

Sigurd smiled. 'Not till you have found the bastard, eh?'

Magnus nodded.

'So be it,' said Sigurd. He gestured to those at the table. 'Tell us about him. One of us might have seen something.'

'Ragnar his name is. About our age. Big. Bristling beard. Sharp eyes. Very sharp. A temper.'

'Drink, does he?' said Ketil, interested.

Magnus laughed. 'Like all of us.'

'No,' said Ketil. 'Not like all of us. This man leaves the fish behind.'

Magnus looked keenly at him. 'A temper, too?'

Ketil nodded. 'He nearly split my nose again.'

Magnus pounced. 'Where?'

'Up around Hordaland. At least I think so. Towards the sea anyway. I do not have a very clear memory.'

'Drinking with him, were you, Splits?'

Everyone chuckled.

'Hordaland?' said Magnus.

Sigurd nodded. 'Two or three days' ride. Over a week on foot, I should say.'

'I shall get there,' said Magnus.

'Do that,' said Sigurd. 'And, when you have finished, come back here. We can use you.'

'Not interested,' said Magnus.

Sigurd did not blink. 'You will be – when you have done what you want to do.'

'No.'

'Just you wait. While the flame of vengeance burns, it keeps you warm. When it goes out, you feel colder than ever. You must put something in its place to keep you alive.'

Magnus was not convinced. 'We shall see.'

Sigurd dusted his hands and poured out some more beer. 'We shall indeed, dear boy. You go in the morning with our blessing. Meantime, eat yourself to a standstill. Who knows when you will eat again?'

He stood up and gestured around the hut.

'Sleep where you like. But not too close to the fire, eh?'

Harold looked at the young man across the table.

'Well? Can you do it?'

Morcar blinked. 'How should I know?'

'Your brother says you can.'

Edwin, Earl of Mercia, grunted in agreement.

Morcar tugged at a wisp of beard below his lower lip.

'I will be on hand,' said Edwin. 'Mercia is next door.'

Morcar swallowed. 'But – the whole of Northumbria. And an invasion on the way.'

'I did not say Tostig would invade,' said Harold.

Not yet, thought Gyrth at the end of the table. But it will not be long, if I know Tostig.

Harold leaned forward. 'You will have time. It is not fighting I want you to do: it is fortifying. I want all the north-east coastal defences overhauled. We must be ready.'

What for, thought Leofwine. Tostig? The Danes? Count Baldwin of Flanders? Could Tostig inveigle his father-in-law to mount an invasion?

Morcar glanced for reassurance to his brother.

'But will they accept me?'

'Aldred in York will see to that. He can stage-manage the northern Witan.'

He probably can, thought Gyrth. Members of the Witan, for all their high rank, would be reluctant to go against the will of an archbishop, especially one with Aldred's clout.

'Talk to them,' urged Harold. 'Get them aside, one by one. Explain that we must have security. Half of them at least must be relieved that we have got rid of Tostig. The other half will think twice before they get involved in plots to get him back.'

Morcar made a face. 'But Northumbria is so big.'

'I shall send Stigand as well.'

Morcar stared. 'Another archbishop?'

Harold made a dismissive gesture. 'Canterbury can spare him. Besides, Stigand is much happier in his counting house than he is in his cathedral. He will raise the necessary taxes for you. I want you to concentrate on the defences. Grimsby, Scarborough, Whitby, Durham – right up to Berwick.'

Morcar's jaw dropped. Harold grinned.

'I am not asking you to do it alone. Edwin will give you some housecarls. Gyrth will deal with East Anglia. There are local reeves and fyrds. The one at Scarborough, I hear, is very good.'

Morcar grasped at a straw. 'Why can you not be here? With your authority—'

'I must go south,' said Harold. 'The new minster. The consecration. We must make a good show.'

Gyrth and Leofwine exchanged glances. Harold had to be there in London. The only show the King was likely to display was a sign that he was going to meet the very St Peter to whom his new minster was dedicated.

Harold fixed Morcar with a sharp eye. 'I am giving *you* the authority.'

It really should be the King giving the authority, but everyone there knew that the King was in no position to do so.

Morcar gave a final tug to his wisp of beard, and heaved a huge sigh.

'Very well.'

'Good man.' Harold stopped himself just in time from saying 'good lad'. He stood up and began to gather his outdoor clothes. 'Oh – and one other thing. As soon as you have set all that in motion, I want you in London. If not by Christmas, then certainly by the end of the Twelve Days.'

Morcar nodded and blew out his cheeks. God's Teeth, this man certainly knew how to get history on the move.

Edric might have expected Gunnar to call.

Gunnar wasted no time on ceremony. 'Well, where is your precious law?'

'Where it has always been – in the hands of the King.'

'And now?'

'Where it should be – in the hands of his new Earl of Northumbria.'

Edric, the Reeve of Scarborough, sat back and gazed at his visitor. Gunnar Palsson was not an impressive sight – short, squat, with a stoop and a thick neck. He looked as if someone had dropped a heavy weight on him at a very early age.

He had been causing trouble ever since the revolt against Earl Tostig had broken out. The countryside was seething with whisper and rumour. Even the appointment of Morcar as the new earl had not stopped the tongues wagging.

'What are you going to do about it?' asked Gunnar as soon as he heard the news.

'What I have always done – uphold the law.'

Gunnar spat. 'You hypocrite! You hated Tostig; admit it.'

'I hated his injustices. But I did not join the revolt.'

'You helped the rebellion just as if you had joined it. You wanted him banished as much as I did.'

'I did not banish him – the King did.' He pushed a cup across the table. 'Drink?'

Gunnar opened his mouth to make a sharp rejoinder, thought better of it, and poured out some beer. Then he had an idea, and came in from a different direction.

'I know why you sit on the fence. Making sure of your – interests.'

Edric gave him as good as he got.

'Gunnar, the law is not a fence to sit on: it is a barrier against chaos. Morcar is now the law. And, whatever the situation, we all make sure of our interests. I value peace and quiet because I hold my land direct from the King; I am a freeman. So are half the citizens in Scarborough, whose welfare I am sworn, as reeve, to uphold. Those are my interests. You are the newcomer; you wait to take advantage of turmoil. Stir the pot, and see what tempting morsels float to the surface.'

Gunnar flushed – thirty years, and still the newcomer. He put down his cup with a bang.

'I came here to talk sense to you, and to talk business. Tostig is gone. We have a boy in his place. It is up to us, as men of affairs, to chase our own fate, make our own fortune. Two minds are better than one on a problem like this.'

Edric shook his head. 'If the heads were turned in the same direction, Gunnar, I agree. But they are not. I look out for Scarborough; you look out for the main chance.'

Gunnar kept his temper with an effort.

'You fool. Who will pat you on the back for "looking out for Scarborough", as you put it? Morcar will have much more on his plate than the fate of a tiny coastal town facing the North Sea, with barely a thousand souls in it. And how many kings of England have visited Yorkshire, never mind Scarborough, in the last hundred years? I tell you, Edric, we are on our own.'

'With our own honour and our own code.'

'Listen to me, Edric. I came here not to argue but to offer partnership. Together we can, with luck and God's favour, do ourselves a spot of good.'

He leaned forward to make his point. The boils on his scaly cheeks stood out from his whiskered face.

15

Edric smiled ironically. 'Go on then, Gunnar. Make our fortunes. Tell me your master plan.'

Gunnar missed the irony. 'I have lots of plans.' He spread his hands. 'Look at me.'

Edric preferred not to, but waited.

'I came here with nothing. Nothing.'

Well, that much was true. Gunnar had been pitched out on the shore from a Swedish merchant ship about thirty years before. Nobody knew what he had done to get himself thrown off, and a week's acquaintance with him was enough to tell anybody that he was not going to give a believable, much less truthful, account of it.

'And I have made something of myself.'

That was true, too. To his credit, Gunnar had worked, and worked hard. Nobody had a sharper eye for an opportunity, or a harder fist when it came to bargaining. One thing had led to another. A lucky chance here, a flinty deal there, a shady profit somewhere else. He was the perfect illustration of the old adage that where there was dirt on top there was silver underneath, and Gunnar never minded how dirty he made his hands.

'I am established. I am known.'

At the end of thirty years, he was known all right. Generally disliked, too. And he was certainly established. If Edric represented the freemen of half Scarborough, Gunnar the Swede now owned the other half.

No presentable Scarborough girl would go near him, so he had married a local ugly duckling, just at the moment when her father was steeling himself to fork out for the hefty charge that the local convent would make to take her in. Then along had come Gunnar, with his usual faultless timing, willing not only to marry her (knowing shrewdly that she would be as grateful as her father), but to waive the dowry as well. Offers like that did not come a father's way every day of the week.

The fruit of the union – not a particularly happy one – was a stringy, chinless son who had many of his father's unprepossessing ways but little of his drive. He was not helped by the fact that he stood by in embarrassed silence again and again while his father made offers to neighbouring parents with marriageable daughters. Everybody knew in his head that, with all his father's property in the offing, the boy was a good prospect; but one look at him told them, and their daughters, all they needed to know. It was a pity to say no to all that money, but the price was far too high. Every instinct revolted. Not even the plain girls wanted him.

Edric was not surprised when Gunnar came out with his next sentence.

'Tell me, Coelwen has a birthday coming up, does she not? An important one.'

Magnus heard the hoofbeats, even though they were partly muffled by the snow. Prudently, he hid under some trees beside the trail.

The party of horsemen drew level with him. He was amazed to see that it was Sigurd and his band. He had a vague memory of some names from Sigurd's casual introductions – Tore, Ivar, Haldor, Finn, Lars – though he could not put the names to the faces. Except Ketil. He certainly recognised Ketil and his split nose.

Sigurd stood in the stirrups and looked about him. 'You might as well come out, Magnus. We know you are there.'

Magnus did so, brushing from his shoulders the snow that had fallen from the branches covering him. 'How did you know?'

Sigurd laughed. 'With the trail you left, you might as well have put up signposts.'

'What are you doing here?'

'Looking for you.'

'Why?'

Sigurd cast a glance to his left and right, as if to collect everyone's agreement.

'We were afraid you might get lost.'

There was a general chuckle. Magnus regained his composure.

'Why?' he repeated more meaningly.

Sigurd laughed again. 'We are afraid you might get into trouble, chasing that nasty Ragnar. We thought we could keep an eye on you.'

'Tell that to the trolls,' said Magnus. 'You are out riding because you are bored to death in that god-forsaken hut.'

Sigurd beamed. 'Absolutely right. Ask Finn here. He has been getting more and more cussed with each passing day.'

Finn had the good grace to grin wryly by way of acknowledgement.

Sigurd cast a gesture about the group. 'We were short of horses, too. So I thought what a good idea to go out and look for some.'

'You mean to steal some.'

Sigurd shrugged. 'If you insist. A mere question of words. The result is the same.'

'You stole them.'

'Have it your own way,' said Sigurd. 'But it kept them busy, eh?' He looked at Finn. 'Killed two birds with one stone. Besides, we needed more mobility.'

Finn shook his head at Sigurd's blatant frankness. It was difficult to argue with the truth.

'So,' continued Sigurd, 'I thought, while we were out, and going west towards Hordaland, why not look for our new friend Magnus, and see if he needs any support from us? It would exercise the horses, too.'

Magnus bristled. 'I need no help for what I am going to do.'

'Surely not,' agreed Sigurd. 'But you can use a meal, I would wager.'

Magnus too found it difficult to argue with the truth. But, unlike Finn, he fought a short rearguard action.

'You are after me,' he said. 'You want me to join your scruffy little band.'

Sigurd beamed again. 'Of course. I need good men. And you are good, or I am much mistaken. Join us, and we shall be that much less . . . "little".'

'Only scruffy,' said Finn.

They all laughed then, and dismounted. As kindling was being collected and a fire prepared, Magnus spoke quietly to Sigurd.

'Will this little jaunt keep them occupied?'

'Not for long,' Sigurd freely admitted. 'But there are times when one lives for the next hour. And this is one of them. Something will turn up.'

'Like me.'

'Possibly. But look on the positive side. We can help you search for him.'

'Ragnar?'

'Yes.'

'Stay out of my way.'

'Keep your temper for Ragnar. When we find him, we shall not interfere. I can even lend you a horse while we are looking.'

'That does not mean I shall join you afterwards,' said Magnus.

'I am prepared to take that chance,' said Sigurd. 'I play the odds.'

Magnus frowned. 'What do you mean?'

'You are young, strong, without any ties of kin. No home. No assets. You will have to find action somehow. When you have got this bug out of your system, you will go looking for it. Here I am, with a good offer. I think the odds are in my favour.'

Magnus had to force a grin. 'You cocky swine.'

Sigurd beamed for the third time. 'So my friends tell me.'

Wilfrid the housecarl heaved his huge shoulders in a sigh of relief, and whispered out of the corner of his mouth to his cousin Oswy.

'Well, they are all in at last. Did you ever see such a gathering? I have spotted thegns here who have not shown their face at the Witan for years.'

Oswy lifted his eyebrows towards the soaring towers of the King's new minster.

'That is what brought them. Curiosity.' He gestured with his head at the huge crowd that scores of other housecarls were keeping back with the handles of their axes.

Wilfrid resisted the temptation to spit. It would not be seemly, he decided, for a member of a guard of honour. Somebody might get the wrong idea.

'Curiosity? Balls. Curiosity may be what brought this lot – the gawpers. But that is not what brought all those in there.' He nodded towards the great west door, which many hands were now in the process of closing.

There came the order to stand down until the service of consecration was over. The twin lines of housecarls broke up into threes and fours, but stayed near the west door. They rested their axes and rubbed calloused hands chapped with the cold. It was noticeable that Earl Harold's housecarls did not mingle with those of the King.

This time Wilfrid did spit, but out of comfort, not disagreement. Now that he was not on parade, he was in a less argumentative mood.

'It is some building, I agree. But I still prefer St Paul's. More homely. You are used to it.'

'All new things take getting used to,' said Oswy.

'Like a new king,' said Wilfrid.

Oswy blinked. 'What?'

'Oh, come on, cousin. Why do you think they are all standing in there and pretending to be gazing in dumb wonder at everything?' He mimicked a herald making an announcement. '"His Majesty's Great New West Minster of London."' He relaxed again. 'Only His Majesty is not there, is he? And everyone knew His Majesty would not be there. Because everyone knows His Majesty is on his last legs – if he is on his legs at all.'

Oswy nodded sadly. 'Poor man. So he may never see it. Never enter the church he has been possessed with for years.'

Wilfrid grunted. 'Oh, he will enter it all right.'

Oswy looked sharply at him. 'You mean—?'

'I do. And we shall get freezing cold mounting a guard of honour for that too.'

Oswy made a face. 'Shame, though. All that time, all that effort, all that hope and devotion – and all you get is a tomb.'

'Saints do not see it that way. I am sure Edward will not mind.'

Oswy looked surprised. 'He is not a saint.'

'He will be, cousin. He will be – mark my words. But they will not be thinking about that, either. They will be thinking about the next king – whoever that is. It is not possible that they can be thinking of anything else.'

Oswy looked shocked and disgusted. 'God – who would go into politics? Thinking about a coronation and we have not buried the other one yet. He is not even dead.'

'It is not politics: it is common sense. We must not have an empty throne. Edward will probably not last till the New Year, never mind till Easter, and the next Witan will not be till then. We can not have an empty throne for three months. It would be asking for trouble.'

'You mean the Bastard?'

'Possibly. So far he has made no move – or none that we have heard of. But the story of the promise is common knowledge.

Edward was knee-deep in Normans for years. He spoke better French than he did English. He could easily have made that promise. It would certainly suit William to say so. But he can make no move till Edward dies. It would look bad. And a bastard can not afford to look bad.'

Oswy nodded, following his argument. 'And then there is the Atheling.'

Wilfrid sniffed. 'Edgar the Atheling. Ha! Last prince of the ancient House of Cerdic.' He laid ironic stress on the last words. 'Twelve years old. Raised in Hungary. I doubt if he even speaks decent English.'

'Blood royal,' said Oswy.

'We want a man, not a boy. If we get the Atheling, just think how many people would be licking their chops – in Flanders, Denmark, Scotland. And I would wager our beloved Tostig would soon be sticking his dirty little finger into the pie.'

Wilfrid flung out his arm towards the new minster. 'And every earl, thegn, bishop and abbot in there knows it. They know that, whoever each one of them wants as king, they must agree on having *someone* before they go home.'

'So it will be Harold?'

'We hope so,' said Wilfrid. 'But then we are biased. What about that lot over there?' He gestured towards the King's housecarls. 'We do not know where their sympathies lie – with England or with the King's Norman friends.'

Oswy looked shocked again. 'But they are English.'

'So is Edward. That does not prevent him from having Norman friends. And who knows – Norman sympathies. Just because Harold's father kicked most of them out, that does not mean that Edward will not try to get his own back. Saint he may be, but he is also devious. I would never trust him. In fact I would never trust half the men in England.'

Oswy made a face. 'Oh, come on, Wilfrid.'

Wilfrid would not be moved. 'Just because you live in England it does not make you English. What about all those in Northumbria? Dammit – *we* live in Northumbria. We ourselves are a handful of generations removed from the Danes.'

'But they are not housecarls like us.'

'True. We are privileged, so we are loyal. But think, Oswy: we have had four Danish kings this century.'

Oswy looked glum. 'You make it sound as if we do not have a hope.'

Wilfrid grinned. 'Oh, we have a hope all right. And the name of this hope is Harold. He is the one they must vote for. And Harold will see to it in the next few days that they do.'

'If they are good Englishmen, they will do that, surely?'

Wilfrid shook his head. 'But they are not all good Englishmen, as I said. Half of them will be saying to themselves, "What will be the best solution for me?" They will need persuading.'

'Persuading?'

'That Harold is the obvious next king. But being obvious does not make it easy.'

Oswy looked even more miserable. 'Still a poor prospect, then?'

Wilfrid grinned again. 'And I shall tell you something to make it even worse.'

'What is that?' asked Oswy, not at all sure that he wanted to know the answer.

'We are forgetting that Edward has actually got to die. If he is not on his deathbed already. And kings on deathbeds make statements. Statements which are very, very powerful.'

Oswy lifted his eyebrows in a cheerless grimace. 'So we have to hope that the King will name Harold in his last words.'

'If he is in a state to mutter any last words at all.' Wilfrid looked around him. 'God, I wonder how long they are going to be. This cold weather. I am dying for a piss.'

*   *   *

Gyrth Godwinson, Earl of East Anglia, took off his cloak, sat down, and kicked a wayward log back into the centre of the flames.

'It can not be long now. Scarcely any food has passed his lips for six days.'

'How is Edith taking it?' said Leofwine.

Gyrth looked sharply at him. 'Doing what our dear sister has been doing for years – playing the devoted wife. Clasping his hand, stroking his brow, massaging his feet, and weeping when anybody is looking. When she runs out of ideas, she sits at the foot of the bed and prays.'

'Is that not rather hard of you?'

'You wait and see,' said Gyrth. 'She is talking Edward and thinking Tostig.'

Leofwine made a noise of disgust. 'What can she do?'

Gyrth looked grim. 'I am older than you. I have known her longer than you have. There is no limit to what our sister might be prepared to do – or at least attempt. She is Queen, for a start. She is closest to Edward. Who knows what she has been whispering into his sick ears for weeks? Certainly since Tostig was banished. I tell you, Edith never gives up.'

Leofwine laughed. 'Oh, come now.'

Gyrth attempted an expression of saintliness. 'Soft and gentle. Clings like cobwebs. Spreads like creeper. Before you know where you are, you are half stifled.'

'And you think she will sway Edward?'

'She always has. It got Tostig Northumbria in the first place. She got Edward to dote on him. That was all her doing. All Tostig had to do was act the part she created for him in Edward's head. Child's play. He was always able to wrap Mother round his little finger, and Edith has taught him to wrap Edward as well.'

'What a good thing he is not here, then,' said Leofwine with heavy irony.

'He will be, brother, he will be – if our dear sister has anything to do with it.'

'Then we see to it that she does not.'

Gyrth raised his eyebrows. 'Oh? And how do you suggest we do that? Tear a devoted wife away from the bedside of her beloved husband? You try, and see what good you will do for Harold's cause.'

Leofwine looked blank. 'Is he so completely under the spell?'

Gyrth shook his head. 'For the life of me I can not tell. Edward is very far from being a fool. And I believe he is genuinely concerned about England. But is his mind still strong enough? That is the problem.'

'What does Harold say?'

'Harold keeps his own counsel on that. But we can hope. Tostig does not possess the entire stock of the Godwin family charm. And *Harold* is no fool, either.'

'So what do we do?'

'We take one step at a time, brother.'

'And what is the first?'

'The first thing is the nomination. That is where we come in.'

'You mean, lobbying?'

'Yes. Why did Harold want everybody at the consecration? So that we can get at them. But it must be discreet. And Harold must stay out of it as far as possible. He must not be seen to be trying too hard.'

Leofwine nodded. 'I know. No visible pressure. No "undue influence".'

'Exactly. Harold wants the throne, but he wants it delivered properly – open election, according to all custom and etiquette.'

A light came into Leofwine's eye. 'Has Harold thought about Stigand?'

Gyrth looked blank. 'What about Stigand?'

'Once we get Harold nominated and elected, we have to get him crowned. Stigand is Archbishop of Canterbury.'

'Ah!' Gyrth nodded. 'Of course. The excommunications.'

'By five successive popes,' said Leofwine. 'Getting crowned by an archbishop who has been sent to Hell five times. Is that "according to all custom and etiquette"?'

'No,' admitted Gyrth. 'But you are forgetting: we have more than one archbishop in England.'

'Aldred.'

'Exactly. In York. He has a much better reputation than Stigand.'

'Not difficult.'

'Stigand will not mind being passed over. He will understand. Anyone who can survive five excommunications is worldly enough to take something like that in his stride. Besides, Stigand will still have his uses. But think, Lef. If York crowns him, it will help to bind the north to the south. Aldred will not be a makeshift; he could be a positive advantage. Harold's dream – a united England.'

In the event Magnus did need Sigurd. It was one thing to locate Ragnar; it was quite another to capture him. If all that had been necessary was an ambush and a quick knife thrust, Magnus could almost certainly have done it by himself.

But he wanted more than that; he wanted a meeting. He wanted Ragnar to see him, to hear him. He wanted leisure to watch Ragnar's face when he, Magnus, recited the roll of crimes, when he reached the burning core of his rage – the death of Sigrid.

Sigurd understood this. All he had to do was wait until Magnus came to understand too. When the time came, it was his band who scouted, who made enquiries, who ran Ragnar to earth, who bound and trussed him, and who delivered him as a living, human carcass.

'There you are,' said Sigurd. 'Now get on with it. We shall wait out of sight.'

Magnus had the grace and intelligence to thank him.

Sigurd made a face. 'I am not sure whether you will be thanking me in about an hour's time.'

It was prophetic. Left alone, with Ragnar helpless before him, Magnus was not prepared for what he felt.

For a start, he knew him. Of course he knew him; their two families had been distant neighbours for decades, possibly generations. He had been taught to recite the ever-lengthening list of crimes and offences and outrages that 'they' had committed against the universally innocent members of his own family. By all the rules he too should have been in the thrall of the blood-feud obsession. None of the men could think beyond it. The older women, too. Some of them were worse. In a way they were even *more* frightening to a young lad with long ears, as he sat listening round the winter hearth.

But that was not how it came to Magnus. To kill a stranger was one thing. Even, in a furtive ambush, to kill someone you knew. By the time you had turned over the body and looked in the face to make sure, it was over; the damage was done. No need to screw up the body to make the final thrust.

But to have the man there, in front of you, tied and helpless, both knowing what was supposed to happen next. A familiar face . . . That was quite another thing.

What made it worse was that he did not beg for his life. He did not try to deny the offence. He did not try to shift the blame.

Nor did he taunt Magnus with what he had done. That would have made it easy. He did not struggle. He did not bargain. He made no attempt to deceive in a bid to escape. That would have made it easy, too.

He just waited.

Magnus considered what the man had done. If it had been a simple case of robbery, or rick burning, even cattle maiming . . . But this man had committed mass murder; he had planned it in advance; he had organised the burning not only of men but of women and children as well. He may not have organised it very well – Magnus' survival was proof of that. But he had willed it. He had deliberately created Hell in the dark – if such a place as Hell existed. Magnus called it Hell because it was the worst place he could think of, real or not.

It deserved the name of Hell because Sigrid had died there. Ragnar may not have struck Sigrid himself, but he was responsible for her death, as surely as if he *had* struck her. When Magnus had burst out through their secret door, he himself was on fire, both in fact and in spirit. In that moment, had he caught Ragnar, he would have lingered over his death with bestial, slavering delight.

That was weeks ago. He had been hunting for so long now that the heat had faded. Never mind, said the old women. Revenge is a dish best tasted cold. The satisfaction is all the greater.

For the life of him, Magnus could not see it like that. And that was because of Sigrid, too. She alone of the female members of his family had stood out against the consuming passion of vengeance. She alone, of all his relations, did not follow the lurid exhortations to pursue the next victim, the alleged author of the latest outrage against family honour.

She always said 'Why?' And she looked in distaste as the rest of her family went red in the face and spat swearwords in their fruitless search for a reason that would satisfy her. In the end they fell back on abusing her for upsetting them.

Now Sigrid, of all people, was dead, victim of the very thing that she had said was pointless. If ever there was a sound reason for revenge, the family said to him, here it was. Even Sigrid herself, they said, would approve.

It did not turn out like that. He may have heard Sigrid's voice in his head in the early days of his search, but that soon faded. He may have carried the image of Sigrid's face in death as he came near the end of his search. But, as he stood there, in front of his enemy, with a naked knife, there was no Sigrid – except for one thing – her question: 'Why?'

But he did it. He did it, because he also had his common sense. He knew that, if he did not, his victim would stalk *him*, with only one aim in mind. The spine of both their families had been broken in the fire and in the fight that followed. Winter had wiped out most of the livestock, deprived of the usual care. Magnus and his enemy were virtually alone. Ragnar's remaining womenfolk would turn into tight-cheeked, avenging furies; God help the man they vented their spleen on, and their curses. There might be very few male members of the guilty clan left, but not one of them, however distantly related, would have any peace. Magnus knew that he could be pursued. That he could never rest – not really rest. A knife had always to be within ready clasp.

He could not stay awake for ever. He had to have company, a group, a band – *something* – in which he could take shelter.

Magnus put the last of the stones in place on the cairn. Whether Ragnar was carrion or not, he had to be hidden – just in case.

'Very sensible of you,' said a voice.

Magnus whirled round. Sigurd had timed his return impeccably. The party gathered round the cairn.

'Well?' said Sigurd.

Magnus swore under his breath. Sigurd was right – damn him. He offered company; he offered protection; he offered food and a roof; he offered opportunity. At that moment Magnus had none of them.

Sigurd leaned forward in the saddle. 'It is not for life; you do not have to marry me.'

Everyone laughed, including Magnus. And that was that.

'I am getting a good deal, too,' said Sigurd, as he handed Magnus the reins of a horse.

Which was true.

Magnus was big, he was strong, he could obviously look after himself. Anybody who could survive in the forest for as long as he had must be good at self-preservation, and Sigurd needed soldiers who were good at that. Magnus came cheap, too. In fact, he came free.

Magnus accepted the lowliest place at Sigurd's board without a murmur. He felt empty, naturally. It was done; it was finished. He could make nothing of it. He could not tell anybody about it. Sigurd, very shrewdly, asked no questions. If able-bodied men were willing to serve in that part of southern Norway, that was enough. Magnus seemed a good prospect. Sigurd liked the look of him. After all, he was not that much older himself.

Sigurd found him unusual, too. He did not brag. He did not even drink that much, as he was to discover. He certainly said very little. That was enough for Sigurd – for the time being, at any rate.

It was enough for Magnus, too. For a while the whole episode haunted him. Haunted him not for what it was, but, oddly, for what it was not. He did not feel pleased at what he had done. Certainly not proud. Not even satisfied, really. It was over; that was enough.

Yet it was not the end of the ghosts. There was still the fire. There was still Sigrid's voice. There was still Sigrid's face . . .

'Woe to my kingdom. Woe to my people. There are those in high places who mean nothing but harm to England. They serve not England: they serve the Devil.'

Those about the bed looked uncomfortably at each other. Where had this sudden surge of energy come from? For the last two days he had been prostrate and speechless. And what did the words mean? Everyone knew that a dying man's pronouncements were of special significance. But those of a king . . .!

'God will lay a curse upon the land. It will be given over to its enemies. For a year and a day after my death, fiends of Hell shall stalk the land, and harry it from end to end with fire and the sword.'

The more the King rambled, the more his audience writhed in both embarrassment and dread. How to stop him? And what did it all mean? There were magic spells in the air. Even Harold felt a twinge of discomfort.

Clearly the King had very little time left. And there was vital business to conduct.

Stigand leaned across to Harold and whispered in his ear. 'Old men's fancies. His mind has gone. Pay no attention.'

'I shall not,' said Harold, 'but *they* are.'

He pointed to the company assembled in the death chamber. Only Queen Edith seemed unmoved, save only insofar as she continued her incessant weeping.

Harold became restive. This was pure drama, almost like a miracle play. Edith was keeping the initiative by her weeping, keeping the performance going, almost as if she were manipulating the dying puppet in the bed to continue its lurid maunderings.

And what had she already been saying to the King when he, Harold, was not there? Was Edward about to pour forth another piece of fortune-telling with talk of Tostig? This had to be stopped. What were they to do – shake a dying man by the shoulders?

It was as if the King had heard his very thoughts. Suddenly he started talking about the Queen, his beloved Edith, his constant and blessed consort, his dutiful wife and daughter . . . Harold began to feel like retching with revulsion.

It got worse. Harold was to nurture, foster, treasure his sister and Queen, was to ensure that every honour that was her due should be paid to her in fullest measure. Harold felt his neck go hot. This was the woman who had always favoured Tostig, and who had, quite likely, shown favour to the idea of Edward's alleged offer of the crown to the Norman bastard all those years ago.

Harold caught Stigand's eye. Do something! It was clearly impossible for Harold to force the King.

Stigand came close to the King and bent down. Nobody heard the whisperings between them. At last Stigand rose and beckoned Harold forward.

The silence became deafening as Harold sat on the edge of the bed. Even Edith stopped crying. The King put out a hand of ghostly whiteness and stretched his fingers. Harold took them. Everybody stopped breathing.

With a voice of such firmness and clarity that they all jumped, Edward said, 'To you, Harold, Earl of Wessex, I commend my kingdom.'

Harold jerked his head.

Gyrth and Leofwine, after a startled glance at each other, fell in behind. Harold led them to his private chamber. He paused at the door.

'Gyrth, get two of my best housecarls – Wilfrid and Oswy will do – and put them outside this room, at ten paces distant, so that they can hear nothing. They are to see that nobody comes nearer. Understand? Nobody.'

As Gyrth hurried off, Harold turned to Leofwine.

'Get Aldred and Stigand.'

Leofwine looked startled. 'Both of them? Together?'

'Both. Together. I intend to be King of all England. That means York as well as Canterbury.'

Leofwine remembered what Gyrth had said, but asked anyway, just to hear it from Harold's lips.

'Who will do the actual crowning?'

'Aldred. Stigand is still under the papal ban. I want nothing irregular. The birth of my kingship – nay, the very conception – will be as immaculate as that of the Holy Child itself.'

Well, there it was. Stigand would have to lump it.

'I shall put him in charge of the funeral arrangements,' said Harold. 'That should help to appease his vanity. Besides, he is a man of practicality. Ask him which he would rather give up – the right to place the crown on my head, or his fees from all those Canterbury estates. He knows what is important right now. He will understand. He will assist.' He chuckled. 'I shall do rather well out of it. Not many kings get two primates by their side at a coronation.'

Leofwine hesitated. 'What about . . . what about . . . you know, Edward . . .' He waved vaguely.

'I have spoken to Edith about that. She and her ladies will prepare the body. She has cried herself into a corner. All that weeping and devotion. She can hardly refuse—'

'—and be seen to refuse—'

'—and be seen to refuse to do what is necessary for such a beloved husband, saint, king and lord. She has been washing his feet for days. Now let her prove that she means it.'

Leofwine began to look a little hustled. 'Is that all?'

'By no means. When you have done that, see the sacristan, and tell him I want the grave prepared at once.'

Leofwine stared. 'At this hour?'

Harold nodded firmly. 'Get the masons and diggers out of bed if you have to. Everyone has been expecting this for days; Edward himself has done nothing but talk about it, when he was not raving. It will be no great surprise.'

'Is *that* all?'

'No. Get hold of Edwin and Morcar. I want a full session of the Witan within the hour, here, in the palace – every earl, bishop, abbot and thegn within striking distance That means most of them. They have been waiting for something to happen. Well, I shall oblige. Edwin can preside. As senior earl, he will not be challenged.'

'Is that not dangerous? Are you sure of Mercia?'

'No,' said Harold frankly. 'Nor am I sure yet of Northumbria, even though I put Morcar there. But if I get you or Gyrth to preside, the Witan will get suspicious. They will suspect that I am staging everything. By putting a man in the chair who has not declared his support of me, I can claim that I am being fair and transparent. Whiter than white. As I said – immaculate.'

'How will you swing Edwin and Morcar?'

'Leave that to me.'

'Do you not think you are being just a little precipitate?'

'No. They are expecting something like this, brother. They have to be. I have the King's commendation. That makes me only half a king. I must have the Witan's election. And as soon as possible. I repeat – immaculate. Beyond criticism.'

'But tonight?'

'At midnight if necessary. We do not give them a chance to steady themselves. We have the initiative. I do not intend to lose it. If the Atheling's party are planning something, we shall catch them on one foot. As for the few who may want the Bastard, we shall, with luck, catch them off their feet altogether. We give them no time.'

Leofwine nodded, if slightly dizzily. He was thrown off balance by his brother's decisiveness and lack of hesitation.

'You have been giving this a great deal of thought.'

'I have had enough time,' said Harold.

Waiting hour after hour in the death chamber, unable to make things happen, unable to show his wishes, furious at the charade of grief being performed by Edith and her women, he had felt impotent. The crazy thought had gone through his head a dozen times: after all these years as the King's right hand – the sword and shield of England – would a capricious twist of fate, a wayward buffet of God's Will, even a malign trick of the Devil, cast this cup, this grail of power, from his hands at the very moment when he was reaching out to grasp it?

He saw Leofwine, waiting as if to hear yet more orders. 'Off you go now.'

As his brother closed the door behind him, another crazy thought also flitted through his head. What would Edward have said if he had had a soothsayer's eye when he was planning his beloved new minster – if he could have seen through the veil of time that, within eight days of its consecration, it would witness a king's funeral and a king's coronation, within hours of each other? Witness too a milestone – a hinge of history – the end of the House of Cerdic, which had ruled in England for five hundred years. Cerdic – the successor of the fabulous, legend-laden Roman Empire, the descendant of Woden himself, the father and founder of Wessex. He and his line were no more. And he – Harold Godwinson – was about to try to fill the gap.

Harold almost shuddered. They were all walking with destiny tonight.

Harold and his brothers entered the hall. The assembly remained standing where they were, in random groups, like guests at a party. They made no attempt to get into any kind of formal shape, to jostle for precedence according to custom, to look for benches to sit on. Late torches burned low in sconces. Tired servants stood about the walls and held candlesticks in their bare hands; it was all Stigand had had time to arrange. They swore silently at hot wax dripping onto their wrists.

The Christmas Witan of England, without a word of command from a chamberlain or a shout from a herald, came to order. The Witan, the men of wit and knowledge, of power and experience, who had advised every king since Cerdic, fell silent.

Earl Gyrth of East Anglia stepped forward. He was to say afterwards that he had no idea where his words were to come from. All the preparation he had had was a hurried conversation in a passageway with Harold half an hour before. The rest he owed to the grace of God and the charged spirit of an unforgettable night.

He informed 'my lords, thegns, bishops, abbots and loyal subjects' that our late holy and venerated sovereign lord, Edward, had, with his dying breath, and before witnesses, which included His Grace Bishop Stigand (he carefully avoided using the questionable title 'Archbishop of Canterbury'), clearly declared that the Earl Harold of Wessex was his God-guided choice as the next guardian of the realm.

As everyone knew, that realm of England was beset with neighbours who wished it harm; it needed, therefore, a strong arm and a trusted one, to steer it through the dangers that doubtless would beset it in the coming months and years. In one sentence, therefore, he took the wind out of the sails of the two parties of possible rivals. Edgar the Atheling, the last surviving legitimate member of the House of Cerdic, was a mere boy, and therefore by definition incapable of becoming the 'strong arm' that the country needed. And Duke William, the Bastard of Normandy, was one of the very threats that beset England at that actual moment. By implication, then, who of the present assembly was going to cast himself in the role of traitor by declaring in open council that he was for William? Promise or no promise.

Gyrth then called upon 'Lord Edwin, of the House of Leofric, Earl of Mercia', to speak as the voice of the Witan here assembled, and expressed the hope that Lord Edwin's words would be guided and marked by the wisdom of the Holy Spirit, concerned as that Holy Spirit no doubt always was for the welfare of England.

Earl Edwin, barely into his twenties, less than half the age of nearly everyone there, licked his lips, swallowed hard and lifted his head so as to make his words carry.

'The voice of the Witan of England, the choice of the Witan of England, is to elect our lord, Earl Harold of Wessex, as King.'

There was the slightest of pauses. Would somebody suggest summarising the deliberations they had just had? Would somebody else ask about the Atheling? Would a brave soul speak up for Duke William? Would a jealous Mercian or a Tostig-lover from Northumbria challenge the privileged position of Wessex? Harold gave a rash protester just enough time to risk his reputation by raising an objection, before stepping forward himself and formally accepting.

Exactly on cue, Leofwine appeared from the shadows on the left, carrying an official axe of state; on the right, Earl Morcar of Northumbria came into the flickering torchlight bearing the crown. There was a distinct intake of breath. The steps of Leofwine and Morcar were clearly audible as they walked towards the new king. Jewels in the crown gleamed dully in the guttering light of the handheld candlesticks around the hall. Over a hundred eyes, possessed by awe of five hundred years of Cerdic's blood, followed it all the way. Harold bowed and took possession.

The deed was done.

Harold wiped his fingers, emptied his cup, leaned back in his chair and looked at his brothers.

'Quite a morning.'

'You have done your duty by him,' said Gyrth.

'A celebration to be envied,' said Leofwine.

Harold chuckled. 'I wonder if they will go to that much trouble for me when the time comes.'

'That is a long way away,' said Stigand. 'You will have plenty to drive that thought out of your head in the coming months.'

Harold nodded. 'Too true.'

'What will you do first?'

Harold laughed. 'Get crowned.'

Gyrth tossed his head. 'I did not mean that.'

'I know, I know. But that really is the first thing. And we must get it right. We are in a hurry, I admit, but it must not look like a shambles. We have got off to a good start with the funeral and the burial.' He turned to Stigand. 'That was fine work you did this morning. Especially the three hundred daily masses for his soul. A nice touch. Your idea?'

'No. Aldred's, actually. He made several useful contributions.'

'He is a good man. Now we must do similar good work this afternoon. The world is looking.' He paused thoughtfully, then said, 'I am sorry about the crown. But you know the reasons.'

Stigand nodded knowledgeably. 'I understand. I bear no grudge against Aldred. He is an able diplomat and a fine administrator. I am more than happy for him to conduct the service. I shall be the one organising everything in the minster.'

'The power behind the throne, eh?' said Gyrth.

Stigand inclined his head a trifle.

Harold peered shrewdly. 'Really? No hard feelings? Remember, I want a united country, and for that I must have a united Church.'

Stigand allowed himself a wry smile. 'A mere twist of Fate, my lord. I was unlucky enough to have been promoted by an antipope.'

'Benedict?'

'Yes, my lord. And to have been excommunicated by his rather more legitimate successors.'

'Five of them,' interjected Leofwine, grinning.

Stigand bowed with aplomb in his direction. 'My lord Earl of Kent is extremely well informed.'

'Never mind the Pope in Rome,' said Harold. 'What I want is a proper coronation here in London. Seemly. Thorough. No rush. As if we do coronations every other month.'

Stigand rose from the table. 'In that case, if your – Your *Majesty* will excuse me, I have further details to attend to. The crowds are already large, and will get larger.'

'You have two corps of housecarls now – mine and Edward's.'

'Nevertheless, my lord . . .' Stigand made his obeisances and left.

Harold thought of other details that he hoped Stigand had not forgotten, and that he wished he had mentioned. What about the safekeeping of the orb and the sceptre? Had they been cleaned and polished? Had he been able to secure holy oil in time? Were all the coronation robes in suitable condition? Had the rats been busy deep in those oaken chests at Winchester? Edward had been King for twenty-four years. Trust Stigand to think of having them brought up to London well before Christmas. Callous and calculating, some might say, but sensible. Stigand was one of those priests who did not let scruples get in the way of practicalities.

And so on and so on. The throne. The carpets. The choir. The bell-ringers in the aisle. The candles and covers for the altar. With all the rush, a detail could easily be overlooked . . . Marshals for the crowd inside the minster . . . Chairs and benches for the dignitaries . . . Oh, and the censers . . .

Harold could not help laughing just a little at himself. His brothers often commented on his cool head and quick thinking. Ha! If they could look inside his head at this moment. Here he was, worrying and fretting like a bridegroom before a wedding.

This would not do. Of course everything would be all right. Stigand and Aldred were able men, and their interests coincided with his own. Stigand was a practical man of business, and a survivor. Harold liked survivors. Aldred had the public reputation – two visits to Rome, one to the Holy City itself, and the Pope's legal confirmation as Archbishop of York. They were the perfect complement to each other. Stigand had the wits; Aldred had the credentials.

Harold was about to overturn five hundred years of history. For that, credentials were important.

That left the family. Surely even Mother could be relied upon to behave herself when one of her sons was being crowned King of England. There would surely be no sighs about Tostig on this day of all days. At least Father would have been proud of him, and of the success of the House of Godwin. How many other Saxon families could boast of having risen in two generations from a humble manor house to a throne?

He tightened his lips. He was King by the choice of the King. He was King by the voice of the Witan, who spoke for the people of England. All that remained was to become King by the Grace of God. And, if Edith began to cry all through that as well, he would have her put out of the minster altogether.

Gunnar Palsson held the package in one fat hand and tapped the other with it.

'Now – are you clear?'

His clerk nodded vigorously. 'Yes, sir. From here, on the morning tide. Then to London. Change ships.'

'Look for Albert the Fleming,' said Gunnar, unable to stop himself from prompting him. 'Down at Deptford. Deptford. Got that?'

'Yes, sir. I have been there before.'

He had indeed. Because he spoke sound English, he would be listened to, and not teased or swindled because of his Danish accent. Gunnar had used him a score of times, but he still fussed. He always found it hard to trust subordinates.

'Very well. Then to Flanders, to Bruges. You go to Count Baldwin, and then the Earl Tostig. You will put this in Earl Tostig's hand. You give it to nobody else. If you can not find him

– and he may well have moved on – come back with it. If you are in any danger, you destroy it. Understand?'

'Sir.'

Gunnar gave him some more money, just in case – though it hurt. But it was practical. He did not want the project to fail for the want of a few pieces of silver. Speculate to accumulate.

It was just a chance; a bow at a very long venture indeed. But worth a try. And he could not see that there was any serious risk attached.

If Tostig could not read the letter, he would have a clerk or two at Count Baldwin's court who could. Bribes would keep mouths shut. Just as Gunnar himself had had to bribe the clerk who had written it for him in the first place. In any case, it was not particularly incriminating. All he was doing was assuring Earl Tostig that he, Gunnar Palsson of the town of Scarborough, was a loyal son of Northumbria, and that he had not taken part in the recent sordid revolt against his lordship – unlike certain other citizens of the town that he could mention. If and when Earl Tostig should return to claim what was his by right, he would find loyal subjects all over Northumbria who would welcome him, and work for his restoration. By so doing, he hoped to merit whatever reward that Earl Tostig, in his custom-ary generosity, cared to bestow.

He had not told his clerk, but he had written three copies and entrusted them to three other clerks, none of whom was aware of what the others were being told to do. Just to be on the safe side.

That was not all. Gunnar Palsson had not got where he was by taking unnecessary chances. He had prepared yet three more letters, with the necessary modifications of names, and was in the process of arranging for their delivery to Earl Morcar as well.

*   *   *

Strong and willing hands heaved mightily to close the great doors of the new West Minster. The roaring theme of five thousand voices outside was suddenly muted to a cavernous bass bourdon of accompaniment. It continued to rumble like a distant ocean through and underneath the entire ceremony that was to follow.

Inside the nave hundreds of eyes were lifted as if by holy cords up to the keystones of the neck-stretching arches, up to Heaven itself, whence the blessing of God would soon descend upon the humble head of the new King of all England. The blessing too of the late King Edward, to whose piety and persistence the whole awesome edifice owed its existence. And of course the blessing of the man to whom Edward had dedicated his offering – St Peter himself. What greater accolade could be bestowed upon a king than to be approved and sustained by the man to whom Christ had entrusted the care of his entire church all those years ago? *'Thou art Peter and upon this rock I will build my church.'*

These were big things indeed. Even before the ceremony began, men crossed themselves at the mere contemplation of them.

A new noise made itself heard. A scuffing of sandals, a rustle of robes, the chanting of a hundred voices. New sights, too. Croziers, staffs of office, mitres, tonsures, black habits, brown habits, grey habits. Bishops, priests, chaplains, monks, vergers, sacristans, almoners, choristers, deacons, sextons, prebendaries, canons, even the men who swept the flagstones. Nobody was going to miss his chance of getting into history.

The procession seemed endless, but of course it was not. There was a final delay while the members of the procession shuffled and whispered and jostled to get themselves into the right places. Even Stigand had not been able to shut out all human nature. The congregation waited patiently. After all, it was a coronation, and they had not had one for twenty-four years.

Suddenly, a whisper at the back told those at the front that the proceedings had begun. Harold made his appearance, flanked and led by more bishops than most could remember ever having seen in one place. Leading them was Bishop Wulfstan of Worcester, by common agreement the most Christian and holy of them all. Once again, Harold was losing no chance to wring the maximum respectability from the occasion. Everything possible was put to use.

The King-elect was conducted to the high altar, where he prostrated himself. The choir sang – in Latin. Priests intoned prayers – in Latin – beseeching God that His servant's hand be strengthened and exalted, that justice, mercy and truth would for ever go before his face. Members of the congregation, barely literate, never mind bilingual, looked at each other, raised eyebrows, sighed and returned to gazing fixedly forward. Their moment would come soon enough.

Harold was raised up, turned round, and brought forward. Wulfstan led him by the hand till he was standing at the head of the nave, and facing the entire congregation. Royal robes were thrown and fastened round his shoulders.

Archbishop Aldred of York stepped up. Raising his voice, he demanded an answer to two mighty questions.

'Do you accept the Earl Harold as your sovereign lord and King?'

The congregation woke up at the sound of English, and in relief gave a mighty roar of assent. For a while it silenced the crowd outside.

'Is it your will that the Earl Harold be crowned as your lord and King?'

Another roar. Know-alls in the crowd without told their neighbours – wrongly – what was going on inside.

Prompted by Aldred, Harold now recited his royal oath: 'I, King Harold Godwinson, swear to preserve peace to the Church of God and to bring peace to all Christian people.'

The congregation had been well briefed. They all said 'Amen'.

'I further swear to forbid all wrong and robbery to men of every rank within my realm.'

'Amen.'

'And, finally, I swear to bring justice and mercy in all my judgements, as I would that God should have mercy upon me.'

'Amen.' Stigand had done his work well.

It was now Aldred's turn.

He prayed that the God who had wrought His mighty works through the hands of Abraham and Moses and Joshua and David and Solomon would shower down upon the shoulders of Harold the King the gifts and graces that all those foregoing heroes had enjoyed in their holy work, and that King Harold would use those gifts and graces to ensure the peace and protection of his people.

'Amen.'

They might not have been clear who Moses and Joshua actually were, but the prayers at least were in English, and they followed the general drift. And they certainly understood very clearly what Aldred was *not* saying.

They understood that England had already had four Danish kings in the last fifty-odd years, and that the present King of Denmark was quite likely to think of himself one day as a possible fifth. They knew that Malcolm, King of the Scots, was no great friend, and regarded the northern counties of England as legitimate territory for hunting and plunder. They knew that the Bastard of Normandy had been trumpeting the story of the late King Edward's promise to him of the crown, and would certainly not be overjoyed when he heard about England's new King. And of course there was always Tostig. The Count of Flanders had married his sister to him, and so was also a potential enemy. And Tostig himself was bound to be up to no good somewhere in any one of those countries – maybe more.

Aldred had ended his prayers. He went back towards the altar, while yet more bishops escorted Harold to the throne.

Harold felt a tightening of the throat. The moment was approaching. The last King had given his approval and his blessing. The Witan had declared their election. The minster had echoed to the acclamation. The oaths had been sworn. The prayers had been recited. God had heard it all. Now was the time for Him to respond with His approval, to hand down from Heaven a measure of His Grace. It was time for the spell of the sacrament.

Aldred returned from the altar bearing a small glass phial. In a shattering silence, during which even the stones were listening, Harold could hear him breathing. Aldred poured holy oil over the head of Harold of Wessex, and by that very act began the process of turning an earl into a king. Not many of the congregation could see clearly, but they knew well what was happening. Even as the Bible had recorded, even as their priests and bishops had recited a thousand times from the Scriptures, even as Zadok the Priest and Nathan the Prophet had anointed Solomon King, so Aldred worked half the miracle that begat a king. As he did so, he prayed that God's Holy Grace might descend upon the head of His devoted servant.

Earl Gyrth stepped forward and offered the Sword of State, which Harold touched to indicate that he would defend his realm and the Church, and smite the enemies of both.

Aldred appeared before him again, with a fresh, rather bigger burden. Harold inclined his head slightly. This was the second half of the miracle. Then, while the stones listened again, Aldred lifted high the crown of England, and placed it, for the first time in five hundred years, upon the brow of an English king outside the House of Cerdic. God was asked to grant to the crown's wearer the gifts of glory and justice and might, in a kingdom that would live for ever.

On the King's one hand, the cross-mounted orb was offered by the Bishop of Durham, and received. On the King's other hand, the sceptre, with its crown of a holy dove, was tendered by the Bishop of London, and accepted.

There remained one more touch to the magic. Aldred would consecrate the Host and administer it to England's new king. In the presence of his nobles, his clergy, his family and his people, Harold would partake of the holiest sacrament of all – the flesh of Jesus Christ.

As Aldred stood close before Harold, he could hear the rumbling in the King's stomach. Time enough to see to that at the banquet later on. It promised to be a memorable one; after all, it was the Feast of the Epiphany.

The miracle was complete. After designation by the late King, after acclamation by the nobles of the realm, after election by the Witan, after coronation by the officers of Christ's church on earth, Harold of Wessex was now, by the Grace of God, King of all England, its guardian and servant, its sword and shield, its judge and lawgiver, its father and protector.

There was no going back now.

Chapter Two

Owen crawled into their makeshift shelter, sat down with a grunt, and wiped the wet out of his eyes. Cold and hunger had pushed them to the lowest ebb of the spirit.

'It is travels again for us, Llew.'

'Where to this time, then?'

'Does it matter? Anywhere, really – nothing could be worse than this.'

'You mean . . . out of Wales?'

Owen shrugged. 'Needs must when the Devil drives. I never thought the day would come when I should hear myself saying that. But what do we have here? Look at us.'

He extended a hand towards the rain-soaked hills around them. 'And look at that.' It was grey and unrelenting as far as the eye could see.

'What do we have here? We shall never make shepherds as long as we live.'

'It is a living.'

'Living do you call it? I call it dying by inches.'

'It is secure. You always have sheep. Well, you do up here.'

Owen fished in his waist wallet for a last, sorry piece of cheese. 'The world is more than sheep, Llew.'

'In the world we had before, somebody was always trying to kill us.'

'Well, at least something was happening. Christ and bloody

Ffestiniog, this is no life. We are archers, Llew. Not serfs to soak in sheep shit all our days.'

'Where do you suggest, then? Gruffydd is dead. The man we followed is dead. Our country is dead; Gwynedd will not rise again in our lifetime. Harold is too strong.'

Owen looked at him. 'Exactly.'

Llew blinked. 'What do you mean?'

'When you look for a man to serve, you do not go to someone with a bloody nose. You look for the man who *gave* him that bloody nose.'

'You mean Harold?'

'Who better?'

'But we have no idea where he is.'

'We have tongues in our heads. We ask. And we use our common sense. A man always knows more than he thinks he knows – if he stops to think.'

Owen held out a chunk of cheese. Llew waved it away. He was hungry, but not that hungry – yet.

'What do we know?' said Owen. 'We know that Harold is King.'

'How do we know?'

Owen waved impatiently. 'It is in the air, Llew. You know as well as I do. Always trust what you get out of the air.'

'Well, so Harold is King. So what?'

'So this. If you were the Bastard of Normandy, would you take that lying down? He has been shouting about the promise of the crown that the Confessor made to him for fifteen years now. So he will come to get it.'

Llew brightened up. 'And what about that oath that Harold swore in sixty-four? You know – at Be-oo.'

'Bayeux,' said Owen. 'Harold swore on holy relics to back him to the throne. The Bastard will shout that from the rooftops as well. Harold is a perjurer, fit only for the flames of Hell. Which is where the Bastard aims to put him.'

Llew stared. 'You mean now we go all the way to Normandy?'

Owen tossed his head. 'No, you pudding. The English are bad enough; who wants to fight for a damned Frenchman?'

'Well then.'

'Well then nothing. Harold is a king; William is a bastard duke with ideas above his station. If you were betting round the camp fire, where would you put your money?'

'I – er – I should imagine . . .'

'Exactly. We all know Wales is best, but there are no Welshmen to fight for at the moment, so we make do with second best. And Harold is the best of the second best. I should reckon that he might be very grateful to a couple of veteran archers – professionals – who serve him loyally in throwing the Bastard back into the sea.'

Llew looked glum. 'We still do not know where Harold is.'

Owen turned to face him full on. 'Llew – you are Harold. You are King. The Bastard is coming from Normandy. You have an army. Where are you going to wait with your army? In York? Chester? Cornwall?'

Light began to dawn. 'Ah . . .'

'By the beard of the druid, Llew. We shall make a general of you yet.'

'So go south?'

'Brilliant. There are not that many counties on the south coast of England. We have tongues in our heads, and we have ears. Besides . . .'

'Besides what?'

Owen popped the last piece of cheese and spoke with his mouth full.

'We shall not have to look far. It will be in the air.'

Harold called the meeting to order.

The protocol of the previous week had disappeared. This was a working council. Not the full Witan by any means. That would have been impossible: the debates would have been endless. Every man would have been speaking for his corner of England. A week beforehand, Harold had wanted every earl, thegn, bishop and abbot in sight gracing his presence. Now he wanted only men of authority, men who would speak for England. Even more important, he wanted men on whose loyalty and efficiency he could rely.

That meant he had his two brothers, naturally – Gyrth, Earl of East Anglia, and Leofwine, Earl of Kent. They were his right and left hands. All the other earls were there. The new ones, Edwin and Morcar, looked very young in that company, which of course they were. Diffident and out of place they may have seemed, but they represented over half the country – Mercia and Northumbria. Stigand sat high at the table. Now that the coronation formalities were over, Harold made no secret of the fact that he valued Stigand's services as a practical man of business. A scattering of senior bishops, too, including Wulfstan, to provide the necessary holiness and virtue. Not that they would be leading troops or presiding at the King's courts, but they added to the aura of respectability that Harold was always anxious to create.

At side tables sat a small cluster of bowed clerks, behind ramparts of papers, quills, reeds, inkpots, sticks of wax, penknives and guttering ends in flat candlesticks. When the decisions had been taken, they would have to translate those decisions into orders and authentications, and attach the vital seals.

Harold began with what he had sworn in his coronation oath – justice. There was to be no break in continuity; orders were to go out to every local government officer. Men were just beginning to get used to the new version of 'shire-reeve' – sheriff. The courts were to continue as if nothing had happened. Which in a sense was true: they were the King's courts; there had been one king; now there was another. The King technically did not die. Another reason why it had been so vital to expedite the coronation. The line was unbroken. The law was to be administered exactly as it had been under the late saintly King Edward.

'Next,' said Harold, in his direct way, 'money.'

Leofwine grinned. Harold took him up on it.

'You may smile, brother, but you know as well as I do that money comes first. Well, second, after justice. And even justice can be made to be fruitful.'

Harold meant fines. A king was obliged to provide his subjects with justice, but he was entitled to the profits of that justice.

'We can not fight the Bastard with empty pockets. I am sure the Bastard is telling his tenants-in-chief right now that he expects their full contribution to his precious invasion – either in men or money. That means everything – taxes, fines, heriot, military service, everything.'

'They will complain,' said Gyrth.

'They always complain. Everybody always complains. But they can afford it. If we could produce all that Danegeld to hold off Sweyn Forkbeard fifty years ago – till he came back for more – I am sure they can cough up enough to keep the Bastard away once and for all.'

Gyrth made a face. Harold leaned forward. 'They pay. We must have funds. If good justice makes the muscle of a nation, so money is the life blood. Do you know why that royal Norwegian bandit is always so successful?'

'Hardrada?'

'The very same.' Harold paused for effect. 'Hardrada's gold.'

Gyrth frowned. 'Why is that?'

The man's treasure chests, they said, were bottomless. The legend resounded across Christendom.

Harold sat back. 'Nobody knows for sure. But he campaigned for years in the east – even beyond Germany, they say. As far as Miklegaard itself, where the streets are paved with gold. Rest assured, he took his share of paving stones away with him when he came back to Norway. More than his share, from what I have heard. He could *buy* England if he wanted to. Thank God he does not. One grasping neighbour is enough.'

Harold went on to discuss a bewildering range of preparations. Orders were drafted for the construction and commissioning of ships, right down to sub-paragraphs for royal foresters, carpenters, shipwrights and makers of sails, ropes, nails, hooks and scores of other pieces of iron equipment. Ignorant bishops wilted under the avalanche of technical terms. Commands were to be sent, over the new royal seal, to every seaport from the Tyne right round to Exeter. Detailed regulations were brought up to date for the calling out of the fyrd, the militias from every county. Harold was not merely Earl of Wessex now; his writ ran right up to the borders of King Malcolm, right down to Cornwall, right over to the Welsh Marches.

His brothers marvelled at Harold's masterly command of detail, his gift for clarity of expression. It became blindingly clear that he had not put all this together in the last couple of weeks; he had been planning it, right down to belts and buckles, for months. To hold all that intent, all that ambition, all that vision, in his head for so long – on his own. Their brother was truly a remarkable man.

Still the commands came like a pent-up torrent through a broken floodgate.

'We get Edward's housecarls to join with mine.'

'Will that not cause more trouble than it is worth?' said Stigand dubiously, glad to have a reason to offer a knowledgeable comment for once.

'I do not expect them to like it, but they will see the need for it when the Bastard arrives. He will recruit every heavy knight he can lay his hands on. I intend to recruit every unit of heavy infantry I can lay *my* hands on. Man for man, I think we have the beating of them, but we must have enough of those men.'

Gyrth looked at Leofwine. Harold saw the glance.

'Yes, and I expect a contingent from each of you. Get your sheriffs to work. I want stores of food, too. I shall have to feed an army somewhere near the coast – maybe for most of the summer. The Bastard unfortunately has not obliged us by telling us when he is going to call.'

Gyrth wagged his head. Those poor sheriffs. They would regret their hard-won appointments by the time the summer was out.

Harold was far from finished.

'At the moment I plan to wait on Wight. It gives us freedom of movement over a wide stretch of coast. And the ships can harbour in the Solent, too. We can not expect them to patrol week after week in open Channel. If he comes from the Cotentin or if he comes from Ponthieu, or from anywhere in between, we can meet him.'

Harold took a deep breath. 'That takes care of the Bastard, so far as we can take care of him.' He grinned to himself. 'I wish it really were as easy as that.'

He lifted his head. 'But that still leaves one other problem, my brothers.'

Gyrth and Leofwine said it together: 'Tostig.'

'Exactly. Dear brother Tostig. Because he is more unstable than the Bastard, that makes it much more difficult. We know the Bastard. I have seen him at work. In sixty-four, remember? He knows what he wants. He makes no secret of it. He plans; he ponders; he pursues his desires with a single mind. So he is to a great extent predictable.

'But our dear brother . . . Well, we all know Tostig. How can we divine what soaring scheme he may suddenly decide to follow if he wakes up one morning feeling more sorry for himself than usual?'

'Tostig is intelligent, Harold,' said Gyrth.

'Tostig is very intelligent,' said Harold. 'That is why he is that much more serious a problem. If he had half the Bastard's fixity of purpose, we should all be trembling. As it is, we have no idea where he may strike.'

Leofwine found himself getting ahead of Harold for once.

'So you will need more than one camp and more than one supply of food.'

'You have it, brother.'

'So we must out-think him,' said Leofwine.

Harold nodded vigorously. 'And, while we are doing that, we must remember that he will be trying to out-think us. I repeat, he is very intelligent.'

Gyrth cleared his throat. 'So it comes to this: we must be prepared to be attacked by a very determined man and a very intelligent man.'

'Yes,' said Harold. He paused. 'And there is one other possibility you must also prepare for.'

Leofwine looked blank. Harold grinned.

'We must bear in mind that Tostig has visited Normandy. After all, Flanders is practically next door. Who knows? With his charm, perhaps he has persuaded the Bastard to join forces with him.' Harold enjoyed the look on their faces. 'Have you thought of that? We must prepare for them to arrive *together*.'

'What do you rate the Bastard's chances then?' said Owen, putting out his hands to the blaze.

A fyrdman eased his weary legs. 'No idea. Jesus! Eighty miles in five days. Harold must be in a hurry. Blast him!'

'But you will fight,' said Owen. 'Despite what we hear.'

'What do you hear?' The fyrdman was massaging his feet, and not looking at him.

54

Owen seized his chance. 'Give us a cup of that broth, and I shall bring you up to date. And maybe throw in a story or two by way of good measure.'

The fyrdman narrowed his eyes. 'What do you know?'

Owen looked mysterious. 'You would be surprised. We travel, my friend and I. We have come a long way, too. We hear things.' He looked sidelong. 'Tell them, Llew.'

Llew came in precisely on cue. 'We have been on campaign with the King.'

The fyrdman sneered. 'You . . . bloody Welshmen? You fought *against* him – and got thrashed.'

Owen twinkled. 'I did not say we were on his side. But I tell you this, my friend. You learn more about a man fighting against him than you do fighting with him.' He laughed. 'Llew and I, we have been beaten by the best in the land. We are experts on Harold.' He paused significantly. 'And on Tostig.'

'What do you know about Tostig?'

'Because *he* thrashed us too. He brought an army to Wales, and Harold brought a fleet. Why do you think we are here?'

'Looking for a fight.'

'Just like you. Only you are doing what you are told; we are doing what we fancy.'

The fyrdman accepted the shaft. This cocky Welshman was good entertainment value if nothing else. Maybe a source of news, too.

Owen read his thoughts. 'A cup of broth says we can tell you things you do not know.'

The fyrdman raised an eyebrow. 'Suppose we do know?'

Owen laid down some coins. 'Then we pay for it.'

Two cups of stew were handed over. Owen kept them waiting while he wiped his lips with the back of a rather dirty hand.

'I am sure you all know what happened to our army. And to our King Gruffydd. But I will wager you do not know what happened to Gruffydd's widow.'

'Well?'

'Married again.'

'Who? The chief druid?' The other fyrdmen tittered.

'No, my friend. Harold.'

'Harold who?'

'Harold the King.'

The fyrdman spat. 'Pull the other leg. He has his Edith.'

'The Swan-Neck?'

'Yes. And a brood of bastards. What does he want with a Welsh widow?'

'Not the comforts of the bed, I agree,' said Owen. 'But there are other reasons. Do you know whose sister Mildred is?'

'Who?'

'Mildred. Gruffydd's widow. She is called Mildred.'

'God – what a name.'

'Never mind that. As with most princesses, it is not their name or themselves that matter; it is their relations.'

'Well?'

'Harold – your new King Harold – has gone and married Queen Mildred of Wales. And why? Not because of her looks. Not because of her fortune.'

Owen let them dangle a moment before clinching it.

'Because of her family. Her brothers are earls.'

The fyrdman stared. 'Earls? What earls?'

'The young brothers – Edwin and Morcar. How to keep a handle on Mercia and Northumbria – marry their sister. A very shrewd move, I should say. Would you not agree?'

The fyrdman whistled. There was a stir round the fire. Owen was pleased with his first foray into the news-bargaining business in England. He grinned cheekily.

'How about another cup on the house?'

'Not yet. We want more than that.'

Owen heaved his shoulders. 'Then I must tell you another story. Want another love story?'

'Try us,' said the fyrdman.

Owen held out the bowls first. Wooden ladles were passed over. 'Help yourself.'

'Remember what I said about "know your enemy"? About Harold and his love life? Well, I would wager you do not know about the Bastard and *his* love life.'

'We did not know he had any.'

'Oh, yes,' said Owen, settling himself more comfortably. 'What about this for starters? The Bastard is six feet tall, and his wife is less than four and a half.'

There were a few chuckles round the fire. 'Makes it a bit difficult,' said someone.

The first fyrdman grinned. 'All right, all right, tell us. How do you know, anyway?'

Owen looked smug. 'It is already as I have told you. I know Harold, if only as a prisoner in his camp. But, prisoner or not, in camp you see things. You hear things. Harold has been to Normandy. Where he swore that oath.'

'Yes, I have heard of that,' said somebody.

'Well, he spent several months in Normandy – sixty-four, it was – and got to know the Bastard very well. He got to know Matilda.'

'His lady.'

'His lady. There were plenty of stories about her. But the best one was about their courtship. Apparently he went a-wooing to her father's court in Flanders. Count Baldwin.'

'Where Tostig married his daughter?'

'No. Tostig married Baldwin's sister. Matilda is his daughter. Anyway, listen, and learn. The Bastard is no ladies' man. He took one look at Matilda and said she was too short. She took one look at him and said he was far too tall. They had a row about that right at the start. They spent the next three days having rows. Just like a married couple. She teased him, and he could not stand teasing. It was so mad he became, they say, that he ended up dragging her round the hall by her hair. They were engaged by the end of the week. They have not stopped rowing ever since.'

'Sounds a bit like *my* wife,' said somebody.

'I tell you, my friends,' said Owen, 'they must have done more than shout at each other: they have had a huge brood of children, and she has not miscarried once. In fact –' he paused to give his next pronouncement more force '– they say he offered Harold one of his daughters as a means of sealing the agreement.'

'What agreement?'

'The one they had the oath about. Harold promised to help the Bastard to the crown when Edward died, and the Bastard offered his daughter as a sweetener.'

'I hope for his sake that she is not like her mother.'

The first fyrdman tilted his head. 'And I hope for his sake that his new wife – the Welsh widow – does not get to hear of it. To say nothing of the Swan-Neck. God – how do these people find the time? Or the energy? He is supposed to be running the country.'

Owen sat back and looked expectant.

'Well, have we earned another cup?'

'*You* may have done, but what about your friend?'

Owen put an arm round Llewellyn's shoulder. 'He tells even better stories than I do. But for that you will have to wait till tomorrow. After supper. Is it a pledge we have?'

Edric, the Reeve of Scarborough, broke a long silence. 'I think you ought to go.'

'Where, Father?'

'To your uncle's.'

'Up in some lonely Yorkshire dale?'

'You will be away from the coast,' said Edric. 'And he is family; I can trust him to care for you.'

Coelwen shook her head. 'What protection do we have out in the country? Uncle will want to look after me, but what does he have? Farmworkers with billhooks and hammers? Surely the risk is greater there than it is here. Here we have walls. Here we have able-bodied defenders whose job it is to keep order.'

'Your uncle will not have sea raiders to deal with.'

Coelwen continued stitching, and spoke without lifting her head. 'How do you know if any "sea raiders" are coming?'

Edric bent down to unlace his boots. 'Tostig,' he said, as if that were enough.

Coelwen looked up and smiled tolerantly. 'Tostig. Tostig. That is all you men can talk about. Tostig is not some will of the wisp who will descend upon us from nowhere. You said your-self that he was hundreds of miles away in Flanders.'

'So he may be. Or may *have been*. But he went there in a ship. If he went there in a ship, he can go somewhere else.'

'But why should he want to come to Scarborough of all places?' said Coelwen.

'Because it is part of Northumbria. Part of his earldom. Or his earldom that was.'

'Father, Northumbria is a big place. Even I know that. He could equally well come and land in the Wash or up on the border. Anywhere.'

'Col, you do not know the full picture. It is not only Tostig, believe me. Although I think he is the biggest threat at the moment.'

'What are the others?'

'Denmark, for a start. We have had Danish kings in England before. Sweyn Estrithson is a typical Danish king. Do you think he is just sitting there in Denmark, and saying to himself, "Oh, fancy that. The King of England has just died. Leaving no chil-dren, too. And the Godwinsons have just fallen out and kicked out one of their clan. And he wants somebody to help him wreak his vengeance. How interesting. What will they think of next? Pass the beer, will you?"'

Coelwen was forced to smile.

Edric jabbed the air. 'And another thing. Tostig's mother and Sweyn's father were brother and sister. What more natural than to try to get your cousin on your side? I tell you, Tostig will try anything.'

Coelwen smiled. 'All right, all right. So Tostig is a threat. Are there any more – besides the Bastard?'

Edric waved airily. 'A mere Norman duke is no threat to England, and certainly not to Scarborough, I agree. And Harold has an army and a navy to deal with him. A jumped-up illegitimate adventurer. He has bitten off far more than he can chew. Besides, he knows nothing about carrying an army across open water. The Vikings have been doing it for centuries. How do you think they got here in Alfred's reign?'

'Well, then.'

'Ever heard of Orkney and Shetland?' said Edric. 'They have ships, too, remember? All Vikings are the same; they are drawn to trouble spots like flies to honey. They will see a power gap, and they will rush to try and fill it. Or at least to cause no end of trouble.

'And you may also care to be reminded that our northern neighbour is not noted for his peaceability.'

'Malcolm.'

'Yes. Like every Scottish king, he raids all over the border whenever he feels in the mood, and we have no border guards to stop him. When was the last time you saw an English king up this far, never mind to Scotland? When Malcolm finds out that Edward is dead, he will chance his arm further south.'

Coelwen frowned. It was difficult to disagree. Even so . . .

'But Father, this situation has persisted for years. Nothing has changed much since old Siward was the earl. For Heaven's sake, he helped to put Malcolm on the throne.'

Edric made a noise. 'If you think that will stop Malcolm taking advantage of a juicy situation, ha!'

Coelwen pushed aside her needlework. 'All that you say may be true. But we have walls here. We have men to defend us. We have the sea for an escape if it gets really bad.' She put her hand on his arm and squeezed it. 'And we have each other.'

She carefully did not say that each of them was all that the other had.

Edric swallowed. 'That – that is true. But, my dearest Col, I not only have you; I have Scarborough. That is my charge, too. I can see danger coming. Is it not common sense to reduce the possible risks? And how can I perform my duties when I have a second loyalty here as well? When I know that, if the wrong situation develops, that second loyalty will become a first loyalty? How do I face the folk of Scarborough then?'

Coelwen dropped her head. She had no answer.

In the silence, Edric got up and pretended to be busy with small household matters. There was one other small matter, too, that he had not mentioned. If the situation were to become difficult, at least she would be away from that gross, greasy Swede.

Harold looked up. 'Have they been housed and fed?'

Gyrth sat down and reached for the beer. 'Yes. Now they wait. What answer do we give them?'

Harold looked inscrutable. 'We let them rest first – after their arduous crossing from Normandy.'

Gyrth leaned forward. 'What do we tell them?'

Harold shrugged. 'What do you think?'

'What? Just "No"?'

'Exactly. But we dress it up a bit. Just as William does. Let us take a leaf out of his book. He is telling the world how much he is in the right. Well, two can play at that.'

'To what purpose?'

'Because it plays the game. It is like a dance. The Normans would liken it to their precious chess. William wants to get himself into the best possible position – the bastard with the purest motives of public virtue.'

'You mean the oath?'

'Of course. I am trumpeted to the world as a perjurer. He has even sent off to the Pope, I hear, to get the official approval of what he is doing. The gall of the man. He knows he is in the wrong; he is a mere duke about to launch an unprovoked attack on an entire kingdom, and he is trying to get a pat on the back from His Holiness.' He chuckled briefly. 'I suppose you have to give him credit.'

'He values world opinion.'

'So do I,' said Harold. 'But I also value the truth. I know what I swore in that oath and what I did not, and so does William. It certainly did not include crowning him King of England. Besides, it was under some form of duress. And no oath under duress counts. *Everyone* knows that, never mind William.'

'What about the promise to marry his daughter?'

Harold laughed. 'Which one – the one eleven years old or the nine-year-old? There is even a rumour that one of them is dead. What does he expect me to do – dig her up?'

'So he is – how to put it . . .?'

'Posturing,' said Harold. 'Besides, whatever age she might be, William knows that I have my Edith, and he must know by now that I have married Edwin and Morcar's sister. Do I excuse myself from perjury by becoming a bigamist?'

'Do you want me to tell that to William's envoys?' said Gyrth.

'No,' said Harold. 'William wants to do the dance, so we shall do the same. Tell them that no King of England can marry a foreign princess without the permission of the Witan. Get that out into the air, as they say, and it will sound well – in

England if not in Normandy. He says he is following the law; well, so am I.'

'So they leave empty-handed?'

'No. They leave with an answer. And, if William is honest, it is no other answer than he could have reasonably expected. We may not have called a spade a spade, but we each know what the other man means. Let him make what he likes out of it.'

Gyrth made a face. 'If that is what you want.'

Harold slapped the table and roared with laughter. 'God's Face, Gyrth. What do you want me to do? Go and tell him that I am sorry, and here is the crown, and I shall marry his dead daughter?'

Gyrth was forced to abandon his frowns. It was Harold who became serious again.

'But we have gained something positive.'

'Oh?'

'Remember they are not speaking with their own mouths; they are saying what they have been told.'

Gyrth became serious too. 'So what was it they said?'

'Not what they said – what they did not say.'

Gyrth waited a moment in growing impatience. 'Well?'

'Tostig. They did not mention Tostig. Do you not see? If Tostig had joined William, William would have said so. He could not have not said so. He knows what a worry Tostig is to us. If he could have let him loose on us, believe me, he would have done so.'

'So that is one worry less.'

Harold shook his head. 'I am afraid not, brother. If William does not have Tostig, he has sent Tostig packing. That means Tostig will be off on his travels again – who knows where? Flanders, Denmark, Germany? Stirring up trouble wherever he goes. If William had taken him on, that would have meant we have only one threat. Now, alas, we have two.'

*　　*　　*

Magnus turned up his nose at the smell – woodsmoke, stale sweat, wet clothes, dogs and fetid air. The doors were opened as rarely as possible. Even so, there were wicked draughts from beneath and above, and from around the hastily fitted shutters. They only added to the discomfort without noticeably reducing the thick atmosphere.

Magnus was accustomed to it, and had tolerated it ever since he had joined Sigurd and his group, but every so often it hit with new force – like now, when he woke up in the small hours. He lay there, with little to think about but the smell.

And the sound – men snoring, dogs whimpering in their sleep, wind whining outside through tall trees, shutters rattling as they let in wayward flurries of snowflakes. The fire in the hearth now offered feeble crackles.

Magnus made a rueful face. Low – just like his spirits. But he had been out of doors and on uncomfortable travels long enough to know that this attack on the mind was a common hazard of the life he had chosen to lead. Or, rather, had had forced on him. The two or three hours before the dawn were always the worst.

If he spent too long thinking during that time, he found it difficult to discover a good reason for anything much. Looking back, what else could he have done? After the fire, he had carried out what he had set himself to do. There was now no quest looming, waiting to be attempted. No unfulfilled duty. So – nothing in front of him. He could still see the hall collapsing in a rushing tower of sparks and flames. So there was nothing behind him. He had long since lost his father and his brother in the feud, and knew his mother had died of grief and exhaustion. Well, that was what they said. More likely, she had simply run out of life. He was doing his best, and failing, to escape the memory of Sigrid.

He looked round the cabin again. It had become more crowded than ever in the last week, as more and more men came in from who knew where. Had they come, like him, simply for food and shelter? Or was there more to it than that?

He had not been with Sigurd very long, but already he was beginning to suspect that these men's motives were not entirely coloured by bodily needs. Sigurd was young, yes, not much older than Magnus himself. But he was tall and strong like him. Good-looking. Well, Magnus could not obviously say that about himself, but he had had his share of reassurance in that quarter from one or two of his female 'acquaintances'. So they had quite a lot in common.

But where Sigurd was ahead of him was in his superb self-confidence. It radiated from him. He was never cast down. He bounced back from continual crises and unfortunate incidents – only too numerous in the life they were leading. He laughed readily. He had a quick wit. He was never short of ideas or solutions. Men responded to this permanent – so it seemed – resilience. Magnus found himself liking him a great deal.

There was another reason – a silly one, really. It was the name. In the jostling, burly intimacy of young men thrown together day and night, there was much teasing, much horseplay – and nicknames. Sigurd inevitably became 'Sig'. Magnus had called his sister 'Sig'. It was quite illogical, but Magnus found himself enjoying the coincidence. It did not matter that it crossed the boundaries of sex. He loved Sigrid and he liked and admired Sigurd. It brought these two people together in his mind. In a curiously comforting way it helped to keep Sigrid alive, however faintly. She was gone, but not completely gone.

So he owed Sigurd more than appeared on the surface. He could not say what brought all these other men to be with him, but he suspected that they were not coming to join him simply for a place by his hearth and a free meal. Although that may have been the reason in the first place – for the early ones, anyway.

Sigurd provided for them – the first demand any group made on a leader. By somewhat questionable means sometimes, as many a local farm could testify. But he was not wanton and he was not cruel. He made men laugh – at himself, at themselves, at life, at everything.

When he set them tedious jobs to do, such as axe work in the forest, or fishing, or repairing their housing, or cooking – well, if the truth be told, all the jobs in that sort of life were tedious – and they began to get fed up, he would come along, crack a joke, make them laugh (he was a fine mimic), and they would return to the matter in hand with a smile on their faces.

They liked him, they came to rely on him, and they were happy to follow him.

Word spread, on the wind, as it always did. Men now began to come for more than a meal and a bed. They started to take pride in belonging to his group, and made jokes about other groups who, it appeared, did not enjoy the same good fortune. Sigurd had magic; he had style; he looked a good bet.

But this would not last for ever. They would have to *do* something. Quite what that was nobody was very sure, least of all Sigurd himself.

He talked round the hearth in the long January evenings, and was full of ideas – building a boat and going a-viking; crossing over to Denmark and maybe finding some land to farm; going to Sweden and joining the great columns of merchants who worked their way down the great rivers in the land of the Slavs; even doing what Hardrada was said to have done – carry on down the great river till they reached Miklegaard itself, where the streets, as everyone knew, were paved with gold. Everybody listened, because it was something to do, and the thoughts of such adventures kept them warm.

As they curled up to sleep, they knew in their hearts that none of this was very likely, and that sooner or later Sigurd would have to come up with a practical idea, which could be of benefit to all of them, or they would begin to drift away, just as they had, up to then, been drifting in. Charm was no substitute for success.

Magnus sighed and composed himself again for sleep. But, before he lay down, he did what nearly all of them did when they woke up before dawn: he heaved a boot at Lars. Somebody had to keep an eye on the fire right through the night – to keep it going and to make sure that it did not set light to anything else. Naturally they took turns. When it fell to Lars to do the job, he usually managed at some time during his watch to go to sleep (he could sleep anywhere). It was pointless to complain, and Sigurd had given up punishing him by giving him extra duty; he simply went to sleep on watch more often.

He was a good companion and loyal, so everyone learned to tolerate him, and simply took the chance. And they enjoyed throwing boots at him.

'You leave by the end of the week, then,' said Harold.

Edwin nodded. Morcar stayed silent. From the habit of a lifetime, he let his elder brother take the lead.

'I would have liked to stay longer,' said Edwin. He had been looking forward to some social life, to a chance to enjoy his relatively new status as Earl of Mercia – for all his tender years, that made him the senior earl after Harold. He had been looking forward to a measure of attention.

'You have heard the news,' said Harold. 'Tostig is not with the Bastard.'

'Good news, then,' said Edwin.

Harold glanced at Gyrth. Clearly this boy had as yet very little political or military instinct. Poor lad; he had not had the time.

'On the contrary,' said Harold. 'He could be anywhere by now. Flanders, Denmark, Germany. And up to no good in any one of them. This is where you come in.'

'What do we do?' asked Morcar, speaking for the first time. With his wisp of a beard, he looked even younger than he was. It was the effort to look adult that oddly took the years away from him.

'I can not be in two places at once,' said Harold. 'If the Bastard has sent his embassy here and received his answer, he will be setting the wheels in motion for the invasion – if he has not done so already.'

'What about the mission to the Pope?' said Edwin. 'Will he not wait for the answer to that?'

'Not if he has any sense,' said Harold. 'He needs six months to build a fleet and collect an army, and he must have it ready for midsummer – for the good campaigning weather. Questions take a long time to get answered in Rome. I know; I have been there. If he were to wait for an answer from His Holiness, it could be halfway to autumn. In any case, whatever the Pope says, William will invade. It is mere blessing he wants from Rome, not permission.'

'If that is the case,' said Edwin, 'what does it matter whether we leave next week or next month?'

Harold glanced again at Gyrth. It was going to be necessary for the boy – and his brother – to have everything spelled out.

'Because war is not about fighting – well, not much. It is about preparation. It is dreary and it is humdrum, but it is vital.' Harold indicated Gyrth. 'I and my brothers have been sending orders to every shire, and every hundred in every shire. I want formal oaths of loyalty sworn to me, in front of full assemblies. Witnesses. Witnesses. I want plans put in place for calling out the fyrd. I want decisions taken about how many stay in their counties and how many come to join my host.'

Edwin began to look uncomfortable. Harold swept on.

'I have put orders out for the minting of new coins. We must have money in circulation. Sheriffs and reeves from each hundred must be given funds for buying supplies, weapons, horses, wagons. I want beacons on every headland from London and Kent right down to Exeter. I want relays of horses for couriers to bring messages to me in London.'

He paused to look at the dismay on the faces of the two young earls.

'I can not do all that in five minutes. That is why I want you up north as soon as possible.'

Edwin turned pale as the implication dawned on him. 'You mean we—'

'Yes, I do,' said Harold. 'All the things I am doing here, on the south coast, I want you to do all the way up the east coast. As far as the Tyne if necessary. We have no idea where Tostig might strike, but, wherever he does strike, we must be ready. Or rather *you* must. That is why you are the Earls of Mercia and Northumbria. Wherever Tostig should choose to land, you must know, you must get there, and with sufficient strength. Any enemy landing force must be struck immediately, and struck hard.'

Their faces seemed to get even longer.

Harold smiled. 'Do not worry. You are earls. You have authority. You have my authority behind you. A king's authority,' he added. He gestured towards his brother. 'And you will have Gyrth in Anglia to tell you what to do if you are in any doubt. Leofwine in Kent, too.'

Harold glanced once more at Gyrth, then looked back at the two young men on the other side of the table.

'Do you know what is meant by "internal lines"?'

Edwin and Morcar both shook their heads.

Harold contained his impatience, though perhaps his measured tones let slip just a hint of it. Certainly it did not escape Gyrth.

'England is being attacked. Or it is going to be. It has two known enemies – the Bastard and my brother Tostig. It may have two more enemies. That depends upon whether Tostig is able to persuade the Count of Flanders or the King of Denmark to join him in his campaign of injured pride and petulant ambition. So we could have four enemies against us. Maybe even five, if Tostig can talk Malcolm into it from Scotland.

'On the face of it, that is a gloomy picture. But it is not as bad as it looks. Four or five partners in crime would find it difficult to work together even if they were under the same roof. Our enemies are spread all over the place. Secondly, our five prize brigands all have ambitions which might well run counter to each other's plans. So that is in our favour too.

'But our chief advantage is where we are – here, in England, *in the middle*. They must go round us all the time. Cover huge distances. At sea. Their lines of communication and supply are dangerously long. We are central; we are compact. We can bring our resources to bear much more easily than they can. We can react much faster to changes in the situation. We are inside; they are running round the outside.' He looked briefly at Gyrth and looked back again. 'That is what we mean by "interior lines".'

Edwin and Morcar mumbled something unintelligible. Harold tried again.

'We agree, I am sure, that we do not like the idea of a Frenchman – an illegitimate one at that – grabbing the English crown. I am even more sure, Morcar, that you would not take kindly to the prospect of my brother Tostig returning to England and snatching back your newly won earldom of Northumbria. Our two houses have not been exactly the friendliest of political partners over the years, but I think we can agree on those two aims. It behoves us, therefore, to work together to secure them. So the sooner you two are in Mercia and Northumbria, doing what I am doing here, the better it will be for all of us. Would you not agree?'

The two young earls managed a slightly more articulate sound of acquiescence. Harold softened his voice just a little.

'Look. I know that what I am asking from you is not easy. Half of Northumbria may have rebelled against Tostig, but the other half are no great friends of Wessex, and would, I should guess, not be averse to having him back. So you have peace as well as defence to organise.

'But, as I said, you have all my authority behind you. You and Edwin are brothers; you should be able to work together. And I plan to come to Northumbria as soon as I can leave the defence of the south. Be assured: by the end of the summer we shall have brushed away the fly called Tostig and drawn the fangs of the snake from Normandy. Then we shall have a good feast and a good laugh.'

When they had gone, Gyrth cleared his throat.

'Well?' said Harold, pouring himself a drink.

'Do you think they are up to it?'

'Probably not. But what else could I do? With reasonable luck they should be able at least to upset Tostig's plans for a while. We know Tostig. He is able, but he is impetuous and he is impatient. Dashing round half northern Christendom as he is, he will have done little preparation. Indeed, he will be giving himself very little time. He has next to no staff and next to no administration. And very few funds. Why else is he going cap in hand to anybody who he thinks will listen?'

'But supposing he does land? What then?'

'He has failed with the Bastard. If he fails with Flanders and Denmark – and neither Baldwin nor Sweyn is a fool – then he will be pretty much on his own. And even Edwin and Morcar should be able to deal with that. It will be little more than a Viking raid. At any rate they should keep him occupied and delayed till I can see the Bastard off, back to Normandy. If I know Tostig, by the time I turn up he will have got fed up again and gone back to his precious Judith.'

'You hope.'

'Yes,' said Harold. 'I hope.'

*　　*　　*

Canon Bernard of Lorraine knew everything. He never moved from the abbey at Waltham, but he knew everything. Men came in to see him from all over England, even beyond. And, when he questioned them, they fell over themselves to tell him the truth, the whole truth, and nothing but the truth.

He was a formidable scholar, they said. He spoke countless languages. He had a gift for inspiring fear. When he lowered his thick grey brows and focussed his gimlet eyes, grown men were known almost to wet themselves. A single meeting with him would be talked about in retrospective sweat in kitchens and guardrooms and taverns for days afterwards.

Two sea captains now stood before him, concentrating fiercely on keeping their knees still. Three days at sea in January winds, and many more hours on unaccustomed horseback, had taken most of the resistance out of them. Bernard's scalding glance took the rest. The canon, having looked them up and down, waved for them to sit. They did, on the very edge of the bench.

Bernard went to the door, opened it, and shouted.

A novice came running, and skidded to a halt just inside the doorway. He gazed in awe at the scale and fittings of the chapter house – a sanctum that was normally denied to humble members of the abbey such as himself.

Bernard did not relax his features. 'What is your name?'

The boy gaped for a moment, and then managed 'Eric, sir.'

Bernard gestured in a lordly way towards the sagging sea captains. 'Food and drink for our guests. Now.'

Eric gaped again. He was a very recent arrival. Bernard took pity on him, but not too much. Authority had to be established.

'Go to the Guest-Master, Brother Edgar. Tell him who sent you. Tell him what we want. Then bring it here as fast as you can. When you have done that . . .' He paused as a look of distress crossed the boy's face. Clearly he was not used to being given more than one instruction at a time. 'When you have done that, see to it that our guests' horses are properly stabled and fed. And those of the escort. See that they are fed, too. Tell Brother Aldric to prepare one of our courier horses, and wake up the rider, whoever he is. You will probably find him in the kitchen or the warming room. He must be on the road to London within the hour.'

As another gape threatened to materialise, Bernard clapped his hands. 'Sharp now.'

When he had clattered off, Bernard relaxed. He took two glasses out of a corner cupboard and poured out some wine. The captains looked at each other. Although this was the chapter house, and normally used only by the abbot for private and public business, it seemed that this rather forbidding canon had the run of the place. It must be the direct authority of the King, they decided.

It was common knowledge that Waltham Abbey had been founded, or, rather, re-founded, by Harold himself, and that he took a personal interest in its welfare. He had personally acquired holy relics for it on lengthy trips around France and Germany. He had acquired Bernard himself from Lorraine, come to think of it. The two captains, having made the acquaintance of both the canon and the relics, were not sure which inspired the greater awe.

Even when he held out the wine to them, they found themselves almost getting up again and ducking their heads. They sipped like fish in a bowl, and held the glasses in gingerly delicacy between the fingers of both hands.

Bernard sat down at the other side of the table, and drew out a fresh folio from the pile in front of him. A quill was scrutinised and selected, a bottle was drawn slightly nearer, and the pen was dipped. The first captain was transfixed by an eye.

'You know why you are here, I take it.'

The man almost dropped his glass. 'Well, in a kind of way, sir. That is, when I docked, I was given money, and orders to come here. King's men, sir, half a dozen of them. They – they – kind of – brought us.'

'Straight-away?'

'Oh, yes, sir, straight-away.' He glanced at his fellow captain, who nodded vigorously in agreement. 'Straight-away, sir.'

'Here. To Waltham?'

'Yes, sir.'

'Do you know why Waltham?'

Two Adam's apples dipped together. 'No, sir.'

Bernard laid down the pen, leaned forward, and put his fingertips together.

'Harold is now our King. I take it you approve?'

'Oh, yes, sir. Certainly, sir.'

'And you want him to go on being King?'

A glance flew between them. 'Yes, sir. Of course, sir.'

Bernard looked down at the backs of his nails. 'England has enemies. Wicked men who would, if they could, take his crown away.'

'Sir.' The poor men could think of nothing else to say.

'We shall try to stop them. To do that we need information. King Harold has given me the responsibility of collecting that information and of passing it on to him. Do you understand?'

A flurry of nods like Lenten lilies in a March wind.

'The King resides at this moment in London, because he thinks that the biggest threat comes from the Bastard in Normandy. This house is a special favourite of the King's. It is fairly close both to London and to the sea. So my charge is to receive every scrap of knowledge that comes in from the Channel and the North Sea. The King's brother Tostig has left Normandy, and he has almost certainly gone to Flanders, to the court of Count Baldwin.'

One man began to fidget.

'Now you –' Bernard stilled him with a basilisk eye '– you have just returned from Bruges.'

'Yes, sir. And he is not there, sir.'

Bernard frowned. 'When did you hear this?'

The man shrugged. 'Oooohh, a week or more ago, sir. And I think it was stale news then. Things travel fast in the taverns and brothels of Bruges.'

'I am not concerned about the dubious ways in which you acquired your information. All I want to know is whether it is reliable.'

'Oh, yes, sir. My brother-in-law. He brought the Lord Tostig to Bruges in the first place. Took him away too. And he never paid, either.'

Bernard grunted as he scribbled. Typical of Tostig. Still short of money.

'Where? Where did he take him?'

'Denmark, sir.'

The second man now showed signs of excitement.

'He did not stay long there either, sir.'

'How do you know?'

'I was in the harbour at the time. I saw his ship leave. It was the gossip of the whole town. The King of Denmark was not taken in by the Lord Tostig. Apparently the Lord Tostig has a temper. Flounces a lot. It was quite a joke.'

'What were they saying?'

'That King Sweyn does not wish to go on his travels again. He has only just finished a long war with Norway, and can not afford another one. He wants nothing to do with my lord Tostig.'

This money shortage seemed to be catching.

The novice arrived with the food and drink. Bernard dismissed the captains, who clattered off with precarious armfuls of cups and platters, and settled down to finish his report.

Two gems of intelligence at one go. But maybe flawed gems.

Tostig was not having a very good month. Kicked out by the Bastard. Turned down by Count Baldwin, for all that his wife Judith would no doubt have pleaded his case with her brother. And now, barely a fortnight later, rejected by the King of Denmark. Strange that a Viking should shy away from the prospect of a good juicy jaunt like that. It just showed you how important money was in these modern times. In the old days, so they used to say in the ancient sagas, a Viking chief, even a Viking monarch, just collected a few ships and some crews of willing adventurers, and away they went. Not any more, it seemed. Progress of a sort, he mused.

He scattered sand over the finished letter, went to the door, and bawled for the boy again.

The letter would be given to the courier, and with luck would be in the King's hands by dawn at the latest. He wished Harold well of the contents. If Tostig was not in Normandy, and not in Flanders, and not in Denmark, where in God's name was he, and what was he up to?

Harold undressed, put on a nightshirt, and flopped into bed. Edith waved away the chamber servants, and poured a drink herself. On second thoughts, she poured two. She came to the bed carrying both.

She held out one cup. 'Hey.'

Harold looked round, grunted, and propped himself on an elbow. They both sipped thoughtfully.

'Do you want to talk?' said Edith after a while.

Harold pushed himself into a sitting position and scooped the bedclothes round his knees. He continued sipping. Edith, from long experience, waited.

'How are the children?' said Harold.

Edith pursed her lips. This was the usual opening. So she played the game.

'Edmund had a fall from his horse last week. Gytha wants to change her hairstyle – again – and Gunnild has just had her first monthly flow.'

She still waited.

Harold finally noticed the silence, looked round, and found Edith looking straight at him. Slowly the corners of her mouth quivered. Then they burst out laughing.

'All right, all right. What do you want me to talk about?'

Edith shrugged. 'Whatever is necessary. But may I make one suggestion?'

Harold nodded. Edith came straight to the point.

'Let us get your – your – er – new wife out of the way first.'

Harold raised his eyebrows. 'What is there to say? She is quite tolerable.'

Edith nodded herself. 'I see. Accommodating, too, would you say?'

Harold grinned. 'Needs of state. You know that. Politics.'

'Yes, I am sure. No wonder you are so tired. The fatigue of public life. Ah, me.'

She put a hand on her chest, and raised her eyes piously to Heaven.

'What else could I do? The opportunity was too good to miss. The most marriageable widow in England – sister of two earls. A perfect alliance. I had to do something to bind those two boys to the kingdom. I need a united England for what is coming. You know that.'

Edith pursed her lips again, and forced her features into a mockery of tolerant understanding.

'What a sacrifice. I am sure it must have been dreadful for you.'

Harold pretended to punch her in the face. 'Oh, shut up.'

'I hope she was not put off by all those moles. In unmentionable places too. Poor woman.'

Harold put on a lofty air. 'Family trait. Very attractive. Tostig has a great wart in between his shoulder blades. He is charming, too – another family trait. He has Judith eating out of the palm of his hand.'

'And our Welsh princess now eats out of yours? Mil— what is her name?'

'You know perfectly well. It is Mildred. But she prefers Gwen.'

Edith smirked. 'With a name like that, I am not surprised.'

'Do not be a cat. Her idea, not mine. She says it is the only thing she got out of Wales that she liked.'

Edith put on a prim expression and smoothed out the blanket in front of her.

'I am sure our . . . *Gwen* will do what is expected of her.'

Harold pretended to look down his nose. 'Naturally.'

'Good for her,' said Edith. She sat back and held the cup in both hands. 'And what is expected of me?'

Harold turned and looked directly at her. 'I expect nothing of you. I never have. All I can do is hope – hope that you carry on loving me.'

'Yes – and a good thing I do, I should think.'

Harold leaned forward. 'I expect you of all people to understand.'

Edith put a hand on his arm. 'Believe me, my darling, I do. But please remember that I am a woman. Do not expect me to like it. I understand that very soon you will have to go to war. But do not expect me to like that, either.'

'What would you have had me do – reject the crown?'

Edith looked down into her cup. 'No. I would not have wanted that. You are Harold; you are what you are. Everything you have done in your life has worked up to this point, even though you may not have planned much of it, even though at times you could not have foreseen it. This is clearly the will of God; this is your destiny. This is the moment and you are the man.' She looked up. 'If you were to turn away now, you would not be Harold, and it is Harold that I love.'

Harold embraced her almost violently, spilling some of the wine on the blanket.

'Careful! I thought you said you were tired.'

Harold released her. 'That was not passion: that was admiration and gratitude. When the real passion comes, then you had better watch out.'

'My, my, what a man. I hope your new Mildred – sorry, Gwen – never sees this side of you.' She put down her cup, then looked up. 'Do you think your plan will work?'

'With Gwen, do you mean? By the Rood, I hope so. Edwin and Morcar are little more than boys. If Tostig got the chance, he could run rings round them. There are plenty up there who would welcome him back, if only for their own selfish ends. If he can stir up trouble against Morcar in Northumbria, there is no knowing what might happen. You know the north: they have never been fond of Wessex. If it were to happen, there would not be much that Edwin could do to help in Mercia. So we must stiffen their spines.'

'How?' said Edith. 'By pulling their sister into politics? Since when have women played a part in running the country?'

Harold gazed at her for a moment. 'I could not run England without you.'

Edith made a dismissive gesture. 'Nonsense. Of course you could – if you had to.'

'Well, thank God I do not have to. And pray to God that being the King's brothers-in-law will help to keep Edwin and Morcar on the straight and narrow. I shall send Gyrth to his earldom in Anglia soon. That will help, too. With Leofwine in Kent, do you see? We shall have the whole of England being controlled by members of one family.'

'Why not go there yourself?' said Edith.

'I intend to,' said Harold. 'Any day now. I have heard news that Tostig has disappeared right off the map. We know he is not in Normandy; he is not in Flanders; he is not in Denmark. So the threat to the south comes only from the Bastard. The clash will not materialise till he has gathered an army and a fleet.'

'And until *you* have,' said Edith.

'Yes. That matter is well in hand. So I have the opportunity to go north and do some binding of loyalties.'

'A Saxon in the Danelaw.'

'True. And they have not seen a Saxon king there for the best part of a century. Well, now I am going. That might make them sit up a bit.'

'Are you going with an army? I thought you said you did not have one.'

'Not a big one, I admit. Not yet. But what I have in mind does not require large armies.' He grinned and chucked her under the chin. 'Tostig uses *his* charm; I intend to use mine.'

Edith laughed. 'Good God! Are you going to get into bed with all of them?'

'I do not believe it. I simply do not believe it.'

Alfred put his hands on his hips and gazed at the other fyrd-men round him. Nobody seemed to take a great deal of notice. Boots were being eased off. Tinder and kindling were being carefully assembled. Men were crouching and stretching as they put together bivouacs and windbreaks. Sheepskins were being teased out of shoulder packs. It was still deep winter. Though there was no threat of frost, a man could easily get chilled after a day's sweating on the march.

Food began to appear as if by magic from folds and pockets and satchels. Smoke started to rise like woody incense from a score of small fires.

Alfred found himself becoming even more annoyed. It was all so deliberate, so ordinary, so domestic – and so slow. He looked at the brindled beards and grey hairs and balding pates. So old, too. These men did not look as if they could become urgent about anything. They were all past it. And so patient. How could men like this work up enough anger to face an enemy?

Alfred burst out. 'Do you not mind? We have been forced to march over a hundred miles, maybe two hundred. We are nearly into Sussex, nearly at journey's end. And now they say we are not going there after all.'

'That is war, son,' said somebody. 'Nobody ever knows what is going on. Least of all the poor devils who have to fight it.'

Another man stopped blowing on his hands. 'This your first outing, then?'

Alfred blushed slightly. 'Well, yes, in a way.'

'Been in the field before?'

'Not a proper campaign, no. It was always my father. But last year he broke a leg, and now I am old enough to—'

'Well, you have to learn sometime. And with a name like yours, you should learn fast. The real Alfred had to. Leading armies before he was twenty, they say.'

'But does it not bother you?' said Alfred. 'Do you not mind?'

A small Welshman put a hand on his shoulder. Alfred looked down at him. An archer. Scruffy, a bit weedy, but with cheery cheeks and a sparkle in his eye.

'What you are learning, boyo, is one of the first lessons in all soldiering.'

'And what is that?'

The Welshman glanced around him and back to Alfred, as if collecting an audience with his eyes.

'You are learning what it is like to be buggered about. It happens in every army in the world. Am I right, lads?'

There were grunts and chuckles of agreement.

Owen the archer had found his way into yet another group, and become one of them. His sympathetic arm round the shoulder of young Alfred took him into the circle round a fire. Llewellyn appeared from nowhere, with an armful of onions. Contributions came in from all quarters to the great pot that was suspended over the flames. Owen cracked another joke or two. Somebody produced a flask of something strong. Treats and titbits were cut up and passed round. Before long, they were taking turns to dip their fingers into the pot, shaking their hands and cursing about being scalded.

'Well, come on then, know-all,' said somebody. 'What do you think is going on? If we are being buggered about, somebody must be doing it. Why?'

Owen was never short of an answer. 'Harold has had some news. Stands to reason.'

'What news?'

Owen pointed southwards. 'We were all on our way to Sussex, yes? Now, our lot have been turned away to Anglia. To Earl Gyrth it is we have to report.'

'In London,' said Alfred, anxious not to appear ignorant.

'Gyrth is Earl of Anglia. He will be in Essex,' said Llewellyn. 'But the King has a secret camp in Essex, near his abbey.' He leaned forward. 'They say he has a special druid there. With a magic eye. Sees everything. And he tells the King what to do.'

There was another chuckle. These Welshmen were incorrigible.

'What is he telling the King now, then?'

'Telling him that there are two threats, not one. It is in the air that Earl Tostig is not with the Bastard. So – he is somewhere else.'

'Where?'

Llewellyn pointed again, this time to the east. 'Out there. So Earl Gyrth must gather an army to watch the east coast while the King watches the south.'

'Llew is right,' said Owen. 'Earl Tostig could come from Flanders or he could come from Denmark.'

82

Another fyrdman made an explosive sound of disgust. 'Suppose he does not. So we shall be told to march all the way back to Sussex.'

There were groans all round.

'No, by God and Holy Snowdon,' said Owen. 'Tostig is not finished yet. Ever heard of Orkney? Ever heard of Shetland? Or Scotland?'

'God's Face, do we have to march to Scotland as well?'

Owen shook his head. 'Have you thought of this? Tostig does not plan to persuade all these princes to come with him. He simply wheedles ships out of them, and builds his own fleet and his own army. Then he can sail up and down the coast and strike wherever he likes. Stands to reason.'

'So we spend the whole blood-blistered year marching up and down the country just in case,' said Alfred. 'I told you—'

'You are right, son,' said Owen. 'We spend the whole year being buggered about. And it would not be the first time. Am I right, lads?'

There was a growl of agreement.

'Tell us a story, Owen,' said someone. 'Cheer us up. We could do with it.'

Owen produced a little wooden ladle from inside his jerkin, and dipped it into the pot. As he licked his lips, he looked at Alfred. 'In honour of our friend here, I shall tell you the tale of your King Alfred, and how one day, instead of fighting the Danes, he burned some cakes . . .'

Waltham Abbey loomed black and menacing between the lurid flashes. The sergeant banged again on the great door with the handle of his sword.

While he waited, he looked at the group round him. My God, what a bedraggled lot. The rain pelted down. Horses stood in pathetic silence, steam rising from their nostrils. Every time the lightning flashed, they started. When the thunder rolled, they whinnied in fear. The stabs of celestial light picked out details of spur and bridle. Nobody said a word. Not a back was straight.

The sergeant looked at the man beside him. He looked exhausted enough to fall off at any moment.

'Where did you say you made landfall?'

'Berwick, in the north.'

'Never heard of it.'

At last there were signs of life inside.

'Who is it at this hour?'

'Messages for Canon Bernard. King's orders. Stir yourself.' After hours in the saddle on an impossible night, the sergeant was in a foul mood.

Bolts were shot back. Beams were lifted. However, only one of the two double gates was opened, and they had to jostle uncomfortably through the insufficient gap.

A frightened gatekeeper looked up at him from under a flapping hood. The sergeant threw back his hood to reveal a mail coif.

'Get the canon. At once.'

The man looked even more frightened. 'At this hour?'

'Get him,' shouted the sergeant, as he dismounted. 'Or you will have even more to be scared about. Move.'

The man was about to go when the sergeant grabbed him by the sleeve.

'Wait. You do not leave us out here in all this. Give us some shelter. And the horses.'

Hunched grooms appeared from nowhere, and the party were shown into a bleak kitchen, where feeble flames flickered in the main hearth. They cast ghostly shadows on the stone walls. Two or three kitchen boys sat up in alcoves and rubbed their eyes.

After an unbearable time, a door opened, and a tall figure appeared. The sergeant moved forward to complain about the reception, but found himself gazing into a pair of eyes that went right through him. He stopped and saluted.

'Sir? I have somebody here with news. And the King did say "any time, day or night".'

An hour later, the sea captain let his shoulders sag. He had been sitting bolt upright under the questioning. Canon Bernard pushed another cake towards him; his exhaustion had not interfered with his appetite.

'Thank you, sir.'

'How long have you been at sea, then?'

'Four days, sir. We were lucky – a following wind. But not too fierce. Rare in January. So we made good speed.'

'Why did you not stop in at the Tyne? Or the Tees? Why beat all the way down the coast?'

The captain looked at him in surprise. 'Time, sir. The roads in winter. It was much quicker by sea.'

Bernard nodded. It was what he would have expected.

The captain, released for a moment from the eye and the grilling, attacked the remains of a cold joint.

Bernard left the kitchen, and went to his table in the chapter house. He sat down, and pulled out paper and ink.

So had they all been wrong? Up to now they had all assumed that Tostig had been simply sent packing by everybody he had turned to – Normandy, Flanders, Denmark. Had they all been too clever?

Was it Tostig who had been the really clever one? Had he been leading them a dance all this time? Was this what he had been aiming for right from the start?

If that were the case, if he had really pulled it off, what a master stroke. It just showed you – never underestimate the ex-Earl of Northumbria.

Well, now they knew. Bernard picked up a quill. Time to begin his report to the King. Two copies, too, with a separate courier for each, to be on the safe side. They would have to go off at once, storm or no storm.

He paused for a moment with his quill in the air. Trust Tostig. And yet – and yet – the irony was that in a way it did have a certain obviousness about it. It was one of those things that you never consciously expected, but, when they did happen, you wondered why you had not seen them coming.

Chapter Three

'Hardrada! Oh, my God!'

Leofwine sat back in shock, and looked away in muted horror, his half-eaten apple still in his hand.

Harold laughed. 'No, he is not that important.'

Leofwine barely heard him, and continued gazing into space.

Gyrth was not as stunned as his younger brother, but he was shaken nonetheless.

'Not far off.' He gazed at the message that had just been delivered, as if looking hard at it might change its contents. Not that he could read it. The courier who had delivered it had been dismissed, but the clerk who had read it out was standing by, with his ears twitching.

'He is human,' said Harold. He pointed hard at the pink-cheeked clerk. 'You keep quiet about all this – understand? Not a word. Well, not till I say so.'

The clerk, overawed into silence at the news, flushed more deeply, and nodded open-mouthed.

Gyrth returned to the attack. 'Brother, we are talking about Harald Hardrada, the King of Norway, the lion of the north.'

Harold pursed his lips and stroked his moustache.

'So? We have been threatened by Norway before. Cnut was King of Norway – King of Denmark, too.'

'And Cnut conquered us, remember?' Gyrth was still in full flow. 'Where are your wits, Harold? We are talking about the greatest Viking alive. Possibly the greatest Viking ever. He would make three of Cnut.'

'Physically, I agree. He is tall.'

Leofwine came out of his trance. 'Tall? He is a giant. They say he stands eight feet high.'

Harold turned to him. 'Lef, you do not believe that any more than I do.'

'But he is a colossal force,' persisted Gyrth. 'He has fought everywhere.'

'And he is over fifty years old,' said Harold.

'Not only has he fought everywhere: he has *won* everywhere.'

'He has just signed a treaty with Denmark. After fifteen years, they agreed to give it best. Neither side could win. Not much of a victory there.'

'He has commanded the Varangians at Miklegaard. The Emperor, no less – his personal bodyguard.'

'The way I heard it, he was responsible for deposing and blinding him. Some bodyguard.'

Leofwine flung the apple core into the fire. 'Stop playing games with us, Harold. We did not expect this. It was bad enough being up against the Bastard; we are now beset by a king, not an illegitimate duke, and by somebody with a towering reputation. You grant that he has a reputation?'

'Reputations do not win crowns,' said Harold.

Gyrth joined his brother. 'Enough, Harold. Talk sense. Be practical.'

Harold threw another log on the fire, dusted his hands, came away from the hearth and came to sit opposite his brothers at the table.

'Very well. Let us talk sense. First, the Bastard. We are not sure that even he is coming, never mind Hardrada. Well, not yet. Oh, yes, I know he has *said* he is coming. Sent a whole embassy to tell us. But he must induce his vassals to come with him. Without them he is impotent. Nor can he force them, or appeal to their sense of adventure.'

'They are his vassals,' said Gyrth. 'Bound by feudal oath.'

'Only in Normandy, and only for forty days a year. As far as I know, there is no law that compels them to serve outside Normandy. And they are not crazy raiders like Vikings. They are cautious men, who have worked hard to get where they are. I know; I have seen them, talked to them, been on campaign with them. Believe me, they are not going to risk it all on a stupid gamble. And that is what it is. Most of them may not be able to read a map, but they know that England is several times bigger than Normandy. They will take a great deal of persuading. If he can not do that, then we can all rest easy about Normandy.

'Second, our lofty King Harald of Norway. Harald the – what was it? – the "Stern Ruler", the man whose policy is stark, whose hand is always "hard". The man with the mighty reputation. My brothers, if you let yourselves be overawed by his reputation, no matter what size it is, you are half-defeated already. In which case a reputation really would win a crown. So we pull ourselves together and refuse to hand him the laurel at the outset. Where is our pride?'

Leofwine flushed, but stayed silent. Gyrth still argued. 'Reputations are not built on air.'

'On the contrary,' said Harold, 'reputations are only too often built on air – most of it hot. It is the heat that makes gossip, makes them talked about. And, when they are talked about, they get exaggerated. So he is now nine feet tall. So he may have blinded an emperor or two. He may have fought all over Christendom for all I know. That does not get him into England. Have you any idea how far Norway is from England? Three hundred miles, I should guess.'

'He could land in Shetland or Orkney,' said Gyrth. 'He is overlord there. Then he could move south.'

'Shetland is ten times further away from Norway than Normandy is from England. Now you tell me – which is the more difficult?'

Gyrth looked at Leofwine. Neither could think of an answer. Harold carried on. 'I grant you we have never faced Hardrada. He is unknown. So he may be good. He may be very good. But he has to get here, across hundreds of miles of stormy sea.

'The Bastard, believe me, is very good indeed, and I *have* seen *him*. And he has only to cross the Channel.'

'What about Hardrada's gold?' said Leofwine.

'Another legend,' said Harold. 'Though, I grant you, a strong one. If he *is* that rich – if he really did loot the paving stones in Miklegaard – he will be able to mount an expedition – true. But to sustain it – that demands good staff work and reliable supplies. And I repeat, his lines of communication will be stretched to the limit.'

'And what about Tostig?' said Gyrth.

'Tostig. Ah – that was something of a shock, I grant you. Though, with our knowledge of him, we should not be surprised that he has sold the idea of such an enterprise to Hardrada. The famous Tostig charm. It tells us too that Hardrada is rather easily led, bewitched by the idea of yet another adventure – at the age of fifty, when he ought to know better. Not the best basis for a successful enterprise. You compare that with the months – possibly years – of preparation that the Bastard has been engaged in.'

'How do you know that Hardrada has not been preparing for years, too?'

'Because a reed or two would have nodded in the evening breeze. Bernard at Waltham would have got wind of it. But there has been total silence. Even Bernard was caught out, though he admits that he ought to have seen it coming. No, if Hardrada had had plans, we should have heard something. He would have been shouting about his so-called claim to the throne through that cousin of his, or nephew, or whatever. But he has only just been shouting about it in the last week or two, according to Bernard. The Bastard has been going on about his precious promise by Edward for fifteen years.

'No – it is a spur-of-the-moment decision. So it is inherently weak. He cannot possibly produce an attack within the next six months. And, even if he did, all the money in the world, and a giant *ten* feet high, will not save a scheme conceived in such haste.'

'I see,' said Gyrth, glancing at Leofwine. 'So we do nothing?'

Harold smiled. 'No, my brothers. We use common sense. We produce a measured reaction. Till we have better intelligence. Bernard will have even more spies out now that we know about this. In Normandy, too – though I hear the Bastard is trying to close the coastline. But Bernard has his ways.'

'All right,' said Leofwine. 'So what do we do?'

'Carry on what we have already been doing: build the fyrd in Sussex and Hampshire. You, Lef, will do it in Kent, and you, Gyrth, will do the same in Anglia. Edwin and Morcar have received their orders to prepare in Northumbria. There is still the outside chance that Tostig has built himself a private little fleet and will descend almost anywhere. And I am building ships as fast as I can to deal with that, and with the Channel.'

'What about Scotland?'

'No news is good news as far as Malcolm is concerned. We have enough worries for the time being.'

'Do you think Edwin and Morcar are up to it?'

'You asked me that before. I am not sure. That is why I am going north myself next week.'

Leofwine got up and prepared to leave. At the doorway of the hall, he turned.

'Do you really find it all as straightforward as you say?'

Harold rolled up the messages and gave them to the clerk, putting his fingers to his lips as he did so. The boy nodded.

'No, I do not,' said Harold. 'But the trick is to make it all *look* straightforward. If you make it look as if you find it easy, it makes the enemy feel that his job is going to be difficult.'

'Hmmm.' It was the best Leofwine could manage. Harold pursued.

'So – if you and Gyrth think I find it easy, you will give that impression to others. And so it will spread, from the top right down to the bottom. I get a reputation for never being upset. You see? I do believe in reputations too. Mine may even give Hardrada something to think about.'

'Sig, I think you had better come quickly.'

Sigurd looked up from his whetstone. 'What is it?' He could hear high voices outside. 'What is going on?'

'Not much. But it is what *might* happen that I am worried about.'

Magnus had already made enough impression for Sigurd to take notice of what he said. This young man had a head on his shoulders. It was not all beer and blood between his ears, as it was with the vast majority of the rest.

Sigurd rose and came to the door. 'Where?'

Magnus pointed.

They were split into two small crowds, about fifteen paces apart. The first group were standing round Ketil – 'Splitnose', as they called him, for obvious reasons: a white scar on the tip was the legacy of a beery brawl several years before. Ketil seemed to be throwing knives at a large wooden target – an upturned trestle, placed on end against a tree trunk, high enough for a man to stand before it without his head rising above the top. And a man *was* standing before it – Ivar the Swede, with the second group scattered on either side of him. He had his arms spread wide, and he was shouting.

'Get to it, Splits. Are your nostrils getting in the way?'

Splitnose tested the edge of his blade. 'Where do you want it? Over the head or between the legs?'

'Not near his head,' said Finn. 'There is no danger of damage there. No brains to spill out.'

There were roars of delight.

'Very well,' said Splitnose, taking his stance. He looked directly at Ivar. 'I hope you have counted them.'

'Two before and two after, just as usual,' said Ivar. 'Come on, Splits – before they get cold feet and change their minds.'

It was then that Magnus realised. God – how long had this been going on?

He started to move forward, but Sigurd put out an arm. 'No, no – let them do it. For a moment anyway.'

The shouts and catcalls from both groups died away as Ketil braced himself for the throw. Ivar stuck out his chin and stood motionless.

'Ha!'

The handle quivered in the pine just two hands' breadths below Ivar's crotch.

There was a roar and a round of applause. Ivar moved away, yanked out the knife, and tossed it back to Ketil.

They both turned to the rest. 'Now – what about it?' They held out their hands.

As he counted out the coins, Finn Arneson said, 'Do we get a chance to win our money back?'

Ivar stuffed the coins into his waist wallet. 'What do you have in mind?'

'Double the stake says you can not do it with an axe.' Finn looked round at the group. 'Are you on?'

Another roar. Finn turned back to Ketil and Ivar. 'Are *you* on?'

By way of answer Ivar went back to the trestle and began to position himself in front of it.

Sigurd removed his arm away from Magnus. 'You are right; it is time we did something.'

He moved forward, went up to Ketil, and laid his hands on the handle of the short chopping axe that Ket was already fondling.

'Let me see that.'

Puzzled, Ket let it go. Sigurd turned it over in his hands, and ran a thumb across the blade.

'Hmm! Very good condition. A pity you should waste a good edge on Ivar's prospects.'

'My axe,' said Ketil. 'I do what I like with it.'

'Not while you are with me,' said Sigurd.

'Not even when I am off duty?'

The voice was level, but the challenge was there. Both groups fell silent.

'Not even then. Certainly not when you are doing things like that.'

'Like what?'

Sigurd suddenly whirled round, took a throwing grip on the handle, and with barely any hesitation flung it. It embedded itself in the trestle, a foot from Ivar's head.

'Like that.'

Ivar went white. So did Ketil. Sigurd dusted his hands.

'You throw axes when I say. I do not want half my men beheaded or castrated for no good reason. Save your balls and your brains for the enemy.'

'What enemy?' said Finn, emerging as a fresh challenge.

'The enemy I shall very soon find for you,' said Sigurd. 'I am going away for a few days to get one.'

'Where?'

'You will hear soon enough. Meantime, get on with that roof.'

Finn looked round as if to collect an audience, and a supporting audience.

'We joined you as soldiers, not as labourers.'

Sigurd was ready for him. 'You joined me as vagrants. Desperate for a roof and a square meal. I have given you both. For that you do whatever I tell you to do.'

Finn tried a more conciliatory approach. 'Come on, Sig. We have worked and sweated. We have just made all those shields you wanted. Though why you want so many I can not imagine. Do we not go into battle with swords as well?'

'You do indeed. The trouble is – and you would know if you had seen a mite more action – that the enemy goes into battle with swords, too. And axes. Have you seen what a battleaxe can do to a wooden shield? So we need spares. Plenty of them. If you go into a fray unprotected, you can be the best swordsman in Scandinavia, and you will not last five minutes.'

Finn gave his shoulders a great heave. Sigurd was right of course. He always was.

'Think ahead,' Sigurd would say. 'Muscles do all the work, like mules, but they need brains to drive them. Bravery and brawn are not enough. Practice too. Practice, practice, practice.'

Sigurd was slowly making a unit out of them. They had trained and marched and countermarched. They had formed open battle order and close battle order. They had practised sword technique and axe-handling. Even sleepy Lars admitted that they were five times better than when they had first come together.

That was the trouble: they were indeed getting better. Ketil's latest antics with throwing knives showed that. But they were getting impatient. Over-confident. Because they were improving, they did not need so much grilling and drilling. They were discovering more spare time. Sigurd could not continue devising work for them very much longer.

The northern nights were still tedious, and they were barely into February. That still meant long hours round the hearth with the wind howling in the pines outside. They could not tell the same stories and laugh over the same old jokes for ever.

Before long, the horseplay, the shows of bravado and the gambling would lead, as surely as night followed day, to injuries and quarrels over wagers and debts. Their cohesion would start to rot – and Sigurd knew from experience that the rot could set in with dizzy suddenness and spread with alarming speed.

It was time to do something. And it was up to him to discover what that something was.

'That roof you were so grateful for needs repairing. I want it repaired by the time I come back.'

'And what if we do not?' said Finn.

'Then you will die of the cold and the damp long before the thaw.'

'We could leave,' said someone.

'You could,' said Sigurd. 'If you want to start right back where you were when you came crawling to me. And it is still deep winter. Fancy that, do you – out there? On your own?'

He looked round at the glum faces, and laughed. Magnus always admired how precisely Sigurd timed his laughs.

'Cheer up, lads. I shall come back with something to make your fortunes. I have an idea.'

They looked at each other. A whole sheaf of eyebrows were lifted. Sigurd was always having ideas.

'What?' said Finn. 'Go on – surprise us.'

Sigurd put a finger beside his nose and tapped it. 'If I said that, it would not be a surprise, would it?'

Eyebrows climbed up foreheads again.

'No – this one really is good. And you will like it, I promise.' He looked round the whole group. 'You mend the house and I mend your fortunes. Do we have a bargain?'

He looked directly at Finn. It was always better to single out the leader and get him to agree. He would do the work with the rest, and none of the rest would want the worry of taking over his leadership.

Finn nodded. 'So be it.'

'Good. I leave early tomorrow, and I am taking Magnus with me.'

'Why?' said Finn, trying to regain a little credit.

Sigurd deliberately misunderstood him. 'Because I am taking only one worker away from you. That way your work on the cabin will not be so hard or so long. That is my sacrifice in the cause of everybody. I look after my men, you see?'

Finn, after a moment, grinned ruefully. Sigurd had outwitted them once again. It was a fair stroke.

As the group split up, Sigurd called Magnus to his side and spoke quietly. 'We leave this evening – late.'

Magnus looked surprised. 'But you said dawn.'

'Dawn was what I said, but tonight was what I had in mind. The sooner we go, the less time they have to think up objections.'

'What are you going to do?'

'I have not the faintest idea – yet.'

Magnus almost spluttered. 'But you said—'

'I know what I said. I had to say something. I had to retain the initiative. Did you have any better ideas?'

'Well – no.'

'There you are, then.'

Sigurd went indoors again, and resumed his work with the whetstone. Magnus followed, and sat down on the opposite side of the hearth.

'Where are you going?'

'Ah – I do have some idea about that.'

'Are you going to tell me?'

Sigurd thought for a moment. 'You will find out soon enough.'

Magnus fell silent. Then a thought occurred to him.

'I had no idea you were so skilful with the axe like that.'

'Neither did I,' said Sigurd without looking up.

'But why? You could have killed him.'

'True. But, from what I saw, it was not going to be long before they changed from throwing things for a wager to doing it in earnest. Magnus, they are bored. They need something new and something exciting. If I wish to continue leading them, I must find it. If they are getting like this sober, what could they be like drunk?'

'But you promised.'

'Of course. If I had said maybe, they would not have stayed with me. They want decision *now*, not half-ideas next week.'

Magnus gaped. 'But you threw the thing at his head.'

Sigurd looked up and grinned. 'It was a fair gamble. If he died, he would not cause any more trouble and neither would the others. If he lived, it would give them all a shock, and it would have the same effect.'

'But you threw it *at his head*,' persisted Magnus.

'Exactly. I thought if I aimed at his head, I had a very good chance of missing.'

'The tortures of the damned, Father. Tortures of the damned.'

Brother Eustace was so consumed with his aches and pains that he could spare no emotion to be frightened of Canon Bernard. He even sat down on a bench without being invited, lifted one foot onto a knee, and began massaging complaining toes.

Bernard smiled sardonically. Brother Eustace was a terrible moaner, but he was a good listener. If he was able to place himself anywhere near a conversation, his good ears, and a near-perfect memory, enabled him to recall every detail of what he had heard – or rather overheard. Because of his monastic education, he was both articulate and coherent. Too many of Bernard's couriers were industrious, enterprising,

even brave, but they were garrulous, and incapable of string-
ing more than two sentences together without tying themselves in knots.

Bernard had to interrogate like some papal inquisitor to get
anything worthwhile from them. They were often so carried
away with their own narrative that they omitted the most
important facts until Bernard teased them out. Brother Eustace
was easy; all Bernard had to do was put up with his ceaseless
complaints.

It began at once.

'A terrible crossing, Father. Waves like mountains. I swear I
shall not be able to eat for a week.'

Bernard met him head-on. 'So you do not wish me to order
anything for you?'

Eustace hesitated. 'Well, perhaps just a morsel. Just enough
to enable me to give you my report.'

Bernard smiled and nodded at young Eric, who smiled back
and went to the kitchen.

'Now,' said Bernard. 'Events. Events. What has happened?'

Eustace knitted his brows. 'The biggest, I should say, is the
Duke's council.'

'Where?'

'At Lillebonne. It is near the mouth of the Seine, not far
from—'

'I know where it is,' said Bernard.

Eustace looked at him, but did not apologise, as almost any
other courier would have done.

'Mmm. The Duke, as I said, summoned his council there.
Not just his senior advisers, like Fitzosbern and Beaumont
and—'

'I know who they are, too.'

'Yes. Well. He had everyone there, every vassal who held land
direct from him.'

'How did you get in?'

Eustace looked at him as if it were a rather unnecessary question.

'They needed the records kept, and, believe me, there were a lot of records. The Duke wanted every single promise and commitment written down, to make sure that nobody could wriggle out of it later. So they used the brothers from the house of St Wandrille. It is only a few miles away.'

Bernard nodded. 'I know. And you just happened to be staying at St Wandrille. How convenient.'

Eustace took down one leg from a knee and put the other up instead.

'You told us to use our initiative, Father. You warned us about the Normans searching for spies. I did not think they would be likely to turn a holy house upside down. And I have been there before. As you are well aware, the vows of hospitality, which—'

Bernard waved him on.

'What happened?'

'It was a long debate, Father. It was a good job my French was as good as it is.'

'Why do you think I chose you?' said Bernard. 'Half French yourself. And a French name.'

Eustace pretended to look aggrieved. 'I thought you chose me because of my quick wits.'

'Certainly not because of your modesty, which, I should have thought, would have been inculcated into a young novice. Now get on with it.'

'As you wish, Father. Well, I must say that it was a triumph for both of them – Fitzosbern and the Duke. When the Duke first put the project before them, they hummed and hawed, and talked about debts and prices and bad times and enemies behind their backs and all the usual things. They said they needed to debate among themselves. So William craftily let them do just that. There they were, in fives and sixes, all round the hall, going on like a market full of old women.

'Then Fitzosbern started circulating among them, and asking them what they wanted and what they were prepared to do. They told him. When he had spoken to most of them, Fitzosbern made them an offer. If they did not fancy talking direct to the Duke, would they let him do the talking for them? Did they want him to be their delegate, to speak with their voice? They thought this was a very good idea.'

For once Bernard did not interrupt with questions. Eustace was bowling along very nicely, and clearly liking it. Bernard found he was enjoying the story for its own sake.

'So,' said Eustace, 'Fitzosbern stepped forward from the gathering and addressed the Duke. First there was a very oily preamble about how loyal and faithful they all were, and how they would sacrifice anything for the good of Normandy and its ruler. Well, they could hardly object to that. But it was softening them up, before the real business.

'Fitzosbern then sprang the trap. He said he had been delegated to speak for the whole meeting. He said that they were willing not only to support the Duke's great enterprise; they would contribute double their usual feudal tribute of men and money to it.'

'Holy Mary!' Bernard found himself reacting like a member of a minstrel's audience.

'That put the cat amongst the pigeons,' said Eustace. 'There were protests and roars of disapproval. In fact, the meeting, to all intents and purposes, broke up. That was when the Duke himself stepped in. He separated them out, and spoke to every one of them – every single vassal – face to face. Not one of them had the gall to say, eye to eye, that he had no intention of supporting such a crazy idea. I watched him. It was a brilliant piece of work. By the time he had finished, they were all on board, so to speak.'

'And that was that?' said Bernard, anxious to bring the interview to an end, so that he could begin writing.

'By no means,' said Eustace. 'That was where we came in. The Duke wanted every single promise and commitment recorded – ships, men, money, everything. I tell you, Father, it took hours. We got cramp, the brothers and I.'

'Was *that* it, then?'

'No,' said Eustace without a trace of apology. 'Then they all had to put their marks – three copies for everybody: one for them, one for the Duke and one for the record.'

Eustace reached out for the plate that Eric had just brought in.

'I tell you, Father, there is no going back now. They are all in it up to their necks.'

Bernard nodded. 'And let us hope that some of those necks get stretched or severed before we have finished. All right, you can go.'

Eustace looked a little dismayed.

'And take the damned plate,' said Bernard.

As soon as the door was shut behind him, Bernard reached for the writing materials.

Well, one mystery was solved. The Bastard at least was coming. Hardrada might be another matter. Time would tell. And still nobody knew where Tostig was, or what he was up to.

'So you are sending her away after all?' said Gunnar.

Edric stopped what he was doing. His shoulders tensed. Gunnar had a knack of appearing not only by surprise, but particularly when he was not wanted. Edric had a small army of workmen round him. They were deep in the business of strengthening the defences of the town, and Gunnar knew it.

Gunnar moreover had a tendency to dispense with the niceties of everyday etiquette, as if to imply that he and Edric knew each other so well that their 'friendship' allowed direct access and intimate forms of address. He had not announced his arrival. He had not even given the customary morning greeting. It was a mercy that he had not clapped Edric on the shoulder. It was intrusive and, repeated frequently, it was infuriating. Yet Edric knew that it had to be tolerated. Scarborough was not a big town. He and Gunnar were the two most prominent citizens. They had to live together. Telling Gunnar to go away, or even to keep his distance, would have made an open enemy of him – far worse than an unwanted 'friend'.

Edric turned round and faced him. His workmen waited patiently.

'Yes. And may I ask how you know that?'

Gunnar presented a smug smile, which only made his lips seem thicker and more unpleasant.

'Servants talk.'

Edric accepted the inevitable. 'I see.' He offered no more. If Gunnar wanted any extra information, he would have to work for it.

Unfortunately, Gunnar *did* want some extra information.

'Where are you sending her?'

'Up into the Dales. I have family there.'

'Remote, then?'

'That is the general idea. It is a lonely village. No raiders would want to go near it; there is nothing worth looting.' Not even worth burning, if the truth be told. In fact, it would be a very well-informed looter who knew of its existence.

Gunnar peered at some fresh timber that the workmen were planing. 'You are taking her yourself, I should imagine.'

'I can not get away. You can see how much needs to be done.'

Gunnar glanced around him. The gate and nearby walls were in the course of being totally overhauled. Half-finished, it all looked a purposeless mess. Gunnar made a wide gesture.

'Do you really think all this is necessary?'

'Yes, I do. We have no idea what might happen. It could be Hardrada who descends upon us. We know now that he is coming – sometime. There is always Tostig. He could be out there anywhere.' Edric gestured towards the North Sea. 'And if the King comes to inspect his defences in the north – and it is in the air that he will, very soon – I do not wish to be found wanting in the discharge of my duty.'

Gunnar nodded appreciatively. 'I rather thought that would be the case. So I have a proposition to put to you.'

Edric did not like the sound of this, but, once again, he did not wish to incur animosity at such a difficult time. He did not like the prospect, but it was just possible that he might be grateful for Gunnar's support in the coming months. Scarborough was a remote coastal town in Northumbria, well away from the main roads and the cities. Not only had no king thought it worth visiting, but very few sheriffs had bothered overmuch with it, either. It remained to be seen whether the new earl, young Morcar, would put it high on his list of priorities.

Edric turned to the foreman of his labourers, whispered a few instructions to him and turned back to Gunnar. 'Let us walk a while. I want to go round the walls, anyway. See what else needs doing.'

'Well?' he said, as they started walking.

'I have business interests in the Dales,' said Gunnar.

'Oh?'

'Sheep, if you must know. Fleeces. I need to make arrangements with certain people, or at any rate to make contact. I can arrange an escort for Col.'

There he was again – 'Col'. The unwanted, intrusive familiarity. It was a close family name, and he knew it.

'I thought you said you were busy here as well,' said Edric.

'I am. So I propose to send Vendel.'

Vendel! His droopy, pigeon-chested son. Ha! Some escort. The boy did not look as if he could even *lift* a sword, much less fight with it.

Gunnar read his thoughts, but did not take offence. 'I can provide able bodied men, well able to take care of themselves and of Col. Vendel will be a pledge of my goodwill and good intentions. Everything will be paid for.'

There was more to this of course. Gunnar was finding a way of putting his son close to Col, well away from prying eyes and interfering fathers. But it would be less of a worry to know that she had some protection out in the wilds like that. Gunnar's men were indeed well able to take care of themselves. They were regularly employed in the collection of debts, and they were not noted for their gentle manners.

On the other hand, Gunnar would want the whole arrange-ment – if things were to work out as he hoped – to be proper and above reproach. He was climbing the ladder in Scarborough society. Indeed, he was near the top, and he would not want any scandal or unfortunate incident to sour the air now that he was so close. So Col should be safe.

Gunnar would pay his men well if they behaved themselves. Vendel had never shown a spark of adventure in all the time Edric had known him. Indeed, it was doubtful if Vendel was even as physically strong as Col, who was a sturdy young woman.

It was just that Edric simply did not like being beholden to a man like Gunnar. You never knew when Gunnar would call in the favour. But – hard times necessitated hard solutions. And Col was a sensible girl.

Gunnar's next remark was a stroke of good timing.

'I see you are not very well supplied with good timber. I can fill that gap. No charge, of course. I am proud of Scarborough too, you know. And I can offer more labour as well. You can get the work finished much faster and to a much better standard.'

He saw Edric hesitate. 'And if the King should come to inspect . . .'

Later, back home again, Gunnar called for some food and drink, and summoned his son.

Vendel appeared somewhat unwillingly, clutching a sheaf of papers. There was ink on the fingers of his right hand.

Gunnar looked appraisingly at him. If he were honest, no, it was not a face or a figure that a father could be proud of. But the boy was intelligent, if not very worldly. Gunnar had put him into a house to make him literate, in the hope that it might stimulate the boy's business faculties. The brothers pronounced him a good pupil, even willing. But, try as he might, Gunnar could not get him interested in business. Not really interested. Oh, yes, he listened, he could carry endless facts and figures in his head, and he was totally reliable. But he had no natural drive, no instinct for it. Gunnar sighed, then beckoned him to sit down.

'Eat.'

The boy did so. For a while no word was spoken. At last Gunnar pushed away his plate and drained his cup.

'I am going to send you up into the Dales. Fleeces again. It is time.'

The boy nodded listlessly.

'And Edric's daughter Coelwen will be going with you.'

'Oh?' Still no sign of animation.

'Edric wants to get her out of harm's way, and I must say I do not blame him. If I were her father, I should do the same. I shall send six men with you. You will escort her to her uncle's manor. You will see to it that she gets there, and that nobody – nobody – takes any liberties with her. I need to be able to look Edric in the face and tell him that she has safely arrived. Do I make myself clear?'

Vendel nodded again, as if it were all routine.

'Good. Be ready in two or three days. Now go and carry on with your scribbling.'

Vendel's 'scribbling' was a tired family joke. Nobody ever knew what it was, and he never talked about it.

When he had gone, Gunnar went out and called for his clerk. He sat the man down at the table, and got the serving girl to clear it. The clerk spread the papers, and cut a couple of quills.

Gunnar marshalled his thoughts. He had done what he could regarding Edric and Coelwen. It was an opportunity and he had taken it. It was not a big step forward, but it was a step nevertheless, though he doubted whether his son would exert himself much to work out or develop the possible advantages of it.

He had offered a significant contribution to the defences of the town, so nobody could doubt his loyalty in that direction. He had already written to Tostig and Earl Morcar, and was still awaiting the possible dividends of those ventures. Now it was time to make further provision, now that the circumstances seemed to have changed in the north.

'Ready?'

'Ready, sir.'

Gunnar started to walk up and down. He always composed better, he found, when he was on the move.

'To His Majesty the most illustrious King Harald of Norway, King by the Grace of God, *et cetera* . . .'

'God blast you – that was my favourite hound.'

The kennel boy stood in mute dejection.

'Not one word of warning,' shouted Morcar, 'Have you any idea how much I loved that animal?'

The kennel master decided it was time to intervene.

'It was not the boy's fault, my lord; he was following orders.'

Morcar whirled round. 'Yours, I suppose.'

'Yes, sir, as a matter of fact it was.'

Morcar kept the flush in his face.

'You could have called me. We could have discussed it. It was my dog.'

The kennel master stood his ground. This was not the first time he had seen his new young earl lose his temper. What was worse, they both knew he was in the wrong.

'We knew how fond of him you were, my lord. That is why we did not want to distress you. That was a mean boar. The dog's injuries were so bad that it would have been cruel to let him live any longer. So I told Sawin to put him down. Believe me, we are both sad at what we had to do.'

Morcar fumed, and tugged at the tiny wisp of hair that he cultivated under his lower lip. All the Earl's servants knew what that meant: that his young lordship could not think of what to do next, in case it made him look silly in front of inferiors.

He was rescued this time by his brother Edwin, who had come into the stable yard, and had been watching. He dismounted, and flung the reins at a groom.

'Morcar!'

Morcar, relieved to have somebody else to complain to, turned to him, and began to recite the whole incident all over again. Edwin cut him short.

'Forget it. Come with me. We have business to conduct. I have heard something.'

After another nervy tug at his chin, and another red-faced, pouting glance at his kennel staff, Morcar whirled away and joined his brother.

Together they entered the kitchen and passed straight through into the hall.

'Something to eat and drink,' shouted Edwin through a doorway.

When they were sitting down, Edwin said quietly, 'You should not go on like that, you know – not to servants. Especially when you are in the wrong.'

Morcar flushed again. 'Not you too. Did you not see—'

'I saw,' said Edwin. 'And I say you were in the wrong.'

Morcar, after a short silence, controlled himself.

'Very well. What is it?'

Edwin threw his gloves onto the table and leaned back.

'Tell me, what are your plans for Northumbria?'

Completely thrown off balance, Morcar said, 'Plans? What plans?'

'Do not play the innocent with me. This is me, Edwin, your brother. I am Earl of Mercia; you are Earl of Northumbria. We are here in York. England is threatened by an invasion, maybe two – possibly even three. I say again: what are your plans for Northumbria?'

Morcar opened his mouth to say something, but Edwin cut him short.

'I shall tell you what your plans are. You are saying to yourself, what is best in it for Morcar?'

Morcar pouted again. 'Are you not saying the same for Mercia?'

'Not quite. Mercia is not in the same danger as you, or rather Northumbria. If Hardrada comes, you will be the one in the way, not Mercia.'

'So?'

'I have heard some news, and I am here now to stop you doing anything stupid.'

Morcar began to bluster again, but Edwin held up a hand. 'Now shut up and listen. I am your brother. I know perfectly well what has been going on in your mind, ever since the coronation. Oh, yes, you gave your pledge to Harold and you bowed before the crown. You were thinking of a crown in England, but not of a crown in a *united* England. You know that Northumbria does not like the idea – never has liked the idea – of a ruler of Wessex lording it over Northumbria. But you and the older earls have put up with it because the blood of Cerdic ran in the veins of our kings. Now it does not. Harold is not of the blood royal. So you think that changes things.'

Morcar did not say anything, but he was not red in the face any more. Edwin continued.

'Well, it does not. Harold is King of England – all England, whether you like it or not. You swore the oath too. If you have fancies about making Northumbria some kind of half-kingdom under Harold, forget it.'

'Harold ruled Wessex like a king,' said Morcar. 'People used to call him the "Under-King".'

Edwin laughed. 'And you fancy yourself as a second Harold? Have some sense. You are not half Harold's age, and you are not half the man Harold is.'

Morcar opened his mouth to reply, when the food and drink were brought in. He and Edwin maintained a loud silence while it was all laid out.

'Do not disturb us,' said Edwin as the servants left.

Morcar, having had just a moment to contain his temper, said instead, 'So what do you suggest I do, O big brother?'

Edwin poured himself a drink. 'I suggest you ponder the possible consequences of what you might be *thinking* of doing.'

'And what is that, O knowing one?'

'Harold is coming north. That is what I was going to tell you. So you can announce to him, face to face, what your plans are. I am sure he will be most interested to hear them.'

Morcar sneered. 'You seem to know everything. You tell me what I am going to say.'

'Very well. As I see it, you have three possible courses of action . . .'

'Here you are, lads. Look what I found for you.'

Llewellyn the archer let a whole cascade of loaves tumble out of his arms. They missed the ashes by inches. A flurry of hands flew out to save them from rolling into the fire.

'Where did you get these?' said Alfred.

'You see, my lad? We are not buggered about all the time.'

'Tell us, damn you.'

Llewellyn composed himself beside the fire, and began to cut up one of the loaves.

'It seems Earl Gyrth is a better organiser than we thought. The camp reeve knew we were coming. You should see the ovens and the spits they have up there.'

'So there is some plan to it.'

'I should say so. Owen agrees with me – eh, Owen?'

Owen nodded with his mouth full, then swallowed hurriedly.

'I was talking with one of the cooks,' he said. 'The King had this camp planned months ago. So, if he had this one planned, he had others planned as well.'

'Where are we, then?'

'Place called Thetford. In the middle of Anglia.'

'Why Thetford?'

'Because it is midway between the great road north and the east coast,' said Owen. 'We can march north or we can march to the sea. I tell you, Harold thinks of everything.'

Alfred was not impressed. 'So we sit on our arses here?' he said.

'Better than marching, I should say,' said Llew. 'Eh, lads?'

'But what do we do?'

'Eat. Plenty more where this came from. All free. First things first. Why should we worry? You know the difference between a young archer and an old one, Alfred?'

Alfred shook his head.

Owen winked at Llewellyn. 'A young archer carries fresh arrowheads in his quiver; an old archer carries food.'

There was a general chuckle. Alfred was not sure whether he was being teased or educated.

'Who are we expecting, then?'

Owen shrugged. 'Your guess is as good as mine. It could be Denmark, or it could be Flanders, or it could be our friend

Tostig. One thing for sure, though. No need for us to learn any more French, my lads. We shall not see the Bastard up here.'

'Who do you think, then, Owen?'

By virtue of his humour, his gift of the gab, and his endless resource, Owen had established himself as the camp sage. Faced with a mystery or a problem, he would lean back on his heels, suck his teeth, and say, 'I have been thinking. And you know, lads, this is what occurs to me.' And away he would go. To back up what he said, he had an anecdote for everything. His stories were coming to be regarded not only with amusement, but with increasing credulity. And nobody could think of a better explanation.

'What do you think, then, Owen?'

Owen wiped a hand across his mouth. 'You know, lads, what occurs to me is this.'

Glances were exchanged and leggings were adjusted to a more comfortable position. The last of the bread disappeared. Llewellyn, who knew the story anyway, went off to scrounge something from the spit.

'On Tostig it is – my money. Of all the brothers, he is the brightest.'

'Brighter than the King?' said Alfred in surprise.

'Yes, possibly. Not better, only brighter. Look at the rest. Sweyn is dead – and thank God. Earl Gyrth and Earl Leofwine – good men, loyal – follow Harold anywhere. But bright?' Owen shook his head doubtfully. 'The youngest – Wulfnoth – well, we do not know. A hostage in Normandy these fifteen years, poor lad. What chance does he have?'

'But look at Tostig. Earl of Northumbria when he was barely thirty. Earl for ten years. Made a good marriage. Very faithful, they say. Does not drink much; never swears.'

'Holy Face!' said somebody.

'True, I say. I have seen him. On campaign. And a man who does not swear on campaign is a rare man. Good soldier, helped Harold conquer Wales. We should know; we were there.'

'You make it sound as if he was the one who should have been crowned.'

'If his mother had had anything to do with it,' said Llew, 'he would have been.'

'All right,' said Alfred, 'if he was so wonderful, why was he banished?'

'Unstable,' said Owen.

'Spoiled,' said Llew.

'Mother's darling,' said Owen. 'Edward thought he was wonderful. Thought the sun shone out of his – well, you know.'

'So what went wrong?'

'Bad justice. He gave bad justice in Northumbria.'

Alfred nodded knowledgeably. 'Ah, yes, the rebellion.'

Owen nodded. 'People will forgive almost anything except bad justice. Even the great Tostig charm could not get round that. He thought he could charm Edward into keeping him there. But Harold and everyone else said he had to go, and the King had to give in. Broke his heart, they say.

'Tostig thought he was hard done by. But then, he would – spoiled and all. No doubt his wife Judith is whispering in his ear, and egging him on. When the old King died, he thought he was going to get Northumbria back. When Harold refused, that was when he embarked on this great quest – revenge. He will do anything and ally with anybody to get it back.'

'He is not so wonderful, then?' said Alfred.

'No, indeed. No, indeed. But he is clever, as I said. And charming. So who will he hoodwink into helping him? Normandy? Flanders? Denmark? Scotland? Or all of them? And who will he be able to outwit? The Bastard? King Sweyn? Earl Gyrth? Leofwine? Harold himself? I tell you, my lads, he could be anywhere, he could land anywhere, and he could be capable of anything.'

'And fyrdmen like us are here to stop him?' said Alfred.

'That is what occurs to me.'

Alfred made a face.

'Christ Almighty!'

Harold indicated a chair.

'Come in. Sit down. I want you to listen to this. It is from Bernard.'

Bishop Wulfstan of Worcester raised his eyebrows.

'I was under the impression, Majesty, that I was here in your company to bring peace, not to discuss impending war.'

Harold hid his impatience. Wulfstan had an unimpeachable reputation for righteousness, holiness, and general all-round virtue. But, like many men with such a reputation, he was too often tempted to wear it on his sleeve. It could at times become a little tiresome. At the very least, not comfortable company. But Harold's brothers were not with him. Gyrth was organising coastal defences in his earldom of Anglia, and Leofwine was doing the same in Kent.

Wulfstan's virtue was the reason Harold had brought him on this peace mission to Northumbria. He would be an invaluable ally in negotiations. Nobody could publicly disagree with Wulfstan without at once putting himself in the wrong. Now, if it had been Stigand, there would have been the very devil. Whereas Wulfstan paraded his virtues, Stigand did not give a fig who knew about his sins, and it did not always produce amenable delegates on the other side of the table. Stigand was good company, but bad publicity.

So – no Gyrth, no Leofwine, and no Stigand. Harold had to discuss the news as it came in with somebody. Somebody knowledgeable, reliable and discreet. And news had just come in from Bernard at Waltham . . .

The courier was exhausted. He had not expected to have to come this far north. Bernard had told him that His Majesty had departed for York, but he had been dismayed to discover that he had already reached Lincoln. He was in admiration for the efficiency of the horse relays that had been organised, but it did not lessen his fatigue.

Harold packed him off to the kitchen, and had summoned his young clerk. He arrived, breathless and pink-cheeked as usual. Harold had sat in total silence, with bowed head, while he read the letter right through.

When he had finished, Harold looked up at him. 'What is your name again, son?'

'Conrad, Majesty.'

'Ah. From Lorraine.'

'Franconia, Majesty.'

'But you came to Waltham with Father Bernard.'

'He recruited me, Majesty. Franconia is near Lorraine.'

'Yes, yes.'

'Sorry, Majesty.'

Harold smiled. 'There will be a lot more of these messages coming, I have no doubt. It is beginning to look as if we shall be seeing quite a lot of each other. So I think you can dispense with the "Majesty" every single time. A plain "Sir" will do.'

Conrad ducked his head. 'Yes, Ma— sir.'

Harold looked him up and down. Slender, fair-haired. Very presentable. The high colour still in the cheeks. He held himself well. His English was good; so was his accent, considering. So far he had shown himself reliable. If this were to go on, he would have to be trusted with an increasing amount of what could be highly confidential information.

Harold decided that he would have to follow his instincts. There was no time for further refinements of research.

'Would you like to continue working for me?'

Conrad blinked, baffled. 'But I already do – sir.'

'No,' said Harold. 'I mean *only* for me. How would that suit you?'

After a second's struggle with the implication of what he had just heard, Conrad's face lit up. He suddenly went down on one knee. 'Sir.'

Harold laughed and lifted him up. 'I am only your King, not your confessor. What I expect from you is not a list of your sins but your silence and total discretion. From now on, you keep your lips sealed as if *you* were a confessor. Is that understood?'

'Sir.'

'Good. Now, wait outside for a while. I am about to summon the Bishop of Worcester. When he comes, I want you to come back in, and read Father Bernard's letter all over again.'

'Sir . . .'

Harold poured two drinks, one for himself and one for Bishop Wulfstan. He looked in Conrad's direction.

'All right. Go ahead.'

Wulfstan put out a hand. 'I can read it for myself, you know.'

'Of course you can,' said Harold. 'But I want to hear it again, to make sure I have not missed anything.' He nodded at Conrad.

Conrad drew himself up and cleared his throat.

'Bernard of Lorraine, canon of the royal abbey of Waltham, to—'

'Just get to the meat of it,' said Harold.

'Sir.' Conrad went a little pink and cleared his throat again.

'"This is a digest of three of the latest items of intelligence which have come in from Normandy. Or, rather, as the Bastard had tried to close the main roads and the seaports, from Brittany and Ponthieu and Flanders:

'"The Duke is mounting a huge diplomatic offensive. Letters have gone off to Denmark, to France, even to the Emperor in Germany. I need hardly stress the importance of three pieces of luck he has had. The succession of the throne of Anjou is now disputed and there is imminent civil war, so border trouble is not expected from that direction. The Count of Brittany is now tame after the Duke's recent campaign. And the new King of France, who is a minor, is in the guardianship of Count Baldwin of Flanders, who is the Duke's father-in-law. So his frontiers are as safe as can be expected.

'"More important, a reply has been received to the Duke's embassy to Rome."'

'Now,' said Harold, 'mark this, my lord.'

Conrad continued.

'"His Holiness, Pope Alexander II, gives his blessing to the Duke's enterprise – his holy enterprise – and by way of blessing has sent a holy banner which is to be carried throughout the campaign. Furthermore, all those soldiers who commit themselves to this holy enterprise can expect to have their sins forgiven and their time in Purgatory cut short by virtue of their noble contribution, to remove an excommunicate archbishop from Canterbury and to remove a perjurer from the throne of England. To accompany the banner His Holiness has sent a ring which contains within it a hair from the head of St Peter himself, the Prince of the Apostles.

'"So it appears that the Bastard is squeezing the very most that he can out of this papal support. I would point out that the Vatican court did not ask to hear from the English side of the case, so I would suggest that their case, being so one-sided, is therefore null and void.

'"I would further point out that His Holiness, Alexander II, is an old pupil of Father Lanfranc, the Abbot of Caen. This busy cleric has no doubt used his wide reputation to impress the Holy Father, just as he has doubtless placed his skills at the Duke's disposal in the drafting of the original application. My guess is that it is due entirely to Lanfranc that this application was addressed as quickly as it was. I know of no other suit to Rome that has been given such prompt treatment. If nothing else, it serves to show that the Duke is at the least very well served.

'"Finally, I have to report that a large amount of evidence is coming to our notice to the effect that the Bastard is recruiting extensively, not only in Normandy, but over a huge area – Poitou, Brittany, Anjou, Champagne, Vermandois, Flanders, Hainault, Frisia, Lorraine, Swabia, Franconia, Bavaria, Burgundy. In the south too – Béarn, Foix, Roussillon, Navarre, Apulia, Calabria, Sicily, and beyond.

'"Our observers have seen new keels being laid down in practically every river from the Couesnon to the Somme.

'"Further bulletins will follow as further intelligence comes to hand.

'"I beg to remain, Majesty—"'

'Yes, yes.' Harold waved a hand again. Conrad gathered up his papers. Harold nodded for him to go, and turned to Wulfstan.

'What do you make of that?'

Wulfstan lifted his shoulders in the smallest of shrugs. 'I am not a warrior, nor yet a strategist. It is not for me to pass comment.'

Harold banged his cup on the table, and forgot formality.

'Oh, come on, Wulfstan. You are an Englishman. What do you make of it?'

Wulfstan allowed the hint of a twitch to appear at the corners of his mouth.

'That God in His Wisdom has removed one of your chief enemies.'

'And what is that?'

'Doubt. It would appear that the Bastard is most definitely coming.'

'What will you do first?' said Oswy.

'Drink some of my own beer,' said Wilfrid without any hesitation. 'God! Get below the Trent and they have no idea what beer is. The stuff we have been putting up with for all these weeks. Bilgewater – straight out of a Grimsby collier.'

118

Oswy eased his horse round a pothole. 'I think I shall go for a good roast.'

Wilfrid looked sharply at him. 'In midwinter? Where will you get that?'

'I have not had a good Lincolnshire roast since November,' said Oswy. 'If I have to kill one of our breeding sheep, I shall have a roast before the next day is out.'

'You must have a very compliant reeve,' remarked Wilfrid. 'I can never get much more than rock-hard salted pork out of mine.'

'Ah.' Wilfrid enjoyed a good moan, and Oswy was content to leave him to it.

After a mile or so, Oswy decided that his fellow housecarl had had enough gloomy brooding for one day.

'Cheer up, Wilfrid. We can put our feet under our own table for a few days, and be beholden to nobody. We can enjoy our own hearth, chase stable boys, gossip with reeves, swagger around our own property, and generally enjoy being the lord of the manor. Even our wives may be pleased to see us.'

Wilfrid made a face, but did allow himself half a grin . . .

The King had needed some persuasion.

'What, now? Do you realise, as soon as I have finished here, it will be the York Witan, then back to London for the Easter Witan at Westminster. And, after that, who knows? Hardrada? Tostig? The Bastard?'

Wilfrid stood his ground. 'None of those invasions will come yet, sir – not before high summer at the earliest. You said so yourself.'

'Tostig might.' It was a conscious effort to break the habit of referring to him – to subordinates – as 'Earl Tostig'.

Wilfrid was not impressed by that, either. 'You said too that the Earls Edwin and Morcar should be able to deal with them on the east coast.'

Harold hoped Wilfrid was right. Stiffening the backs of these two young noblemen was the main reason for his making the trip all the way from London.

Wilfrid, and men like him, needed to be listened to. What this housecarl had done was raise a problem that, Harold knew, was going to plague him right through the coming year: how to hold able-bodied men in readiness for long periods. Nobody had any idea when these invasions would come, or where, or – at the moment – how many. But, if he was to stand any hope of success, he had to be ready. Invasion armies had to be attacked immediately; speed was of the essence. Bridgeheads could not be allowed to grow.

That meant having fighting groups available to deal with any crisis at any time – and at any place from the Scottish border at Berwick right down and round to the Channel coast as far, possibly, as Exeter, maybe even further.

It was bad enough trying to keep these men from getting bored and fed up. It was worse knowing that the vast majority of them had duties and worries that drew their minds away every evening as they sat before campfires and let their thoughts run free in the chill evening air.

Wilfrid and Oswy were not mere fyrdmen, contracted to serve so many days a year. Nor were they the rag-and-tag that attached itself to any army in the hope of quick and easy reward – little loyalty or staying power. These were housecarls – professionals. Men of status. They were landowners in their own right, many of them. Most of them would follow Harold to the death – Harold knew that – but they merited consideration. No commander could afford to take loyalty like that for granted.

These men had worries, just like kings. Harold knew, and Wilfrid knew that he knew. That was why he felt comfortable standing his ground.

Harold looked into Wilfrid's fierce grey eyes. 'Where do you live – on the coast, is it not?'

'Yes, sir. Near Grimsby. Two villages not far. Oswy lives at Little Coates and I have my holding at Great Coates.'

'Close to each other, then?'

'Yes, sir. We are cousins.'

Harold pretended to shiver. 'On the Humber. God's Face – I bet that is cold.'

'It does blow a bit, sir,' admitted Wilfrid. 'But it is good land. And there is the fishing.'

Harold nodded. 'How long would you want?'

'A day's riding each way – say a day and a half. With a good horse. Three or four days to put our affairs in order . . .'

'. . . and kick a stable boy's arse.'

Wilfrid grinned. 'Something like that, sir.'

'Very well. Be back on the seventh day.'

'Thank you, sir.'

'I shall be in York by that time.'

'Sir.' Wilfrid moved to go.

'You can do me a favour.'

'Sir?'

'Think what we may have to do in the coming months,' said Harold. 'A great deal of marching. I know God gave us two legs each, but He also put horses on earth to help us get around with greater comfort and speed.'

'You want horses, sir?'

'Yes – anything remotely usable. I do not mean these great galumphing Norman destriers – nobody has those, up here or anywhere else. I mean anything with four legs that can carry a man and rest his legs on a long march. You can have them back at the end of the year.'

'If they last that long,' said Wilfrid.

'In that case I shall pay you for them,' said Harold. 'Is that a bargain?'

Wilfrid made a wry face. 'Oswy and I will do our best, sir. I hope you are just as grateful when you see them.'

*　　*　　*

In the nave of the great minster at York, Bishop Wulfstan of Worcester administered the Host to a long line of communicants.

It was the last step in a carefully prepared procedure that Harold had worked out with Wulfstan on the journey north. First, long before the King's arrival, had come the summons to attend – delivered to every thegn, abbot and senior cleric the messengers could reach in the north, allowing for Pennine snow and Cumbrian rain. Most of these men had been unable, or unwilling, to make the long journey south for the consecration of the Confessor's new minster, and so had been absent from the assembly that had elected Harold King.

Well, now they could have no complaint; here they were being given the opportunity to elect Harold King, in person, on their own home ground.

By arranging that Archbishop Aldred should be given plenty of business to conduct in London, Harold ensured that his friend Wulfstan was given all the scope he needed to parade his authority and his forbidding virtue, with no rival to outshine him.

There was a giant procession through the streets of York, bursting with heralds and outriders and escorts and chaplains and choirboys and rustles of monks from every one of the surrounding houses – pipes and drums and tabors and staffs of authority and swirling incense and anything else a harassed mayor could think of at the last minute. At the centre of it all was Harold on a splendid horse, caparisoned to kill, waving and shouting, exchanging jokes and catcalls with the crowd. Then came every member of the newly summoned Witan. Harold wanted to make quite sure that they got a good view of the crowd, and a sharp impression of their excitement, and of the general goodwill that was being created all round them – whether they liked it or not. Finally, Bishop Wulfstan himself, in full pontificals, crozier and all, surrounded by a screen of yet more clerics and chaplains, frowning severely and fully living up to his meticulously advertised image of episcopal sovereignty and celestial holiness. It was quite a show; the participants enjoyed it almost as much as the crowds, which caused the streets to bulge. Harold offered up a silent prayer of thanks that the Almighty had looked so kindly upon his efforts as to have brought out the sun.

When the congregation had settled itself in the nave, Wulfstan, in a chasuble even more magnificent than all his other vestments, came forward, and proceeded to preach a sermon laden with references to sovereign power and the authority of the Church and the paramount importance of loyalty to an anointed king, and numerous references to Zadok the Priest and Nathan the Prophet and Samuel and Eli and Saul and David. Its message was enveloping, all-embracing and unmistakable.

Before the congregation could recover, Harold stepped into Wulfstan's place, and looked searchingly at the front rows, trying to meet as many eyes as possible.

This was the arena; this was the contest; this was the year's hinge. Which way would the door swing?

'My lords, last year this illustrious province of Northumbria rose in revolt. The late King, Edward of noble memory, would have brought fire and the sword to put down that revolt. It was I who persuaded him that the people of Northumbria deserved mercy and justice. Peace, not war. Thanks to my advocacy, there were no hangings and no persecutions. The King listened to your case, and recognised that you had been the victims of injustice, at the hands of the Earl Tostig – my brother. I make no excuse for him.

'The result was that Earl Tostig was banished, and a new Earl, my lord Morcar, was appointed in his place. I am now King. I have confirmed Earl Morcar in his position of Earl of

Northumbria, and, at Westminster, he, and the rest of the Witan there assembled, elected me King. Many of you now here, my lords, were unable to come to London because of the winter weather.

'So now I come to you. With an escort, not an army; with persuasion, not power; with fairness, not force. I have here, to show you, one of my new coins – here it is. It is stamped with one word: "*Pax*" – "Peace". I have the new dies with me, for minting here in York. "Peace". Peace for England. All England.

'I come here with an ideal, a dream. A dream of a united country. I come to you not as Harold of Wessex but as Harold of England. As I speak these words, our country is beset by enemies on every hand – in Normandy, in Flanders, in Norway and quite possibly in Denmark, Scotland, Orkney and Shetland.

'These enemies will not be attacking Northumbria or Anglia or Wessex; they will be attacking England. That is how they see it. We shall defeat them, never fear. But we shall not defeat them as Northumbria, or Anglia, or Wessex, great though they all are; we shall defeat them only as England. If we try to stop them, each on his own, as Wessex or Anglia – or Northumbria – we shall fail, and all will fall under the yoke of a Frenchman or a Dane or a Norwegian. All will have gone – Wessex, Anglia, Northumbria – all will have gone, because England will have gone.

'I do not want that to happen. I do not believe that anyone here wants that to happen, either. I was elected King to stop that happening. Without Northumbria, I am in some doubt as to whether I can do it. But *with* Northumbria, with the noble north, with all of you behind me, I have no doubt whatever that it can be done. And done triumphantly. We shall clear the shores of England. And Wessex and Anglia – and Northumbria – will come into their true greatness. We shall fling this foreign flotsam back into the sea, and live – together – in peace and safety.'

This was the moment.

'Will you have me as your King?'

A servant took away the bishop's ceremonial robes, and left a simple gown in their place. Wulfstan slipped it on, tied the cord round his waist, stretched, and subsided onto a bench.

'No question, Majesty. It was a noble effort. God was truly with you this day.'

Harold nodded, slightly mystified. 'It sort of came to me. It was almost as if I was listening to myself.'

Wulfstan poured a drink. 'Never underestimate the power of theatre. We in the Church are experts at it. And you – may I take the liberty of saying? – are learning fast.'

Harold grinned. 'And just a little of the Will of God, too.'

Wulfstan nodded solemnly. 'Just a little. But God prefers it if those He helps show some willingness to help themselves first.'

'Do not expect God to do *all* the work, eh?'

'Indeed. You have it.'

Harold heaved a huge sigh. Wulfstan put a hand on his arm.

'More to the point, you have given Edwin and Morcar no escape. With the Witan behind you, they have three choices, two of them impossible: they must either be secret rebels or they must turn to Tostig and become open rebels. Either way they go against the categorical verdict of their own Witan. Either way spells disaster. They have no choice but to be faithful.'

Magnus shook his head.

'I can still not believe it.'

Sigurd lifted his head from his horse's neck, where he had been whispering fond nothings.

'Nevertheless.' He looked very pleased with himself.

'Trondheim!'

'It is only a capital town, like any other capital town.'

'I have not been to any,' said Magnus, 'so I would not know.'

'Always go to the centre if you can.'

Magnus shook his head again.

'But to him.'

'And always right to the top – if you can.'

Magnus stared. 'How on earth did you do it? How did you know?'

Sigurd laughed.

'I can not let you go on thinking like this – I shall start believing it myself.' He shot a warning glance at Magnus. 'But this is only for you – not the others. Your word?'

'My word.'

'It was not brilliance, however much I may be tempted to claim it. It was not a stroke of fortune. It was not God intervening, with all due respect to the Almighty.'

Magnus frowned. 'Well, then?'

'It was the odds. The odds looked good. It was worth a try. We would have achieved nothing if I had not tried. Just as it was with Ivar and the axe.'

'You will have to explain.'

Sigurd patted his horse. 'You will agree I needed to come back with something. If I did not, I should soon have had nothing to come back to.'

'So?'

'I knew what was in the air. It was all over Norway. If he was planning something like that, he would be at his capital, ready to receive tribute and other contributions. He would need to coordinate everything. You agree?'

Magnus nodded.

'He was buying,' said Sigurd. 'I had something to sell – you, and Ivar, and Finn, and the rest. And not just off-scourings

– well trained. I had seen to that. And you were my best testimony.'

Magnus stared. 'So that was why you took me?'

'Not the whole reason, but certainly part of it. If he thought there were plenty more where you came from, it was going to make things easier. Moreover, I could bring you all at any time. All he had to do was give me a date. I knew he was rich. I knew he was needy. That helped.' He paused. 'There was something else, too.'

'What was that?'

'My name. Sigurd. I knew his father's name was Sigurd. Indeed, many men call him Sigurdsson. I knew that would attract him. Familiarity. Always a winner.'

Magnus marvelled at this man's superb confidence. Sigurd smiled smugly.

'Knowledge, dear boy. Not luck – simple facts.'

Magnus frowned. 'I knew most of what you have just told me.'

'Exactly. But you did not know what to do with it.' He tapped himself on the chest. 'I did. That is my gift. I know an opportunity when I see one. I work out the odds. If they look good, I strike. Because timing is important, too. Two months ago, he had not thought of it. Two months hence, it might have been too late; he would have gone.'

Magnus had a thought. 'Do you think our lot will see it like that?'

'They will by the time I have finished with them. Stand by and listen. And learn. I am good at selling, too. Remember the story of Eric the Red? He told people he wanted men for an adventure – a new life – in a wonderful green land to the north. In fact he called it "Greenland". And they joined him. Could not wait. When they got there they found that it snowed for three-quarters of the year. So they complained. "Why did you deceive us?" they said. "Why did you call it 'Greenland'?" they said. "Simple," he said. "If I had not, you would not have come."

'That is what I shall do. I shall offer them something they can not refuse. What do you think they will choose? To stay on and shiver out the rest of the winter in a moth-eaten log cabin in the forest, or join the greatest Viking alive and run wild in a whole new kingdom? I tell you, dear boy, the year of Our Lord one thousand and sixty-six is beginning to look good.'

What he did not tell Magnus was that Sigurdsson's daughter clearly liked the look of him. And he rather liked the look of her.

Chapter Four

Edith gazed at Harold's back. 'Do you not think you were hard on him?'

Edith did not sit down. Harold turned and looked up, and patted the mat beside him invitingly. Edith shook her head, and drew her shawl more tightly round her. She looked up and down the bank either side of them.

'Not warm enough. Besides, you will not talk much. Put a fishing rod in your hands, and you are useless for all practical purposes.'

'The only chance I have had for weeks. Would you deny me that?'

'Would you deny Edmund the chance to behave like a prince?'

'No. Nothing would please me more than that he should behave like a prince. I do not want him to behave like a spoiled prince.'

'Give him a chance, Harold. His father has been King barely two months. He has to learn.'

Harold drew in his line. 'Then he has to learn fast.'

He paused with a fresh piece of bait in his fingers. 'Edith, we are not of the House of Cerdic. We do not have the leeway of tradition, which makes allowances. Nobody will make allowances for any of us. We have to get it right, from the very start.'

'Edmund behaved badly, I grant you. But he has us to correct him.'

'That is what I have just done – corrected him.'

'With the flat of your hand? In front of servants?'

'Especially in front of servants. They were the ones he was rude to. One day neither you nor I will be here. He must learn to do it himself. He must bear himself like a prince without fault.'

'Even though he knows he will never be King?'

Harold was ready for her. 'It is God who makes the laws, not I. God and His Church. It is not up to me.'

'But it is up to you to marry and father legitimate princes, eh?'

Harold did not even look up. 'You are speaking as Edmund's mother, for which I respect you. But you would not say that, speaking for yourself. You would understand, for which I love you.'

Edith made a face at him behind his back, then came and sat down on the mat.

'I spoke to Bernard before I came out to look for you. He says there is news of Tostig.'

Harold picked up his rod again. 'Scraps. Bits and pieces. He flutters to and fro like a sparrow trapped in a hall. It looks as if he is frustrated every time. But we hear only of his failures. Tostig is clever. Perhaps he is collecting small successes all the time, which we do not hear of, because our spies do not see them.'

'For example.'

'Tostig is clever, I repeat. You know him only as a charming brother-in-law.'

'Albeit a rather unreliable one.'

'Nevertheless . . . I know him as a brother, from the cradle. I also know him as a soldier. We fought together in Wales. I tell you, he is good. I know him as a fellow earl, as a ruler.'

'And a bad one.'

'Yes indeed. A very bad one. So we got rid of him. Now we know him as an enemy. But put together all his many gifts, and we have a very threatening enemy. Do you know what I think?'

Edith put her hand through his arm. 'What do you think?'

'I think he has been collecting all this time.'

'Collecting?'

'Ships. And crews. Every time he is turned away, the ruler who turns him away lets him have a handful of ships. Why? To get rid of him, to stop him being a pain in the neck, to allow them to get on with their own plans. And, if he can do a spot of harm to me while he is playing with those ships, fine. If my attention and my resources are drawn elsewhere, it can not but do them good. Money well spent, would you not say?'

Harold made a fresh cast, and sat in silence. Edith looked sidelong at him. This was the man who had been her friend and lover for nearly fifteen years. It was what they called in the Danelaw a 'handfast' marriage – legitimate and normal in the Scandinavian society from which it had sprung. And Edith was a daughter of the Danelaw, raised in Norfolk. She had never felt second-class because of it.

Neither did Duke William, Harold's enemy in Normandy. He too, a descendant of Vikings, was the fruit of a handfast union. But men were so accustomed to calling him 'the Bastard' that it had become a virtual nickname, like 'Hardrada'. William was content to ignore it, so long as nobody with more arrogance than sense made a reference to 'the son of the tanner's daughter' in his presence, and then his wrath could be terrible.

The recent reforming popes had not helped matters by insisting on the necessity of marriage as a guarantee of legitimacy. So both men carried a burden of sorts.

Edith understood all this, and she understood equally well that there were much bigger burdens on her lover's shoulders. Crowned and anointed Harold may be, but he was not of the House of Cerdic, and to many Englishmen this was of the highest importance. It was a matter of five hundred years of tradition and continuity. It was a matter of the very soul of Wessex.

There still lived a descendant of that distant Cerdic. Edgar the Atheling was a mere boy, who had lived all his life in Hungary, to escape Danish enemies. But the blood of Cerdic ran in his veins. There was still an 'Atheling' interest in England. Thanks to the old Norman friends of the late King, there was a 'Norman' interest too. And Wessex was not exactly doted upon by either of the two other most powerful earldoms, Mercia and Northumbria. Two more toxic herbs in the brew were the King of Denmark and the King of Scotland, each on the lookout for rich pickings in a turbulent time. And there was always Tostig out there somewhere, with a great big spoon waiting to stir the pot.

As if that were not enough, into the kitchen had stepped Harold of Norway, the Stern Ruler, whose titanic reputation dwarfed those of all the others put together.

Edith felt a great fullness of heart. Here was this man, surrounded by a forest of demons, and he was blithely casting his line as if he were a shepherd boy taking time off from the sheep.

On an uncontrollable impulse, Edith put her arms tight round his shoulders and kissed him.

'Hey – careful! I nearly had a bite.'

On another equally powerful impulse, Edith punched him.

Owen arrived rubbing his hands, and snuffing the evening air.

'Holy Mary and Ffestiniog, that is fresh meat. Where did you get it?'

'Ask no questions and hear no lies,' said Llewellyn. 'But I tell you this: the very last chickens these are, between here and Colchester.'

Owen sat down and put out his hands towards the flames.

'Oh, the blessed warmth. You have no idea, Llew, how lucky it is you are.'

Llew adjusted the spit, and drew his knife in preparation for sharing out the rations.

'Camp fatigues? You call that lucky?'

Owen looked at the circle of shivering workers who were trying to make themselves comfortable. 'Lucky – yes. Anything that is not to do with building bloody beacons. I tell you, Llew, I would have lit one of the damn things if nobody had been looking. The wind up there is like a thousand knives. They say Earl Gyrth is a cold man. Being as how he is Earl of Anglia, I am not surprised. I reckon the coast of Anglia is only a league or two from the edge of the world.'

'Stop talking, Owen,' said Alfred. 'And you, Llew, start sharing.'

Round went the chicken and the bread. Spoons were dipped into the pot, in the slender hope of trapping an onion among the bubbles.

For a while very little noise was made, as everybody made the best supper they could. But, slowly, eyes were taken off the food and cast upwards into the night sky. Men looked at each other, as if each were waiting for somebody else to start the conversation. Owen looked at each man in turn.

'You will not see much tonight, boys. Too much cloud.'

'Thank God,' said somebody.

'But it is still there,' said somebody else. 'Behind the cloud.'

'Still a long way away,' said Llew. 'What harm can it do?'

That was the signal for a dozen forecasts to come tumbling out.

'No good will come of it; it never does.'

'They say kings die. Just like Pharaoh.'

'Who is Pharaoh?'

'Some king or other. He died in the bulrushes, they say. Drowned.'

'Should have looked where he was going.'

'It is not for mockery. There will be a famine – you wait and see.'

'Just like this camp, then. We shall be used to it by the time it comes.'

'No, I mean it. All over the kingdom. Mark my words.'

'Earthquake, too. Well, that is how I heard it.'

'Who told you? Has he seen this – this thing?'

'Seen it for myself. All hairy. With a great tail.'

'It glows, like a fiery worm. Right up there. See it for miles.'

'It brings bad things,' said Owen. 'Do you not know about the last time it came? It brought the death of the King and the invasion of the Vikings. They were the scourge of God.'

'How do you know? Were you here to see it yourself? Fancy you being that old, Owen.'

'For truth it is,' said Owen. 'It will be bad for somebody.'

'Never worry, Owen,' said Alfred. 'Perhaps it will be bad for the Bastard, not us.'

'Or Tostig.'

'Or anybody,' said Llewellyn. 'Let us hope it will be bad for every prince, then we can all go home.'

Loud laughs were lifted into the evening air, but searching faces were lifted, too. Not very sure faces . . .

Brother Eustace advanced into the presence. Even from the back view, Canon Bernard of Lorraine was able to inspire reverence. Eustace coughed gently.

Canon Bernard turned round. A wayward eyebrow stuck out. He had clearly been tugging it – always a bad sign.

'You sent for me, Father,' said Eustace, quaking inwardly at the awful prospect of further travel that was about to be laid before him. 'Where to this time?' he said, dreading the answer.

The canon allowed himself the faintest of sardonic smiles,

then gestured towards three long trestle tables against the wall. They were almost groaning under the weight of paperwork.

'There.'

Eustace blinked.

'We have to reduce this to manageable proportions,' said Bernard.

'Father?' Eustace was still groping for the right question to ask, and still wincing at the possible answer.

'On those tables,' said Bernard, 'lie all the letters and reports that have come in, and a copy of every message I have sent to the King. They are now so numerous as to be an unwieldy mass. I want you to prune them.'

Eustace let both his own eyebrows take flight up his forehead. Bernard waved an impatient hand.

'No histrionics now, Eustace, please. There is work to be done, and you are my best scholar.'

Eustace forgot his fear so far as to preen himself a little. Bernard, having achieved the desired effect, got down to business.

'You will go through all these documents, and pull out all those you think are worthy of my further attention.'

Eustace now looked more cheerful. 'And burn the rest.'

'No, you idiot,' said Bernard. 'Just put them on another table. You never know when somebody will tell us something quite random, and something which hitherto has looked useless in one of those papers will suddenly become important. I want to be able to find it quickly.'

Eustace looked worried. 'How do I do that, Father?'

'You use your common sense and your brains. You can read nearly all of them. You have French, Latin and German. And, I would wager, Flemish as well.'

Eustace began another preen, but Bernard cut him short. 'I shall let you off the Norwegian and the Danish. You will soon learn to recognise those writers who can not string two sentences together without tying themselves in knots; those who can watch a busy seaport all day and see nothing; those who talk for pages and say nothing; those who have all the facts and understand nothing.'

'What do I look for, Father?' said Eustace, becoming more practical.

'Anything military. News of any kind of gathering, large groups on the march, camps near the coast. Pay special attention to reports from the seaports – shipbuilding, cargoes of sailcloth, nails, tar, hemp, timber. Then there are the more difficult ones.'

'Father?'

'Messages from foreign courts – which prince is visiting whom? Which bishop or cardinal is on his travels? That sort of thing. Royal rumours, gossip. Anything. Oh – and something else.'

'Father?' Eustace was beginning to wilt.

'Fresh material is always coming in. The piles of messages will change; some will get bigger than others. That in itself will tell you something. For instance, the Normandy traffic is getting thicker. We are fairly sure now that the Bastard is coming. But he has to hold his motley army in camp till his fleet is ready, and he has to hold his fleet till the weather is right. Believe me, he will have his problems. And, when he does come, it will be with worried vassals and a bag of riffraff recruited God knows where, in a fleet thrown together with half-seasoned wood.'

Eustace nodded. He was beginning to understand.

'Flanders has gone quiet,' continued Bernard. 'Tostig was not able to inveigle the Count into his adventures, for all that he is the Count's brother-in-law. So he has gone off in a huff.'

'As usual,' commented Eustace, feeling more at home with the project.

'Indeed. Then there is Denmark. I do not rate Denmark very highly. If King Sweyn has just signed a treaty with Norway after fifteen years of war – which he has – he will not have much energy or liking for another military venture just yet.'

'That leaves Norway,' said Eustace.

Bernard inclined his head by way of approval of Eustace's perspicacity. 'Well done. Sweyn in Denmark may be a spent force at the moment, but Hardrada most certainly is not. He is the one who has upset the apple cart. I should have seen it coming, especially with his character and his reputation – which almost certainly bewitches himself as well as everybody else. Now it looks as if he and Tostig have got together. I would almost wager that Tostig put him up to it. What is worse – we know roughly where the Bastard has to strike, if he strikes at all. But Hardrada can strike anywhere, from the Scottish border right down to Essex. And Hardrada brings in two more troubles.'

'Father?'

'Scotland for one. Malcolm will watch out for any juicy morsels that float to the top of the pot. Orkney and Shetland for another. Jarl Thorfinn is no great threat on his own, but Hardrada is his overlord. Their joint resources may well prove menacing. Keep an eye open for that.'

'It seems, then, Father, as if most of the messages will come from the north,' observed Eustace.

Bernard smiled his approval. 'Well done again, Eustace. It looks as if we shall need a headquarters in the north. Another Waltham in York.'

Eustace began to suspect something. Just reading messages: it had been too good to be true.

Canon Bernard stood up and smoothed his erring eyebrow back into place. The shadow of a grin flitted across his granite face.

'Fancy a journey to York, Eustace?'

Eustace managed a wan smile. He too should have seen it coming.

'If it is your pleasure, Father.'

'Would you like to rest?'

Coelwen lifted her eyebrows. 'We have been on the road barely more than an hour. I am not a frail Lenten lily.'

Vendel blushed. 'I am sorry.'

Coelwen immediately regretted what she had said. Vendel had not deserved it. He had spent much time since dawn – and indeed most of the evening before – attending to every detail of the coming journey. Many times he had asked if there was anything he might have overlooked for her comfort. She had been dismissive, almost abrupt – the result, she had to admit to herself, of her annoyance at having to make the journey at all. It was not Vendel's fault, as she well knew.

She disliked the idea of leaving Scarborough, and had argued again with her father, but his reasons were unanswerable, and she knew him well enough to know that pleading with him would not achieve her aim. Her father loved her – which was indeed the whole point of her journey. She had no choice but to accept. She was her father's daughter. She had been brought up to understand, almost from swaddling clothes, that tears would not get her anywhere. Reason and common sense would, but not tears. He was a rare father, and she, in consequence, was a rare daughter.

Perhaps it was the price she had to pay for the fact that Edric had had no son. Coelwen had learned boyish things. She had been given responsibilities beyond her years, and was expected to live up to them. She was treated as a reliable member of the household, not as a mere adornment of it. After her mother died, she was treated too as a companion. Her father was her best friend.

She shared her father's distaste of Gunnar. She shared his annoyance at being beholden to this overweight, objectionable Swede. For all his clumsy attempts at neighbourliness, it was obvious what his motives were. Gunnar never appreciated that everyone always knew what his motives were; he honestly thought he was manipulating them. When they fell in with what he wanted, he could not see that they were only tolerating a situation that they could not avoid.

It was for this reason that everyone disliked his son Vendel. Everyone could see what his father was trying to do for him and with him. Again, it was not Vendel's fault. Because he was a dutiful son, people assumed that he was party to his father's clumsy, often tasteless, schemes. Because he was completely overshadowed by his father's overbearing personality, he rarely spoke in his presence, much less imposed himself on the conversation. So everyone assumed he was a mouse. Because he had few if any redeeming physical features, everyone assumed he was a graceless mouse. Neighbours, if asked, would have struggled to put their attitude into words. They would have patched up a verdict rather to the effect that it was not so much that there were unpleasant things about him as that there was absolutely nothing about him. They could think of nothing to say.

Edric and Gunnar had, naturally, dominated the farewells. Edric by his lack of fuss. He and Coelwen had long since said everything that was necessary; each knew exactly how the other felt; each perfectly understood the other. They embraced, once – that was all. Save that Edric gently tweaked her nose, something that had given her pleasure since the cradle. She smiled, and turned away to the horse that one of Gunnar's servants was holding. Mounting the box, she settled herself in the sidesaddle and put on some gloves. Edric never took his eyes off her.

Gunnar dominated of course by never stopping the fuss. The horses were too fractious; the wagon needed its coverings properly lashed; the bodyguard were harangued about good manners, about the roads, the rate of progress, the weather, the danger of outlaws. Vendel was harangued about absolutely everything. It was a bravura performance for an audience of whom none spared a glance.

The column at last wended its way through the renovated gateway. Edric watched till they were all completely out of sight round a bend. He nodded briefly to Gunnar, and returned to his repair party on the walls.

Vendel rode beside Coelwen at first, and tried to make conversation. But Coelwen confined all her remarks to commonplaces with her maid on the other side. Thora had plenty of commonplaces to talk about; she was a very poor horsewoman. After a while he gave up, and rode with the front three of the escort. The other three engaged in desultory chat with the driver of the wagon. It was anything but a merry company.

It was after the hour that Vendel tried again. It was then, after her riposte about the Lenten lily, that Coelwen began to feel ashamed of herself. But, when Vendel retreated a second time, she found it difficult to repair the damage. He was too far away again with the escort.

It was the maid who rescued the situation. She complained of a need of nature, and Coelwen had her excuse. The request was, naturally, of an embarrassing nature, but at least they had to speak to each other. Vendel stopped beside the first accessible wooded patch. As Coelwen and Thora made their way towards it (Thora would not go by herself), Vendel sharply told the escort to keep their dirty mouths shut.

Gradually, very gradually, it became easier. By midday, she was content to share his company for the meal. He was grateful to get away from the escort, with whom he had little to share beyond a common interest in his father's business.

Coelwen asked politely about Vendel's work for his father, and Vendel put similar wary questions about the new fortifications of Scarborough. The answers on both sides came readily enough. Each was mildly, and quite pleasantly, surprised.

The weather turned suddenly bad shortly afterwards. The rain came in sharp, cold, and low-slung. Few clothes were going to stand up to it for very long.

Vendel came alongside again.

'I think we should take shelter, my lady.'

Coelwen felt an absurd surge of vanity at being so addressed. But all she said was, 'What do you suggest? Out here in the open?' Still the faint tinge of annoyance.

Vendel took no offence. 'There is a house not far, round that bluff. The brothers there taught me my letters. I know the Prior; he will welcome us well enough. There are good facilities for guests.' Well, good by the standards of Yorkshire, and he did not suppose Coelwen was very well acquainted with many houses elsewhere.

'Very well.' There was no other answer Coelwen could give. Thora was already weeping with misery.

'Damn him, crown and all. I might have guessed it. It is just the sort of thing he would do.'

Oswy grunted as he lifted the saddle off his horse, and staggered across to a side stall, where he dumped it noisily.

'You wanted to stay longer,' said Wilfrid, doing the same thing.

Oswy turned and spread his hands. 'He has not been such a stickler before. A day or two more or less.'

Wilfrid tackled more straps and buckles. 'He has not had a couple of invasions to deal with before.'

'Tostig is not here yet, or we would have heard. And the Bastard is in Normandy, with no army at all yet. We could be a month late, and no harm would be done.'

'You are not charged with defending a kingdom; he is. And you are too taken up with that wife of yours. I was only too glad to get away from mine.'

Oswy unstrapped saddlebags and bedding roll. 'Speak for yourself. Harold has a wife; why does he not stay with her?'

Wilfrid laughed. 'He has a mistress, too, and manages to find time for both. God – what energy.'

A stable boy hovered expectantly, hoping for a tip. 'Can I take that, sir?' He stretched out a hand towards a long, thin package.

'Hands off,' said Oswy. 'Nobody touches that but me.'

'Sorry, sir.'

Wilfrid tapped him on the shoulder. 'Do you know what that is?'

The boy's eyes snapped. 'I can guess, sir.'

'Then you should know better. Nobody touches a housecarl's axe but a housecarl.'

'Can I see it, then, sir? Just see it?'

Wilfrid smiled. 'What do you want? A sight of the axe or a tip?'

'The axe, sir,' said the boy without hesitation.

'Good for you, son,' said Wilfrid.

He undid the package, and carefully took away the leather bindings. That left a sort of glove round the head, held by long laces round the handle. As if by magic, half a dozen other boys had appeared from nowhere, and now gathered close. A dozen eyes glowed as Wilfrid undid the knots and slowly drew off the glove.

There was a distinct intake of breath. 'Holy Virgin!'

Wilfrid allowed them a good look, then moved to replace the glove.

'How many have you killed with that?' said somebody.

'Enough,' said Wilfrid. 'Things like this are trouble. Keep away from them, and ask no questions. They are not for the likes of you. Off now!'

Disappointed, they drifted away. Wilfrid stopped the first one. 'Here you are: that is for wanting the axe more than the penny.' He slipped a coin into his hand.

The boy whooped in delight. 'Thank you, sir.'

Wilfrid pointed at the gear that he and Oswy had taken off the horses. 'Get your mates to help you clean all that leather, and there may be some more. By tomorrow morning.'

As they walked towards Morcar's hall, Oswy returned to his bad mood.

'So we shall see nothing.'

'If you wanted to see things that badly, you should have torn yourself away.'

'You were just as keen to get home as I was,' said Oswy.

Wilfrid agreed. He had been. Keen simply to be among things that were familiar to him. The King had put it perfectly: ' – to kick a stable boy's arse'. Well, he had done that – several times. He had talked with his reeves and his haywards, inspected his boundaries, checked his barns and the remains of his winter stores. He had enjoyed his wife, till she began to get used to him and nag.

But, as the week of leave had continued, it was Harold that he thought of more and more. Big things were happening in and around England, and he could not wait to become part of them again. He had visited Grimsby, watched the ships, gossiped with captains, picked up news from the North Sea, which washed up all sorts of information from Denmark, Norway, Scotland, and the northern isles, for the man with ears to listen. He might even have collected one or two things which that know-all priest at Waltham had not heard about.

None of it was the same as being at the King's side. Compared with the King's court and camp, anything that happened at puny places like Little Coates and Great Coates was going to look pathetic. He had overstayed his leave only to please Oswy and his wife, though he could not for the life of him work out what Oswy saw in her.

When they returned to York, it was to discover that the King had, not unexpectedly, left for the south. But what was unexpected was that he had left orders with Earl Morcar. His Majesty's two housecarls, Wilfrid and Oswy, were to remain with Earl Morcar's growing army of fyrdmen, and begin a programme of military training. In preparation for the coming campaign.

It was infuriating, but it made sense. Any group of fyrdmen anywhere in the kingdom could always do with a dollop of military training, and who better than the professionals at the King's side?

It made sense, but it was infuriating. For all Wilfrid knew, Harold was in the process of arranging similar programmes with battalions of fyrdmen down the whole east side of England, maybe even in Sussex as well, and using housecarls to put them into operation. It was an obvious way of keeping men occupied while everybody waited for something to happen.

In their own case, and bearing in mind that they had been, technically, absent without leave, it was easy to see that Harold was punishing them and playing a joke on them at the same time. He and Oswy had wasted time kicking one stable boy's arse too many – very naughty. It was typical of Harold. Wilfrid cursed; he could almost see Harold grinning.

'The Countess Gytha and Her Majesty Edith.'

Gytha swept past the hapless page with an imperious wave of a heavily ringed hand.

'Generous of you to see us.'

Harold, who had risen, ignored the irony. He waved away the tonsured clerks who had been at a huge trestle table, chest-deep in documents, lists, returns, writs and requisitions. In the flurry of gathering, some sticks of wax fell on the floor. One of the clerks stooped to begin collecting them. Harold whispered, 'Not now. Mothers do not wait for the national business.'

The clerks grinned, and carried off as much as they could.

Harold cleared a couple of chairs, shooed away a dog and gestured for his mother and sister to sit down.

'Mother, you know you do not have to make application.'

Gytha settled herself in her chair, and folded her hands across her stomach. The skin of her knuckles bulged slightly against the rings and formed almost a mounting of flesh for the gold. When Harold saw those hands folded, he knew – had always known since he had been a boy – that he was in for a talking-to.

'You have so little time for family now.'

Edith sat upright and righteous, as if she were a child expecting a blessing from a priest.

'My dear Edward would see me at any time of the day. Day or night,' she added primly.

Harold sighed inwardly as he sat down. It was going to be one of those conversations. It was notorious general knowledge, or at the very least common palace gossip, that the late saintly Edward had never sent for his wife after sunset, for any reason whatever, but no purpose was to be served right now by referring to anything so mundane as the truth.

All he said was, 'I do have a kingdom to run.'

'So did Edward,' said Edith, right on cue. 'And he gave endlessly of his time to daily columns of petitioners. He listened, he was patient, and nobody went empty-handed or ungrateful away. He could decline a request with such gentleness and grace that the petitioner went away praising God for His Majesty's kindness.'

Not when he was getting ready to go to the hunt, thought Harold, but knew there was no point in saying so. If he left his mother and sister unanswered long enough, they would get to the point of their visit.

Gytha pointed to the retreating clerks. 'What were those men?'

'I am organising the small matter of the defence of the realm, Mother,' said Harold. 'We need ships. We must build new ones, and requisition old ones, over a very wide area. They must be properly equipped and victualled, and crews must be found for them. Instructions have to go out. It takes time.'

'Whence are you expecting this . . . "invasion"?' said Gytha, deliberately loading the stress.

'I am sure you know about William of Normandy,' said Harold, delicately avoiding the routine reference to 'the Bastard', so as to give Edith no excuse to put a pained expression on her face. 'Now we have a second threat – from Norway.'

'Hardrada?'

'Exactly. It has shifted the whole focus of operations up to the north. As you know, I have recently returned from York, where I was able to win over the Witan there.'

'The Northumbria Witan,' said Gytha, who knew perfectly well. But this was her entry. Here it comes, thought Harold.

'The Northumbria Witan,' he repeated. He was not going to make it easy for her. His mother would have to come clean.

Gytha twiddled a ring. 'I take it Tostig was not represented there.'

'You take it correctly,' said Harold. 'The Witan was universal in its endorsement of me as King. No dissentient voice.'

Gytha tightened her lips. 'Poor Tostig. Not a voice to speak for him.'

'Oh, yes, he has,' said Harold. 'And that voice is here now, doing just that. Tostig has a great ally in you, Mother. The best ally a man could have.'

'And a sister,' said Edith, anxious to claim her share of the credit for loyalty.

Harold leaned his elbows on the table. 'Look. Let us have a few things out in the open. You are seizing the chance to speak to me now, because you know Gyrth and Leofwine are away in their earldoms, busy carrying out my orders for the protection of the realm. But, if you think you will have greater influence over me when I am separated from my brothers, you still have some things to learn about me.

'That is the first thing. The second thing is that I am knee-deep in organising the defence of England against not one invasion, but two. That concentrates the mind most effectively. And I apologise if I can not give you both the day-to-day attention that you seem to feel is your right. You know perfectly well, Mother, that I honour, love and revere you, as I have always done. And you know perfectly well, Edith, that I have so far carried out my promise to Edward to give you all deference and respect as pertains to your rank and your position.

'That leaves Tostig. You both love him; you both favour him. Gyrth and Lef and I all know that, and we can live with it. You are human, and you must have your preferences. But I am the one who is King, never mind by what agency, never mind whether it is fair or just. I am King.

'It follows, then, that you must accept my decisions regarding what is best for England. And, take it from me, Tostig is not good for England. He is, as we speak, dashing all round England's neighbours, trying to drum up support so that he can regain his earldom of Northumbria – the earldom he was legally deprived of by decision of the Witan – the earldom he lost because he gave bad justice, or no justice at all. And now he is raising his hand against the country of his birth. If that is not high treason, I do not know what is.'

Edith looked at her mother, in effect handing over the initiative to her. Gytha unfolded her hands and extended them in a gesture of urgency as she leaned forward.

'Could you not talk to him? If you are so well informed about his movements, you must know where he is. Could you not make him see?'

Harold shook his head. 'I am sorry, Mother, but I do *not* know where he is. All I find out is where he has *been*. And, even if I did know, it would do no good. You understand that better even than I. When Tostig feels aggrieved, the red cloud comes down. He simply does not listen. Besides, my guess is that he is bewitched by Hardrada. And better men than Tostig have been bewitched by Hardrada. He does not have to swing a sword. If he so much as swings his reputation, half the north is paralysed in awe.'

There was a pause. At the end of it, Gytha gathered up her skirts. 'Come, Edith. There is no mercy here.'

Harold watched her sweep past the gaping page.

His mother had many virtues, but thinking like a monarch was not one of them. It was hardly to be expected. The Lady Gytha thought like a mother, and, second, like a countess. But, now that Earl Godwin had gone, she thought mainly like a mother, and why should she not?

She had seen her eldest son Sweyn die, ambushed or taken ill unto death on his return from a pilgrimage. Nobody was sure. Her youngest son Wulfnoth was a hostage at the court of the Bastard in Rouen. If and when hostilities broke out, as they were almost certain to sooner or later, a danger loomed over Wulfnoth's head. That would be two sons gone.

And now Tostig. If he continued with his cruise of revenge all round the north, he would find himself, again sooner or later, on a battlefield on the opposite side to Harold. Gyrth and Leofwine too. What mother would not want to remove him from such danger?

Alas! He was not on the throne to cater for his mother's sensibilities. It hurt, but there was nothing he could do about it.

Harold got up, went to the door and called his clerks back again.

As they set out their table and their equipment, Harold contemplated one last possible move in the game. Of course, if

Tostig were successful and brought Hardrada over to become King, he, Harold, would be dead, and so, almost certainly, would Gyrth and Leofwine. And his mother would have lost three more sons.

Earl Morcar of Northumbria looked at his brother, Earl Edwin of Mercia, and raised his eyes heavenwards.

His sister pretended not to notice the move, and made herself comfortable in front of the blaze.

Morcar came out into the open. 'Do you really need that wrap, Mildred? It is surely not cold in here. We have two fires and countless candles. Is this your way of saying that our hospitality is not good enough?'

'Morcar, if you had been living for nearly ten years in Wales, as I have, you would understand. It only stops raining there in order to snow. Gruffydd was not generous with the firewood, either.'

The poverty of the late Welsh king, and his meanness, were common knowledge in the north. The latter was almost certainly the result of the former, but that did not stop those around him, and everybody else, from seeing it rather as a character flaw than an economic necessity.

Morcar sniffed. 'He has made a skinflint out of you. You are always wrapped up against everything.'

'If you had had to watch out for yourself as much I had, you would have become the same. I learned very soon that the most important thing was to get warm, and stay warm. I vowed that I would never be cold again. I do not intend to start now. I did not notice that you came to visit me in Wales to see how I was.'

'Mildred, that is not fair. I was hardly of an age—'

'Packed off without a word.'

'Politics, Mil,' said Edwin. 'You are the daughter of an earl. You understand that. You got a crown out of it.'

'And now what do I have? Widow's weeds and exile.'

Edwin gasped. 'Mil, what more do you want? You are out of Wales, which you hated. I did not notice that you were broken-hearted over Gruffydd's death. You have a private fortune. Now that you are married to Harold, you are a queen twice over.'

Mildred knew this was true. Ten years before, she had travelled to Gruffydd's court as a shivering spinster. After ten years of chill living and even chiller care, she had returned as a woman of the world, with an unassailable position. And now she was a queen for the second time.

'Edwin is right, Mildred,' said Morcar, pleased to be on safe ground.

'And my name is Gwen,' said Mildred, also feeling for safe ground.

Morcar sighed. 'Very well – Gwen.'

It was the one piece of Wales that she had enjoyed acquiring, and she intended to keep it.

Both the brothers found her difficult to deal with, and tried to avoid her whenever possible. They had not invited her to York, and welcomed her only out of good manners.

It was Harold's idea. Harold had instantly seen the value of snapping up Gwen (even he had become used to her insistence about the name) as a queen. Now he had the means of welding Wessex, Mercia and Northumbria into one gigantic family complex. Gwen appreciated the intelligence of the stroke. And she was fully aware of the reason Harold had sent her to York.

She broached the subject with what had become her usual directness. She reached out for a small tart, and ostentatiously pulled her fur wrap even more tightly round her.

'They tell me you are having trouble making up your mind.'

Edwin sighed. This was typical of the new Mildred – all right, Gwen. She sailed straight in with bows fully strung and arrows at the ready.

Morcar swallowed. 'What do you mean?'

'I mean,' said Gwen, 'that you gave your oath of loyalty to Harold at the Witan, and you are now wondering how you can get out of it without putting yourself in the wrong.'

Edwin was forced to smile. His 'new' sister had hit the nail right on the head.

Morcar began to tug at the wisp of beard below his lip. 'I want what is best for Northumbria. I am, after all, its earl.'

It was a feeble effort. Gwen shook her head. She found herself agreeing with Harold . . .

'Give the boys a talking-to. They will take it from you. That is what they need, not a king's anger. There is good in both of them.'

In fact, Gwen found herself agreeing more and more with Harold the longer she was with him. His common sense appealed to her newly won wisdom, quarried in pain and embarrassment among the grey mountains and the mangy sheep. Her new marriage, even as early as this, was showing signs of being more than yet another political deal, in which she was the helpless currency handed over as payment. Dare she think it, there was a distinct possibility that they could become a sound working partnership, with respect on both sides . . .

However, first things first.

'Morcar, you are nineteen years old. Harold is over forty. How can you possibly think of yourself as an equal?'

'It is not that. I want to be an earl, not a king. A great earl. Like Siward. Like the great earls of the past.'

Gwen shook her head again. 'My dear, you are simply writing sagas for yourself. Men who want to make history do not write it first in their heads. They do what they can do at the time.'

'I told him,' said Edwin. 'I told him the same.'

Gwen turned back to Morcar. 'How can you match Harold or Hardrada? Or even Tostig if it comes to that? You must learn. And you learn by doing what is in your power to do.'

Morcar stopped pulling at his chin. 'I have it in my power to decide the fate of Northumbria.'

'Not if you contemplate treason, however attractive or profitable it may seem. No great career was built on treason. You saw the example only a few years ago. Look at Macbeth.'

'I can make offers to Tostig or Hardrada that they could not refuse.'

'Quite possibly. But what would you get out of it? I tell you – disappointment. At the very least. Partners in treason do not stop at a second act of betrayal.' Gwen made a puffing sound of contempt with her lips. 'Tostig and Hardrada could run rings round you. You would never become a second king in Northumbria in a thousand years.'

Morcar bridled. 'I never said I wanted to.'

Gwen looked at Edwin, and back at Morcar. 'No – but you thought it.'

Morcar blinked in mortification. Gwen pursued him.

'Morcar, think. Look around you. You live in a world of great men – Harold, Hardrada, Thorfinn of Orkney, the Bastard of Normandy, the Emperor Henry of Germany, the Guiscard in Italy. You are nineteen; you can not match them.'

'I said that, too,' said Edwin. 'I said that.'

'Do not try to imitate them. You will fail. Make your own destiny, with the resources at your disposal. You have a great earldom. You have it in your power to help Harold to expel two men, maybe three, who do not think of England, only of their own fortunes. If you help Harold to victory, how much more secure will your earldom become. And, if I prove fruitful, do you realise that you and Edwin will become uncles to a king? *Then* you could become a truly great earl of a truly great Northumbria.

'Is that not enough to be going on with?'

*   *   *

Vendel tried to hide the stammer. 'Would you like to see the *scriptorium*?'

Coelwen could not think of a good enough reason to say no. In fact, as time had gone on, she had found it more and more difficult to think of good reasons not to fall in with what Vendel suggested.

It had begun early in the morning. They had hoped – all of them – that the rain would have spent itself by the end of their first night in the monastery. But when they rose, yawning almost in time with the eternal bell that announced the different services of the Divine Office, as laid down by the blessed St Benedict, it was clear that no serious improvement could be realistically hoped for.

The sky was of a lowering, enshrouding, permanent dark grey. The wind blew with a steady but chilling insistence, capable of eroding the will of the hardiest traveller. The drizzle penetrated everywhere; no tunic, gown, hood, cape, or cloak could keep it out; no material – the thickest worsted, the toughest leather – was proof against it.

Both Vendel and Coelwen were raised in Yorkshire. Each had travelled the moors since they were infants, each for their own reasons. Each understood the situation. When Vendel spoke of waiting another day, albeit with hesitation lest Coelwen should turn down the corners of her mouth, he was surprised at her ready agreement. Coelwen had her share of pride, but she also had her share of common sense, and she had no desire to get herself soaked to the skin within a couple of hours.

'I shall see the Prior and the Guest-Master,' said Vendel. 'I am sure it will be all right.' Coelwen nodded. Vendel was about to turn away when a thought struck him. He turned back.

'Would you like to meet him? The Prior, I mean.'

Coelwen hesitated. In a house where the entire population, except for a few menials in the kitchen, was male, she had fully expected that she and Thora would be left to their own devices for the entire day.

'I have told him about you,' said Vendel. 'He would be happy to meet you.'

Again, Coelwen could think of no other answer but yes.

The Prior was indeed happy to meet her. Out on those remote moors, with no company but the brothers he saw every hour of the day, and half the night, he was pleased to meet any visitor. Even more so when he discovered how personable she was.

It was a rare pleasure too for Coelwen, to be treated as an equal, as a favoured equal, by so impressive a figure as a prior. With a small slice of luck, it would have been the Abbot himself, but that dignitary had house business in York, and would not be back for several days.

Free from the slightly inhibiting presence of the Abbot, the Prior rather let himself go, and spent considerable time showing his guests – both of them – many of the various chambers of the house.

If the truth be told, the Prior was deriving equal pleasure from the meeting, as he was keen to ply Coelwen with questions about what was going on outside the confines of the house. Indeed in Yorkshire generally, in England, throughout the whole of the north. It was a dramatic time, and the Prior was anxious to catch in the net of his questions any butterflies of rumour and gossip that were fluttering around the country. The Abbot was no doubt using his own visit to York to do exactly the same, and the Prior saw no reason why he should not try to do some netting on his own account.

If a house were to survive, it had to be up to date on who the important and powerful people were, and where the next dramatic news was likely to come from.

So names like Morcar, Edwin, Harold's new queen, Hardrada, and of course Tostig yet again came into the conversation.

Coelwen used her position as the daughter of a town reeve to good effect, and supplied the Prior with welcome news about her father, about Gunnar, about the new defences of Scarborough. The Prior nodded sagely, and asked yet more questions.

Coelwen derived yet more pleasure from her new, and unexpected, role as local expert. The Prior was better informed about the affairs of Scarborough than she would have expected. She soon saw why.

'You must understand that Vendel is well known to us,' he said. 'For several years he studied here.'

'Yes,' said Coelwen. 'I heard.'

Of course – the Gunnar connection. That man got everywhere. But she now felt relaxed enough to ask, 'Was he a good pupil?'

'He was indeed,' said the Prior, nodding vigorously. 'Willing, industrious and adept. With an excellent memory. We were sorry when he had to go.'

Coelwen turned to Vendel. 'Was there no desire on your part to stay?'

Vendel sidestepped. He opened his mouth, and there was a slight pause while he fought for speech. Coelwen had noticed this before. It was not that he repeated syllables; it was just that sometimes the words simply would not come. She had noticed that the escort made fun of him behind his back, and cruelly mimicked him. She did not like that.

'My father needed me back for the business. It was only to learn my letters that he sent me here.'

'And your numbers, and your Latin,' said the Prior. He glanced at Coelwen. 'And very good he was, too, at all of them. He has a fine hand.'

Coelwen smiled in approval. It was then that Vendel seized a chance.

'Would you like to see the *scriptorium*?'

While she was framing an answer – which looked as if it was going to be yet another agreement – he said, 'It was where I learned everything.' He smiled. 'I can show you the very desk at which I stood.' He turned to the Prior. 'I presume it is still there, Father.'

The Prior allowed himself the shadow of a smile. 'It is. And so are the letters of your name – carved most shamefully, I may add.'

When they entered, Coelwen saw Vendel almost open like a flower, despite the fact that it was empty because of the appalling weather and the terrible draughts. He looked all round and sighed deeply.

'They often had to kick me out of here,' he said. 'They used to say I had taken root. I enjoyed *everything* about this place.'

Coelwen shivered. 'Even the draughts?'

Vendel grinned. 'Even the draughts.'

Coelwen noticed that there were now no silences interrupting his speech.

Looking back on the whole day, she was forced to admit that she had enjoyed it very much. If her father had not sent her away, this would not have happened. So she at least was grateful for Tostig's being such a nuisance.

'There you are, lads. What do you think of that?'

Sigurd made an expansive gesture towards the longship behind him. It positively shone with newness. Almost too much so. Some surfaces needed more planing for comfort's sake. Ropes were hard; canvas was unyielding. Everything was stiff. It all reeked of haste.

There was a moment of hesitation, almost of disbelief.

'Believe me, it is ours,' said Sigurd. 'He gave it to me himself.' He waved invitingly. 'Go and have a good look.'

That was enough. With a noise that sounded almost like a roar of excitement – certainly of anticipation – Finn and Ivar and Ketil and the rest swarmed aboard. Even Lars was wide awake.

Sigurd leaned contentedly against a bollard. Magnus looked keenly at him.

'You look like the fox who has swallowed the goose.'

'So would you if you were in my shoes.'

Magnus folded his arms and tilted back his head. 'All right, all right, what is it? What is up?'

Sigurd's smile of smugness spread almost to the back of his neck. 'Just look at them. Like children with a new toy.'

'How many of them have any idea how to operate it?'

'Very few, I should say,' said Sigurd with his usual disarming frankness. 'But I expect them to learn. They learned how to fight; now they can learn how to sail. We have plenty of time.'

'Who is going to teach them? You?'

Sigurd laughed. 'Christ and Odin, no. I know nothing. But I do know how to buy knowledge, and I do know how to learn.'

'Where is this wonderful knowledge market?'

Sigurd waved all round him. 'We are in the biggest seaport in Norway. It is bursting with the greatest mass of skill and experience in all the northern seas. Men from everywhere, with knowledge of the whole world, are here to join in his great adventure. They can not resist it. Magnus, there are men here from Brittany and Muscovy, the ends of the world. The word is out. If we can not hire what we need here, we have no business owning a ship.'

'You need money to hire it. Where are you going to get that?'

Sigurd shook his head. 'Dear boy, you really are the greatest miner of misery. You can dig it out anywhere.'

Magnus persisted. 'Well?'

Sigurd grinned. 'He not only gave me a boat; he gave me some money, too. He has sense. The one is no good without the other.'

'I see. He has gold to spare of course.'

'Yes, he has actually. Bottomless barrels of it. Ask anybody.'

It was Magnus's turn to shake his head. Only a fortnight before, this young man was practically beleaguered in a ramshackle collection of cabins on the edge of the snow-laden forest, at the head of a gang of beefy bully-boys with more muscle than sense, and fast becoming bored out of their sanity. Now he was welcomed in the court of the greatest Viking alive; he had persuaded that Viking to grant him untold favours: more recruits for his contingent; bed and board; an introduction to his daughter; a brand-new longship; and now, it seemed, a small fortune, too. It was a staggering achievement.

'Sigurd, how do you do it?'

'Charm, dear boy. Charm. Works wonders. You catch more flies with honey than you do with vinegar.'

Well, it was that, of course. Magnus himself had felt the impact. But clearly it was more. It was talent for one thing. Sigurd was a born leader, and a great Viking monarch would know all about leadership. He could spot it in others, too, and would be bound to encourage it; it could not but enhance the chances of success in his own great enterprise. A half-dozen leaders like Sigurd in an army could triple its effectiveness.

It was not only talent; it was confidence. It was no use a man having exceptional gifts; he had to believe in those gifts, and in himself. If he did not, nobody else would. That was Sigurd's gift: he made his men believe in him – though admittedly there had been a few moments of doubt two or three weeks ago. But the general verdict was sound; Sigurd's men, nine times out of ten, believed that he was capable of almost anything.

Talent and confidence, plus a shrewd eye for an opportunity, produced the final ingredient – luck. Sigurd was lucky. Witness what he had achieved in the last fortnight. But only Sigurd could have done it. The circumstances were there for anybody to see, but only Sigurd had the wit and the imagination, and the pure cheek, to make something out of it.

Sigurd would have summed it up by saying that he had weighed up the situation, and decided that the odds looked good. So far, he was being proved abundantly right.

What Sigurd had done with his motley of log-cabin layabouts was obvious to anybody with a grain of sense, and Sigurd made sure that the right people noticed. Small wonder his command had been extended with more recruits. The great man was clearly impressed with him.

But the great man was also noted for his caution. He appreciated talent, but he did not fall in love with it. Having rewarded it, he now proceeded to test it before he trusted it. Hence the longship. There was a commission waiting for Sigurd. Magnus was determined to find out what it was. The fact that Sigurd held him back from swarming aboard with the others was a good sign that he, Magnus, would hear before the others did.

Magnus tried again. 'Come on, Sig, what are you so devilish pleased about?'

Sigurd waved again to the longship, where Ketil and Ivar were already competing to see who could climb higher up the shrouds. Shouts and hoots came from all over the deck. Somebody had already fallen in the water.

'Look at that. They will not be bored now for months.'

'Will the novelty not wear off?'

Sigurd shook his head. 'There is no novelty to wear off once you get to sea, there is only hard work. They will be too busy, too tired and too seasick to worry about novelty.'

'Will they not begin to wonder where they are supposed to be going?'

Sigurd grinned. 'Wherever it is, they will be pleased at the prospect, because by that time it will be an improvement on sailing a longship. They will not care where they are going; all they will want to do is get there.'

'And where is "there"? Where is he sending us?'

Sigurd put on his fox-eaten-the-goose expression again.

'My idea, not his.'

'What?'

'Yes. We were discussing his plans the other day. As you know, he is going to use his powers as overlord in Orkney and Shetland.'

'Thorfinn?'

'Yes. He plans to use the islands as jumping-off points for the invasion. Very sensible of him.'

'Good of you to say so.' Magnus shook his head again at this man's nerve.

'Thank you. And did you know that he plans to take his wife and his daughter with us?'

Magnus stared. 'Take them to war?'

'Take them, yes. But not to war. He plans to leave them on Orkney.'

Magnus loaded his voice with irony. 'So that he can send for them quickly for the coronation when he wins.'

'Yes,' said Sigurd with total seriousness. 'Something like that.'

It seemed that there was more than one man brimming with confidence.

Magnus looked hard at Sigurd. 'How do you know all this? Are you a member of his senior staff already?'

Sigurd grinned. 'No – not yet. That comes later. But I have struck up, shall we say, an acquaintance with his daughter, the Princess Maria.'

Which was true. Hakon, Ivar, Ketil, Lars – everybody had noticed. Once again, his cheek was breathtaking. What was even more amazing, the Princess Maria seemed to enjoy his attentions. Sigurd had come in for a good deal of chaff from the likes of Finn and Tore and Haldor and the rest. Which he had dealt with in his customary breezy way. Nobody ever got the better of Sigurd in verbal fencing.

'I had my common sense,' continued Sigurd. 'I looked around me. What could I use?'

Magnus pretended to be totally ignorant. 'I have no idea. What could you use?'

Sigurd, after a brief glance at him, explained. 'We had a king who wanted to make a reconnaissance for his main expeditionary force. We had a proud husband and father who wanted to take his queen and his daughter on campaign, but who would be understandably concerned about their safety, comfort and welfare. We had a promising young officer who had just been given command of a new longship and who needed to train a fresh crew.

'So I say to the King, "Majesty, how would it be if I took my men and the ship you have so generously given me, and use a voyage to Orkney to give them the necessary training, and to give the ship the needful sea trials? In Orkney, I could negotiate with Jarl Thorfinn. I could assess the facilities for harbourage, supply and forage. And I could arrange suitable accommodation for Her Majesty and Her Highness – of sufficient levels of comfort, and safely distant from the main theatre of operations that you anticipate off the coast of England."'

Magnus pulled up his sagging chin.

'And he agreed?'

'Of course he agreed. What better offer could he expect? It will fit his plans perfectly.' He paused to give effect. 'It will fit mine, too.'

'How?'

Sigurd leaned forward. 'Do you not see, dear boy? If I bring this off, he will give me a whole squadron of ships.'

Magnus laughed so loudly that some of the gang on board looked up from their gambolling.

When Magnus saw, he dropped his voice in wary discretion. 'And no doubt you will use the opportunity to get to know the

Princess somewhat better? I suppose you have already asked for permission to take her with you?'

Sigurd twinkled. 'I am working on that.'

The King raised his head and smiled a welcome.

'Good of you to come to London. I know you hate leaving Waltham.'

Bernard acknowledged with a dip of the head. One of Harold's most appreciated gifts – at any rate appreciated by those who worked closely with him – was that he understood the pressures under which they worked. Whether he was talking to an archbishop or a sergeant of archers or a lowly carter, he made them feel that he spoke their language.

Perhaps it came from the fact that Harold knew what it was to be a subordinate. A *second* son, for example. Then a *junior* earl. Then, as people said, an *under*-king. If he had been born into the royal house of Cerdic, he would have grown from the cradle steeped in the knowledge that he was special, separate, that the normal rules did not apply to him. Harold was all too normal, sometimes disconcertingly so. His earthy rebukes to those who put on airs and graces in his presence were painful to those on the receiving end, and often entertaining to those who witnessed them.

It made men like Bernard respond so much the more. Harold could, and did, command intense loyalty from people in all walks of life because he was so human.

Harold pointed to a seat opposite him. 'You have eaten?'

'Yes, sir.' He smiled and put up a hand as he saw the King reach for a jug. 'And drunk, sir, thank you.'

'What do you have for me that is new?' said Harold.

'Tostig mostly,' said Bernard. 'My agents bring news of his travels from Flanders to Denmark.'

'What is he up to?'

'Recruiting, from what we can gather. Ships and crews. Frisia. Schleswig. Germany. Maybe even the Baltic.'

'Quality?'

'Riffraff for the most part. Out for the main chance. Not much staying power. But by this time he could have twenty or thirty ships, maybe even more.'

'No serious invasion threat,' said Harold.

'No, sir, but more than enough to cause damage and distraction, and upset local morale. And he could land anywhere.'

'Do you think he will get anything more from Flanders or Normandy?'

'Frankly, no. But he could be given harbour facilities. My money would be on the Bastard. Maybe a raiding force based on the Cotentin. It will cost William virtually nothing; it will not get in the way of his own preparations in the mouth of the River Dives; and could be a wretched nuisance to you. If it fails, he is no worse off.'

Harold nodded in acceptance. 'Now, what about the north? What is Hardrada up to?'

'Like the Bastard, preparations. My ships all talk of the same thing: every fjord in Norway is teeming with ships of every shape and size. It is a wonder there are any forests left, so many trees are being eaten up by the saws and the axes. That means he is buying a whole world of naval supplies.'

'He can afford it, several times over.'

'Indeed he can. So he has the advantage of us there. And gossip says he will not be short of manpower, either. They say the roads of Germany and Muscovy are being pounded by the feet of thousands who think they will get a share of his fortune when he sets sail.'

Harold laughed. 'It seems we shall be the focus of attention for every rogue in Christendom. Hardrada is pulling them in from all over the north, and the Bastard is scooping them up by the wagonload from all over the south.'

'And that is why you have summoned me here,' said Bernard.

Harold looked sharply at him. 'Yes,' he said in his direct way. 'I want to know – from you, face to face – what you think. My resources are limited. Where lies the greater threat?'

Bernard returned his gaze. 'I speak honestly, but, remember, my lord, not infallibly. My information is irregular, inconsistent, imperfect and incomplete.'

'But there is nothing imperfect about your judgement,' said Harold. 'That is what I want. The decision based on that judgement will be mine, and mine alone.'

'Very well, then. There are two dangers – the Bastard and Hardrada. Tostig makes a lot of noise and gets a lot of attention, but he is no more than an annoyance. I suspect to everybody. The Bastard will let him have nothing but a quay or two in the Cotentin. He will never share his expedition with him, much less his command. He wants England, he wants all of England, and he wants no partners. Tostig comes nowhere.'

'And Hardrada?'

'The Bastard thinks at his planning table. Hardrada thinks on his feet. He too will make use of Tostig if the opportunity permits. He might make promises to him. He might even share his expedition with him. But he knows Tostig has no long sight. He has confidence in his own ability to outwit him. A broken promise will be nothing to Hardrada. And Tostig will go off in a huff yet again.'

Harold smiled. Poor Tostig. Bernard continued.

'So, of the two, Tostig is more likely to join with Hardrada. That makes the threat from the north that much bigger, if only in appearance. Add to that the possibility that Hardrada has Orkney and Shetland. And that Scotland and Denmark could still come in at the last moment, once they see which way the cat appears to be jumping.'

Bernard paused. 'Which is why I was pleased to respond to your summons, sir.'

'Ah,' said Harold. 'I thought you sounded suspiciously will-ing. What is it you want?'

'In the light of what I have said, I think it is time to shift my headquarters to the north.'

'To pick up the intelligence earlier.'

'Yes, sir. The Bastard may be the better commander when it comes to it, but his Normans, by all accounts, are not falling over themselves to join him. Whereas one rarely sees a Viking reluctant to join a scheme to cause alarm and confusion anywhere in the world. Their king has spent his whole life causing alarm and confusion. It is the breath of life to all of them.'

'Where do you want to be, then?'

Bernard shrugged. 'York would appear to be the obvious place. The river estuary comes quite close, which will make it easier for my captains.' He smiled. 'They hate riding.'

Harold nodded. 'So be it, then. But you will keep a deputy at Waltham, to gather up the bits and pieces.'

'Of course. Do I have your authority to organise the horse relays and couriers?'

Harold nodded again. He was rising when Bernard said, out of the blue, 'What do you make of this star?'

Harold looked surprised. 'The one with the tail?'

'Yes. It has caused quite a stir where I have come from. Even among the brothers. I imagine it will come in for a lot of comment everywhere.'

Harold was direct once again. 'Does it trouble you – as a man of God?'

'No. Does it trouble you as a king?'

Harold sat down. 'Perhaps I should try to give an honest answer. No – I do not like it. I do not understand it. I would rather it were not there. But, as for a sign of impending doom, anything could be interpreted as a sign of that – a poor harvest, a big thunderstorm, a sudden outbreak of cattle plague, a baby with six fingers. So why worry? We all have to face doom some time or other.

'As for its being a sign of God's displeasure, I think of all the signs I have been given of God's favour: my family, my Edith, my good fortune, my new role as the defender of England. More recently, the holy oil that Aldred poured on my head, which sanctified my kingship. I am king by the Grace of God. It seems to me that God does not hand out such favours with one hand and take them away with the other. God does not play games.'

Harold poured himself a drink. 'All I should like is a sign or two of God's interest at least in my problem. So far, I have had to put up with signs, rumours, whispers, possibilities, the odds of this, the odds of that.' He took a draught. 'Right now, Bernard, I could do with a good, old-fashioned event.'

Chapter Five

Harold woke to find his shoulder being shaken. For a moment he could not make out the face behind the candlestick.

'Sir.'

Harold recognised the voice. 'Bernard.'

Despite the urgency of the situation, Bernard almost smiled to himself. Any other prince would have instantly demanded to know what he was doing there, and why he had the nerve to interrupt his sleep. Harold always understood. Bernard appreciated the King's confidence that he, Bernard, would not have done such a thing without very good reason. All Harold wanted to know was the reason.

'Well?'

'A rider has just come in. It is Tostig again, sir.'

'What has he done now?'

'Landed.'

Harold stopped rubbing his eyes. 'Where?'

'Wight. The Isle of Wight.'

Harold sat up properly, and motioned to Bernard to sit on the bed. 'Well, at least he has surprised us – damn him.'

Bernard put down the candlestick. 'Well, sir, you told God you wanted an event.'

'And only a couple of hours ago.' Harold tilted his head. 'God has a trick of answering your prayers and rapping you over the knuckles at the same time.'

'I am sure He knows what is best for us, sir.'

Harold made a face to shake off the sleep. 'Well, come on, then, what has happened? Where is he now?'

'Gone back to his ships.'

Harold frowned. 'So it was just a raid?'

'Looks like it. He sent in several shore parties. Some of them trashed and burned, just to cause trouble and fear. The others took food mostly, and any weapons they could lay their hands on.'

Harold was unimpressed. 'Impulse. No planning. He is short of supplies almost before he starts. And he causes damage just because he could not find as much as he wanted. Typical Tostig.'

'Either that or it was all the Bastard would give him.'

'Mmmm. Could be. How many ships *did* the Bastard give him? How many did he have?'

'Possibly none. What he had with him he had gleaned from Flanders months ago. As for numbers, you know the locals, sir. Surprised and frightened. We have been told anything from twenty to two hundred.'

'And he has gone again, you say?'

'Yes, sir.'

'Did any of our fleet see him?'

'No. Neither coming nor going.'

'Well, hardly their fault. The Channel is a big place. And most of them are watching higher up.'

Bernard scratched some stubble. 'This could be the Bastard's way of causing a diversion. Tostig is not much use, so send him westwards to cause a stir and draw our attention, while he prepares to cross where the Channel is narrower.'

'He is not ready to invade yet,' said Harold.

'No,' said Bernard. 'But it gets us *thinking* about the westerly route – the Cotentin to the Isle of Wight. Anything that gets the enemy even thinking about the wrong thing must be a good idea.'

Harold nodded. 'True. So what you are saying is that, wherever the Bastard is going to strike, it will not be on the Isle of Wight.'

'Certainly not the Isle of Wight, because he will have to re-embark and land again in Hampshire. And he will have given the game away. Unless –' Bernard paused '– he is running a double bluff.'

Harold shook his head. 'No, no. We do not get drawn into that territory. Let the Normans play their chess. You can get too clever. I saw them doing that when I was there in sixty-four. They tied themselves in knots trying to work out what I was up to. It made life much easier for me; I just did the next thing, and they spent hours wondering what my "game" was. No – we keep it simple. Tostig has been and Tostig has gone. He has taken supplies. He can not possibly intend simply to go back to Normandy and sit on his hands. He can not have any reason whatever for going westwards. So he is coming up the Channel eastwards, so far as the wind will allow him.'

'He is taking a chance. Our ships could catch him.'

'Even Tostig knows he is taking a chance being out in the Channel at all. But he could be working his way along, causing trouble, taking supplies, splitting our forces and maybe preparing to join his own squadron with the Bastard's fleet somewhere near the Narrow Seas.' Harold grimaced appreciatively. 'Not a bad idea. And, if Tostig does get caught, he is no great loss to the Bastard, and it may have taken our eyes off the vital thing – himself. Clever.'

'So where does that leave us?' said Bernard.

'It leaves us with a possible change of viewpoint. We have been moving to the conclusion, during the last few weeks, that the real threat comes from the north. Curious, is it not? We started the year firmly convinced that the biggest menace came from Normandy. Then you brought news about the Bastard's troubles collecting his army, so we began to wonder.

Then we had the thunderbolt that Hardrada was on the move. And, with his reputation, our whole focus of attention shifts to the north. The more so with Tostig's connection with Northumbria.

'Now comes this escapade of Tostig's. Suddenly, an invasion from the south becomes more real again. What do we do? React to the danger of the greatest reputation? React to the latest piece of news? React to my instinct about the Bastard? Use our common sense? Take a chance and concentrate our forces? Spread our butter right across the bread? What?'

'You are the King, sir. I await your orders.'

Harold smiled ironically. 'Well, I wanted the crown, eh? Here is God giving me what I want again.' He became practical. 'I think we hold to our conclusion that Tostig will move eastwards, and hope he will not be a nuisance on the way. Presumably, when he gets off the coast of Ponthieu, he will go to ground, or rather harbour, till the Bastard is ready, then come over with him.'

Harold looked at Bernard. 'Do you still now want to move to York?'

'On balance, sir, and despite what we have just heard, yes. I think I would go not for the timing of the threat but for the size of it.' Bernard lifted his shoulders. 'In the end, sir, it may come down not to how clever we are at gazing into the future, but to how fast the carpenters and shipwrights can do their work in Normandy or Norway. Even more simply, it may come down to which way the wind blows when they have finished their work. One thing is for sure: the same wind can not bring both the Bastard and Hardrada at the same time.'

'Jesus and Mary.' Alfred groaned as he stretched his legs and flexed his bare toes. 'All day – the whole damned day. And for what?'

'For twenty miles,' said someone. 'And we are only halfway there.'

Alfred grimaced as he massaged his feet. 'What did I tell you? We shall spend the whole year marching up and down. First towards Sussex. Then to Anglia. Now where the hell are we going?'

'Hertford,' somebody said.

'Where is that?'

'Down towards London. Not far from Waltham.'

Alfred grunted bad-temperedly. 'What is so special about that?'

'That is where Harold has his secret meetings with that priest of his.'

Alfred looked blank.

The next man round the fire turned to him and grinned. 'You know – Llew's druid. The one with the magic eye. The one who tells the King what to do. Like now; he tells him to bugger us about – just like Owen says.'

'Oh, him.' Alfred gazed sourly into the flames. 'Bloody little Welshmen. What do they know?'

'More than you – which is not difficult. And they earn their keep.'

Which was true. Owen had gained a reputation for being adept at ferreting out any news that was flying round the camp, indeed round the shire. Llewellyn had shown endless resource in obtaining unofficial rations. Nobody had the bad sense to ask him where or how he acquired them.

Right on cue, Llewellyn appeared, almost staggering under the weight of a young deer carcass. He flopped it onto the ground.

'There you are, my boys. That should keep the wolf from the door for a while.'

'God, Llew? How did you come by this?'

Llewellyn pulled out a broken shaft. 'We are archers,

remember? And quite small ones. Nobody notices us. We get overlooked. We are those "bloody little Welshmen".

Several pairs of eyes turned towards Alfred, who covered his embarrassment by taking out a knife and starting on the dismemberment of the deer. Others joined him. There were a few awkward laughs. Somebody patted Llewellyn on the back.

Conversation declined and spirits rose as the joints were turned on makeshift spits. When the hot meat was passed round, even Alfred's mood began to soften. He managed a joke to greet Owen when he arrived.

'Hurry up, Owen, or you will miss the treat. Llew here is feeding the five thousand.'

''Tis pleased I am to see you, my dears,' said Owen, as he sat down.

'Do not tease us; there is only one deer you are interested in.'

Owen joined in the laughter and began to try to catch up.

'Well, come on, Owen, tell us. What have you heard? What are we doing here? Where are we going?'

'If you guess we are being buggered about, you are right. But it is not Earl Gyrth who is doing it. It is Tostig.'

'Tostig.'

People began to sit up.

'Right,' said Owen. 'He has landed near Southampton, and is marching on Winchester. That is what they are saying. The King is gathering the fyrdmen from a dozen counties to go and meet him. Earl Gyrth says we have to – what is the word? – "concentrate". Yes, "concentrate" on Hertford.'

'Why?'

'To wait and see which way he goes.'

'It could be anywhere.'

'Not if Harold has anything to do with it.'

'You mean Llew's druid.'

'Not a druid. A cardinal.'

'What is a cardinal?'

'A big red priest,' said Owen, never stuck for an answer. 'He plots and he plans, and he draws great big maps and he moves all the county fyrds around on it. Just like the Normans.'

'The Normans?'

'Yes. In their game of chess. They move men of chess around a great board, and they sit and plot and plan.'

'Are we on this great board?'

Owen nodded conclusively. 'We are. But we are very small men of chess. The great ones are kings and bishops and knights. We are the smallest. We are called pawns. We are the least important.'

'Nothing has changed, then. Just like real life.'

'All the best games *are* like real life,' said Owen.

'So what is our big red cardinal telling the King to do?'

'To sit and wait and see.'

'In Hertford.'

'In Hertford.'

Alfred felt a return of his sour temper. 'So we march, then we sit, and we march, and sit again – and nobody tells us anything.'

'That is what war is about,' said a grizzled fyrdman. 'If you had done five minutes' service, son, you would know that.'

Alfred spread his hands. 'So we do nothing about it?'

'Oh, yes,' said Owen and Llew together.

'What?'

'We make ourselves comfortable – all the time. And we look ahead. Like Llew here – with his bow.'

'Look ahead to what?' said Alfred.

'To the next thing.'

'And what is that?'

'Tomorrow's camp. We do not loiter and linger and moan about how hard life is: we make a good pace, and we get to the campsite early, and we get the best places and find the best things.' He paused. 'We use our wits – just like Hardrada.'

He had timed it perfectly. A chorus of questions rose at once.

Owen crossed his legs and selected another small joint. 'Is it a story you want?'

'It is. You know it is.'

'Well, all right, then. Pay attention. Hardrada was in a position just like this,' he began. 'It was when he was the captain of the Emperor's bodyguard in Miklegaard. He and the Emperor's marshal, called Georgos, had orders to march to a certain spot and make camp. Hardrada made his men march fast, and reached the camping ground first. He chose to put up his tents on some rising ground near a wood. When Georgos arrived some time later, he found that his men had nothing left but some water meadows beside a large stream. It was wet, naturally, and it had no shelter.

'He went to Hardrada and said, "I am the senior commander. I order you to take down your tents and make room for mine."'

Owen put on a suitably hectoring tone.

'Hardrada said, "We got here first. That is what counts. Besides, I am the commander of the Emperor's bodyguard, and I take orders from nobody but the Emperor."

'They argued for a long time, and men began to fasten sword belts. But other men with longer heads came between them. It prevented the bloodshed, but it did not stop the dispute.

'"We must find a way of resolving the dispute without any shame to honour," they said.

'Everybody gathered down by the stream to watch and witness. After much talk, they agreed to draw lots. Two small discs of wood were fashioned of identical size and shape. Each side was to put a mark on their own disc – Georgos for his imperial troops, and Hardrada for his Varangians (that is what they called the Emperor's bodyguard – Varangians). They were to go into a box. A senior officer was to be blindfolded, and he was to put in his hand and draw out one of the discs.'

Owen put a finger beside his nose. 'Here is where Hardrada showed his cunning. He said to Georgos, "Show me what your mark is, so that I do not make the same one and cause confusion." Georgos did so. And Hardrada said, "That is good. Now we know."

'When the blindfolded officer stood ready to make his choice, Georgos and Hardrada stood on either side of him. When the officer drew out one of the discs, Hardrada seized his hand, and snatched the disc. He looked at it and said, "Ah, it is ours. So we win the campsite." At once he threw the disc into the river.

'Georgos said, "That is cheating. How do we know that the disc was yours? We have only your word for it."

'"Nonsense," said Hardrada. "Look at the disc that is left in the box. It will have your mark on it."

'They looked. And of course it did.

'"There you are," said Hardrada. "Then the other one must have been mine. We win."'

There were a few chuckles. Alfred frowned. 'But how could he know? Why was he so sure?'

There were louder laughs. 'Oh, Alfred!'

'How long, Sigurd?'

'Well before dark, I should say, my lady.'

'Come right in. Sit down. We know each other well enough by now. No ceremony.'

'My lady.'

Sigurd crept in below the canvas screen and sat down opposite Queen Ellisif. My lady drew a handsome bearskin more tightly round her shoulders, and leaned back against some rough cushions. They did indeed know each other well enough by now, though Sigurd was still wary about opening a conversation – especially after the shocks at the start of the voyage.

For a while the only sounds were the usual ones – flapping canvas, grinding of rowlocks, Rolf's words of command, creaking of timbers and a score of other noises that all ships made at sea.

'Not long, then.'

'No indeed, my lady.'

Sigurd thought back over the events of the last week or two. He had learned more in that time than in the last six months. Most of it was due to the woman at her ease in front of him.

The first shock had been her mere arrival. Her sudden appearance on the quay took his breath away. He dared not ask straight out what she was doing there; one did not ask questions like that of queens.

He had been hoping, with the confidence of the charming man, that he would have persuaded King Harald to let him take the Princess Maria with him to Orkney. He had sown the seed by throwing the casual idea into the conversation. He had courted Maria, so that she too would fall in with it, and use her own charm on the King to get him to agree.

Then Sigurd had weighed in with a dozen good reasons why the Princess should make the trip. The ship needed sea tests. The men needed training. It was necessary to make diplomatic contact with Orkney and Shetland, to acquaint Jarl Thorfinn with the King's plans. Arrangements would have to be made for providing supplies for the great enterprise. More arrangements were necessary for the accommodation of the Princess Maria and Her Majesty Queen Ellisif. A silver tongue was needed to help persuade Jarl Thorfinn that it was to his advantage to provide hospitality and support, and nobody had a more winning tongue than his servant Sigurd.

And what better enhancement of the embassy could there be than the presence of the beautiful and resourceful Princess Maria, who also could see the many advantages of her presence in that embassy? And, it could be fairly said, could it not, that his servant Sigurd and the Princess Maria made a handsome couple, well able to make a most favourable impression on the great Jarl?

The King listened, his wayward eyebrow lifting yet another fraction in quizzical contemplation as he stroked his flowing fair moustache.

But it was not Princess Maria who arrived on the quayside; it was her mother, the statuesque Queen Ellisif. Her lofty manner, combined with her impressive height, made a strong impression. Her instinctive air of command made a stronger one. Her Slavonic accent, which in a young woman might have inspired gentle affection, in a middle-aged one induced, at the very least, wariness. And there was no chance of one's being able to smile at her imperfect command of a foreign language; in twenty years of marriage to Hardrada, she had gained a near-perfect fluency in Norwegian, albeit with that eastern accent that was so distinctive. Indeed the adjective 'distinguished' demanded to be added.

Sigurd had of course met her already, at her husband's court, and several times when she had accompanied her daughter in his presence. Watchful politeness and careful choice of words in formal surroundings was one thing; learning how to cope with constant company on a North Sea voyage was quite another. So much time was spent almost literally on top of each other. There was little space or privacy in a longship, even one modified for a queen.

It did not help matters when Sigurd discovered, right at the outset, that Her Majesty had an unnerving habit of coming straight to the point, and calling a spade a spade.

It began on the very quayside.

'I suppose you thought you would get Maria, eh?'

Sigurd scraped hastily from the bottom of his barrel of charm.

'Well, no – um – not exactly. I simply thought, Majesty, that Her Highness would make a splendid ambassador. And such a voyage can be something of an ordeal for someone who—'

'For someone who is old like me?'

Sigurd had enough sense to see, and just in time, that, if he tried to dig himself out of this hole, he would succeed only in making the hole bigger, until he disappeared from view.

He bowed low. 'It is not for a humble servant to pass comment, either by deed or by implication, on Majesty's gifts and talents. I am at Your Majesty's disposal in all things.'

Ellisif smiled sardonically. She would enjoy putting this bumptious young man in his place, if only for the pleasure of watching him extricate himself.

'Did you honestly think that the King and I would place our daughter at risk in such circumstances, and with such untried company?'

Sigurd acknowledged the thrust. 'I beg pardon, but I had been led to believe – by His Majesty – that a certain level of esteem had lodged itself in His Majesty's mind. After all, he did commission this voyage, with me in command.'

'Esteem is one thing. Trust is quite another. And before trust comes test. That is what you are about to embark upon. And I am here to observe how well – or otherwise – you discharge the responsibilities which have been placed upon you.'

Sigurd wilted again.

'And let us clarify one more thing,' added the Queen. 'You may be in charge of the mission, but you are responsible to me, and the responsibility for the ship lies with Rolf of Bergen. Is that understood?'

Sigurd nodded.

'Furthermore,' continued Ellisif, 'Rolf has authority to hire any other crew as he sees fit. And, judging by what he has already told me, and from what he has seen on board so far, he will see very fit very soon.'

'Majesty.' Sigurd felt himself sinking further into the ground. The more so as some of his own contingent were watching and grinning.

Ellisif caught them at it. She turned full face to them. 'And if I see or hear any insubordination from any of you, to me or to my officer, Sigurd, you too will feel the sharp side of my tongue. If I choose to tell the King, you will also feel the sharp side of his lash.'

The more she spoke, the keener became the Slavonic accent, especially the odd vowel sounds and the typical liquid *l*'s, but the authority and the menace were as clear as a Nordic spring. Rough salutes were offered, heads were lowered and shoulders were bowed to deck duties. Magnus was most impressed. Hearing stories about the Queen was one thing; actually seeing her in action was quite another. The stories, he could see, had not been exaggerated.

Sigurd tried to make up for his bad start with the Queen by trying to spoil her. He bowed and scraped; he fetched and carried; he fussed and worried. Was this all right? Was that all right? Was Her Majesty comfortable? He was sorry about the lack of comforts aboard, but he had tried within the limits of the ship's design and space. And so on.

Queen Ellisif put up with this for about half a day. She summoned him to her shelter in the stern, and told him to keep the crew at a distance. When he had done that, she fixed him with a steady eye.

'Young man, the charm which you so freely brandish may impose on my daughter, but it cuts no ice with me, because I know what your motives are, and I rely on my husband to do all the flattering necessary as far as I am concerned.

'In any case, you are wasting your time. You are dealing with a princess of the House of Rus. My father is Prince Jaroslav of Kiev. Have you any idea what my country is like? I was raised in a land of snows in winter, burning sun in summer, and floods in autumn and spring. I have slept in sledges; I have rocked on rafts on the swollen River Volga; I have faced ice in the Baltic Sea. I do know something of travel. So do not cosset me. And never cosset me for reasons of your own. Do I make myself clear?'

Sigurd bowed his head and said quietly, 'As clear and sharp as a diamond, Majesty.'

'Good. So now we understand each other.'

She liked this young man. She saw the same talents in him as her husband did. Given time, training and the opportunity, he could rise fast and give good service. What if he *was* reaching above himself with Maria? The girl obviously liked the attention, and, if he really did rise as high as his ambitions drove, she could, frankly, do a lot worse.

After all, Harald had first arrived at her father's court in Kiev with little more than what he stood up in – part vagabond, part refugee, part pure adventurer. True, her father had made him wait several years, but Ellisif had to admit – if only to herself – that she had been rather taken with him right from the start.

She pulled herself together. Harald as a courtier was in the past; Sigurd as a possible son-in-law was in the future. Right now he had to be ridden on a tight rein. But he would respond, she felt sure.

She also liked the big lad who seemed to be his constant companion. Not that she saw much of him; the poor devil spent most of his time hanging over the gunwale.

In the event, the voyage passed satisfactorily enough. Rolf was a stern captain, but trained Sigurd's men with a firm but fair hand. Sigurd himself had plenty to do learning much of what they had to learn. The rest of the crewmen Rolf had hired saw to the emergencies that any voyage threw up, and they made good speed.

Magnus did his best, but felt wretched most of the time. As he leaned and groaned and strained, he reflected gloomily that he did not seem to have very good relations with any of the four elements that made up the world. It had been fire which had driven him away from his home. His stomach was now telling him that water, in large quantities, did not agree with him. He needed air, of course, but he wished it did not come in such vicious, stormy quantities, and so mercilessly cold. All that was left was the earth, and, the way he was feeling at that moment, a six-foot hole in it did not seem all that unattractive.

All the time, Queen Ellisif made her presence felt, not so much by what she said as by what she did not say.

She did not complain and she did not fuss and she did not nag. She did not hide herself and she did not get in the way. She made no attempt to interfere with the handling of the ship. Nevertheless, her comments generally, when she chose to make them, were timely, well informed, and helpful. She was probably the most travelled person aboard.

The captain, Rolf, after a brief period of cool reserve, became increasingly willing to listen to her. Sigurd had long since learned his lesson, and was the soul of correctness. The crew, after their initial awe, also grew respect for what she said. Once they had learned where lay the boundaries in their respective behaviour towards her – which they did very quickly – they lost their nerves. She had a trick of passing a remark with a completely straight face, which in fact masked an incisive sense of humour. Whenever she appeared, it was not long before a laugh arose around her. By the time they arrived at Orkney, the whole ship's company was eating out her hand.

King Harald had sent warning ahead to Jarl Thorfinn, and a welcome was provided commensurate with her rank. She accepted it with a manner that indicated that she had expected nothing less.

Before long, Thorfinn found her equally unstoppable. She took Orkney hospitality – not noted in the northern world for its opulence – in her stride, without a word of complaint. She travelled with him over not only Orkney but Shetland, too, without turning a hair.

She was indefatigable at the feasting table. She was moved to say to Sigurd one evening during a lull in proceedings, 'These islanders, boy. They have no idea what drinking is; they should see a harvest festival by the Volga, or a Christmas feast at my father's court in Kiev.'

She was equally obdurate at the bargaining board. She had come with a list from her husband, King Harald. Harald was Thorfinn's overlord, but demands from an overlord three hundred miles away across a stormy sea had a habit of getting watered down. After a few days of Queen Ellisif's attentions, those demands regained their original strength, even perhaps developed some more.

Thorfinn had initially rubbed his chin and scratched his cheek. By the time Ellisif had finished with him, he had agreed to provide the necessary harbourage. He had promised two score ships. Crewmen were pouring in from both groups of islands. Food and drink were guaranteed. Ellisif had inspected, and loftily approved, the accommodation that was being provided for herself and her daughter Maria. And Thorfinn's own son, Paul, had been commissioned to lead the whole Orkney and Shetland fleet to wherever King Harald decreed the rendezvous.

Sigurd had prided himself on his ability to extract gifts and favours from people; as he watched Queen Ellisif, he freely acknowledged that he was in the presence of a master, or rather mistress, of the art.

Thorfinn came down to the quayside in person to see them off. As he bent to kiss the Queen's ring, he said, 'I look forward to your return, Majesty.' Despite the fact that he still looked a little bemused, he clearly meant it.

For the whole of the return journey, Sigurd could not do enough for her, and this time *he* meant it, too.

They stood together at the rail watching the coast come closer. The Queen drew her bearskin round her shoulders once again.

'One way and another, not a bad trip, would you say, Sigurd?'

'I would indeed, Majesty.'

Sigurd reflected that, the way things had turned out in his relations with the Queen, and bearing in mind his intentions regarding the Princess Maria, he might have done himself a bit of good too.

'Close ordaaaaaaaaaahhh – *now!*'

Wilfrid's voice echoed down the line. There was a shuffling and wriggling from five hundred feet. A distinct murmuring, too.

'How much longer, I should like to know,' muttered one fyrd-man to his neighbour. 'Close order – open order – close order. Where does he think we are – on a dance floor?'

The neighbour growled. 'Fat-gutted Yorkshire bastard.'

'You!' bawled Wilfrid.

He walked swiftly towards him. The line went silent. Eyes and eyebrows rose heavenwards. This was not the first time. Wilfrid thrust his moustache under the fyrdman's nose and told him what he thought of the man's standard of drill. While he was about it, he added further unwelcome details about the man's standards of dress, his dexterity – or lack of it – with the basic weapons, and his general attitude. He concluded with observations on his personal character and the illegitimate features of his family background.

The rest of the line were by now so familiar with it that they were mouthing Wilfrid's last words in time with him.

When he was satisfied that he had conveyed the general drift of his thoughts, Wilfrid stumped back to the middle of the open space at the entrance of the camp, and stood beside Oswy. He was preparing for another word of command when Oswy whispered in his ear, 'Dismiss them. Give them a break.'

Wilfrid turned and glared at him.

'Do it,' said Oswy.

After another pause, Wilfrid did. 'Ten minutes,' he shouted. 'Then we go again. Awaaaaaayyyyy – *now!*'

Wilfrid glared again. 'For what good it will do.'

'It will.' Oswy always had more patience than Wilfrid. And Oswy knew him so well. 'I know what you are thinking: we could be doing so much more good at Little Coates and Great Coates than we can here.'

'You can say that again,' growled Wilfrid.

'Yes,' said Oswy. 'Good for ourselves. I agree. But not for Harold. We are both Harold's men – remember? We are both housecarls.'

Wilfrid grimaced. 'But we make no progress. I would work like the Devil if I could see some results.'

For over a week, they had moved from one fyrd camp to another, all over Anglia, doing very much the same thing in each place. It was a good thing they had one of Earl Gyrth's reeves to accompany them, or they would have had trouble getting any fyrdman to turn up for a parade at all.

They had long since given up on marching practice. The men simply laughed.

'You stupid bastard. We spend all our days on our feet, and half of those days getting from one spot to another. Our legs are as good as yours. We do not need to be told how to put one foot in front of the other.'

They listened in surly silence while Wilfrid and Oswy lectured and hectored about the construction of a shield wall; gave lessons about the making of simple wooden shields; explained certain sequences of command; went through the meaning of various trumpet signals.

As Wilfrid complained to Earl Gyrth when he visited, 'Most of it goes in one ear and out of the other.'

Gyrth listened sympathetically, and nodded. 'Never mind; any training is better than none at all. If anything sticks between their ears, it will help to keep their heads on their shoulders.'

Wilfrid was not comforted. 'You would think we were on the other side, sir,' he said, 'the way they moan.'

Gyrth nodded again. 'Soldiers always moan. So do you – you are moaning about *them* now.' He glanced at Oswy, who grinned.

Wilfrid agreed, but grudgingly. Gyrth looked at him for a moment, then turned to the fyrdmen, who were loafing almost within listening distance. Suddenly, he clapped his hands and shouted, 'Come round here, lads.'

They did, jostling and curious. Gyrth stood on a convenient boundary stone near the camp gate.

'Well, are you all having a nice time with Wilfrid? Loving every minute, eh?'

There was a ripple of laughter.

'Yes, I know,' said Gyrth. 'But listen to what he says, and Oswy here. They talk a lot of balls half the time, but the other half is good sense.'

'How do we know which is which?' asked somebody.

There was another laugh.

'That is the problem,' said Gyrth. 'You do not. You have to listen to all of it to find out. But the sense is there, and you know it is. They have forgotten more about swords than you will ever know. They will give you the beating of these longship scum. They want to send them back where they came from.

'And so do you. I know that. Nobody here wants to welcome these carrion from the sea, do they? Does anybody here doubt that we can thrash them?'

He waited just for a second. 'Of course not. Well, listen. Listen to Wilfrid and Oswy, and we can do more than thrash them; we can destroy them, send the survivors scuttling to their salt-soaked rowing boats – and never dare to come here again.'

There was a ragged cheer. Gyrth seized the moment.

'Do what Wilfrid and Oswy say, and your swords will put the fear of God into them. They will be so scared, so mad to get away, they will not have time to be seasick; they will have done it in their leggings already. What do you say?'

'We shall murder them, sir.'

'Right, lads. Now then, into line, get those swords out, and show Wilfrid what you can do. Go on, surprise him. He likes surprises.'

There was a roar of goodwill. Gyrth turned quietly to Wilfrid and Oswy.

'Now get on with it. Make the bastards work.'

'Well, was it good or was it not?'

'It was good. I thank you.'

One did not have to be a fortifications expert to see that. Gunnar had well and truly delivered on his promise. Edric's men had worked hard, but they all knew that their success had been made possible by the quality, and the amount, of first-class timber that Gunnar had produced. Edric himself knew that Scarborough's defences had not been so sound since he had become the town reeve.

So why could he not enthuse? As soon as he asked himself the question, he knew the answer. He hated being beholden to Gunnar – for anything. However, he knew too that his most important concern at the moment should not be his feelings towards this squat, sweaty Swede, but the town's preparedness for the possible dangers of the coming summer.

He still had no idea whence those dangers would come. Tostig was out there somewhere. No reliable evidence had reached Scarborough – well, none that he was aware of. All sorts of stories were still in the air: Tostig was in Normandy; Tostig was in Flanders; Tostig was in Denmark; Tostig was in Norway; Tostig was on the high seas somewhere, anywhere.

And which prince had he talked into helping him? The Bastard? The Count of Flanders? The King of Denmark? Hardrada?

Or was it the other way round? Which of these foreign princes was simply using Tostig for his nuisance value?

Or – again – was Tostig operating entirely on his own? He was a selfish man. With the selfish man's narrow vision, was Tostig merely working to get himself back into power in Northumbria? It was most unlikely that he would succeed, but that would not stop him trying.

Or – yet again – was Tostig being vastly overrated? Was it that they thought of Tostig all the time because he was the one they knew best? After all, he was the one who had been Earl of Northumbria. But now that he was gone, was that how they should think of him – as gone? And the real threat had not yet materialised. When it did, whence would it come? From the south or the north?

Edric was not short of advice. Most of it was useless, because the givers were even more ill-informed than he was. Gunnar's comments were not to be trusted, because the man was not to be trusted. And as for the gloomy forecasts about doom and tragedy brought about by that damned star . . . Edric credited himself with a fair ration of common sense, and he knew he would not have been made reeve if he had not shown more than average steadiness under pressure. Nor did he think of himself as a superstitious man. Yet he had to admit – if only to himself – that he would rather the wretched thing were not there. He defied anybody to claim that he *enjoyed* it.

Edric sighed. There was so much that a man did not know. Probably never would know. That was why they were all enjoined to listen to the men who claimed that they *did* know. And why was that? Because they got everything they said out of a huge book in a foreign language that few could read and even fewer could understand. And why was the book always right?

Because we, the priests, say it is right. Not much of a recommendation, if you stopped to think about it.

The trouble was that thinking about it got you nowhere. In fact, it only made things worse; you ended up not knowing anything, and worried to death. Holy Blood – he had enough to worry about without that as well. So – Devil take the star. He had probably sent it in the first place, so he could damn well have it back.

Practicalities. Events. Realities. Those were what he had to deal with right now. That was his job, and God would not punish a man for doing his job.

He, Edric, had remained loyal to King Harold. He had fulfilled his responsibilities, and made Scarborough as safe as was allowed by the knowledge and resources at his disposal. He well understood how limited that knowledge was; indeed the one event that was likely to be most certain was that, whatever happened, he would be surprised. By the same token, his resources, for all Gunnar's contributions, were also inadequate. If an earl, a count, a duke, or – worse – a king were to bring his full force against Scarborough, the result would not be in doubt. All Edric could hope for was that he might be able to delay the progress of that earl, count, duke or king just long enough to give King Harold a little advantage of time.

Well, if that was the limit of his capabilities, so be it. He would have done his duty, and his best. He could face the King afterwards – assuming, that is, that he would be alive to face the King afterwards.

Thanks be to God, he had got Coelwen out of it, though even that was tinged by a sense of incompleteness, because he was beholden once again to Gunnar. The break was not clean; that tie of obligation clung like a tiresome cobweb across the eyes in a disused cellar.

'It all looks a good piece of work,' said Gunnar, bringing him back to the matter in hand. 'What else do you have to do?'

Edric responded, almost grateful for having something straightforward to talk about.

'Precautions against fire, mostly. The more we use wood to defend ourselves, the more we lay ourselves open to it. I am building cisterns as near the walls as possible. I have a team of carpenters and coopers knocking together scores of buckets.'

'If they are made in such a hurry, they will surely leak,' observed Gunnar.

'True. But they will hold water long enough to carry it from the cistern to the wall. I have also cleared spaces behind the walls, for braziers.'

'To heat water?'

'Yes. To give them hot heads when they try to climb the ladders.'

'Do you have enough poles to push the ladders?'

'Yes,' said Edric, anticipating another offer of help. Perversely, he was trying to avoid having to accept.

Gunnar looked along a section of wall. Parts of it still showed white where the adzes had scraped away much of the jutting surfaces on the new timber he had provided.

'What about skins?' he said.

Edric swore to himself. Trust Gunnar to spot the one weakness. Yes, he was short of skins – very short. That was the irony. He would have cisterns to hold the water, and buckets to carry the water. But the one thing he also needed to prevent the spread of fire was enough skins to soak and hang over the walls. And Gunnar had noticed. Edric knew at once what was coming next.

'I can get you some. We slaughtered more animals than usual last autumn. The local seers had said it would be a worse winter than usual.'

'Was it?' said Edric.

'No. But by the time we found out the damage had been done. But I have them still stored up country. Vendel can go and get them – no trouble.'

Edric knew he had no choice. 'Then I shall be grateful.'

'Just doing my bit,' said Gunnar.

Doing his bit. Edric kept a straight face. The only 'bit' Gunnar ever did was to do himself a bit of a favour. But hard times needed hard decisions.

'I thank you once again.'

When Gunnar had gone, Edric was glad there had been no more questions. Otherwise he might have had to talk about some of his plans to deal with the worst possible situation. Common sense told him that, if the town were to be attacked, it would probably be captured; the only question was how long it would take. The best he could hope for was delay, to give the King whatever help that would provide.

That meant he would have to make plans for possible evacuation. Once again, it was quite likely that the town would be destroyed, but there was a slender chance that some of the townsfolk would be able to escape, and he had to provide for it. In such a scene of disaster, with besiegers on all sides, escape by land could be almost impossible.

Even if he could not evacuate people, it might be possible to get some news out before the ring of siege became complete. So he had arranged for reliable couriers, and relays of horses, to take news to York.

There remained one final hope. Scarborough was a port, albeit a small one. There was a clear chance, albeit a slender one, of escape by sea. If the town were to be attacked, you could rest assured that there would be Viking ships offshore, so the chance was very slender indeed. Nevertheless, Edric knew that Hardrada would be interested in destruction, and his men would be interested in loot, and a whole town sitting helpless would be a great deal more attractive than a single ship scuttling away full of refugee civilians with nothing but the clothes on their backs.

One thing that Gunnar was not going to find out about was the ships that he, Edric, was quietly preparing in a cove further up the coast.

Gunnar, on his way to give Vendel his orders, felt well pleased with himself. He had placed Edric under yet another obligation. He had secured another opportunity for Vendel to go up country. And who knew? Perhaps there might arise the opportunity to visit Coelwen. He had been surprised when Vendel had returned from escorting Coelwen in a suspiciously good mood. None of the sullen silence of his usual behaviour.

There was a second surprise when he told Vendel he would have to go again. His willingness was astounding. Gunnar lifted his eyebrows. Perhaps his long-term plans were working out even better than he could have hoped. Well, fancy that. But time enough to tell Edric when the relationship showed more definite signs of maturing. Plenty of time.

Gunnar felt yet another twinge of surprise when he thought about what he had just offered to do for Edric. A second journey, with all the expenses involved. A second free gift of supplies and equipment for the defence of the town. What on earth was he about? Here he was, a man who prided himself on his ability to spot the main chance, and he was allowing himself to be drawn into the welfare of Scarborough itself. Thor and thunder, was he getting involved in a noble cause?

He had long considered the likelihood of disaster, and had taken steps to avoid it. He had already written oily letters to the (former) Earl Tostig, to the new Earl Morcar and to the invader Hardrada. But suppose the ship was not going to sink after all. Suppose King Harold came through it all. Suppose – miracle of miracles – Scarborough itself survived.

It was time to write another letter.

*   *   *

191

Coelwen pulled back the shovel, and slid the loaves carefully onto a tray. For a moment she allowed herself the luxury of simply sniffing. She never tired of the smell of fresh bread.

She did not have the easy skill of the bakers in Scarborough, naturally, but she had helped to run her father's household ever since her mother had died. As the years had gone by, her duties had multiplied and her skills had grown. She was by now an accomplished housekeeper.

She was a practical girl, and kind by nature. She was sensible, too, and understood clearly the debt she and her father owed to his brother. These were difficult times, and her uncle had his own problems. For instance, he was short-staffed; he had lost three of his best workers to Earl Morcar's fyrd, and had no idea when he was going to get them back – if at all. Word was already floating around the north that the King had camps for fyrdmen all over England. Since nobody had any idea – not even the King – where the blow would fall, there was no way of knowing how long he would have to keep these men in readiness.

Coelwen was well aware that her uncle would have to work his remaining men harder. He himself was already doing a much longer working day than usual, and the tiredness was beginning to show in spats of impatience.

Worse, his wife was no longer in the best of health. She caught fevers and bad humours easily. Coelwen had noticed, too, that she did not seem as sharp-witted as before. She would start to say something, and drift off into another topic. She was becoming absent-minded.

So Coelwen's immediate future was clearly set out before her. She must do what she could. Before very long, she was taking on household chores as naturally as if she were at home. Her uncle was showing signs of relying on her just as her father did. When the time came for her to return home, she could see that it was going to be a wrench for both of them.

She was beginning to feel responsible for the household. In a perverse way, she quite liked it, in the way anybody likes to feel that they are indispensable.

And yet – and yet – she still missed her home, and her father. She missed her own bed, her own trinkets, ornaments, special treasures. She missed the familiar layout of her father's house. She missed calling her pets by name.

It was an odd limbo. She was in this family of her uncle's, and clearly welcome, but she was not *of* it. Her aunt was not well, but she was not an invalid, and she still appeared daily in the kitchen. She was causing mishaps with her faulty memory, but it was still her kitchen, and Coelwen had enough sense, and kindness, not to try to take her place. But it was frustrating.

The mixture of busyness and frustration, of familiarity and loneliness, of welcome and exile, made her ill at ease. This in turn made her wonder whether it really had been a good idea to leave Scarborough. Should she have been more determined to oppose her father?

The sudden arrival of Vendel took her mind off all this. She surprised herself at how much she was pleased to see him.

'I have been to Father's holding to collect some skins.'

'Skins?'

'Skins – to hang on the walls – against fire.'

'Ah. Yes. Yes, of course.'

There was a pause.

'And your father offered them to my father?'

'Yes. The town needed them.'

Coelwen understood perfectly well the nature of the relationship between Vendel's father and her own. For that matter, so did he. But, like their parents, neither of them wanted to come out beyond the protection of formal manners. There was nothing to be gained by the truth at this moment.

'That was very good of him,' she said.

'Yes.'

There was another pause.

Vendel made a vague gesture. 'I was not far away. I thought I would just come and see that you were settled in all right. You know – comfortable.'

'Yes. Yes – thank you.' She extended her hand to indicate the kitchen.

'As you can see, they are keeping me busy.'

Vendel managed a ghost of a smile. 'Yes. Yes – I can.'

A sudden gust of wind blew against the open door and flung it back against the wall. Drops of rain were blown in. Coelwen went to fasten the latch.

'You must stay the night. It looks bad out there.'

'Thank you. Thank you very much.'

Coelwen swallowed. 'You – er – you have some men with you?'

'Two.'

'We can put them in the barn. The loft is warm, and there are sheepskins up there.'

By the time they were resting after the meal, conversation had become a little less stilted.

Coelwen broke off the end of a loaf as she recalled the evening, and quietly chewed. Vendel had said how good it was, too.

They had talked about the monastery, and about his time there. He told her about different styles of writing, and qualities of parchment and vellum, and illustrations, and a host of other things. She did not understand everything he said, but she enjoyed listening to him. He talked now without a trace of shyness or restraint. Very little stammer, either.

She felt sorry that she had no things like that to talk about.

He took a deep breath, as if considering whether he should say what was in his mind. At last he took the plunge.

'I write things too, you know.'

'Yes. You said. The Scriptures. It must be very interesting.'

Vendel waved. 'No, no. I do not mean copying: I mean writing. Composing. I write –' He hesitated once again. '– I write poetry.'

'Ah.'

'I have memorised a few pieces. Would you – would you –?'

'Yes, I would.'

As Coelwen wrapped the loaves and stored them in a pantry, she recalled his voice, the blushes, the slight sweat on the brow. But, again, no stammer. He recited beautifully.

Coelwen, not having any letters herself, was in a poor position to judge it all. Nor did she understand all the phrases or the vocabulary. But the timbre of Vendel's voice, the rhythms of the lines, the cadences, all combined to make a most enjoyable noise.

'Is it permitted, Maj— sir?'

'Come in, come in. It is time we got something clear. Sit down.'

Conrad gaped. Harold flapped his wrist towards a stool. Conrad subsided, still with his mouth open. Harold leaned on his elbows at the table.

'When you came to work for me, it was as a bringer of letters, a reader of letters. Is that not so?'

Conrad nodded uncertainly, having just managed to haul up his lower jaw.

'Well,' said Harold, 'I am pleased with your work. You have not only discharged the duties you were given, but you have shown initiative too. You do not put boundaries to your responsibility. I like that.' Here Harold smiled. 'But you do not know what you have let yourself in for. If a servant is good, a sensible lord does not take burdens off his shoulders; he lays even more on. You have been alive long enough to know that – yes?'

Conrad nodded slowly, warily. Harold continued.

'These are difficult times. A king must take difficult

decisions. To do that he must have information he can rely on. He must have servants he can rely on. He has no choice but to trust them. He does not have time for the luxury of testing them and examining the results. He has to follow his instincts. Do you understand what I am saying?'

Conrad nodded again, slightly more surely.

'I am charged with the protection of England. My servants must share that charge. England can stand or fall on their decisions and actions just as easily as it can on mine. Now – Father Bernard brought you here from Franconia. Father Bernard has made England his cause. Are you also willing to make England your cause?'

Conrad opened his mouth to reply, but Harold held up a hand. 'Think before you answer. You were born German; you only live here. If you have any doubts, you must say no, and I shall think none the worse of you for it. Indeed, I shall respect you for your honesty.'

Conrad opened his mouth again, and again Harold held up his hand.

'Hear me out. Father Bernard is going to move shortly – north – to York. What you have in your hand is probably his last despatch from Waltham. Am I right?'

'Yes, sir.'

Harold smiled. 'So far in this conversation you have spent most of your time with your mouth open. But what I want, as I said before, is a man who can keep his mouth shut. If Father Bernard goes to York, I shall be receiving many more despatches. Brother Albert will continue to send me information from Waltham. There will be many others from all parts of England. Those like Father Bernard's will be valuable. There will be many others which are – well, not so valuable.

'I need somebody to sort them out. I need a filter of news. I need an interpreter. I need a reader. I need a secretary. Do you know what a secretary is?'

'Yes, sir.'

'Good. I need a secretary I can call on at all hours. I need a secretary who can think for himself. I need a secretary who can make decisions. I need a secretary I can trust, because, like me, he believes in England. Now – are you that man?'

Conrad was gaping again.

'I have finished,' said Harold.

Conrad came out of his trance, and threw himself on his knees before Harold.

Harold tossed his head. 'God's Blood! A simple "yes" will do.'

Still on his knees, Conrad smiled hugely. 'Yes, sir.'

Harold clapped his hands. 'Good. Now, what have you got there?'

Sigurd leaned over from the quayside. 'Come with me.'

He turned away and began walking without waiting to see if Magnus obeyed.

Magnus looked enquiringly at Finn and Ketil. They both shrugged. Magnus threw the hammer in his hand to Ketil, and climbed out of the ship.

Sigurd wove his way through a forest of timber piles, massive coils of rope, and great folds of sail canvas. They passed ships of every size and style, in every stage of construction and repair. Sweating teams of labourers were lugging masts, humping boxes, rolling barrels, heaving baskets, hauling on ropes. Shipwrights, carpenters, coopers, smiths, sailmakers, charge hands and foremen were surveying, squinting, waving, warning, shouting and swearing.

The impact of hammers, the rattle of pulleys, the grinding and groaning of timbers, the slapping of ropes, all contributed to a general, all-pervading roar of industry and purpose. The sheer scale of it was crushing.

Magnus had gone to and fro from their ship a hundred times

197

but, every time, he had been absorbed with what he had been instructed, or was preparing, to do. He had become so accustomed to the route from his bed to the deck of his ship that he did it almost in a sleep-walk; he took little or no notice of what was going on around him.

Now, as he followed Sigurd, with nothing to think about except obeying Sigurd's order, he was able to take in the full panorama of it all. The shock was almost physical.

He had known that Trondheim was a great port, and he had already spent several weeks there, on and off, but now, as he looked to right and left, it was as if he were seeing it for the first time.

For the first time, too, he began to get an impression of what a colossal enterprise the King was engaged upon. He shook his head in wonder as he thought of the sheer expense of it all, and wondered if there was another king in Christendom who could find the funds for it. Only perhaps the Emperor in Miklegaard. But then the story was that Hardrada had helped himself to a large slice of those riches when he was in the Emperor's service, so it made some kind of sense. Had he really looted a pile of those legendary golden paving stones from the streets of the city? If he had, well, good luck to him.

He had been forced to leave Norway at fifteen, after seeing his brother killed in battle. He had been forced to seek his fortune in a host of wild eastern countries, men said, against bandits, barbarians and savage tribesmen whose very names were so outlandish that nobody civilised could even pronounce them, much less understand their tongue. He had served an emperor, worked for a prince of the Rus, and collected this enormous fortune. Then, fifteen years later, he had returned with this fortune, and a Kievan wife, and won further laurels as the greatest Viking monarch of the whole north. Magnus was quite sure that no other man could even have contemplated such a venture as he now saw being prepared.

Sigurd echoed his thoughts when he caught up with him. 'You are right: only Hardrada could think of this. And only a man like Hardrada can bring it off.'

'So you think he will?' said Magnus.

'Oh, yes,' said Sigurd. 'Whether he does or not, I want to be there. What about you?'

Magnus found himself agreeing, though he was not quite sure why. But, then, he had not seen as much of Hardrada as Sigurd had. And then again, he was not bewitched by Hardrada's daughter.

'Where are we going, Sig?'

'Nearly there.'

They were round at the other side of the harbour by now. Sigurd stopped beside a ship on a completely different scale from anything Magnus had seen before. It was longer, broader, stronger, taller than any other vessel. Magnus leaned back and gaped at the mast. How had they got it up there?

On the dockside a large space had been cleared, and most of it was occupied by a sail of cloudlike proportions. Crouched all over it was a small army of sailmakers engaged on stitching a device onto it. Magnus cricked his neck to work out what it was, and gasped when he realised.

It was a great black raven, complete with slavering beak and bloody claws. He did not need Sigurd's whisper that it belonged to Hardrada. This was the King's flagship and this was his banner, his symbol, his signature on the sea. Sigurd himself was whispering not in order to muffle his words, but because he too was short of breath.

They both had a heart-stopping vision of the impact such a sight would have on those who saw such a vessel bearing down upon them with a following wind.

'God and Odin!' said Magnus, invoking both, just to make sure.

'I would wager that Hardrada will get both to bless it,' said Sigurd. 'Look at that.'

Approaching from the direction of the town was a procession. At its head was an array of monks, priests, chaplains and choristers. Behind them came a bishop, in full pontificals.

Magnus gasped. 'What on earth is that?'

'A bishop,' said Sigurd. 'Never seen one before?'

'No.'

'Nor has anyone else, I should guess,' said Sigurd. 'There is only one in the whole of the north. Hardrada must have got him here all the way from Denmark, even maybe Germany.'

'God, what influence!'

'I told you only Hardrada could mount an expedition like this. Well, only Hardrada could get a bishop to move hundreds of miles just to bless a ship. I tell you, he could move the Holy City if he took it into his mind to do so.'

Magnus suddenly had a thought. 'How do you know what a bishop is, then?'

Sigurd made a smug face. 'I have just come from the court.'

Magnus tilted his head. 'State secrets again, eh?'

Sigurd grinned. 'Something like that.'

'Another chat with Maria, was it?'

'Her father tells her everything.'

'And she then tells you. How fortunate.'

'Not luck, dear boy. Pure charm.'

'What a gift. Tell me, what is it like to be so favoured – unlike the rest of us mere mortals?'

Sigurd raised his eyebrows. 'Well, I came and told you. You should be grateful.'

Magnus nodded. 'Ah, yes. A chance to impress me.'

'Of course. When you tell the others all about it, you will exaggerate, and they will believe you. If I exaggerate, they will not believe me.'

They watched while the procession drew level with the ship. Behind the bishop came the Princess Maria and the Queen herself, Ellisif.

'Where is the King?' whispered Magnus.

'Ill,' said Sigurd. 'The flux. Over-eating again. But he wanted it to go ahead, because they had already organised the crowd. Look around you.'

He was right; the harbour had mysteriously filled to bursting point. Magnus had been so dumbfounded that he had scarcely noticed.

'If it goes well,' said Sigurd, 'my guess is that they might do it all over again tomorrow. By then he may be here himself.'

They watched while the ceremonies were conducted – the prayers, the singing, the blessing. More prayers and chants. Then the holy water. Some of the crew stood like statues, and blew the wayward drops off their faces.

Maria and Sigurd managed to exchange a whole flight of facial expressions while it was going on. Ellisif smiled drily.

When it was all over, and the bishop and his train had departed, the Queen and the Princess remained to have a closer look at the ship. With an imperial gesture, Ellisif told the court servants to keep their distance.

She waved at the ship. 'Well, Sigurd, what do you think of her?'

'I am truly amazed, Majesty.'

Ellisif raised her eyebrows. 'For once, Sigurd, I believe you are speaking the truth.'

During this exchange, the Princess Maria had gone aboard, and was roaming like a prowling wolf all over the deck, peering, examining, pulling, pushing, trying, testing.

The crew fell back, but looked anxiously in Sigurd's direction. He, too, began to be concerned. Ellisif caught his expression.

'Have no fear, Sigurd. We have never stopped Maria exploring. She has steady feet, steady nerves.'

Sigurd saw the Princess stop beside some of the new shrouds, and look up. Ellisif smiled.

'She can also climb like a cat.'

As if to prove it, Maria put her foot on the first rope rungs, and climbed a step or two.

Ellisif leaned forward and asked quietly, 'Do you think you will be able to control her? I tell you, *we* have trouble. If you are not sure, you had better give up now.'

Sigurd did not answer. He was watching Maria. She went up five or six more rungs, turned, let go one hand and waved vigorously.

Ellisif returned the wave. Sigurd made a feeble imitation of it.

Suddenly, Maria was falling. Before anyone could blink, she was in the water. There was no cry from her. It all happened so fast that for an instant the watchers could not believe their eyes.

Then they heard Maria shouting. And it was not distress; it was annoyance.

Sigurd rushed to the edge and dived in. Maria did not show much sign of gratitude.

'All right, all right. I can manage.'

She did. Sigurd was forced to keep away while she swam the short space to the dockside. A dozen hands were extended. She ignored them all, and heaved herself out of the water.

Maria found herself looking her mother in the face.

'Are you all right?' said Ellisif.

'Yes, yes, perfectly all right.'

Sigurd had by this time joined them. They stood face to face, dripping all over the dock.

'What happened?' said Sigurd.

'No idea,' said Maria. 'Everything went black for a moment. But only for a moment. By the time I hit the water, I was awake again. It was nothing.'

'But you should be more careful,' said Sigurd.

Maria wrung out some of the more voluminous parts of her dress. 'No fussing, please, Sigurd. I fell in the water, that is all. Served me right. Now get out of my way and let me go back to get out of these clothes.'

And she was gone. Sigurd found himself looking at the Queen.

Ellisif smiled slightly. 'See what I mean?'

Sigurd for once did not have an answer.

Neither did the Queen. This was not the first time something like this had happened. She hoped Maria's father did not know.

'Come!'

The door opened, and Conrad almost crept in.

Harold looked up from a fishing line he was untangling.

'How many times do I have to tell you? You are my secretary; you have access to me.'

It did not take the worry off Conrad's pink face. 'But how can I be sure, Maj— sir, that you are alone?'

Harold pointed to the door. 'Because you ask the housecarl on duty outside. He will not eat you.' He chuckled to himself. 'Some of them are quite human. If I am with any of my family, then you knock and wait. If I am not, then you knock and come in. Even if I am with company. They will probably need to know the details of what you have to say.'

Conrad drew himself up. 'Sir.'

Harold pointed a fishing rod at him. 'Remember, you are now a member of my headquarters. We are a team; we work together. When I want you to stay away, believe me, I shall tell you. And I shall probably shout at you. Are you ready for that?'

Conrad smiled in spite of himself. 'Oh, yes, sir. Father Bernard shouts – now and again.'

Harold smiled too. 'Good. Now – what do you have for me?'

Conrad waved a document. 'From Brother Albert, sir.'

'Is it important?'

Conrad looked baffled. 'It is not for me, sir—'

'Ah, but it is,' said Harold. 'This is a good chance to test your judgement. Is it long?'

'Yes, sir.'

'Is it a bit too long? Could it have been said in a shorter space?'

Conrad hesitated.

'Go on. I am employing you to think.'

'Well – yes, sir. Brother Albert does not have the skills of Father Bernard. I have often said—'

'I do not wish to know what you said. I want to know what you think. If Brother Albert's report is too long, then I want you to shorten it.'

Conrad frowned. 'You mean, to go away and—'

'No, I mean to stay here, and tell me the important bits.'

'Now, sir?'

'Now.'

Conrad swallowed. 'Well, sir, there has been another council in Normandy. The Bastard – the Duke of Normandy—'

'The "Bastard" will do perfectly well; that, after all, is what he is.'

Conrad nodded. 'Sir. The Bastard summoned his second council at Bonneville-sur-Touques. It is a small river, sir, in—'

'I know where it is. Carry on.'

'The council—'

'What were the decisions taken?'

Conrad peered at the despatch. 'None that I can discern, sir. The main decision to invade has been taken. The Bastard has simply reinforced his decision, and made doubly sure of his main vassals' support. They have promised soldiers, and money, and, especially, ships.'

'Are they built yet?'

'No, sir. Not on the evidence of this.'

'Good. Anything else of importance?'

Conrad peered once again. 'No, sir.'

Harold sat back. He surprised himself by how intently he had been listening.

'There, now. That did not hurt, did it?'

Conrad had to smile. 'No, sir.'

'That is what I want you to do. Can you do it?'

Conrad smiled more broadly. 'Yes, sir, I think so.'

'Good. Now, off you go.'

As Conrad reached the door, Harold shouted after him.

'What are you?'

Conrad turned. 'Your secretary, sir.'

'And what do you have?'

'Free access, sir. Except—'

'Except for the family. Good. Now push off.'

When he had gone Harold laid down the fishing line, and gazed into the fire.

It had been a busy week, but a fruitful one. And it was beginning to look as if it had been a decisive one, too.

The Whitsun Witan had gone well; they had conducted quite a lot of business. More instructions had gone out to the mints. His new pennies were becoming familiar currency, and funds were flowing. More judges had been appointed. Harold had sworn, at his coronation, to bring justice to his people, and he could not delay that merely because of a threatened invasion – even because of two threatened invasions. More requisitions had been agreed – for food, drink, equipment, horses and wagons. Further orders had gone out about the assembling and deploying of the country fyrds. More couriers and warning beacons had been arranged, particularly on the south coast, even though it looked quieter now that Tostig had moved on from the Isle of Wight.

Harold had shadowed him in Hampshire and Sussex as Tostig moved eastwards. When his brother descended suddenly upon the town of Sandwich, Harold had been too late to stop his destruction, and his virtual kidnapping of crewmen for his longships, but his arrival nonetheless had driven Tostig to pull away again, with his unwilling pressed men crowded on board.

Instead of running back to Normandy or Flanders, he had last been seen moving north. Whether or not it was to Denmark, Norway, Scotland or Orkney, it was definitely north. And so far there had been no battle. All resources were intact. After prodigious efforts of supply, and a great deal of persuasion, Harold was managing to keep his Channel fleet on active patrol, and they were herding Tostig off the premises. The county fyrds were all on active alert.

That was the positive news. The negative news came with Conrad's despatch about William's council at Bonneville-sur-Touques. There was no mention of orders for actual movement, or dates of embarkation, or anything remotely like that. His vassals had only *promised* ships; they had not delivered them. Harold's spies had talked of assembly harbours virtually empty. William's new ships, however numerous they may be, were not yet ready for sea.

So, at the very least, there was breathing space in the south. Tostig had, with the direction of his withdrawal, confirmed that conclusion. If further confirmation was wanting, another spy ship had told Bernard in York that there was a lot of activity in Orkney. Men and ships were gathering in Scapa Flow. And Orkney's overlord was Hardrada.

Harold leaned back and put his hands behind his head. It looked, then, as if Bernard was right. It was not the south; it was the north.

Chapter Six

'Well, what are you going to do about it?'

Morcar refused to meet his sister's eye. He tugged at the wisp of hair beneath his lower lip. Gwen looked at Edwin. This was typical Morcar. They would have to get a decision out of him.

Gwen leaned forward. 'Morcar, Northumbria is under threat. An enemy force is off the coast somewhere.'

'We do not know that for sure,' said Morcar, relieved to correct his sister on a point of fact.

'If you see storm clouds,' said Edwin, 'you know you are going to get some rain. And we shall get wet.'

Gwen joined in. 'We know Tostig has left the Channel and is working his way up the east coast. He will certainly strike again, as he did in Kent and the Isle of Wight.'

Morcar looked as if he were about to win another point. 'Why should he not raid in Anglia, then?'

'Use what little sense the good Lord has given you, brother. If you were Tostig, where would you want to land – in your brother Gyrth's earldom, and be thrown out, or in your own old earldom, where there might still be some supporters?'

Gwen returned to the attack. 'Edwin here has brought the Mercian fyrd.'

Edwin looked slightly alarmed. 'Only part of it.'

Gwen made a dismissive gesture. 'The rest is on its way; you said so yourself. In a short while, we shall have men from the midland shires as far south as Hereford.'

'Yes,' said Morcar gloomily, 'and who is going to feed them?'

'That is my worry,' said Edwin. '*I* am the Earl of Mercia, not you. The point is that they are at your disposal.'

Morcar stood up and walked agitatedly up and down.

'Yes, that is all very well. But what about the York Witan? Tostig used to ignore them, and look what happened to him. I have to get their approval, and that takes time.'

'Stuff and nonsense,' said Gwen. 'We are not talking about everyday government; we are talking about defending the realm against an outside enemy. The Witan is only an excuse and you know it. If Tostig lands, we have to strike, and strike quickly. By the time you have summoned the Witan, and they have talked their heads off, he could be halfway to York – here.'

'Suppose he comes in force,' said Morcar, stopping for a moment.

Edwin shook his head. 'More excuses, brother. We know that he was driven off from the Isle of Wight; Harold and Leofwine drove him off the Kent coast. Denmark has given him nothing, and I doubt if the Count of Flanders has. Dammit, man, what are you afraid of?'

Morcar whirled on him. 'Curse you, I am not afraid.'

Before he could go further, Gwen joined in again. 'You are afraid,' she said. 'But you are afraid only of doing something wrong.'

'You are afraid you won't do something to make yourself a great earl.'

'Forget the sagas, Morcar,' said Gwen. 'Look at the situation. Use your common sense. Use us. We are your family, and we would not give you bad advice. Edwin has the fyrd. You have your own men.'

'What sort of earl do you think your own people will make of you,' said Edwin, 'if you let Tostig roam at will all over Lindsey and the north-east?'

'Any prince must defend his people – whatever kind of prince he is. If you do not do that, you are no prince at all.'

Morcar sat down, heaved an enormous sigh and looked at them both. He looked beaten. But he had stopped tugging at his little beard.

Gwen resisted a temptation to put her arm round his shoulder, but she made her voice more gentle.

'You want to be a good earl. Well, be one and protect your people.'

Edwin offered a last word. 'Tostig is after Northumbria, and that is yours. Are you going to give it to him?'

Gwen leaned forward. 'And if you succeed, you never know, Hardrada may get cold feet and not come at all. And you will be the liberator of the north.'

Morcar nodded glumly. 'Yes, there is that, I suppose.'

Gwen looked at Edwin. That should do the trick.

Edith eased off her shoes. 'God, Harold. I am exhausted.'

'You wanted to come.'

Edith flopped back on the bed and stretched. 'I ache everywhere.' Then she smiled. 'I will be little comfort to you tonight.'

'Oh, yes, you will.'

Edith groaned. 'Oh, Harold, please! I have never felt less like it. Have some consideration.'

'I do not mean that,' said Harold. He leaned down towards her, put his face very close to hers and pretended to threaten. 'I have other plans for you this evening.'

He rose from the bed, went to a large chest nearby, poured two drinks and brought them back with him.

'Here. This will help. Travel is always tiring.'

'You are always doing it.'

'Oh, you learn a trick or two.'

Edith sat up and began sipping. 'Well, I am glad I do not have to do it all the time.'

'You did not have to do it this time.'

Edith looked sharply at him. 'Yes, I did – if I wanted to see anything of you.'

Harold sat down again. 'It is a busy situation.'

'Yes. And, because I understand something of that situation, I want to get as much of you as I can. Times like this are going to get rarer.'

Harold nodded thoughtfully. 'They will indeed.'

Edith snuggled close as they sipped. 'How far is it from London to here?'

'London to Leicester? About a hundred miles, I suppose.'

Edith grimaced. 'No wonder I ache all over.' Then she remembered something. 'What are these "other plans"?'

Harold grinned. 'I want your brain right now, not your body.'

'Thank you very much.'

'Oh, shut up and listen.' He put down his drink and turned back to her.

'Gyrth is in Anglia. Lef is in Kent. Both of them are trying to guess where Tostig will come ashore next. I have nobody else close.'

'Your mother and your sister?' said Edith with a touch of mischief.

'I mean somebody close who *understands*.'

Edith pretended to look put out. 'So you are making do with me.'

'Yes. Now stop complaining and listen. I want to go through my plans and ideas, and I want to find out what you think of them.'

'I am not a general.'

'No. But you are a sensible human. If there is a human flaw, you will find it, and you will tell me the truth. Ready?'

Edith sat up very straight in a parody of the attentive pupil. 'Ready, sir.'

After a final significant glance at her, Harold began.

'As you know, I have decided that the main immediate threat is more likely to come from the north than it is from the south. I still think the Bastard is the greater danger, because I know more about him, but I do not think he is ready. Hardrada probably is ready by now. Or, if not, very nearly.'

'What does Bernard say?'

'He agrees with me. He also thinks my immediate worry is Hardrada. That is why he asked to be moved to York. And I said yes.'

'Has Hardrada moved?'

'Not yet. Not to England, anyway. But Bernard tells me his ships have made contact with Orkney. So something is up. I propose to send more spy ships up there to sniff around. Scotland, too.'

Edith pushed back a lock of hair. 'Do you think Malcolm is a danger?'

'Not by himself, no. He is not an attacker; he is a scavenger. He will wait to gobble the pickings after the party. Unless . . .'

'Unless what?'

'Unless somebody pushes him.'

Edith's eyes lit up. 'Tostig.'

'Yes. He has tried the south coast, and we have seen him off. Now he is working his way up the east coast. Leofwine can see to him off the Thames, and Gyrth can look after himself in Anglia.'

'So he is getting closer to Scotland.'

Harold nodded. 'Looks like it, yes. But I am wondering now if he would dare to go that far unless he had safe news about support from Hardrada.'

'Not much to go on, is it?' said Edith.

'No. It is not. But it is all I have. That is why I want those spy ships out, more and more.' Harold smacked a fist into his other palm. 'News. I must have news.'

Edith frowned. 'Are you still watching the Bastard?'

'Oh, yes. Because I concentrate on the north, that does not mean that I forget the south. But all the present signs are that Hardrada will come first. And it is the first invasion that I must meet. What would be the point of peering into the Channel mist and wondering about the Bastard, if Hardrada's creatures are wasting the north behind my back? I must protect my people. Or at least be ready to protect them. Nevertheless, the southern fyrd is there. And the navy. Why do you ask?'

'Because,' said Edith, 'I was wondering if you were losing sight of one important thing.'

'Oh? What is that?'

'That you are a Wessex man. You are a king, but you are a Wessex man. There is your heartland. You must never leave Wessex bare.'

'I agree,' said Harold. 'But I wanted to hear you say so. Never fear, I shall keep the southern fyrd in full force, as long as I can feed them. But I have told Edwin to move the Mercian fyrd towards York, and Gyrth can send us some more from Anglia, unless Tostig attacks there.'

'What will you do?'

'Wait.'

'Here?'

'No. I am here to find out what is in the air in the north. Bernard expects trouble, but he sees little sign of it yet. When I have had a good look round, and seen my northern judges and taxmen, I shall go back south again.'

Edith groaned. 'Oh, no. When?'

'Not for a few days. I tell you, being a king is no holiday.'

'Neither is being a queen, I should think. I am glad I am not.'

'I hope you mean that.'

'Not much choice, have I? Are you going on to see *Gwen*, or *Mildred*, or whatever she calls herself?'

Harold grinned. 'Cat.'

Edith lifted her eyebrows. 'I have every right to be – under the circumstances.'

Harold showed no sign of embarrassment. 'In answer to your question – no. I shall not go on to see her. From what I hear – the last message Conrad showed me – she is managing very well with Morcar. She might actually put some fight into him. It will take a load off my mind.'

Edith laughed. 'I did not think you chose queens for their skill in man management. I thought it was for something else.'

Harold laughed too. 'I save that consideration for you.'

'Flatterer.'

Harold turned to pour out another drink. 'You keep an honest tongue in your head, or I shall change my mind and make you ache in all sorts of other places.'

'Where is your captain?'

Magnus turned, and gasped. It was the Princess Maria, by herself. She laughed.

'I said, "Where is your captain?"'

Magnus came out of his trance. 'Rolf? He is with your father, I think. He is having a meeting of senior commanders. Must be getting near the time.'

Maria waved away the idea. 'I do not mean your sea captain; I mean your brave soldier captain – the intrepid Sigurd Olafson. They told me he was here.'

'Who?'

'That buffoon you have with the split nose.'

'Ketil?'

'Yes, probably. Now, where is he?'

'Ketil?'

Maria bent down from the quay. 'Sigurd, idiot.'

Magnus grinned, leaned back and pointed aloft. Maria leaned back too.

213

'Holy troll! I did not think he would have the guts.'

Magnus liked Maria. She gave as good as she got. Rather like her mother. Magnus and the rest of the gang felt at home with her. Now was a good chance for some teasing. He waved upwards.

'Do you fancy going up there to tell him?'

Maria was already grabbing the lowest rungs on the shrouds. 'I mean to do just that.'

Magnus gasped again, and looked in horror at Ivar, Lars, Finn and the rest. They too had their mouths open.

At last Finn found a voice. 'Are you going to stop her?'

Magnus shook his head. 'It is Sigurd she is after. Let him do it.'

Finn shook his head. 'God help him when her mother finds out.'

Ivar grunted. 'May all Valhalla help him when her father does.'

When Maria was halfway up, she called Sigurd. Sigurd almost fell off when he looked down to see who it was. He waited, ashen-faced, till she climbed up beside him.

'What on earth are you doing here?'

Maria settled herself and looked about them. 'I should have thought it was obvious. I came to admire the view.'

'Are you crazy?' said Sigurd, hanging on for dear life, in case his nerves weakened his grip.

'No,' said Maria cheerfully. 'Just curious. But I am pleased to see you are concerned.'

Sigurd contrived to pass a swift hand across a damp brow. 'Your father will kill me if he finds out.'

Maria continued to gaze. 'I doubt that. He is rather keen on you. Must be your name.'

'What?'

In spite of his nerves, Sigurd was baffled.

'Your name, idiot,' said Maria, still looking away. 'His father was called Sigurd, and his martyred brother was called Olaf. And you are called Sigurd Olafson. I hope you have better qualifications than that.'

She turned back to look at him as a thought struck her. 'I thought *you* were rather keen on *me*. And now I find that all you are worried about is whether my father will be angry. Not much to come all this way for, is it?'

Sigurd found his wits. He had already known Maria long enough to realise that she relished repartee. Still grimacing at the breeze, still clinging tightly, he managed a grin and said, 'If you get yourself down off these wretched shrouds, I shall make you see that it is well worth coming all this way for.'

Maria grinned back. 'Now, that is a fair offer. Come on – race you down.'

'All right – half an hour. Then we go again.'

Wilfrid turned away and went back to where Oswy was unpacking what was left of their marching rations.

Alfred watched him go. 'That bastard. Does he never get tired?'

'He must be twice your age, Alfred,' said somebody.

'He has been doing it all his life,' said Alfred, easing out his knees and waggling his ankles.

'You wanted to be a fyrdman,' said somebody else.

Alfred threw the remark over his shoulder as he massaged a calf. 'I wanted to do some fighting – for England. I thought that was the general idea.'

'You will, Alfred, you will.'

'Yes, but when, for God's sake? We have marched over half the realm. We have loaded wagons. We have built beacons in the freezing cold. We have sat and sat till our arses go solid. And now we are marching again. And nobody ever says why.'

'We told you. That is what soldiering is all about.'

Owen leaned forward, as if he had been waiting for the right time. 'You wait till you see what they have in store for you at Lincoln.'

Alfred turned round. 'What have you found out, you little Welsh ferret?'

Owen pretended to look right past Alfred towards the other fyrdmen. 'Do you think he is old enough to be told?'

There was a chuckle all round. Alfred looked from one crinkled face to another.

'Well?'

'It is a surprise they have for you, Alfred.'

Alfred fidgeted. 'Out with it.'

Owen glanced again at the others, and grinned.

'Tell me, Alfred, what do you do first thing in the morning?'

Alfred looked puzzled. 'What do you mean?'

'What I say. What do you do first thing in the morning?'

'Get up.'

'Yes. And then?'

'Have something to eat.'

'Yes. But before that.'

Alfred frowned. There were more laughs. A voice said, 'Go on. Tell him, Alfred.'

Alfred frowned again. 'Have a piss. Why?'

'Well done, Alfred. And then, when you have had something to eat, what do you usually do?'

Alfred looked from one face to another.

'Tell him, Alfred.'

Alfred began to look angry.

A fyrdman leaned forward. 'You have a shit.' He looked around him. 'Well, *we* all do.' There was another laugh. Alfred looked at a total loss.

Owen began to feel sorry for him. 'There are only about thirty of us. We can do it under a bush somewhere and nobody will notice. Now – supposing it is a whole army you have who stop the night. Two thousand. Three thousand. Five thousand. What then?'

Before Alfred could conjure up an answer, Owen did it for him. 'You have to arrange it so that they all do it in the same place, or at least in as few places as possible, or you would not be able to move for shit.'

Alfred found a voice. 'What has this got to do with me? We are not an army.'

'No, Alfred. But one day soon an army may pass this way. An army on its way from London to York, to fight Hardrada.'

'An army in a hurry,' said a fyrdman.

'An army which must arrive not stinking of shit,' said another.

'And not exhausted from digging privy pits,' said a third.

Alfred began to gape. 'Do you mean to tell me that we are going all this way to Lincoln simply to dig privy pits?'

'That, and a few other things,' said Owen. 'Like collecting firewood, preparing trivets, building shelters, making ovens.'

'But why us?' said Alfred.

'Because we are here,' said his neighbour.

'They are building marching camps like this all the way along.'

'Along where?'

'Along the road from London to York,' said Owen. 'The King still does not know who will strike first – Hardrada or the Bastard. So he sits in London and watches. If the Bastard comes, he has only about fifty miles to go. If it is Hardrada, he must go north – best part of two hundred.'

'Why does he not sit in the middle? Then he would have equal distances to go.'

'London is the centre; London is the heart; London is the soul. That comes first.'

'Yes,' said a listener. 'And his precious Edith is somewhere near London.'

'And his precious druid sits in Essex and gazes into his crystal ball,' said another.

'I heard his druid—'

'His cardinal.'

'All right – his cardinal. I heard he has gone north. Right up to Orkney. Send out the fleet; catch Hardrada at sea. By God – that would shake him.'

Owen felt that the discussion was slipping out of his hands. He was the one who told the news.

'We do not dig privy pits for this cardinal; we dig them for the King. If he needs to march north in a hurry, he must have all the time he can get. If the camps are ready, his men will not have to spend hours digging and cooking. They can spend more time on the road, and get there faster. And better fed.'

'Camps?' said Alfred, alarmed. 'How many do we have to dig?'

'We are doing one by Lincoln. There will be one at Doncaster, I should not wonder.'

'Further south, too.'

'Are we doing all of them?' said Alfred in consternation.

'No, son, rest easy. The King has other privy-diggers besides you.'

Another chuckle rippled round the group.

'Fancy digging one for us tonight, Alfred?'

Alfred glowered.

Owen patted him on the shoulder. 'Do not take it too much to heart, boyo. Our next rest will be our last for today. And I have an idea that my friend Llew will have something for us.'

Right on cue, Llew appeared from nowhere in particular, with two large bulges in his jerkin.

'Here. Hide these somewhere.'

He passed over two chickens with their necks already wrung.

'Where did you get these?'

'Ask no questions,' said Owen. 'I bet the King does not ask his cardinal how he got his news. He is just grateful. Well . . .'

'And I tell you what, Alfred,' said Llew. 'You make the fire when we get there, I shall cook the birds, and Owen here will tell you a story.'

'About privy pits.'

There was a roar of laughter.

'No,' said Owen, 'but I shall tell you about the time Hardrada went campaigning in Miklegaard, and put out the Emperor's eyes.'

Alfred winced. 'God Almighty!'

A fyrdman patted him on the knee. 'When you have heard that, you will much rather dig privy pits than go up against him.'

The second peal of laughter reached Wilfrid and Oswy, as they packed their satchels for the road.

'God – they are cheerful. I wonder what caused that.'

Oswy slung his bag over his shoulder and hung his axe once more from his belt.

'Will you still go?'

Wilfrid nodded. 'I think so. You can handle them. And I can look for both of us. If Harold ever finds out, it is only I who will get into trouble, not you too. I shall take a horse.'

'Will you tell them?' said Oswy, nodding towards the fyrdmen.

'No. You can tell them when I have gone. Chances are they will not notice; they will be too busy moaning.'

Oswy grinned. 'I bet our Alfred will have something to say.'

Wilfrid fastened his belt. '"Our Alfred" does not have property on the north coast, where either Tostig can raid, or even Hardrada himself.'

'If that happens,' said Oswy, 'you will not save it.'

'No,' said Wilfrid. 'But I can warn the people who live there. Our people. And they can take good care to be somewhere else.

It is your wife and family too, remember. We can always rebuild property. People take a bit longer.'

'What are you doing here so late? You know I am usually in bed by this time.'

'I too,' said Edith primly. Harold ignored her. Edith contrived to make the most mundane of everyday actions sound virtuous enough to get you straight into Heaven. She would expect a bishop's blessing for washing her hands.

Harold shut the door behind him. 'I am sorry, Mother. But I have news of Tostig. That was why I asked both of you to be present. I thought you would both like to know.'

Tostig, damn him, was the favourite not only of his mother, but of his sister as well.

The Lady Gytha went pale. Edith forgot her airs and graces, and sat down beside her. Harold noticed.

'You have no need to fear. Tostig is still in one piece. But he has attacked the coast of Lindsey.' He paused. 'And he has been driven off.'

Both women always found it difficult to absorb news that reflected any kind of discredit on their beloved.

'How do you know?'

'I have heard from Gyrth.'

Edith sniffed. 'What does he know?'

Harold sighed. 'It may have escaped your memory, sister, that our brother is Earl of Anglia, and has been watching the coast for weeks. And Lindsey is just to the north of Anglia. Of course he knows. It was some of his troops who helped to expel him.'

'Well, he would say that,' said Gytha. 'He has no love for Tostig either.'

'I have it from Bernard, too,' said Harold. 'In York. Morcar took a large section of his fyrdmen to Lindsey. In fact, he was in command. Gyrth only sent extra troops. There might have been some from Edwin, too – the Mercian fyrd. But it was Morcar who led. Good for him. At any rate, Tostig has gone – again. He has descended, out of the blue. He has caused trouble. Morcar has rapped him over the knuckles. And he has gone.'

Edith glared, but became practical for once. 'Where?'

Harold sat down. 'Scotland. Well, that is our best information.'

'You are sure he is well?'

Harold nodded wearily. 'I doubt if he ever came ashore.'

Tostig was in fact not without physical courage, and would probably have relished being in the centre of the trouble-making, just for the hell of it. But Harold, unlike Tostig, did not like causing trouble if it could be avoided, and he saw no use, nor any credit, in making his mother and sister worry to no purpose. One white lie more or less. Who knew? Perhaps even sister Edith might have seen virtue in it.

Tostig was certainly alive; he did know that. And had gone off to be a nuisance somewhere else. Scotland, in all probability. Or Orkney. Or – an outside chance – he could be sailing direct to Norway, to put his head together with Hardrada.

Well, let him go. It was one headache less, at any rate for the time being. It had been clear from the Lindsey raid that he did not have many ships at his disposal. So the Count of Flanders had given him nothing. Neither had the Bastard. Nor, it seemed, Denmark. Even some of those men he had pressed into his piti-ful little flotilla when he raided Sandwich had apparently escaped. That was what Gyrth's report said. So he was low on manpower as well.

Harold took his leave of his mother and sister, and walked down the cold corridors to his own chambers. The housecarl on duty outside came to rigid attention.

'Evening, Eric.'

'Sir.'

Harold took off his belt and shoes, poured himself a drink, and leaned against the pillows on the bed.

The situation had improved quite considerably, when one came to think about it.

Tostig, obviously, was out of the way, which had to be a good thing. If he came back, it would almost certainly not be by himself. He had been given a bloody nose three times now, and not even Tostig in the most monumental of sulks was stupid enough to invite more. He had suffered casualties each time, and had been given no reinforcements. It began to look more and more as if the only way he was going to get back into England was in the train of Hardrada. So he had become a fringe consideration; the only real threat at the moment was Norway.

News had come from Brother Albert in Waltham that the Bastard was still not ready. That talkative monk – what was his name – Eustace? – Eustace had reported that yet another council had been assembled at Caen, and perhaps a few more vassals had been persuaded, pressurised or blackmailed into promising their support. But councils and promises did not make an invasion force; ships and soldiers did. And the word was that William's Channel ports did not look very busy. So the precious commodity of time was still available in the south.

It was narrowing down. Norway, almost for sure. Orkney and Shetland were rising on the likelihood list. Scotland was still only a maybe. And Tostig, of course, drooling frustration, spite and revenge.

There was another aspect, too, which had become apparent. Tostig had been seen off, but he had been seen off by Morcar. Helped by Gyrth and Edwin, yes, but the leadership and the initiative had been his. So he deserved the credit for the victory, however modest it was. Harold raised his eyebrows and made an appreciative face. Gwen must have given him a really rough going over, to be able to put that much fight and decisiveness into him.

It would encourage him, too. He was very young to be in such a situation of responsibility, and he would need all the encouragement that there was going. He was not a secure defence, but, with his brother Edwin, he was now at least a less uncertain defence than he had been a fortnight ago. Northumbria was safer – only marginally, but it was safer.

Harold put down his cup, let himself slide further on the bed, and put his hands behind his head. For a moment, he pictured his mother and sister in their chamber now that he had gone. Edith was probably praying.

He sighed. What did he have to do to win their favour? For years he had served the Confessor as virtually an under-king. He had practically run the country for him. Achieved a far higher status than his father. His brothers Gyrth and Leofwine were earls as well. He had married the sister of an Earl of Mercia and an Earl of Northumbria. He had become a crowned and anointed king. And he was, by common consent, the best choice in all England to lead the fight against the many dangers that threatened the kingdom.

And all they could do was blame him for what had happened to Tostig. Tostig – who had been deservedly expelled from his earldom for rank injustice (or, worse, no justice at all), who had consorted with England's sworn enemies, and who had raised arms against the country which had given him birth. Tostig could do no wrong.

For a moment he wallowed in self-sympathy. What a family! Elder brother Sweyn, who was such a bad lot – a proven murderer – that nearly everybody heaved a sigh of relief when he managed to die (or get murdered – nobody was quite sure, but it did not matter) on some remote pilgrimage or other. His mother pining for a spoiled third son. His sister pretending to be devoted to the memory of a ghost of a king, and actively favouring the memory of a traitor brother. Poor baby Wulfnoth, still a helpless hostage in Normandy – though William, to his credit, had not harmed the boy. Only Gyrth and Leofwine were faithful.

This would not do! He sat up again, and poured himself another drink. If that was how the land lay, so be it. The fewer people you had to rely on, the fewer there were to let you down.

'Try it again.'

Willing hands – well, perhaps not quite so willing as at first – swung the great oak doors of Scarborough to the closed position; and heaved and puffed at the massive beam of a bar behind them. It was the complete trunk of a tree; it had taken days of work with axes, saws, and adzes to get it to something like the right shape. Two smiths laboured for a week to forge the iron clasps and fit them to the inside. It took a score of strong men to lift the beam and fit it. Accidents had caused three broken arms, countless bruises and smashed fingers, even a couple of hernias.

But the drill was improving. The men were becoming a team, and they were beginning to take pride in their greater speed. Edric could not see what else he could do to improve the gate.

He squinted up at the gatehouse. Slits for archers, poles to push ladders away, traps through which the boiling water could be poured, endless rows of buckets. Gunnar's skins were draped everywhere. Vendel had delivered two enormous loads. Along the walls there were rough-hewn catwalks for sentries, though Edric doubted whether any enemy force could creep up unobserved. If the Vikings were coming, they would be coming by sea, and there was no way a squadron of longships could come ashore without being seen.

If the sentries could not see, the lookouts on the hill certainly would. It reared close and steep right outside the town. Its narrow paths wound and twisted to the summit in gradients that would give pause to the hardiest of sheep. A deserted monastic chapel teetered on the summit. It still had a useful purpose, if only to give shelter to the lookouts in bad weather. But it was a precarious vantage point; in some places the hillside fell almost vertically to the sea.

The men talked loud and long about how they were going to 'see off' the invader, without having any clear idea of what that invader might be. The walls were stout, and in many cases quite new. They were well supplied with weapons. Edric had prudently hired a small squad of fletchers, whom he had worked overtime to provide with thousands of shafts. Spear handles a-plenty had been fashioned and hoarded. Smiths had been sweating producing heads. Teams of boys had been coming in and out for days, lugging nets full of stones for ammunition to be loaded on the catwalks and in the gatehouse. Edric had sent teams around the neighbouring fields and settlements, requisitioning flour, salt meat and any vegetables they could lay their hands on. Unlike many town elders, who looked down on country yokels, Edric had always believed in maintaining good relations with the surrounding hinterland, particularly village reeves and local millers. One never knew when one would need their help.

Suddenly, all the preparation, all the boasting, all the speculation had been suspended in an instant by a cry from the top of the cliff: 'Sail-ho!' Those without keen ears soon picked up the signal being flashed from a metal disc in the sun.

Every eye in Scarborough turned seawards.

That was the first shock – that there was a sail at all. After all the thinking and the planning and the guessing, to have actual physical evidence. To see something!

The second shock was the direction. The ship was coming up from the south, and clearly moving north. That started the nerves.

They were soon stilled when sharp eyes saw the number of ships behind the first one. This was not the thousand-ship fleet that rumour had spoken of, the one that Hardrada was supposed to be gathering in Norway. And, anyway, how could he be approaching from the *south*? Norway was three hundred miles to the north-east.

When the sharpest eyes had done with counting, and the know-alls had at last finished pontificating, the Great Invasion proved to be a matter of only a handful of ships – twenty at most. Inhabitants were surprised to find that their relief was tinged with slight disappointment. So it was not going to be a great drama after all; the eyes of England were not going to be turned towards Scarborough.

Worse, they showed no sign of turning towards the shore. The disappointment became even more palpable. Not only was there no Great Invasion Fleet. This squitty little squadron was not going to invade at all; it was holding to its course due north. Scarborough, it seemed, was not worth invading.

One man voiced the mood of many. He looked up at the gate-house. 'What have we been doing all this for, then?'

Edric had not even bothered to correct him. When the real trouble started, he would find out soon enough.

Besides, Edric knew something the man did not: a courier had come in late the night before, with news of Tostig's brief landing in Lindsey, and his rebuff at the hands of Earl Morcar. Edric raised his eyebrows in appreciation. Good for the lad. Perhaps there was more in him after all than everyone thought.

That ragged little flotilla that had crept past was almost certainly the remnant of Tostig's expedition. Almost certainly, too, on its way to take refuge with Malcolm in Scotland; or, if it was up to it, creeping across the North Sea to sit at the coat-tails of Hardrada, like a cat begging for milk.

It was good news and bad news. It was another indication that an invasion from Norway was more certain. At the same time, it was encouraging to hear that Morcar had won a military success. It might put enough courage into him to dare to oppose a Viking landing, should it occur in Yorkshire. And, if Earl Edwin brought the fyrd of Mercia as well, there was a good chance of success. At the very least, Edric's town of Scarborough could hope for some support if the worst were to happen.

Edric sighed. No. When all was said and done, this was mere speculation. The north-east coast was long; Hardrada could land anywhere, and nobody had the faintest idea where that would be. There was no protection from the sea. King Harold's fleet could never reach Yorkshire; they had their hands full in the Channel with the Bastard.

Remembering a conversation he had recently had with Gunnar, Edric made a noise of disgust in his throat. Gunnar, of course, had seen the worst side of it, and had taken predictable precautions to save his hide. They had met in the street outside Gunnar's house . . .

'Ah, there you are,' Gunnar had said. 'I was coming to see you.'

This from the middle of a turbulent scene that spoke loudly of hasty departure.

'Going somewhere?' said Edric, with a flat face.

'Getting some more skins. I noticed some gaps on your south-facing walls. Thought I would do you a favour. Is there anything else you want?'

Edric cast an eye over some of Gunnar's wagons. 'Do you always take furniture when you go to collect skins?'

Gunnar cast a sweaty glance back in the direction of Edric's eyes.

'Oh, that? Just sensible precautions. Sensible precautions. Anybody else would do the same. You sent Coelwen away; I am sending away some valuable possessions.'

'*Sending?*' said Edric. 'Or taking?'

Gunnar did have the grace to blush through his damp cheeks. 'No. No. Vendel is taking them.'

Edric nodded. 'Ah. I see.'

Gunnar writhed. 'Well, I shall go to keep an eye on the more valuable stuff, naturally. Vendel is a good lad, but he lacks experience. Experience, you see. I do not need to tell you the value of that.'

'Ah.'

Gunnar continued to suffer. 'But I shall be back. With those skins. Rest assured.'

'When?'

'When?'

'Yes, when?'

Gunnar made futile gestures. 'Well, when the time is ripe. When the coast is clear.'

'It is clear now. They have gone.'

Gunnar turned to see to a wayward knot on a wagon. 'It is all very well for you, Edric. You are of this town. You are part of it.'

'So are you. You have been here for over thirty years.'

Gunnar did not lift his eyes from his fingers. 'But I do not belong.'

'Belong? You own half of it.'

'It is not the same. You know that.'

'If you stayed, you would,' said Edric.

'Would what?'

'Belong.'

'You have that fox-who-has-eaten-the-goose expression again.'

Sigurd's smile stretched even further. He clapped his hands. 'A command, Magnus. A proper command.'

He slapped a timber, picked up a scrap of frayed rope and tossed it overboard. He walked up and down, punching the air. He could not stay still.

'Well?' said Magnus.

Ketil, Ivar, Finn, Hakon and the rest appeared from nowhere and formed a tense crowd round him. Lars for once looked wide awake.

'What I said – a proper command.'

'How many ships?' said Ivar.

'Not sure yet,' said Sigurd, losing just a little of his bounce. 'Thirty, maybe forty. Could be fifty.'

There was a ragged little cheer, which seemed to restore Sigurd to his previous mood of elation. He flashed a wide smile again at everybody.

'Just think, lads. A whole squadron. Could be nearly a quarter of the whole fleet.'

'So we are going, then?' said Finn, who was usually the most sceptical.

'Oh, we are going all right. I have just come from a meeting of squadron commanders. The last ships are in from the Baltic ports, and they say that dozens more are gathering in Orkney and Shetland. We might also get a few from Scotland.'

Finn pursed his lips. '"They say".'

Sigurd turned to him. 'Go and ask him if you doubt me. Go on. Go up to him and say, "You are talking too big for your boots." Try that.'

'Go on, Finn,' came the chorus.

'Ask him.'

'Tell him you do not believe him.'

'Say the invasion is a bundle of bombast.'

'Only let us be there.'

Finn swore, and walked away in a gale of scornful laughter.

Everyone turned to their work with a real will. As each became occupied with his own duties, Magnus sidled quietly up to Sigurd.

'Fifty?'

Sigurd looked round to make sure they were not overheard. 'A trifle optimistic, I agree. But it is a definite separate command, and it is mine.'

'But Rolf will get us there.'

'Naturally. He expects us to do the fighting, and I expect him to do the sailing.'

'Especially if things go wrong, and he is needed to get us back.'

Sigurd did not look put out. 'Why do you wear a belt? To stop your trousers falling down. That does not mean that you expect them to.'

'So you think we shall conquer England?'

Sigurd looked him directly in the face. 'I should not have put it as bluntly as that, but, since you mention it, yes, I do.'

He looked around him again, to make sure once again. 'Magnus, we are talking about over two hundred ships. That does not count the transports. And more to come in from Orkney. You should see the supplies he has been hoarding, ever since he first got the idea. He may be a gambler, but he is not a stupid gambler.'

'So he thinks the odds are good.'

'Yes. So do I. Remember, I always say that you do not gamble unless the odds are good. Look at England. Harold their King has his hands full with an invasion from Normandy. That is not rumour, or "they say"; the Bastard has been talking about it for fifteen years. That will keep Harold down south, and leave the back door open for us. Hardrada knows this. God and thunder, man, if anybody ought to be able to weigh up the odds, he should. Have you any idea of the places he has been? Russia, Poland, Bulgaria, Miklegaard, the Holy Land, Sicily, Greece.'

Half of these places were mere names to Magnus, but the list was nevertheless impressive; the names, if not loaded with information, were certainly loaded with legend. And Hardrada was at the heart of them.

'And I tell you something else,' said Sigurd. 'His treasure. It is absolutely vast. I have seen some of it. Maria and the Queen took me to have a look. One thing is for sure: this expedition will not founder for lack of money.'

Magnus did not argue. He was delighted, of course, that something definite was happening, and he was pleased for Sigurd that he had been awarded his own command, and it looked a significant one. It was just that Sigurd was a trifle too excited. Up to now he had always displayed a nice touch of distant appraisal, and he had been no respecter of authority or reputation.

But now he was behaving, just a little, like a young boy with his first toy sword. His enthusiasm was beginning to affect his hitherto sharp judgement. Understandable, of course; he had worked and waited for this moment. Indeed, he had created the opportunity in the first place, by turning up at Hardrada's court, and snapping up any chance that presented itself. He had shown superb cheek by paying attention to the Princess Maria, apparently with considerable success. And it was clear from their first voyage to Orkney that Queen Ellisif liked him.

Perhaps the King, too, liked him, for his very cheek, for his skill at making his own luck, for his willingness to take risks – calculated risks. But Hardrada was known for his caution, and he was not going to be swayed by the likes of Sigurd, not to the extent of making a mistake in the name of affection.

Magnus wondered. Was Sigurd the Great Charmer falling victim to the magic of an even Greater Charmer? Any man who could put together a fleet of this size and power in six months, from all over the north, for a project as huge and daring as the conquest of a foreign country three hundred miles away, must have powers well beyond those of the average man, even beyond those of the talented man. Hardrada was special.

Magnus watched Sigurd cracking jokes with Ivar and Ketil and Haldor and Tore. They were all behaving like overgrown boys. Well, there was no harm done – yet.

Sigurd broke off for a moment, and glanced towards Magnus. Sigurd valued what Magnus thought, and right now he could almost read what Magnus was thinking. His face was a picture.

Sigurd went to the side of the ship and climbed up into the shrouds. Everyone was used to his doing this, so he was left alone.

He gazed out to the sea, the North Sea that they were soon to cross – three hundred miles, clouds, storms and all.

Yes, Magnus had a point, damn him. It almost certainly was not fifty. The ships were not going to be Norwegian, either. They were going to be everything else. Ships and eager crews were turning up in Orkney, in dribs and drabs, from all over the place – Orkney itself of course, but Shetland, too, Iceland, Scotland, even Ireland. There was a rumour that King Harold's wayward brother, Tostig, might be there, and nobody knew what he had with him.

Sigurd had been put in charge of this motley array. He did not know whether to be pleased or disgusted. He had said as much to the Queen, when she had come up to him after the commanders' meeting . . .

'Well, are you satisfied?'

Sigurd unburdened himself as much as he dared.

The Queen raised her eyebrows. 'My God, you are a hard man to please. Have you any idea how hard I had to work to get you that much?'

Sigurd stared. 'You?'

'Mm. And Maria, too. You should be grateful.'

'But it is all bits and pieces. I do not know how many, I do not know where each one comes from, I—'

The Queen raised a hand. Sigurd stopped. Ellisif smiled gently.

'Do you think the King has got where he is by trusting every likely lad he comes across? I have told you before. He likes you. And he would like to trust you. But, before he does that, he has to test you. You are being tested. As I said, be grateful. Ask Maria; she will say the same.'

Maria did.

'Idiot – you are twice as bright as half the commanders in that fleet. All you have to do is prove it.'

'Well, I hope you are right.'

Maria looked searchingly at him. 'You have doubts, then?' Sigurd hesitated. Maria pushed him. 'The truth now.'

Sigurd tossed his head. 'Of course I do. You just get good at hiding them. I had doubts running that gang of mine, out there in the forest. Could I hold them together? Could I find a purpose for them? Then I came to the court. Could I get to the King? Could I induce him to take notice of me – a complete nobody? Then I saw you. Could I get you interested in me?'

Maria smiled. 'Well, you did that all right.' She leaned forward. 'Sigurd, we all have to carry something. You have doubts. Father has bad dreams. Mother has second sight, which sometimes causes trouble. I have these moments when everything goes black. But none of them lasts long, and we are all here when they are over. Your doubts go, too, do they not – soon enough?'

Sigurd nodded, if a trifle glumly.

'And nobody notices?'

Sigurd agreed again.

'Well, then,' said Maria. 'Be grateful and get on with it. And learn a little Irish and Icelandic. I shall expect to find you fluent before we arrive.'

Sigurd stared. 'You mean you are coming with us?'

Maria looked innocent. 'Yes. Did I not mention it? Careless of me.' She smiled wickedly. 'Mother said she had such a good time with you that she wants to do it all over again. And I want to find out what I missed.'

Coelwen was touched. She turned the brooch over and over in her hands.

'Vendel, it is beautiful.'

Vendel made a dismissive gesture. 'The workmanship in the setting is not of very good quality, I regret. Perhaps, when this trouble is over, we can get it improved. But it is amber, I assure you.'

At the mention of the word 'amber', Thora craned her neck to have a look, too.

Both of them continued to make noises of appreciation.

Vendel smiled. To be sure, it was not of the highest quality – far from it. In fact quite low down the list of goods that came in on the latest of his father's ships to reach Scarborough. The way things were going, it would probably be the last merchant ship to call there for quite some time to come.

Gunnar had not even bothered yet to price it. Vendel saw its possibilities at once. Amber had an almost magical reputation everywhere. Many people had never even seen a piece, never mind owned one. He held it up so that his father could see.

'Do you mind?'

Gunnar understood at once. 'Go ahead. I wish you joy of it.'

He really did. If the boy's relationship with Coelwen was going that well, he could have it, and with a father's blessing.

Coelwen felt genuine gratitude. She was not the most sophis- ticated of girls, by virtue of a childhood in a chilly northern coastal town, and she had the normal feminine susceptibility to jewellery. To her it was wonderful.

Vendel fished in a pocket and brought out a smaller package. He presented it to Thora, with a deep bow of mock obeisance.

'For my lady's maid.'

Thora did not know what to do with herself. She made flut- tering little movements with her hands, and blushed to her temples.

Coelwen laughed. 'Well, open it, silly.'

To be sure, it was not very big, and it was not very wonderful, but it was amber. And – the most important thing – it was for her, and only for her.

Thora clasped it to her chest, ducked her head and made a little curtsey.

Vendel felt absurdly pleased with himself. He could not remember the last time anybody was glad to see him. He had never been especially close to his mother, save in the embraces and fussings of early childhood, and, although he respected his father's achievement and inherited his business sense, he could not for the life of him find his father likeable. He, Vendel, was good at business, and knew he was, but it did not interest him. He had simply lived each day as something to be got through.

The monastery had been a revelation, an epiphany. He could not now imagine a world without words. He almost felt sorry for Coelwen that she did not have any.

He loved everything about words. He appreciated the order in which they came in the sentence. He relished deep meanings. He pondered the Scriptures, not because he was holy, but because their text was so subtle; it was for the sake of the words, not for the divine message. With his excellent memory, he had found the endless rules of Latin grammar and syntax no problem. He could feel the hair rise on the back of his neck just to open the pages of a great book in the abbey library, and let his eyes take in the pattern of lines and columns, the regularity of the writing, and the dazzling colours of the illustrated initial letters. It was a delight just to run his fingers over a folio of expensive vellum. He felt physical pleasure to open an inkpot, sharpen a quill, mix colours – anything to do with the business of writing. The Prior, who could see what an apt pupil he had, used to let him loose in the *scriptorium* after the brothers had finished their copying duties for the day.

He had no wish to become a novice, though he would have jumped at a chance to stay in the house beyond the period for which his father had contracted. But his father had put him there for a purpose, and, when that purpose had been fulfilled, had taken him away again without another thought. It never crossed Gunnar's mind that there might be something else to the business of learning to read and write. It was a means to an end, and that was that.

Vendel had no choice but to obey. He had no funds of his own, and the abbey – a modest one – could not afford to keep him without a fee for his keep. So, as usual, he had tightened his lip and done what his father said.

He had agreed to escort Coelwen and her maid to her uncle's manor simply as part of filial duty. When Coelwen put on airs and graces at the outset, he had taken it as yet another instance of the world being an unfriendly place, especially as he had tried really hard to be considerate. Thora's whining did not help.

But thereafter the world changed. To his amazement, he found Coelwen easy to talk to. And she actually listened. They shared jokes together. Thora lost her pout. Even more stagger-ing, he plucked up the courage to talk to her about his poetry. And she listened to that, too. Whenever he had to visit his father's property in the Dales, he found himself coming to call on her because it never occurred to him not to.

When he gave her the present, he liked the plain way she thanked him. No airs and graces this time. No silly simper. Not clutching it to her chest as Thora did.

Quite simply, it was such a relief. Genuine human contact.

Coelwen offered him something to eat and drink, and all three sat down at the table together. Thora said little, because she was so absorbed in her amber, but, whenever she looked at Vendel, her face shone with delight. It was quite likely that, in her short life, not many people had taken much notice of her, either.

'Why are you here this time?' said Coelwen.

Vendel's face hardened. 'Father. He told me to bring his furni-ture here.'

Coelwen widened her eyes. 'His furniture?'

'And his valuables.' He sneered. 'He thinks the ship is sinking, and he is getting out while the going is good.'

He saw the alarm on Coelwen's face, and hastened to correct himself.

'I am sorry, Coelwen. Scarborough has not been attacked. And is not going to be. Well, certainly not yet. We simply saw a squadron of ships sailing by, and Father immediately feared the worst.'

'Is there danger?'

'No. Not so far as we can see.' He let slip a ghost of a smile. 'We have no fortune-teller in the town. Your father has worked hard on the walls and the gate.'

'The skins.'

'And the timber. Believe me, the town's defences are now as strong as I have ever seen them. Your father has done wonders.'

'And the squadron of ships?'

'Sailed right past. Up to the north.'

Coelwen frowned. 'So why has your father sent you away with his property?'

Vendel's face went even harder. 'Because he is a coward.'

There was a short silence. Not only was Vendel being painfully honest; the fact also came as no surprise to her. She had known Gunnar all her life. She now felt sorry for his son. She searched hard for something to say.

'Why bring it here?'

Vendel shrugged. 'Can you think of a safer place?'

'But Vikings attack churches and monastic houses, too.'

'Not any more, I hear. Norway has gone Christian. Hardrada's brother is now called "St" Olaf.' He added wryly, 'Now that he is dead.'

'Have you spoken to the Prior?'

'Not yet. I came to see you first. But I shall. Never fear; he will do what Father is asking. I am carrying a nice fat fee.' He patted his waist wallet.

'Where is your father now?'

'On one of his manors lower down the Dales.' Vendel tossed his head. 'He has taken root there. Unless I can shift him.'

'Why would you want to do that?' Coelwen wished she had not asked as soon as the words were out.

Vendel looked bitter. 'Would you like to have a father who is so spineless?'

Coelwen thought of her own father, standing in front of the walls he had built so well, and tweaking her nose as he said goodbye.

'No.'

'Well, neither do I. I am going back to try to put some fight into him. If your father can stay with his town, so can mine. Dammit – he owns half of it.'

Coelwen felt sorry for him again.

'God go with you, Vendel.'

'Amen to that,' said Thora, who had not missed a word.

When Vendel had gone, Coelwen gave a lot of thought to what he had told her. Vendel clearly knew his place at a time like this. Coelwen looked at Thora without really seeing her. Where was the right place for a daughter of the Reeve of Scarborough?

Conrad put down the letter he had just read out. Harold came out of a reverie and looked at him.

'What do you think, Conrad?'

The King motioned to him to sit down. With no hesitation now, Conrad did so. He had gained in confidence with each passing day. He came straight to the point.

'I think Father Bernard is in need of assistance and support, sir.'

Harold nodded. 'I agree. There is far too much beginning to happen in the north.' He gestured to the letter. 'And now we have Tostig on our plate again.'

'He may be just licking his wounds, sir,' said Conrad.

'It is not only Tostig I am concerned about. It is where he is – Scotland.'

'Malcolm has not moved, sir. All Father Bernard said is that

Earl Tostig has taken refuge there.' Conrad was careful to allo-
cate a title to Tostig, albeit one that was out of date.

'You do not know my brother,' said Harold. 'Tostig sit still
and mind his own business, when he is eaten up with spite
and swearing revenge? Never. Even as we speak, I would
wager he is turning the famous Tostig charm on Malcolm.
"Oh, yes, Malcolm, my dear brother has his hands full with
Hardrada and the Bastard – and me. He can not be everywhere. You will have free pickings in the fells and the Dales
right down to the Derwent and the Mersey." I can hear him
saying it.'

'That is not true,' said Conrad, daring to disagree. 'The north
is protected. Earl Edwin has the Mercian fyrd, and Earl Morcar's
writ runs almost to the border.'

Harold laughed. 'Conrad, the absence of truth has never got
in the way of what Tostig says when he wants something.'

'So what do we do, sir?'

'We take precautions, that is what we do. Malcolm has not
moved yet, I agree. But we want more information about him.
We want more information, too, about Orkney and about
Norway. If I can find enough extra eyes and ears, we might get
information about Ireland.'

'Ireland?'

'Yes. Bernard says so. You read it out to me. There are ships
coming in from Ireland and Iceland.'

Conrad gaped. 'You surely can not send a ship to Iceland?'

'No, I can not,' said Harold. 'We must remain practical. But I
want more information from everywhere else. And Bernard
needs assistance. Qualified assistance.'

Conrad frowned. 'Sir?'

'Where is that fat monk?'

'Brother Eustace?'

'Yes.'

'In the kitchens, I should think. He enjoys a good meal.'

'The man is a glutton,' said Harold. 'But I do not care how hungry he is; he is a good listener, and he has a capacious memory. He can also read and write, and he speaks foreign languages.'

'You mean send him back to Normandy?'

'No. Normandy is getting too tight for him. William closed the ports weeks ago, and Eustace can not take refuge in monasteries all the time. And he has to cross the Channel somewhere. It is getting more difficult. I do not want him to get caught; he is too valuable.'

'Are you thinking of sending him to Father Bernard?' said Conrad with a tinge of surprise in his voice.

'Yes.'

Conrad smiled. 'He will not like that.'

'He is not here to like it. Bernard was going to take him before, but he wriggled out of it. To be fair, he really was ill for a while. But he is better now. Well, he has a surprise coming.'

'He is a terrible traveller, sir.'

Harold looked thoughtful. 'Suppose he has somebody with him to chivvy him along.'

Conrad inclined his head to indicate partial agreement. Harold leaned forward.

'Can you ride?'

Conrad stared. 'You mean . . .?'

'Can you ride?' repeated Harold. 'Not like a farm boy on a mule; I mean really ride.'

Conrad smiled. 'I was raised in a lord's stables.'

Harold sat back. 'There you are, then. I must have had second sight when I chose you.'

'You want me to go to York?' said Conrad.

Harold nodded vigorously. 'Yes. And I want you to get Eustace there, too. I shall send a couple of housecarls with you, for safety's sake.'

'What do you want me to do when I get there, sir?'

'The same thing you are doing for me. Be Father Bernard's secretary. Eustace and you, between you, can be very useful.'

Conrad looked worried.

'What is the matter?' said Harold.

'Father Bernard, sir,' said Conrad.

Harold laughed. 'You sound as if you are more frightened of him than you are of me.'

'I am,' said Conrad with feeling.

'Just do your job,' said Harold. 'Help him with messages coming in, and drafting them out. Use your common sense, speak up, and tell the truth. Father Bernard values them just as much as I do.'

Conrad looked doubtful. 'If you say so, sir.'

'I do say so.'

'What about my work here, sir?'

'Nobody is indispensable,' said Harold. 'I shall miss you, but I shall manage. Right now Bernard has more need of you than I do.'

Conrad looked as if he were summoning up his courage. 'Sir?'

'Yes?'

'Does that mean that I shall go back to working for Father Bernard?'

'No. Not for good. When this is all over, you come back to be my secretary. Does that satisfy you?'

Conrad stood up and grinned broadly. 'Yes, sir.'

'And you can face Father Bernard?'

'I can now, sir.'

'We whipped them, Gwen. We whipped them.'

'Yes,' said Gwen. 'I heard.'

Morcar flung his gloves to a valet and strode towards a table by the wall, throwing his next remark over his shoulder.

'Is that not so, brother?'

Edwin sought Gwen with his eyes. They exchanged glances.

Morcar looked down at the food and drink laid out in front of him, and spun round to glare at a servant by the door leading to the kitchens.

'Is this what you call a dinner for weary warriors? For whippers of scum? God, man. Send me the duty cook.'

As the man scuttled away, he came to sit in front of Gwen. Edwin took a chair by their side.

Morcar could hardly get the words out quickly enough.

'It was total surprise. We had total surprise. You should have seen their faces. Within an hour we had them on the run.'

Gwen listened patiently, then said, 'Were there any casualties?'

Morcar grinned broadly and shook his head. 'Us? No. Not unless you count two broken legs and a cut or two. We got about twenty of them.'

'Dead?'

'Prisoners. I tell you, the rest were running too fast.' He stood up and began walking up and down. 'It was like chasing deer off a garden patch.'

Edwin and Gwen exchanged glances again. This time Morcar noticed. He stopped pacing, put his hands on his hips, and leaned forward.

'Tell me this, brother. Has Tostig gone or has he not?'

'He has gone,' said Edwin.

'And has he taken his ships with him?'

'He has taken his ships with him.'

Morcar stood up straight again. 'Well, there you are.'

The duty cook arrived in some disarray.

'Ah, about time,' said Morcar. He pointed to the table. 'What do you call this? Scraps for a serf's supper? Now – bestir yourself and put out something that befits the occasion. Your master, the Earl of Northumbria, does not return from victory every day of the week. Move!'

He began to chuckle to himself. 'Complete surprise. Complete surprise.' It was as if he could not stop laughing at a private joke. Excusing himself about a call of nature, he left the hall.

Gwen looked at Edwin. 'Well?'

Edwin went to the table himself and poured a measure of beer. He stretched a hand for some dark bread and cold chicken, then came back to sit beside his sister.

'There is one true part in all that: we did catch them by surprise. Half of them had dispersed to steal supplies or to loot valuables. The rest were on guard. Tostig is no fool.'

'And did they run?'

'Yes, but not for the reason Morcar suggests. Tostig did what any sensible commander would do when a situation becomes untenable: he got out. If the odds are against you, you quit. We must have outnumbered them five to one.'

'So it was not –' Gwen laid on the irony '– a great victory?'

Edwin laughed.

'Hardly any fighting at all. Tostig conducted a perfectly orderly withdrawal. He has his faults, but he is a good field commander.'

'What about all these prisoners?'

'Not prisoners – deserters. They were the sailors he pressed into service when he raided at Sandwich. Only too glad to have a chance to get away and join us.'

'Is that all?'

'Oh, we did catch a few genuine prisoners. Men who were too taken up with looting to notice that we had arrived. Our broken legs were the result of careless chasing over broken ground.'

Gwen put her hands on her knees and hunched her shoulders. 'So where does that leave us?'

'Alone,' said Edwin. 'Morcar is right about one thing: Tostig has definitely gone, and taken his ships with him. And he was not able to take much else with him.'

'And Morcar is pleased with himself.'

'Very.'

Gwen made a grimace of appreciation. 'Something, I suppose.'

Edwin took a sip of beer. 'Sister, you know the danger now as well as I do. Morcar now thinks he is a great general. You saw him. He can not sit still for excitement. Do you know what he said to me on the way back here?'

Gwen smiled. 'Go on.'

Edwin shook his head. 'He said, he said, "The sooner Hardrada comes, the better I shall like it." I tell you, it scared me half to death. Hardrada!'

'Well, we wanted to put some fight into him,' said Gwen.

'Yes,' said Edwin. 'But not that much.'

Chapter Seven

Edith muttered an imprecation.

'God, what was that?'

'Another shutter, I should think,' said Harold. 'That is the third blown off in two days. You should be used to it by now.'

Edith pulled the blankets up higher. 'I hate storms – always have. Can you not do something about it?'

Harold looked incredulous. 'The storm?'

'No. The shutters. That chamberlain ought to be boiled in oil. I would wager he puts half the maintenance money in his own pocket.'

'I can not be everywhere,' said Harold. 'Why not boil him in oil yourself? You make *me* feel small enough times. And the children.'

Edith did not know whether to frown or smile. 'I can not be everywhere, either. And I do not wear a crown, remember? And another thing. Why is it, the only times we can get to talk to each other, it is time to go to sleep?'

'I have long days.'

'You found time before.'

'I was not King before.'

Edith was having a moan, and they both knew it. Harold simply waited. He was a very difficult man to annoy. Edith wriggled closer.

'I am sorry, Harold.' A vicious gust howled, and rattled numberless things outside. 'But it is a bad storm.'

'It is indeed. But you know the saying: it is an evil wind that does no good to anybody.'

Harold fell silent. After a minute or two of waiting, Edith made a noise, turned over, and pulled the blankets right up over her head. Harold smiled, and gave an absent-minded pat to the mound made by her hips under the bedclothes.

Edith was right. Storms were not nice things. But this particular one might, just might, do him a bit of good. It was bad news for his fleet, of course. What a good idea that he had decided, at last, to disband them and send them up the Channel to London, to revictual and refit, just before this most recent storm struck. August had been a dreadful month – rain and wind all the time. It was not really like that, of course, but, to a fleet constantly on patrol and enduring all the weather, and becoming steadily more depressed at the lack of action, it must have seemed like that.

At any rate, the majority of the fleet had missed the worst of it. However, it gave them a nasty chase up the Channel, and it gave a mauling to the laggards who were the most inefficient, or the slowest to obey the King's orders. Teach them a lesson, thought Harold.

More to the point, one good thing about a storm was that it had no favourites. Harold knew that William's fleet would be suffering just as much as his. Even more satisfying, it would be bad not only for his ships at sea, but for his ships in harbour in the mouth of the River Dives. The further ahead he may have reached with his assembling of the invasion force, the more crowded the Dives harbourage became. The mind boggled at the damage that could spread as scores, perhaps hundreds, of ships were thrown up against one another in such a limited space.

If he had prudently – and, if Harold knew his William, he had – kept his supplies ashore till the last minute, there was still the problem of protecting them. He had a whole army encamped close to the shore, and that army needed feeding. The longer he, William, had to wait, the hungrier they became, and the more bored and – thanks to the weather – fed up. And they were not all Normans; rumour had it – and Bernard's despatches confirmed it – that soldiers of fortune had been streaming in from every corner of Christendom (apart from those, of course, who were now pouring into Hardrada's headquarters in Norway for the other invasion). What a motley pack of hounds to keep on the leash.

William's headache, then, apart from the weather, was discipline. How was he going to stop the army running unchecked over half Normandy on a summer spree of looting and pillage that would not be much of an incentive to make fellow Normans support the Duke's Great Enterprise of England – however justified he was trying to make it, with his talk of broken oaths and papal banners?

Harold slid down in the bed. So God was giving the Bastard a whole Channel-ful of problems. Good. Long may it continue.

But God had no favourites, either. If food was a problem to Normandy, it was just as big a problem to England too. Harold looked up at the beams. He had taken a chance with the navy, sending them home, if only for a few weeks. How long could he hold the army? It was not only a case of feeding them; it was a case of getting in the harvest to produce that food as summer turned into autumn. William's troops were mostly professionals. Riff-raff, many of them, maybe, but professional riff-raff. Many of them mercenaries, contracted for hard cash. Soldiers, not farmers. Far too many of Harold's army were men of the land. Contracted to serve only for a limited time each year.

That limit had been passed, and they were serving now only out of goodwill. It said a great deal for their loyalty and patience. But the harvest would have to be gathered. If he did not send them soon, they would go anyway, and he would have no legal machinery to stop them. Worse, the recent weather did not offer much hope of a good harvest, either. September had better be warm and dry, or the whole of England would suffer.

He felt Edith's steady breathing.

News! News! He needed news. He always needed news. When would Hardrada sail? How big was the force he was putting together? What would Malcolm do in Scotland? Denmark and Flanders were quiet; did that mean they would remain quiet? And, of course, the eternal question; where was Tostig?

And then the mysteries: how long would the bad weather last? When would he have to send the fyrd home? Where would the Bastard plan to strike? More immediate, where would Hardrada strike? When he did, would Edwin and Morcar be up to it? Would Northumbria be loyal to the crown, or loyal to the ties of Scandinavian blood that had run down the centuries?

Harold made a face. He had heard that Hardrada's Queen, Ellisif, was supposed to have second sight. He shut his eyes. He could do with a dash of that.

Ellisif, Queen of Norway, leaned back in her chair, and winced yet again at the gales of laughter and roars of delight that echoed round the enormous hall. Apart from the church of St Olaf, it was far and away the biggest building in Trondheim. For hours now it had been crammed to the rafters with as much of the King's invasion forces as could squeeze themselves in. Hundreds, perhaps thousands, more were jammed in crowds round huge fires outside, roaring as yet another mighty log was thrown onto the flames and showers of sparks flew like fireflies into the darkening summer sky.

Sigurd leaned across to the Queen and said, 'Well, does this compare with your harvest festival on the Volga or wherever it was?'

Ellisif smiled. 'Well, perhaps it does come just a little close.'

There were calls for order as yet another guest, as monu-mentally drunk as his predecessors, rose shakily to his feet at the top table, and declaimed yet another cascade of slurred couplets, which he called poetry, which he claimed he had composed that very evening. There were nods and growls of approval at each turn of phrase, and more roars of appraisal as the speaker waved, bowed, and slumped back onto his chair, which teetered backwards for a sickening moment before restoring itself and throwing him forward till his face hit the table. This was met with delirious howls of delight and bawled catcalls.

The verses, such as they were, all forecast honour, loot and glory in fulsome quantity. The coming invasion of England would dwarf all previous Viking adventures in size, scope and success. The very gods in Valhalla would applaud in appreciation.

Ellisif, even after twenty years of listening to it, could not, for the life of her, understand this culture of spontaneous versify-ing. She had sat on her parents' knees and taken in her share of baby stories; she had learned to repeat the details of a hundred folk tales as told to her by her nursemaids; and she had sat round the fire in her father's hall and listened to countless minstrels. But the attraction of this practice, which was clearly a national obsession with her husband's people, completely escaped her.

Harald was as much bewitched by it as the most drunken of his followers. Indeed, he 'composed' many of these snatches himself, though Ellisif had never caught him in an unguarded moment putting one of them together. Indeed, she had never caught anybody making one up. It was all a huge conspiracy, she thought, in which the conspirators pretended to see a great deal of significance in order to puzzle and baffle outsiders. It was a great big private game, which looked like an orgy of beer-bloated ramblings, for the simple reason that that was exactly what it was.

Harald was never happier than when he was on his feet at similar gatherings, drinking and declaiming and collapsing amid bedlam.

Mind you, thought Ellisif, this was a special gathering. The great expedition was now ready, or as near ready as it was ever going to be. Every squadron of longships was now in harbour, or further out by the Solund Islands, awaiting only the word of the King. From all over Norway they had come; from Frisia, Finland, Scania, Schleswig, Sweden; from Hedeby, Lubeck, Rostock, Memel, Riga, Novgorod, and as far afield as the great rivers of Rus. And that was only the fighting ships. Beside them was drawn up a second fleet of transports – ugly and sluggish to be sure, but, given reasonable luck, enough of them would get there to be able to feed and supply the whole force till they could get to work on the necessary business of looting in England. When they reached Orkney, more would come in from Iceland, from Ireland, Shetland, and, with luck (if Malcolm could be persuaded to open his mean Gaelic purse) from Scotland. Earl Thorfinn himself would provide another squadron from his own resources. And his son Paul. Well, that was what he had said.

A special gathering indeed. Ellisif smiled. Perhaps Harald could be forgiven for letting his hair down just a little. He had worked prodigiously ever since January. Ellisif was proud of him. Nobody else in the whole of the north could have put a force like this together. And behind all the charm and the magic there worked a very shrewd brain. Because he looked spectacular, it was tempting for a sceptical onlooker to suspect that he was all show and no substance. Her husband was nobody's fool. Moreover, he was well aware of the effect he had on those around him, and he shamelessly played on it. Like so many charming men, he could turn on the charm like a tap – as she herself was well aware. But he could also turn on the reality when it suited him. He relished causing shocks; it gave him an advantage. It was always useful to be able to catch either friends or enemies off balance.

She watched him. Yes, perhaps, on occasions like this, he did behave like an overgrown boy, but she knew, better than anyone else, that behind the façade was a very brave man, a ruthless one, a lucky one, a resourceful one – and, incidentally, a rare lover, too.

'Will you excuse me, my lady?' said Sigurd.

Ellisif turned to him. 'What?'

For once, Sigurd looked almost shy. 'I promised that I would spend some time with the Princess Maria.'

The Queen laughed. 'And she would never forgive you if you let her down. Make sure you come up to expectations.'

Sigurd wove his way past a forest of outstretched arms and proffered pots towards the main door. He could drink and carouse with the best of them, but this evening had taken its toll even of a young man like himself. He had one more reason to admire the Queen; she seemed to take it all in her stride. She was indeed a fitting consort for a man like Hardrada.

And Maria was a fitting daughter for both of them. She did them credit. Like them, she would appreciate direct action. Sigurd took a deep breath. So it was up to him to get on with it.

Maria had left the party some time before. The King never minded her attending such gatherings, and she was well able to take care of herself. Not that any wayward young warrior would dare to take liberties, with her giant of a father within striking distance – literally. The crooked eyebrow would rise, the broad moustache would bristle and, as likely as not, a ham-like hand would knock the offender off his feet.

For all his enlightened attitude to Maria's upbringing – an attitude he shared with the Queen – he still behaved like a fussy hen whenever Maria was in a large gathering involving a lot of young men – even fussier as the hour grew later. It was as if he thought she was still ten years old.

Sigurd had taken great care to give no offence in that direction, because the more he had come to know Maria, the more he realised that she was worth a great deal more than a casual adventure.

He knew the King liked him. The favours he had already received would not have come his way if he had not. As he had found out, the King liked to test before he trusted. Well, so be it. Sigurd could not complain of that. Now – what would the King's reaction be to what he had in mind?

They were about to venture on the quest of a lifetime. Well, of Sigurd's lifetime, for such exploits were bread and butter to Hardrada. He had spent a lifetime as a soldier – before he became King of Norway, as a professional soldier, selling his sword everywhere from the Baltic to the Black Sea, from Sicily to the Holy Land. He took life-and-death chances all the time. Here he was, at fifty, when even the majority of Vikings would have long since hung up their weapons, doing it again.

But he felt sure, too, that Hardrada was not as simple as that. He was suspicious and he was cautious. Witness his wariness with Sigurd himself. Witness the many stories of his shrewdness, craftiness and cunning. This was one of the reasons why Sigurd responded to him. Harald weighed the odds, but, when they looked good, he had the courage and the confidence to take a calculated risk. Sigurd liked that.

He braced himself. Now he himself had to take an even more daunting calculated risk . . .

'About time,' said Maria, when he arrived.

Sigurd walked up to her, kissed her, and stood back.

Maria raised her eyebrows. 'Is that all I get?'

'Yes,' said Sigurd, 'for the time being. Just one thing: are you really willing to go through with this?'

When Maria stretched up to her fullest height, she was the image of her mother.

'Yes. Are you?'

Sigurd turned to go.

'Where are you going?' said Maria.

'To do what you said – go through with it.'

'Now?'

Sigurd stopped in the doorway. 'Can you think of a time when he will be in a better mood?' . . .

On his way back to the King's hall, he bumped into Ketil and some of the lads.

'Sorry, Sig.'

Ketil backed out of the way, stumbled and fell. There were muffled snorts of delight. Glances were thrown around the whole group.

Sigurd put his hands on his hips. 'What are you lot up to?'

Ivar put a finger beside his nose. 'Not for your innocent ears, Sig. Not for the likes of caps' shiptains.' He giggled helplessly.

'He means scodron c'manders,' said Finn, by way of being helpful. He put a finger to his temple by way of explanation. 'Tight as a Jew's jewel box.'

'Where are you going?' said Sigurd. He pointed behind them. 'The beer is that way.'

Ketil drew himself up. 'Going t'bed Had enough. It is a wise man who knows when he has had enough. Eh, lads?' He leaned back to Sigurd. 'All going t'bed, Captain, like good boys.'

Several of them almost doubled up with hysterics. Sigurd looked around. 'Where is Magnus?'

Ketil glanced vaguely about him. 'Coming, coming, Captain.' He dropped his voice to a confidential whisper. 'A bit on the slow side, our Magnus.'

What Ketil meant, thought Sigurd, was that Magnus was usually the last to fall in with some of the more outrageous escapades that Ketil and the rest were always thinking up. What *that* meant, of course, was that Magnus had more sense.

Sigurd left them to it. He had better things on his mind.

Ketil watched him go, then gestured. 'C'mon, lads.'

They fell in behind Ketil as he made his choppy way to the barracks where they all slept. It was a sort of barn, too, containing many of the stores Sigurd had laid in for the voyage. The King had let him have the use of one of the hall's outbuildings, on the edge of the great square in front of the church of St Olaf. It was as secure a place as one could wish for in the whole of Trondheim, apart of course from the King's private quarters. It was yet another sign of the favoured treatment the King was offering to Sigurd.

Even so, they all had to take turns to mount guard, hour by hour. Stealing stores from other crews was almost as big a local obsession as reciting drunken verse.

Ketil put out a hand. 'Shh!' He pointed. 'There he is.'

Sprawled up against the door, his head on his chest, was Lars.

'What did I tell you?' Ketil put out a hand. Ivar fumbled in a pocket and handed over the wager.

Ketil peered blearily at his palm. 'Come on – you said double. Two to one was the deal.' He put out his hand again. Ivar swore and paid some more.

'Just look at him,' said Hakon.

Lars lay amid a pile of hay bales, which he was supposed to be stripping in order to stuff some fresh palliasses for everybody. It was one of the chores that a night sentry was expected to do. Lars had managed barely two before he had fallen asleep.

They crept closer. 'Careful now.'

'You could drop an anvil beside him and he would never hear it,' said Hakon.

'Shh! No chances,' said Ketil. 'We want this to work.'

With infinite pains so as not to make a noise, but giggling all the while, he fished in his tunic pocket and pulled out some long tapers, two of which he tied to the toes of Lars' boots, so that when they burned down they would reach the flesh. He slid several more into the folds of his cross-gartered leggings. Meanwhile, Finn produced a piece of twine and tied his feet together, leaving just enough room for him to hobble.

He put a hand behind him. 'Where is that flame?'

At that moment, Tore arrived, carrying a piece of burning wood he had snatched from the nearest bonfire, almost falling into it in the process.

'Here.'

Immediately behind him came Magnus. 'What are you doing with that torch?'

'Watch,' said Ketil, as he leaned down and put the flame to the tapers.

Magnus let out a gasp of horror. 'Are you mad? Look around you.'

'Oh, shut up,' said Ketil. 'Just a bit of fun.'

'Fun?' said Magnus, pointing towards the palliasses and the straw bales, and the piles of timber nearby. 'You can send us all up.'

'Oh, it will not get that far. Lars will put it out for us with his dancing.'

More helpless roars of laughter.

'There he goes.'

Lars had woken up. After a second of stupefied staring, he had leaped to his feet, and of course immediately stumbled because of the hobbling twine round his ankles. A few stray wisps of straw were ignited by the tapers. As Lars shook his feet in panic, more sparks and fragments came together and spread both smoke and fire.

Ketil and the rest hooted with delight and chanted to encourage Lars. 'Up now, Lars. Feet up. Hup, hup, hup! Dance for us, Lars.'

Magnus flung himself forward to try to extinguish the flames, which were now spreading with frightening speed. Finn put out a foot to trip him up. As he fell, Finn said, 'Magnus, you are such a spoilsport.'

By this time, some of the palliasses had begun to ignite. When the flames spread to the nearby bales, Finn and some of the others began to sober up. A little late. A gentle evening breeze began to blow the flames further. Some sparks drifted towards the thatch on their barracks roof.

Magnus scrambled to his feet. Suddenly, Sigrid's face, never far from his memory, rose agonised before his eyes.

'Water,' he roared. 'For God's sake, get some water.'

Ivar wiped his eyes, and peered blearily at Ketil. 'Do you know what, Splits? I think our Magnus may be right.'

Sigurd pointed at what was left of the barracks.

'You idiots. You raving lunatics. Do you realise what you have done?'

They were all standing in a penitent line. Finn winced as yet another hot iron was driven through his head.

'We did save most of the stores, Sig.'

'No thanks to most of you. Nobody took any notice of you.'

'They did not take much notice of you,' said Finn.

'Exactly. It needed the King himself to take charge and get things going. That is the point. The King now knows how stupid you were.'

'We saved the stores,' repeated Finn. 'What is he so upset about?'

'It is what we nearly lost that troubles him.' Sigurd pointed across the square. 'See that? The church? The church of St Olaf? The King's brother? His holy body is in that church, under the altar. If that had gone up, he would have thrown you on the flames with his own hands.'

Ivar tried next. 'Everybody was drunk last night, Sig. Including the King. It was just bad luck.'

'Try telling him that.'

There was a silence. At the end of it, Ketil said, 'So what is he going to do with us?'

'Nothing,' said Sigurd. 'Well, nothing with most of you. He knows you are fools with nothing but beer and blood in your heads.'

'Why is he so sure?' said Tore, aggrieved.

'Because I told him,' blazed Sigurd. 'You were not *worth* hanging. So he left you to me.'

He paused, and noticed a distinct murmur of relief run through the line. Seeing Hardrada drunk was frightening enough; seeing him furious did not bear thinking about. So they owed that much to Sigurd for diverting the King's awesome wrath.

'What are you going to do with us, Sig?' said Hakon.

'Punish the one who was responsible.'

Sigurd could not hang them, obviously. Nor could he dismiss them, or he would have lost half a crew. At a time like this, it was unthinkable. But he had to do something. Magnus wondered what it would be.

'We were all responsible,' said Finn. 'We were all drunk.'

'But you were not asleep.'

Lars became alert and pale. Sigurd walked up to him. 'If you had been doing your duty, they would not have been able to do what they did – no matter how drunk they were.'

Lars went even paler. Sigurd went back to stand before all of them. He turned round to face them.

'Lars will stay behind. The rest of you – get to your duties. And, next time Hardrada comes after you, I will hand you all to him on a plate.'

Lars looked absolutely stricken. As the group broke up, some of them patted him on the shoulder. Not even Finn dared think of an objection.

Magnus went quietly up to Sigurd. 'Is that all?'

Sigurd looked round to make sure that he was not heard.

'It is all I *can* do. But I have hit them where it hurts. They are not afraid of fines or whippings. They know I can not hang every one. But they *are* afraid of being left behind. After all that we have been through. And now that we are about to sail.'

'Lars is finished. You have broken him.'

'A small price to pay – one man. It could have been all of them, if Hardrada had had his way. We have got off lightly. And they –' he gestured towards the others '– they know what can happen to them. I have made my point.'

Magnus shrugged as if to accept.

Sigurd grunted. What a good thing it was that he had been able to put his question to the King before it had all happened. The next worry was: would the King stand by his word?

That reminded him of what might have happened. He turned back to Magnus.

'One thing, though.'

'What?'

'Thank you for what you did.'

'Me? I did nothing.'

'No,' said Sigurd. 'But you did try.'

'I know something about fire,' said Magnus.

'God's Eyes – more privy pits!'

Alfred threw his spade on the ground, and collapsed into a sitting position.

'One thing, Alfred – you should be good at it by now.'

Alfred opened his satchel, took out what food was left, and swore again.

'Where is Doncaster, anyway?'

'Further north. On the great road to York. The old Roman road.'

'God – do we have to dig them all the way to York?'

'Take heart, Alfred. Perhaps we can use the old Roman ones. They should have stopped smelling by now.'

Alfred snorted in disgust, lay back, and rubbed his eyes. 'I could sleep for a week.'

'Shelter first,' said a fyrdman.

'Food next,' said another.

'Then weapons,' said a third.

'Why?' said Alfred. 'We never fight anybody.'

'But you may – one day. That is why we are here.'

'You could have fooled me.'

'Not difficult, apparently.'

Alfred bridled at the remark. 'My sword is ready whenever it is needed.'

'Oh?' said his neighbour. 'When did you last use it?'

Alfred hesitated. 'My father gave it to me.'

'When did he last use it?'

Alfred hesitated again.

The fyrdman nodded. 'Forgotten, eh? Too long ago when you sat on the old man's knee?'

Alfred began to get angry. The fyrdman put up a hand in token of peace.

'No offence, son. But we have been watching you.'

Alfred blushed. 'Well?'

'You work hard – we grant you that.'

'And you eat hard,' said somebody else.

'But war is a funny thing. It is like a lullaby. Because nothing much happens, you get lulled to sleep, and you can easily think that that is all there is to it. Then something does happen, and you are caught with your trousers down.'

'Beside the privy pit.'

Everyone roared.

The fyrdman persisted. 'What I mean is, whatever it is you have to do, always remember to keep your weapons in good order.'

'They are,' said Alfred.

'Oh? Stand up. Put on your sword belt.'

He watched Alfred fumble. 'See what I mean? Now – pull it out.'

Alfred clapped his hand to the hilt, and took a few seconds to find a comfortable grip.

'It has to be faster than that,' said the fyrdman. 'You must find that grip in an instant. And know it is comfortable. Now – pull it out.'

Alfred pulled and twitched at the belt, gripped the scabbard, took a deep breath and pulled. There was friction. It did not come out easily, and it did not come out in one go.

'You could be dead by now,' said the fyrdman.

Owen and Llew had been watching all this, and felt a little sorry for Alfred. Owen patted him on the shoulder.

'You are new, son, and you do not know what to look for. We have all been doing these fatigues, and you have got so tired and fed up with them that you have not noticed what else we do. It is only routine. Just a short time each day. But it has to be done. A man is as good as the edge of his sword.'

'What about you?' said Alfred.

Owen and Llew looked at each other. 'We?' said Owen. 'We are only as good as a piece of twine. We are only as good as our bowstrings. A tiny thing you could almost carry in your mouth. Get it right, and we are deadly. Get it wrong, and we are dead ourselves.'

'War is all about doing things for just a short time,' said Llew.

'What do you mean?' said Alfred.

'Think about it,' said Owen. 'Think about your life since you joined the fyrd.'

'It is all about "–oring",' said Llew.

Alfred frowned.

'You never have enough of anything. So you spend most of the time "moreing".'

'You spend a third of your day snoring.'

'Half the rest of the time it is raining and pouring.'

'You are always made to do routine household chores – choring.'

'If you want to survive, you must always be storing.'

'If you are lucky and they turn you loose in the town, there is always a spot of whoring.'

'If it comes to a battle, you keep your spirits up by roaring.'

'Then you go into the line and you spend about five minutes goring – the enemy.'

'Only five minutes?' said Alfred.

'That is all the time you can keep your sword arm up. You have to hope that the enemy's sword arm gets as tired as yours does.'

'And, if it is not any of those, it is one more thing,' added Owen.

'What is that?' said Alfred.

Owen and Llew chanted in chorus. 'Boring.'

Everyone clapped in appreciation and agreement.

Alfred looked downcast.

'Never mind, boyo,' said Llew. 'Luckily you have a couple of chaps like us around, who can take your minds off the boredom by doing yet another thing.'

Alfred looked up. 'What?'

Owen and Llew looked at each other and grinned. 'Telling tales – storying. It does not quite fit but it is close enough.'

Everyone clapped again. 'Tell us a story, then.'

Llew looked at Owen. 'What shall we give them?'

'Give them the enemy,' said Owen. 'On a plate. That will make him easier to eat when the time comes.'

Llew nodded firmly. 'I agree. Gather round, lads, and we will tell you all about Harald Hardrada.'

Alfred took off his shoes and made himself a cushion of dried bracken. Guy ropes were tightened on the canvas shelter they had rigged up between some slender coppice trees. Somebody made up the fire. A goose that had strayed too far from its home yard was cut up and the pieces spitted over the flames. Llew passed round some small apples he had scrumped from a nearby orchard. The company gradually settled down.

'Is it a story you want, then, boys?' said Owen.

'Yes. And it had better be a good one,' said Alfred. 'Something to make me forget my feet.'

Owen laughed. 'Oh, you will forget your feet, I promise,' he said. 'When you have got to know him.'

'Who?'

'Hardrada.'

Alfred put on what he hoped was a knowing expression. 'How do you know him? Have you met him?'

Owen looked at Llew and looked back at Alfred. 'Tell me, do you know God?'

Alfred looked blank. 'I have not met Him.'

'I did not ask you that. I said do you know Him?'

Alfred waved a vague hand. 'Well, in a way.'

'Is He with us?'

'I hope so. Yes.'

'All around?'

'Yes.'

'All the time?'

'Well – yes.'

'He runs things.'

'Yes.'

'He controls the world – our lives. Whatever happens, you say it is God's will. Yes?'

Alfred's frowns got deeper and deeper. 'Yes.'

'So you know what He does?'

'Sort of, yes.'

'You do not have to see Him?'

'No, I suppose not.'

'But you know what He has done in your life?' said Llew.

'So you know Him,' said Owen. 'You do not need to have met Him.'

Alfred's brow was now a positive lattice of lines. 'No, I suppose not.'

Somebody laughed. 'He has got you there, Alfred.'

'Well,' said Owen. 'I hear about Hardrada. I listen. I catch what is in the air. I meet people who *have* met him. I pick up stories, hints, rumours. I see what he has done. I think I know what he is going to do – well, try to do. I build a picture. When that picture is complete, I know him as well as if I had seen him. I know Hardrada.'

'Will we know him, then, when you have finished?' said a fyrdman.

'Yes,' said Owen. 'But you will know a different man from me. You will listen to me and you will build your own picture, and it will not be like mine, because you are not like me. But it will be a true picture, and you will believe it, because it is you who have built it.'

'Hmm!' grunted the fyrdman.

Owen leaned forward. 'And I tell you this, my lusty privy-digger. When you have heard me, you will tell others that you too know Hardrada. That is the way it goes.'

The fyrdman leaned back, put his hands behind his head, and said, 'Prove it. Tell us.'

Owen laughed. 'I thought you would never ask.'

He pulled his legs into a crossed position, spat out the remains of an apple core, and wiped his fingers on his leggings.

'Do you see Alfred here? A big strong lad, is he not?'

There were amused chuckles of agreement. Alfred did not know whether to bask in the compliment or get annoyed at the chaff.

'Well,' said Owen, 'Hardrada is one and a half times as big as Alfred.'

'So he would make three of you and Llew,' said Alfred, delighted to get some of his own back.

Owen was not a whit put out. 'No doubt. He is not only tall. He is splendidly proportioned. His hands and feet are well made, and his chest is deep. He keeps his fair hair quite short, but he cultivates a broad moustache. One of his eyebrows is higher than the other.'

'They say he is so strong that no other man can swing his axe,' said Llew.

'His coat of mail,' said Owen, 'is a wonder to behold. It even has a name. He calls it Emma.'

'Emma!'

Owen nodded solemnly. 'So they say. Some coat, eh?'

'And this coat of mail,' said Llew, 'is not like any other coat of mail you may have seen. It reaches right down his calves. He is protected all over. The links in it are so strong, it is said, that no weapon can penetrate it. And his helmet gleams like silver. You would pick him out of any line a mile away.'

'He is always victorious,' said Owen. 'The only time he was defeated was when he fought alongside his brother, the blessed St Olaf, at the Battle of Stiklestad. But then he was not in command. He was only fifteen.'

'Fifteen?' said Alfred. 'In battle?'

Owen nodded again. 'Remember his great height. At fifteen he was already taller than any ordinary man.'

'And you should see his battle standard,' said Llew.

Alfred reacted with recognition. 'You mean like the King's? The Fighting Man?'

'Yes. And the other – the Dragon of Wessex. Well, Hardrada has a great white banner, which flutters the length of five ells. And on it is a great black raven. Its claws are red with blood, and more blood drips from its beak.'

Alfred gaped.

Owen fixed him with an eye. 'And he calls it the Landwaster.' He sat back, looked all round the circle, and said it again. 'Landwaster.'

'God Almighty!'

Alfred swallowed. One or two men crossed themselves.

Owen looked at Alfred. 'You see? Now you know him.'

The fyrdman with his hands behind his head said, 'Nobody is that marvellous.'

Owen turned to him. 'Then you know him, too. You have heard me tell of him, and you know him – but you know a different Hardrada.'

'How many more are there?' said Alfred.

'As many as there are of us here. And everywhere else. Every man will carry his knowledge of Hardrada in his own head.'

Another member of the company grumbled. 'Well, I must say you have been a great help.'

'Better to overestimate your enemy than to underestimate him,' said Owen.

'Why not tell us the truth? Then we will not get him wrong either way.'

'Because nobody knows the truth – not the full truth. Only God knows all the truth, and I am not God. I simply tell stories – which are part of the truth. They are possible. It is good to know what this man is capable of – what is possible. That way you can prepare. That way you have a chance.'

'Thank you very much,' said Alfred.

Llew laughed. 'But I wager you have forgotten your feet, Alfred. Admit it now.'

'Go on, Alfred.'

Alfred did have the good grace to grin. 'Well, just for a bit.'

The fyrdman patted his shoulder. 'Good for you, son. Now, before you go to sleep, put some work in on that sword. That will be your preparation.'

*   *   *

The Prior looked up in surprise from his accounts. The Guest-Master did not normally bring business to him at this hour. Especially with news as mundane as this.

'How many?'

'Just two, Father Prior. And a couple of servants.'

'Well, give them something,' he said, lowering his head. 'You know, the usual things.' He was not paying proper attention; the accounts demanded concentration.

The Guest-Master held his ground. 'No, Father, these are different. You know them.'

The Prior looked up again. 'Who?'

'Those friends of Vendel. The young woman, remember? And her servant.'

'Vendel? Is he here too?'

'No, Father. Just the two women.'

The Prior thought for a moment. 'Well, give them something, anyway. Then send them on. They do not live all that far away. We can not have favourites.'

'They are in a bad way, Father. They have been travelling two days. And this weather ...' The Guest-Master gestured expressively.

'Well, take them to the kitchens.'

'I fancy the infirmary would be better to begin with.'

The Prior raised his eyebrows. 'That bad? Very well. I will come and see them in a little while. As soon as I have seen to these.' He indicated the folios on his table.

It was getting dark before the Prior was able to keep his word. When he finally reached the infirmary, both Coelwen and Thora were on their feet.

'So you are better already?'

Coelwen ducked her head. 'Much better, Father. We just needed to dry out.'

'And eat.'

Coelwen smiled. 'And eat. Are our servants well?'

'Cared for. Dried out as well. Now, young woman, what are you doing running around the Dales in weather like this?'

Coelwen sat on a bed, folded her hands and lowered her head. 'Not easy to say, Father.'

'Try,' said the Prior. 'I am used to listening. I am a priest as well a monk.'

While Coelwen had tripped and stumbled her way to an explanation, the Prior listened without making any comment. When she had finished, she looked up at him. 'Do you understand?'

'Very well. Your heart is with your home and your father.'

'Yes.'

'Will you not make it difficult for him?'

'At first I thought so, yes. But not now. Then I talked with Vendel. He was . . .'

She tried to slide round what Vendel had said about his father, but the Prior nodded as if she had said it all out loud.

'His father, eh? And he feels shame. And that made you feel shame?'

Coelwen nodded. 'Something like that.'

The Prior sat back. 'Well, if you have attempted such a difficult journey, almost by yourself, in such bad weather, you must feel strongly. And your motives are good. You are not thinking of yourself.'

'Oh, but I am,' said Coelwen. 'I do not wish to feel such dishonour.'

'Nothing wrong with having a conscience for a guide,' said the Prior. 'But what can I do? I can not take you.'

Coelwen looked as if she was getting towards some kind of difficult point.

'No. But Vendel could. You know where his father's manors are. You could get a message to him.'

The Prior smiled. 'And you could stay here while we fetch him.'

Coelwen fidgeted. 'Would it be a great inconvenience?'

'No. Hospitality is part of our calling. It may take a few days, especially if he is in Scarborough.'

'He told me he would be back here this week.'

'Ah.' The Prior smiled. 'So you have been planning this for some time.'

'The matter has been troubling me for some time.'

'It has, Father, it has.' Thora had been following intently.

'I see. It has to be Vendel who escorts you, I take it?'

'Yes, please, Father,' said Thora. Then she realised she had spoken out of turn, and blushed.

Coelwen came to her rescue. 'We are used to Vendel, and we did not want to be a nuisance.'

'Of course, of course,' said the Prior. 'Do you like him?' he added innocently.

'He has served us kindly,' said Coelwen, sliding slightly away. 'He speaks very well of you and of this house. He obviously loved it here. Did he . . .' She hesitated. 'Did he ever speak of becoming a novice?'

'No. And I do not think he ever would. Certainly his father would not have it.'

'When he is fully adult, he could make up his own mind,' said Coelwen.

'If he had the money to do it. There are fees, you know. Hospitality is free; study and the novitiate are another matter.'

'Yes, I see.'

'And you must remember that he is the son of his father. He may be more worldly than you think. He understands figures, and he knows his father's business very well.'

'He loves writing and books. He writes poetry, too.'

'Words do not make a vocation,' said the Prior. 'He is an intelligent, thoughtful young man, but he is human like everyone else. Look at his new beard.'

'What about it?'

'Do you not think it hides a slightly receding chin? Oh, no, he is concerned with the affairs of the world.'

'Well, I think it suits him,' said Thora.

Conrad and Brother Eustace had been standing uncertainly at the door. It took two more imperious waves from Father Bernard's hand before they found the courage to come forward. The dreaded eyebrows bristled. Conrad and Eustace looked at each other.

'Sit down.'

It was a great relief to both of them. Conrad had become used to sitting in his King's presence, but wanted confirmation all the same from this awe-inspiring man. Eustace simply jumped at the chance to relieve his aching muscles. Bernard looked at his long face.

'If you start complaining . . .' he said, and did not finish the threat. 'Even you have to admit that Earl Morcar keeps a good table. However lowly your position at it, you were given enough to fill even that capacious stomach.'

Eustace burped. 'My worry now, Father, is indigestion. Coming so soon after the ride here from Waltham. It has totally upset the balance of humours. I shall take days to recover fully.'

Conrad smiled. The ride to York had been a constant paean of pain from Eustace, and he had scarcely stopped even after they had arrived.

Bernard already knew of Conrad's gifts; after all, he had recruited him. His judgement had been confirmed by the King. Harold had slipped a remark to Bernard when they had last spoken in London: 'The boy has a head on his shoulders.'

Bernard had taken pains to get them both included at Earl Morcar's table, so that they could observe the people round it. Eustace was intelligent and a good listener. Now Bernard wanted a return on his experiment – a full report. He clapped his hands and leaned his elbows on the table. 'What I want now is your opinions, not your complaints.'

'Sir?' Eustace looked puzzled. Conrad was becoming used to being asked for his opinion, so he took the lead in replying.

'Opinion of what, Father?'

'Everything. Let us start. Look around that table in your mind's eye. Start with the Queen. What did you think of her?'

'Queen Mildred?'

'Gwen. Remember to call her Gwen, if you do not want your ears pinned back.'

Conrad grinned. 'Sorry, Father. I think she is a forceful character. She says what she thinks, and she means what she says. That is unusual for—'

Conrad stopped himself, for fear that he had said too much. Bernard finished it for him.

'You mean unusual for women to have such opinions.'

Conrad came straight back. 'I mean that it is unusual – almost irregular – for the likes of us to pass comment on queens.'

'But you think she is like that?'

'Yes, Father.'

'I agree. She speaks with authority, not just with wilfulness,' added Eustace, who was finding his voice.

'Do you think she influences the Earl?'

'Oh, yes,' they both said together.

'For the good? Do you think she will put some fight into him?'

'Surely, Father, she already has,' said Eustace. 'That landing in Lindsey – surely that is a good pointer.'

Conrad did not look convinced. Bernard noticed. 'Well?'

'You heard him talk, Father. I think she has put too much fight into him. He thinks he can thrash Hardrada.'

'You think he can not?'

'No, sir, not the way he is talking. He is underestimating Hardrada. He could rush in, make a vital mistake.'

'You have seen the figures for the northern fyrd,' said Bernard. 'They are favourable.' He pushed some papers towards Conrad. 'Only estimates, I know, but they give you some idea. And remember, Earl Edwin will soon have the full Mercian fyrd here, too. Plus their own domestic establishment of housecarls.'

Conrad shook his head. 'We can not be sure, Father. Look at that report you have just received from the spy ship that came into the Ouse yesterday. According to him Hardrada has mustered over two hundred ships. And that does not count the ones he expects to gather in Orkney. Say forty men to a ship – that is eight thousand men.'

Bernard made a private note of Conrad's excellent mental arithmetic. Eustace was still struggling.

'Those two hundred may not all be full-sized longships,' said Bernard.

'No, Father,' said Conrad. 'But it is *possible*. And add on the ones he will pick up in Orkney. It could come to ten thousand.'

'Why look on the worst side?' said Bernard.

'Because we must not underestimate him,' said Conrad.

Bernard smiled. 'Well done, my son. I was hoping you would say that. I wanted you to agree, but I did not want you to do it simply in order to please me.'

Conrad's cheeks flushed with pleasure.

'So,' said Bernard, 'we come to the heart of the problem. This despatch I am about to send to the King.' He tapped the table with the pen. 'What advice do we give to him? Do we think that Earl Morcar can hold the north? Even with the combined fyrd and the housecarls? Do we recommend he send more troops? Do we recommend that he keep several hundred in readiness? Or do we suggest that he come himself? And when?'

Both Conrad and Eustace looked worried.

'Well?' said Bernard. 'Do we?'

'You are a powerful man, Father,' said Conrad. 'I am not. Neither is Eustace here. If we said Earl Morcar could hold the north, and the King did not send any more men, and we were defeated, then they could say that we lost the whole of England for them. All on our word.'

Bernard laughed. 'I am only asking for your advice. I do not promise to take it. And, if it does turn out the way you fear, the chances are that none of us will be here to face the consequences, so there will be no need to worry.'

He tapped the letter again. 'Now, what do I say? Can Earl Morcar hold by himself?'

They hesitated.

'Think what you are offering,' said Bernard. 'Not orders. Not recommendations. Not even advice. Only opinions. And you see only half the picture – if that. It is the King who sees it all. He must look to the south as well as the north. He must deal with the threat of the Bastard. Remember too that he can not keep his southern army in readiness much longer.'

'The harvest,' said Eustace.

'Exactly,' said Bernard. 'And if he disbands that, and keeps only his housecarls and a few mercenaries, and marches north with them, he leaves the south almost naked.'

'God!' said Conrad, as the extent of the problem dawned on him. Immediately he gasped at the realisation of the blasphemy, and crossed himself.

'Now do you see the burden he carries?' said Bernard. 'It needs a strong head. It is not a head that will be swayed by the word of people like us. But he likes to hear what we think, because he trusts us. Nevertheless, he is the one who will decide, and he will never blame us for speaking the truth as we see it. Even if it turns out that we are wrong.

'Now – for the last time – what do you think?'

*   *   *

Gunnar followed his son into the stable. 'Where are you going?'

'To see the Prior.' Vendel gave orders to the grooms. He barely turned his head towards his father.

'You mean to see that girl.'

'Ah – she has become "that girl" now, has she? It was "Col" before.'

'Admit it – you are keen on her.'

'She has been polite to me.'

'I should think so. Can you not see?'

Vendel paused and looked across a horse's back.

'Father, it is you who can not see. She is the first person who talks to me as a human being, not as a business rival or a likely prospect.'

Gunnar changed tack. 'If you are not after her, what are you going to do there? You have plenty to do here.'

'She wants me to take her to Scarborough.'

Gunnar stared. 'She has only just left.'

'She wants to go back. She feels her place is there.' Vendel looked at his father again. 'I feel mine is there, too.'

Gunnar glared. 'What is that supposed to mean?'

'What I say. Father, Scarborough is the only life I know. Our home, our whole fortune, our fate is there, whether we like it or not.'

'Our fate is what we make it,' said Gunnar. 'I was thrown up on the beach at Scarborough when I was fifteen. I made the most of my fate. I did what seemed sensible at the time. All I am asking you to do is the same. Make the most of what is before you.'

'We do not know what is before us.'

'If Hardrada gets here, we shall.'

Vendel shook his head. 'England has been invaded before. An invasion either succeeds or it fails. Even if it succeeds, the whole population does not die. Most of it survives.'

'Only those who look out for the main chance survive.'

'And I think our main chance lies in Scarborough. It does not lie in skulking in a few mangy farms out here in the Dales.'

'You are being swayed by sentiment. That wretched girl again.'

'So she is a "wretched girl" now. Father, look. You may not have asked to be dumped on the beach at Scarborough. But you were, and you have made a good fortune out of it. You have put thirty years into Scarborough. Will that count for nothing? You own half the town. Does that count for nothing? Your tenants look to you for security and protection. Do they count for nothing? You tell me your greatest wish is to build a fortune for me. Does that wish count for nothing?'

Gunnar sneered. 'Do not talk to me about business. A fat lot of interest you have shown in it. Every scrap of interest has to be dragged out of you.'

'But I *know* the business,' said Vendel. 'And I know that it is worth trying to save.'

'A bit late now.'

'Nobody knows,' said Vendel. 'But we must give it every chance. We must give Scarborough a chance.'

'Pure romance,' said Gunnar. 'That girl again. She has turned you soft.'

Vendel shook his head. 'Whether she has turned me soft in the heart does not matter; she has not turned me soft in the head. And now I tell you we have to go back. All the signs point that way.'

'But the risks, the risks,' said Gunnar.

'All business is a risk. How often have you told me – the greater the risk, the greater the profit? It is all about the odds, Father.'

'They are terrible at the moment,' said Gunnar.

Vendel looked hard at him. 'For Scarborough, for the business, or for you?'

The spots on Gunnar's face seemed to glow redder. 'How dare you.'

'Then prove me wrong,' said Vendel. 'You know as well as I do that the odds are least bad in Scarborough. It is thanks to you that I know. Even if Scarborough gets reduced to ruins, some-body will have to rebuild the ruins. Are the odds not good for that?'

He finished strapping up the last of the saddlebags.

'Now – are you coming or not?'

'The usual trouble?'

Magnus looked up. Above him stood Queen Ellisif, wrapped in her familiar bearskin. She looked kindly down at him and smiled.

'Bad, eh?'

Magnus nodded miserably. It was fairly obvious. He had been lying almost doubled up in a feeble effort to tense himself against further onslaughts of nausea. His arms were clasped round his body.

'Is it usually like this?'

'Always,' said Magnus bitterly.

'You had better come in with us. At least you can get warm.'

Magnus did not argue. He crawled into the shelter at the stern, and allowed the Princess Maria to wrap a sheepskin round his shoulders.

'I do not know what Sigurd would say. *You* are supposed to be looking after *me*.'

Magnus had been quite proud, almost touched, that Sigurd had given him this duty . . .

'I have my squadron.' His voice had bulged with pride. 'But I must show Maria that I think about her.'

'I am sure she understands,' Magnus had said.

'Do you understand? Do you mind?' said Sigurd.

'No. I am flattered that you trust me this much. And in any case –' he grinned ruefully '– I shall get seasick wherever you put me.'

'You can join us again in Orkney,' said Sigurd.

Magnus had nodded. 'So that I can get seasick with you all the way to Scotland. Thank you.' . . .

Maria offered him something to eat. He waved it away almost with horror.

'Why did Sigurd choose you?' said Maria in her direct way.

Magnus shrugged. 'Perhaps he thinks I am slightly less stupid than some of the others. You know what they say – all beer and no brains. Well, I have just a few. That is what he says.'

'You are too modest,' said the Queen. 'I have heard him speak of you. He says you have a very long head.'

'Do you have a wife?' said Maria, slightly changing the subject.

Magnus shook his head.

'Any plans?' said the Queen.

Another shake of the head. 'I have nothing to offer.'

'Why is that? You look as if you come from a good family.'

Magnus sighed. 'There is no family. It was wiped out in a fire.'

The Queen looked intently. 'A feud?'

Magnus nodded.

The Queen nodded too. 'What a curse that is. Harald would like to get to grips with that ghastly institution – when he has the time.'

'A bit late for me,' said Magnus sadly.

'You never know,' said Maria. 'Perhaps on this quest you will make your fortune. There is a whole country for the taking. You could finish up even better off than you were.'

'Maybe. Maybe.' He did not feel like concentrating on future good fortune. The present *bad* fortune was quite enough to think about for the time being.

The Queen looked at him, looked at Maria, and nodded for them to go outside.

'Let him rest for a bit,' she said as they leaned on the side of the ship.

For a while they said nothing, each occupied with her own thoughts. Then Ellisif said, 'Are you happy about all this?'

Maria answered without any hesitation. 'Sigurd? Oh, yes.' She turned to her mother. 'Are you?'

'Yes. I am. I am happy about *him*. I am not so happy about you.'

Maria turned in alarm. Ellisif looked her straight in the eye.

'I have been watching you. You have had two attacks since we left home. True?'

Maria shrugged a trifle too casually. 'Nothing. They were nothing. A few seconds only.'

'But you do . . . go, do you not? You do not know what happens?'

'I come back, almost straight away.'

'Do you feel ill at all when it comes?'

'No. Not at all. How can I, when I do not know what is going on?'

'So you feel well in yourself?'

Maria nodded vigorously. 'Oh, yes. Yes.'

Ellisif looked thoughtful, and turned back to gaze at the waves.

Maria put a hand on her arm. 'You will not tell Father?'

Ellisif continued to look out to sea. 'No.'

'And you will not tell Sig?'

'No. Well, at any rate not yet. He, and your father, have quite enough to think about at the moment.'

'Thank you,' said Maria simply. She shivered slightly. 'I am going back inside. Magnus will be asleep. I shall not disturb him.'

Queen Ellisif drew her bearskin more tightly about her, and leaned her elbows on the salt-soaked timber.

If there was really anything seriously wrong with Maria, it would soon be a problem for Sigurd, so he would have to be told sooner or later. Time enough to worry about that when the moment came.

Maria had pestered her mother to persuade her father to let her come on this adventure. It was partly because of Maria's problem that Ellisif had agreed. But she found that Harald had taken very little persuading. He needed no persuading at all to agree to Ellisif herself coming. It was as if he had been waiting for her to ask. His consent sounded almost like a sigh of relief. Now why was that?

She turned and looked at him, up in the bow with the captain.

Harald was fifty now, almost fifty-one. Why had he embarked on this quest, at an age when nearly every other warrior would have begun to think about grandchildren on the knee? Was it that he was still prey to the overgrown boy's desire for simple adventure? Did he feel that, at fifty, this would be his last campaign? He had fought through every season almost non-stop since he had fled from the battlefield where his brother had died, over thirty-five years ago. Was it that he could not think of anything else to do? Was he bewitched by the great goddess of ambition, by the desire to go out in a blaze of glory?

Or would he in fact surprise them all, as he had so often done in the past? Had he carefully calculated the odds, and decided that this was an opportunity not to be missed? After fifteen years in a vain attempt to conquer Denmark, now this chance had suddenly arisen – the chance to win an even greater country, half of which had been Scandinavian for nearly two hundred years. A split country, and a disputed crown – what better chance did he want?

No wonder he wanted them both there with him. If he had half a sense of destiny, he would want no other. And he had left Aud behind. No question of wanting his handfast mistress with him. It was Ellisif he wanted. What if she had been unable to give him the son that Aud did? It was herself, Ellisif the Queen, daughter of Prince Jaroslav of Kiev, that he wanted with him on this greatest of all adventures. And Maria. Who knew? Perhaps he too had noticed Maria's trouble. It was always a mistake to underestimate him.

Ellisif lifted her shoulders in a great shrug. They said she had second sight. Not really true. What she saw was not foresight; it was insight.

Did Harald see the same things as she did?

Chapter Eight

'Well, what do you think?'

Leofwine gazed out from the swinging shutters, and put out his hands to hold them back from banging against the stonework.

'You are the King, not I. It is too big a decision for the likes of me. I am only an earl.'

Harold made a noise of impatience. 'God's Teeth, Lef, you are the Earl of Kent. I am not. You know much more about the weather here than I do. I am not asking for your decision; I am asking for your opinion. I take the decisions. I alone.'

Leofwine let go of the shutters, which promptly banged shut again, and continued to rattle throughout the conversation.

'I am sorry, Harold. I was not thinking.'

'Well, all right,' said Harold. 'Now I am asking you to do just that. For the second time, what do you think?'

Leofwine pushed open the shutters again, and peered out. The sky was grey and cheerless; the wind threw gusts of drizzle into the chamber where they stood. Leofwine let the shutters close again, then walked across the room and opened shutters on the southern side. Sheltered from the wind, the shutters behaved themselves. Through the window the white horses leaped all over the Channel.

Leofwine turned and gestured back. 'See that? Still from the north.'

'I can see that,' said Harold. 'What I am asking you is: how long do you think it can go on?'

Leofwine pulled a face. 'When you get a bad summer to start with, you usually go on getting it bad, and you spend the whole summer being miserable, hoping against hope that the weather will change. But it very rarely does. Not till it is too late to do any good anyway.'

'That is the sort of information I want,' said Harold. 'Thank you.'

He turned away and paced up and down past a table at which sat a tense group of clerks, quills poised, left elbows spread, ready to write out his orders. A boy was preparing candles and seals.

If Lef was right, he could count on more bad weather, a few days at least. It tallied with his own experience. This wind would coop William in his assembly ports and main harbour. By the same token, it was laying out the red carpet in the North Sea. If Hardrada did not sail with a following wind like this, he was not the warrior he was supposed to be. Successful warfare was all about timing. He could not hope for a better chance than this. If he hung on till October, he would have not winds to deal with but storms. And the campaigning season would be over anyway.

Finally, there was the harvest. It would not wait any longer.

Harold stopped pacing, and looked at Leofwine. 'Very well. We let them go.'

He turned to the eager clerks. 'Get out the orders we drafted for the dismissal of the county fyrds. Copies to every camp. Copies to every detachment commander below a line from Anglia to Hereford. They all go home. But they stay in readiness for recall at a week's notice. Special orders for fyrd commanders and shire levies within forty miles either side of the Great North Road.

'All housecarls will stay with me. County headquarter house-carls, too. Every available horse to be requisitioned and held in the housecarls' camps. Ready to move at three days' notice.'

Harold fixed the chief clerk with his eye. 'Nobody gets up from the table till every order is in the very hands of the courier and on its way. Is that clear?'

The man bowed his tonsured head. 'As crystal, my lord. It shall be done.'

Harold nodded. 'Get the guard commanders. Tell them to dig every courier out of the kitchens at once. They saddle their horses, and they wait outside, here, till the seals are on. Come and tell me when they are all ready for the road. I want a word with them.'

The chief clerk bowed again. Harold looked sternly at every face at the table.

'We are depending on you.' He turned to Leofwine and jerked his head. 'Lef.'

As they went downstairs to the courtyard, Harold said, 'Well, we have done it. England is half naked. What is the betting Hardrada catches us in the bath?'

'Or the Bastard,' said Leofwine.

Harold laughed. 'Or both of them. And it would be just like Tostig then to descend on Wales.'

'Well, so much for that.'

Queen Ellisif drew her favourite shawl more tightly, and turned away from the sea. The ships were practically invisible in the evening murk.

'Now we do what women always do.'

'We wait,' said Maria.

'And we worry. We are never at peace. We worry when they get too close, in case they make us mothers; we worry when they get too far away, in case they make us widows.'

'But there are some in-between times, surely,' said Maria.

'You know there are,' said her mother. 'That is what makes all the waiting worthwhile.'

Maria looked at her sidelong. 'Have you never had any regrets – about all this waiting, I mean?'

Ellisif met her eyes. 'Do you not think your father is special?'

'I think he is one in a million,' said Maria.

'Well, if his daughter thinks he is one in a million, just imagine what his wife thinks.'

Maria smiled, and took her mother's arm.

'Which reminds me,' said Ellisif. 'I take it you think our Sigurd is one in a million, too.'

'Oh, yes,' said Maria.

'And you have told him?'

Maria squeezed the arm. 'I have proved it to him.'

The Queen looked quizzical. 'Very resourceful of you.'

'I am my mother's daughter,' said Maria. 'If you can do it in the stern of a longship, so can I. All it needs is a little planning.'

Ellisif pursued the matter. 'No sudden dark moments?'

'None. Why do you ask?'

'Because they say it can be brought on by intense excitement.'

'Really? Then I had a lucky escape, did I not? All the same . . .'

'What?'

Maria smiled wickedly. 'What a wonderful way to go.'

The Lady Gytha twiddled a ring.

'Well, what are you going to do now?'

'Nothing, Mother.'

'Nothing?'

'That is what I said – nothing. That should please you. So Tostig is safe. You can stop worrying.'

'Keep a civil tongue in your head,' said the Lady Gytha.

Two table servants at the end of the hall gaped. My lady was talking to the King.

Harold ignored them. If his mother wished to bring up topics like this in front of an audience, she would have to put up with his answers.

'I have to treat all this as a joke, because you are being impossible, and you know it.'

'I will not be humoured.'

'Then be reasonable.'

'I have not said anything yet.'

'No. But you are thinking it. I am your son; I know. Alas – I am not your favourite son.'

'All I have asked is what you are going to do.'

'And I have told you – nothing. Because there is nothing to be done. I have no news – or not enough for me to make a proper decision.'

'A nice way out, then.'

'There you go again – being impossible. Mother, you know as well as I do – the most difficult thing to do is nothing.'

'Could you not make an approach? Must it always be war?'

'I am the one being attacked,' said Harold. 'It is not up to me.'

'I should have thought it was all the more up to you – to try and make peace.'

'With whom? Hardrada? Who has two or three hundred longships on the high seas as we speak, on his way to Orkney? Or the Bastard who sits in his seaports with hundreds more? How do you suggest I get to them?'

'Tostig is not with them.'

Harold tossed his head. 'Ah! So there it is. We come back to Tostig again.'

'Of course,' said Gytha. 'He is the one who knows both of them. Get him to talk to them.'

Harold leaned forward and spoke slowly as if to a child. 'Mother, I have not the faintest idea where he is.'

'You have spies and couriers. You could find out.'

'Mother, Tostig has spent every waking hour since we banished him talking to my enemies in Normandy, Flanders, Denmark, Norway, Scotland. Even if we did get him to the table to talk, what would you want me to do – let him have England? Summon Hardrada and the Bastard to the meeting so they can carve up England between them, while I go and live in Ireland?'

'Tostig is English too. Give him the chance to come to some agreement.'

'Mother, he is a traitor. He has sworn my destruction. He has raised arms against his own country, and against his own family – me, you, Edith, Gyrth, Leofwine, everybody.'

'Give him a chance,' said Gytha.

Harold looked at her and sighed. 'I will say this: if ever I am in a position in which I have defeated Tostig, I shall offer him his life if he goes away and does not bother England any more. Will that satisfy you?'

Gytha folded her hands in her lap. 'It seems to be all I am going to get.'

'I tell you this,' said Harold. 'If the situation were reversed, it is more than I would get from Tostig.'

The stable yard near the minster was seething. Everybody had his own urgent business. It was a wonder they did not trip over each other.

Steaming horses were led away by soothing grooms. Boys staggered under the weight of freshly unbuckled leatherwork. Servants bustled to and fro under the eye, hand and voice of hectoring stewards. Hooves clattered on the cobbles; doors slammed; pots rattled; swearwords filled the air.

The couriers were led away to Father Bernard's chambers to make their reports. Everything was happening at once. News was arriving from Orkney, from Scotland, from the Forth, the Tyne, the Tees – each message, it seemed, bursting with more urgency than the last. Each courier was convinced that his message was the most dramatic of all.

Hardrada had moved to strike. He had ships from Norway, from Shetland, from Orkney, from Scotland, Ireland, Iceland, the Faroes, from the edge of the world. He had two hundred ships, three hundred, four hundred, a thousand. He had five thousand men, eight thousand, twenty thousand. Observers from lonely headlands, peering into the mist, and loafers in busy harbours, running out of fingers to count on, had allowed their enthusiasm and imagination to get the better of their own eyes.

Lonely rides on horseback, bad weather, fevered imagination, together with the desire to be the bearer of the most important news, had had the usual inflationary effect on the figures.

Father Bernard listened to every breathless account, asked the usual questions, received the usual assurances that he was being told nothing less than the unvarnished truth, and packed off the tellers to some refreshment and rest. From time to time he glanced at Conrad, and they often shared a wry smile at the most outrageous stories and numbers.

When they had all gone, Bernard beckoned to Conrad, who was prompt to place before him the necessary papers, pens, and ink. He looked absently into Conrad's face, dipped his pen and began to write.

My lord King,

We have movement at last. All the accounts speak of invasion from Norway. That much seems sure. Contingents of ships, and detachments of men, have been identified from Shetland, Orkney, Scotland, Ireland, maybe Iceland. My lord Tostig's standard has been recognised, though his squadron is not estimated as large.

Estimates of numbers are unreliable, but your Grace will do well to prepare for an invasion force of not less than five to seven thousand – maybe more. It is difficult to hazard a higher figure without becoming alarmist.

There seems to have been a rendezvous with Earl Tostig either in the River Forth or the River Tyne. At any rate, the combined fleet has begun to move down the north-east coast. Their purpose would appear to be twofold: to forage for supplies, and to ravage and lay waste what is not needed or what can not be taken away. In a word, terror.

My guess is that he is coming south by the seaward route for two reasons: one, he can stay near his ships, and, therefore, his lines of communication; and, two, movement is easier by sea than it is by land. However, he can not stay at sea for ever, because he must be looking for a decision; he is trying, I should say, to provoke the Earls Edwin and Morcar to battle on the one hand, and to undermine civilian morale on the other. By these means, he hopes to unsettle the earls, and to hustle them into hostilities without sufficient preparation either of forces or of the ground.

It follows, then, that he will not stay on the coast for much longer, but turn inland, to reach York, because he must know that the earls' main force is to be concentrated there. We do not know if the forces available to the Earl of Northumbria and the Earl of Mercia will match those at the disposal of King Harald of Norway. If he can take the capital, he will dominate and he will have the initiative. And I do not need to remind you of the age-long sentiment of Northumbria's capital towards the Scandinavian countries. Such a situation, I respectfully submit, should not be allowed to come about, and all our resources should therefore be channelled towards preventing it.

Bernard looked up from his writing, and fixed Conrad with his fearsome eye. 'Listen to this.'

He lowered his eyes and read out what he had just written. Then he looked up again.

'Well, do we spell it out even more?' he said.

Conrad licked his lips. He was being asked about the very fate of England. His answer – his – that of a mere novice brother – was about to go to the King of England, who was charged with the fate of everybody. And what did he – Conrad the novice – know about high politics? But he had been with the King long enough to conceive a high regard for him.

'No, Father. I think, when the King reads this, he will know what to do.'

Gyrth threw his travelling cloak onto a bench, and came forward to the fire.

'Is there news?'

He shivered, rubbed his hands, put them out to the blaze, then turned his back and rubbed his buttocks.

'God's Face, this weather.'

Harold beckoned to a servant, who instantly left the hall to get some refreshment.

Gyrth stood up straight, looked at Leofwine, then at Harold. 'Well, is there?'

Harold grinned and winked at Leofwine. 'Is there what?'

'News!' exploded Gyrth. 'Harold, this is no time for playing games. I have ridden a long way from Anglia.'

'And Lef has come up from Kent,' said Harold.

'So he should be feeling as I do,' said Gyrth. 'True, Lef?'

Leofwine folded his arms. 'Come on, Harold. Time.'

Harold nodded, and became serious. 'Very well. But my first answer to you, Gyrth, if I am to be truthful, is going to annoy you. The correct answer to your question, "Is there news?" is "Yes and no."'

Gyrth sat down with a bump. 'Explain yourself.'

'We have too much news from the north, and not enough from the south. In fact, practically none at all from the south.'

'Well, tell us anyway.'

'Bernard has been writing endless despatches for the last week. His men have been practically falling over each other on the road south.'

'What does it amount to?' said Gyrth.

'Invasion,' said Harold.

Gyrth whistled. 'So he has really done it?'

'Looks like it. Bernard mentions ships from all over the north. As far north as Iceland and as far east as Finland and Rus.'

'Is Tostig with them?' said Leofwine.

'So it would appear.'

Leofwine made a noise of satisfaction. 'At last. Out in the open.'

'Do we know how many?' said Gyrth.

Harold shook his head doubtfully. 'You know what men are like when they are asked to count. They do their best, but . . .' he left the sentence unfinished.

'What do you think?'

Harold shrugged. 'Best not to alarm ourselves. Just concentrate what we have and hope for the best.'

'What *do* we have?'

'Well, obviously, we have the northern host – Edwin and Morcar.'

'Are they up to it?'

'Do you mean the host or Edwin and Morcar?'

'Both.'

'Their numbers may not be enough. And Morcar is in charge.'

'Well, you put him there.'

'No. We – the Witan – put him there. But you know Morcar. Poor lad – he should not be in command at a time like this.'

'Then change him.'

'No,' said Harold. 'Especially at a time like this. To say you do not trust your commander on the ground would be the worst I could do for morale, for everyone. Right now they are all facing Hardrada. Not the prospect of Hardrada, the chance of Hardrada, the possibility of Hardrada, but the man himself.'

'You said we should not be swayed by reputations.'

'True. I am not. I hope you and Lef are not. But Morcar is barely nineteen. Edwin is not much older.'

'They have seasoned men in the fyrd. They have their housecarls.'

Harold shook his head. 'Firmness comes from the top, not halfway down. I have one hope.'

'What is that?'

'Morcar chased Tostig away from Lindsey. The success may have gone to his head, but at least he is full of fight right now.'

'So what are you saying?'

'That he may inflict damage on Hardrada, but he is not likely to chase him off as he did Tostig. Hardrada will run rings round him, but Morcar may slow him down.'

'You were not saying this a couple of months ago.'

'No. But I have been thinking. And things have been happening. Bernard tells me that Hardrada is pillaging and wasting his way all down the north-east coast. He hopes to burn away all support for me. He knows Wessex is not popular in Northumbria, and I can not rely on instinctive loyalty as I can in Wessex. The north is half-Danish, as you well know. If Hardrada can get it across that peace under him means the end of burning, and loyalty to me means more burning, guess what might happen.'

'So?'

'So – we must do something, and not just wait and hope.'

'We have done nothing but wait all summer,' said Gyrth.

'True. And now is the time to do something else. It is the fire, Gyrth. Fire does things. A King must protect his people, and *must be seen to protect his people*. If York burns, I shall never be able to hold Northumbria. People will say I deserted them, Morcar or no Morcar.'

Gyrth glanced at Leofwine. 'So you will go north?'

'Yes.'

'You have disbanded the southern fyrd, and left the south half naked. Now you will take away the rest of the army and leave it *stark* naked.'

This time it was Harold who glanced at Leofwine. 'Yes.'

Gyrth shrugged. 'Well, you are the King. It is your kingdom.'

'What would you do, then?' said Harold.

Gyrth looked again at Leofwine. A smile slowly spread across both their faces.

'The same as you, I daresay.'

They all three laughed outright.

'All right,' said Gyrth. 'Now. Practicalities. What arrangements have you made? Oh – and what about the small matter of the Bastard?'

'He is the other half of my answer to you,' said Harold. 'Remember I said, "Yes and no"? All the news is coming from the north. The south is practically silent.'

'Apart from the wind,' said Leofwine.

'Exactly,' said Harold. 'The Bastard can do nothing in this weather. I am not even sure if he is ready. Some of our spy ships talk of his moving his entire expedition from the Dives to the Somme. It may shorten the crossing for him, but it will take time. Moreover, it speaks of indecision. Always a bad sign. Whatever it says, he still needs the wind. Without that he is helpless.'

'And another thing,' said Leofwine. 'Harold has sent the fyrd home. They will be fully occupied, and an army needs to be fully occupied. William has an entire expeditionary force shivering in wet tents – baffled, uncomfortable and bored out of their wits. He has a far bigger problem than we do at the moment.'

Leofwine laughed again. 'All we have to worry about is Hardrada.'

Gyrth pulled a wry face, and repeated, 'So we go north?'

Harold nodded. 'I have sent out the orders. Every southern housecarl, whatever his household, will concentrate just outside London, on the north road. Sheriffs of counties within fifty miles of the road will recall their fyrds and have them rendezvous with us as we go north. With any luck we shall also pick up handfuls of country lads keen to have a crack at the enemy.'

'Not much use,' said Gyrth.

'Maybe not,' said Harold. 'But they add to the numbers. They add to the initial impact. And that will be our greatest asset. Hardrada is counting on meeting Edwin and Morcar, and no one else. He knows – or he thinks he knows – that I am watching the Bastard all the time and have my hands full down here. We make a dash. The camps all along the road are ready and supplied. Every manor for miles either side of the road has had my men requisitioning horses. They may not be able to fight on the battlefield, but they will help to *get* us to the battlefield.'

Harold punched a fist into his other palm. 'And we shall be the last people Hardrada expects to *find* on the battlefield.'

'Suppose he has beaten Edwin and Morcar by that time,' said Gyrth.

'Then he will be celebrating. We shall surprise him even more.'

'Suppose Edwin and Morcar win,' said Leofwine, with a grin.

'In that case,' said Harold, 'it will be all of *us* who do the celebrating.' He too grinned broadly. 'And, if Hardrada beats us, the Bastard becomes *his* worry, not mine. I do not see how anything can go wrong, can you?'

Magnus looked eastwards to catch the first sign of dawn. He shivered and tried to bury himself inside his sheepskin tunic.

The weather had been improving since they had left the Forth – no doubt about that – but the winds could still be uncomfortable. The sun, though bright, had not been strong. And the nights still made you think of winter.

Taken together, it did little to lift the spirits. The hour made the situation worse. Everyone knew that the sentry turn of duty just before dawn was always the worst. Magnus had no idea what it was, but those few hours lay like a great load on the spirits. Nothing ever seemed attractive, or optimistic, or encouraging.

Sentry duty anywhere was never something you looked forward to. It was particularly irksome when nobody could see what on earth was the point of it. Ever since it had left the Forth, the King's great fleet of longships had had total freedom of the sea. When they had landed, the army had run riot all over the north-east coast of England, with barely a flicker of resistance. And that had been speedily dealt with. It was little more than brushing away a few flies.

Wherever they had stopped to make camp, Hardrada had decreed that sentries should be posted – in large numbers – round both fleet and army camp – day and night. For a man whose reputation was based on daring, dashing exploits, he fussed about detail like an old woman. Everything must be just so. And there was no threat whatever that men could see.

Magnus sighed. It must run deep in the King's character. He was a great leader and a towering personality, and most of his men worshipped him, but he had a deep-set suspicious streak. Perhaps this was more easily noticed by those who had most recently joined him, like Sigurd and his squad of bully-boys. Which made it all the more remarkable that the King had shown him such favour. But even Sigurd came up against this suspicious vein in the King's character. Look how the King had put him down by refusing to let him take Maria to Orkney the first time. Then giving him a squadron, but giving him all the bits and pieces – the renegade little groups of ships from Iceland and Ireland and the Faroes and so on.

As for instance now; Magnus, in his pre-dawn depths, was quite sure that Hardrada made Sigurd's men do more sentry duty than his own precious veterans. The Irish and Icelanders complained of the same discrimination. The islanders grumbled, too.

They grumbled, but they did not complain. Nobody dared. Besides, they knew, deep down, that Hardrada was being a careful campaigner. The enterprise must succeed. Everyone felt the force of his hand, and accepted it. He was not called the 'Stern Ruler' for nothing.

It was Hardrada's way of keeping order. Everyone had to work for his favour. What was it the Queen had said? 'He tests before he trusts.'

Magnus was also fairly sure that Sigurd and his lads were being made to do not only more sentry duty than the favoured Norwegians, but more of the dirty work, too. The voyage south had not been the greedily awaited procession of victory . . .

At first they had tensed themselves for opposition. After all the months of waiting and training and travelling, at last they would have some action. Tore and Finn and Hakon and the rest could not wait to get ashore. If Ketil sharpened his axe once, he did it a dozen times. Sigurd did not crack as many jokes as usual. There was no gambling on board.

But the beaches were empty. The coastal settlements were empty. Half the farms were empty. Horses were there for the taking in the stables. When they rode round the country looking for supplies, they found livestock, unharvested crops, stores, groaning orchards, bursting chicken coops – all almost pathetic in their availability.

The cheers and the roars of anticipation became snarls of disappointment. It was all too easy. They felt like children who had torn open the wrappings round a present and found nothing inside.

So they began to burn. It was part of Hardrada's orders. They knew that. But they were doing it now out of frustration, not obedience. Indeed, Sigurd had to give strict orders to stop them burning valuable provisions in their anger.

Hardrada needed those supplies; he could not possibly carry everything required for a whole campaign on the longships, even in the fat, wallowing supply tubs.

He did not mind about the burning. In fact he had ordered it – in moderation. He knew it spread terror and sapped morale. It was simply another weapon of war. But he could not let it blaze out of control; the food was more important. So the men were annoyed that they could do little more than burn, and they were annoyed when they were told to stop the burning.

Tempers began to fray. It was all becoming a bore. Magnus could see that as well as Sigurd. He told him so.

'Did you foresee this?'

'No,' said Sigurd candidly. 'We shall just have to hope for something to turn up.'

'Like what?'

'Like some opposition in Scarborough. That is our next port of call, I believe.'

Sigurd looked keenly at him. 'Will that do?'

'No,' said Magnus equally candidly.

'Ah.'

Magnus looked at him, awaiting a question. But none came. Sigurd was never one to pry.

Magnus did not see the burning in the same way. To the lads, even Sigurd, too, it was a tiresome chore. To Magnus it was a vehicle of dread and loss.

He could not look on flame-licked timbers or roaring thatch without curling his nostrils over the smoke, without feeling helpless, without remembering the blind stumbling, the groping, the running of the eyes, the choking. Above all, feeling his ears torn by Sigrid's screams. After all his desperate efforts, it had been to no avail. She had gone, and left seared into his memory a face that was a mask of terror and agony. And he had been forced to leave her like that. Suspended in a rictus of horror between life and death, or rather between death and decent burial.

It had been the same wherever they had stopped: in the Forth, the Tyne, the Tees – those were the names, Sigurd said – and now Cleveland and Whitby (men who went a-viking usually knew their geography).

The only thing that could drive the flames out of his head was the, by now, familiar nausea once he got back on board ship. So much for the procession of victory . . .

Magnus, almost enjoying his misery, decided that he had plenty to be miserable about – the sickness, the flames, the wanton destruction (mercifully, most of the inhabitants had fled, so there had been little killing, which he had been able to avoid) and the merciless company of Sigrid's face.

He stirred restlessly. God and Valhalla – please bring the dawn, and please bring it quickly.

He stood up. Perhaps a walk might help to ease his mind.

He had gone hardly a few steps when he tripped over a recumbent body. It swore. The voice was familiar. He bent down to look in the face.

'Lars! What in the name of Odin are you doing here?'

Lars put an urgent finger to his lips. 'For God's sake keep your voice down.'

'But how did you get here? You were told by—'

Lars waved the words aside. 'Yes, yes, I was told. We all know that. But I could not stay. Could you?'

'So what did you do?'

'I stowed away.'

'Where?'

'On the King's ship.'

'What?'

'It was the biggest. Besides, Sig was the one who dismissed me, not the King.'

Magnus could hardly contain himself.

'But he knew. Suppose he found you.'

'His own ship would be the last place he would look. Besides, he had the Queen on board. Maybe their last voyage together?' Lars grinned. 'What do you think he would be thinking about – me?'

Magnus shook his head. 'Lars, you are impossible. And you have not learned. Look at you.'

Lars looked blank. 'What do you mean?'

Magnus pointed to the ground. 'What are you doing when I find you? Fast asleep.'

Lars put on a lofty expression. 'The King followed his instincts. I followed mine.'

Morcar tugged at the tuft of a beard under his lip. His brother, Earl Edwin of Mercia, looked at Father Bernard, who stood patiently with the latest reports in his hand.

'You are quite sure?' said Morcar.

Bernard bowed. 'Quite sure, my lord. This is from one of our most reliable observers.'

Morcar began pacing. Edwin and Bernard exchanged glances again.

Up until now it had been a very different tune. Morcar had revelled in his 'victory' over Tostig in Lindsey . . .

'Seaborne carrion,' he had said. 'They can not stand and fight; they fly to their precious ships at the first sign of determined resistance.'

'Hardrada is rather different,' observed Edwin.

Morcar snapped his fingers. 'Pah! More seaborne carrion. Besides, look at us. Look at the men we have now.'

It was true, to a certain extent. The full fyrd of Mercia had arrived. More men had come in from Anglia, and the shires of Nottingham, Northampton and Derby. The northern shires, too – Cumberland and Westmorland. Extra housecarls had been mustered from every available county headquarters. But Morcar's administrative system, in tatters when Tostig had been banished, was nowhere as good as the King's. Nobody really knew how many men were actually involved. Morcar did not have the experience to know the respective value of each contingent. (Edwin, only a few years older, knew that his own judgement was not much better.) Even feeding them was already stretching York's resources.

Morcar, however, was bewitched by mere numbers, which of course he overestimated.

'We have ten thousand, maybe twelve thousand, brother. When we muster in force, Hardrada will take one look, and turn back to his ships. And I shall be merciful and let him go. Imagine – defeating the greatest Viking without even fighting a battle . . .'

Now that the enemy was forty miles away, just above Scarborough, Morcar did not look so decisive or confident.

Edwin looked at his brother. The more Morcar pulled at that wisp of fair hair, the younger he appeared. Edwin felt a sinking of the heart.

For one thing, Morcar had never commanded so much as a thousand or two in the field, never mind the twelve thousand he was boasting about. They were simply numbers to him. He had no experience of deployment. He had never been on full campaign, certainly not in high rank.

For the third time, Edwin glanced at Bernard.

Bernard felt sorry for both of them. They were both too young. But Morcar was the Earl of Northumbria, and that was that. Bernard cleared his throat.

'My lord, suppose we strike at their next landing. It is said that the sooner one strikes back at an invasion landing, the better one's chances of driving it into the sea. Every hour makes them stronger.'

Morcar stopped pacing. 'Nonsense. By the time we get there he will have gone again. And we shall have to wait for news of his next landing.'

Well, thought Bernard, there was something in that. Far be it for a mere member of the Holy Order of St Benedict to correct a nobleman on the art of war.

Edwin saw deeper. He knew his brother. Morcar was simply putting off a decision. As it happened, he might be right about the difficulty of chasing a seaborne landing, but sooner or later Hardrada would land, and stay. Morcar would have to decide then.

'We could deploy around the Ouse Estuary,' said Edwin. 'That must be where Hardrada is aiming for. He has to invade, and that is the best place. The river comes right into the heart of the county, and he can penetrate right up to York.'

Morcar began pacing again. 'No. No. We must not be drawn. We have to defend York. It is the capital. What would Harold say if we lost York?'

Edwin fell silent. His brother did not know what to do.

'Go on, Father. Admit it. That was better than Bertha could have done.'

Edric smiled as he wiped the last piece of bread round the wooden plate. 'Yes. It was.'

Then he fell silent, and looked away at nothing.

Coelwen waited a while, then leaned forward. 'Is it really very bad?'

Edric looked at his daughter. Her face was always so open, her eyes so clear, her look so direct. He resisted the temptation to stretch across and tweak her nose.

'Hardrada has been in the Tyne and the Tees. He has ravaged Cleveland. He must be in Whitby by now. Scarborough lies in his path.'

There was another silence.

'So we shall be next.'

Edric heaved a great sigh. 'It looks like that. Unless . . .'

'Unless?'

'Unless he simply wishes to make a point. When he has done enough wasting, he may decide that he has made that point. He may feel that Northumbria has been frightened enough to offer surrender.'

'You mean Earl Morcar?'

'Yes.'

'Do you think Morcar will give up as easily as that?'

Edric cocked his head. 'Hard to say. He is very young.'

'He has Earl Edwin with him. That may put some fight into him.'

'Possibly.'

'So Hardrada will not have made his point.'

'No.'

'So he will go on wasting.'

'Yes.'

'So we are back where we began.'

'Not necessarily.'

'How?'

Edric took a draught from his cup. 'My guess is that Hardrada wants York. That would make sense. The man who controls York controls Northumbria. He could burn a dozen Scarboroughs, but without York he is still out there on the edge.'

'So we are still next?'

Edric smiled. 'Do not be so hasty to welcome disaster. As I said, he wants York. Now there are two ways of getting to York. One is down the coast to the Ouse Estuary, up the river, then up the River Derwent to York. And he could take his ships with him.'

'And the other?'

'Straight across country,' said Edric. 'As the crow flies. It is only forty or fifty miles. A quick dash with a picked body of men, and he could do it. Surprise, you see. Earl Morcar has no more idea of what he will do than I have.'

'What do you think?'

Edric pushed away his plate. 'For the life of me I do not know. All I can do is prepare for what could happen. What they say – prepare for the worst, and hope for the best.'

Coelwen stood up and began to clear the table.

'What does Gunnar say?'

Edric grunted. 'Gunnar? He talks a lot and says nothing. I must say his son is proving himself a lot more practical and sensible than his father at the moment.'

Coelwen made a noise of agreement. 'He was kind to me.'

'I do not mean simple kindness. I mean common sense. I may have misjudged that young man. There is more to him than first meets the eye.'

'He shamed his father into coming back, you know.'

'Yes, so I gather.'

'Did he say so?'

'Who – Vendel? No. He would not. But you can guess. For a start, you only have to look at Gunnar.'

Coelwen nodded. 'Yes. Do you know what Vendel said to me? He said his father has spent most of his time since he got back by digging a great hole in the floor at the back of his house.'

Edric stared. 'Gunnar? When did he last do manual work?'

'No, no. Not Gunnar himself. His servants. Vendel thinks he is going to bury his treasure.'

Edric grunted again. 'It is going to take a large hole, with what he has accumulated all these years.'

'Are you not disgusted?'

'It is no more than I would have expected.'

'Vendel is ashamed of him.'

Edric looked keenly at her. 'You seem to think very well of Vendel.'

Coelwen returned the look. 'As I said, he was kind. And he is easy to talk to.'

'Is that all?' said Edric.

Coelwen patted his shoulder as she passed behind him to clear more things off the table.

'That is all. I promise you.' She laughed. 'I should not like to make you cross with me a second time.'

Edric turned and looked up at her. 'A second time?'

Coelwen stopped for a moment. 'Coming back.'

Edric stood up too, picked up the last knife and spoon, and put it carefully on the tray she was carrying.

'You know full well that I could never stay cross with you.'

And then he did tweak her nose.

'I do not believe it. I simply do not believe it.'

Alfred could think of nothing else to say. 'I just do not believe it.'

'You learn to believe anything in wartime,' said Owen.

Alfred gazed at him. 'But *south – again*?'

'Not all the way this time, boyo. Only fifty miles or so.'

Alfred stared again. 'Only!'

Owen continued munching. 'That is what they say.'

'How do you know?' said Alfred.

'The same way he knows everything else,' said a neighbour. 'He is a Welsh wizard.'

Owen shrugged. 'I go around. I talk. I exchange gossip.'

'How do you know if it is true?'

'I do not,' said Owen. 'That is the whole point of gossip. But it oils the wheels. People talk. You have to sort out the wheat from the chaff – the news from the gossip.'

'And you are expert, I suppose,' said Alfred.

'I have heard enough of it,' said Owen. 'And what I do not hear, my friend Llew does. It is a perfect arrangement.'

Alfred looked at a loss. 'How do you do it? Look at what we have been doing. Working ourselves to a shadow – building camps, setting up beacons, digging privies, making ovens. And in between we march, march, march.'

'At least those fat-bellied housecarls have gone,' said a fyrdman. 'By the way, where did they go?'

'Pushed off,' said Alfred with a sneer.

'You mean deserted?'

Owen shook his head. 'Housecarls do not desert. It is maybe they heard something.'

'Have you?' said the fyrdman.

'Not yet,' admitted Owen. 'But—'

'Tut, tut,' said the fyrdman, shaking his head. 'Slipping, eh?'

Owen was not abashed. 'Time and patience, patience and time.'

Alfred swore. 'What difference does it make? Now we do nothing but hump bags of corn. Where is the news in that?'

Llew placed a finger beside his nose. 'Ah, my young friend, you see only the work. We look for the reasons behind it.'

'How do you look for them?' said Alfred.

A fyrdman leaned forward. 'It is called experience, son. The reasons are there if you know where to look.'

Alfred turned to him. 'All right, know-all. What are they?'

Owen tossed a chunk of cheese towards Alfred. 'What he means, my little druid, is that we have seen things like this before.'

'Where?'

'I have been in Wales with the King, when he fought against Gruffydd – our king. And beat him, more is the pity. These lads here have fought with Earl Tostig when he invaded Wales in partnership with the King, or they have been in the northern wars with Siward and King Malcolm.'

'Or back in the days when Earl Godwin was invading,' said a fyrdman, 'to get his earldom back. Some of us have fought all over the place. Or at least were prepared to fight.'

Alfred looked from one to the other. 'But what does it all *mean*?'

'We can not tell you that – not for sure,' said Owen. 'All we can do is guess.'

Llew joined in. 'That is all war is – guessing. Guessing what the other man is going to do.'

'Nobody knows – not even the King. He has to be the best guesser of all.'

Llew pointed vaguely out towards the road they had just come in from.

'Look at Harold now. He has the Bastard waiting to jump at us from Normandy.'

'He has the King of Denmark,' said Owen, 'who may invade or he may not.'

'He has the Count of Flanders.'

'He has Earl Tostig, who might be anywhere.'

Alfred jumped to interrupt. 'You said he landed at Lindsey, and Earl Morcar shooed him away.'

'Maybe. But we have no idea where he is now. So just think of all the guessing the King has to do.'

Alfred sat back to digest it all. The fyrdman leaned forward again. 'It is a wonder he is able to come to any decision at all.'

An idea occurred to Alfred. 'All right, then. So it is hard to make the right decision. Then tell me, O wise one, why do we have to go back down south again? Surely the Bastard has not landed, not with these northerly winds? That is what you told me.'

'We do not go all the way,' said the fyrdman. 'Besides, the King has troops nearer the south than we are.'

'Then why not send us north to deal with Hardrada?'

'Because he has Earl Morcar there.'

'Then why move us around like counters on a board?'

Owen wiped his mouth and dusted away some crumbs. 'This is what occurs to me. We all know that Hardrada is coming. Well, we do now. The King hopes that Morcar can cope with it. I think Harold is waiting till he is more sure.'

'Till he can guess better,' said Alfred with a touch of irony.

'If you like,' said Owen. 'But he must be ready. He must be ready for anything. You know what it is like when you try to avoid a slap in the face; you get a kick in the arse. Well, that is what the King is doing. It is waiting in the south he is, for the Bastard. He has put Morcar in the north, to meet Hardrada.

'Now, if life does what life always does – messes us about – he must be ready to deal with it. The word is "flexible". Ever heard of "flexible", Alfred?'

Alfred tossed his head. 'Of course.'

'So,' said Owen, 'he must be ready to move his army from the south to the north – quickly.'

'Which is why we have been building camps,' said Alfred. 'I am not stupid.'

Owen looked at him. 'No. Well.'

'But look at what he wants us to do now,' said Llew. 'We are moving food. Food goes off. That means that the King thinks—'

'– or guesses.'

Llew smiled. '– or guesses. Guesses that he will need to move soon.'

'In other words,' said Owen, 'something is going to happen.'

Llew pointed to his friend and laughed. 'See Owen there? Second sight he has. Just like Hardrada.'

Alfred fell for it again. 'Does he really? Have second sight?'

Owen nodded firmly. 'So they say. He has bad dreams, and they often come true.'

'Let us hope he has one soon,' said Alfred.

Llew grimaced. 'Trouble is, he has visions, too.'

'Visions?'

'Oh, yes. His brother is a saint, you see.'

Alfred stared. 'A man like Hardrada, who spends all his life killing people, has a brother who is a saint?'

Owen nodded portentously once again. 'St Olaf. King too, once. Till they killed him.'

'Then why did they kill him?'

Llew shook his head. 'Good people tend to get killed. Perhaps that is why God makes them saints – to tell everybody what a mistake they made.'

Alfred looked about almost with desperation. 'Then what are we up against? A seven-foot devil who has a brother with a foot in Heaven.'

Owen laughed. 'Difficult, eh? Never mind, boyo. We have King Harold to do some good guessing for us.'

Llew joined in. 'And rest assured – you will have the chance to swing your Dada's sword. Keep it sharp, lad.'

It was the faces that Edric was to remember.

His brain took in the helmets, the mail, the swords and axes, the whole panoply of conflict. His training and experience noted the numbers – not all that many, he observed. Well, not as many as he had expected, with all those ships out there. He noted, too, the fact that they had acquired an unnerving number of scaling ladders. How on earth had they acquired those?

But it was something beyond all that which made him reel, if only for a moment. It was the faces – all, naturally, looking up. Looking up at his walls, his gatehouse, his sentry catwalks, his arrow slits. It was as if they were trying to tear down the defences of Scarborough with their eyes alone. Surveying, squinting, judging, sweeping, blazing. Beneath them were the open mouths, the bared teeth. For that moment, Edric stood as if transfixed, his sword arm loose at his side.

Then one of them threw a ladder against the wall beneath him. It reached nearly to the very top. As it fell towards him, Edric found himself noticing that it had been very well put together. Another mark of Hardrada's generalship. Thorough.

The noise it made falling against the woodwork brought Edric out of his trance. He raised his arm.

'Make ready.'

Palms were spat upon. Poles were grasped. Buckets of boiling water were lifted to knee height. Mats of stones were dragged just a little closer, to make sure. Swords left scabbards. In the streets of Scarborough below and behind, eyes were lifted, towards the reeve of their town. With that, and with the enemy below on the outer side, Edric suddenly felt as if every eye in the whole world were watching him.

The first of the enemy was halfway up the ladder.

'Now!'

As his men roared into action, and as the first pole was thrust out, Edric noticed another ridiculous detail: the man on the ladder had a curious scar right on the end of his nose . . .

Edric almost cried out with relief. Another few minutes and his muscles would have let him down. Men around him were bent over with exhaustion; some were on their knees. All were wheezing like old men at the top of five flights of steps.

Along the whole length of the town wall it was the same. After a while people began to peer over. So did Edric. They could scarcely believe the quiet – or the emptiness.

They had gone. Almost as fast as they had arrived. Not so much as a single body had been left behind. The wounded had been dragged away. Barely a bloodstain remained.

On the wall, buckets still stood in good order. The ladder poles did admittedly lean rather drunkenly against the parapet. The braziers still smouldered. Water was everywhere, of course, but there was amazingly little disarray. The skins on the walls had done their job; there was no discernible threat of fire. In the streets of the town behind them the fire-fighting squads had been alert and energetic. Barely any thatch was smoking. Edric allowed himself a brief moment of satisfaction at his thorough preparations.

Yet only a few minutes beforehand the scene had been one of shouting and bellowing, of order and counter-order, of crashes and splinterings, of swearwords and imprecations, of cries of fear and surprise and bloodcurdling menace. Muscle and nerve had been strained to the limit on both sides.

Suddenly, there had come orders from some hidden source. The surprise of their going was almost as great as the shock of their coming. It was difficult to believe that the uproar they had all suffered a few minutes ago had actually taken place.

All around Edric men began to congratulate each other. Who were these much-vaunted Vikings anyway? They look tough enough safe behind the shields on their precious longships, but, give them some proper action, against men, and they vanish like morning mist off the sea. It all sounded very pretty.

Edric looked at Vendel. Once again, his opinion of the boy had gone up – quite a lot. He had appeared on the parapet without any warning, had sized up the situation, and had done his bit to the limit of his modest strength. But the spirit was there. Edric found himself nodding in appreciation. Good for the lad.

'Where have they gone?' said Vendel, frowning.

'Back to their ships, I hope,' said Edric.

Vendel lifted his eyebrows. 'To stay?'

'Could be. They would have stayed closer if they had intended another attack. Look. The road is clear as far as we can see.'

'Why? They must outnumber us ten to one.'

'I know.'

Edric frowned too. This was not what he had prepared for. He had planned for a white flag demanding surrender. He had considered the possibility of being by-passed altogether, particularly likely if Hardrada's main objective was the Ouse or York, or both. He had steeled himself, naturally, for a blood-and-death struggle on the walls, with next to no hope for any kind of relief from Earl Morcar, much less the King. In any case, the attack had come so suddenly that he had had no time to send off a courier with the news. The chances were that he would have been caught anyway, because the enemy was all around the town.

Was this not just like Life? Whatever you prepare for, you get something else.

Edric peered over the parapet of the gatehouse again. There was still nothing there.

Vendel echoed one of his thoughts. 'If he intended to pass us by, why did he bother to attack at all?'

'The only reason I can think of,' said Edric, 'is what happened at Cleveland. He found no resistance there. He probably found none in the mouths of the Tyne and the Tees. So he expected none here. Perhaps we gave him a shock.'

'But he could wipe us out,' said Vendel. 'Look at the fleet he has out there.'

Edric could find no immediate answer. A thought suddenly occurred to him.

'Where is your father?'

Vendel's face hardened. 'I have no idea.' He paused, and looked away. 'Nor do I care.'

Edric looked at him. The boy was clearly feeling it very badly.

Edric peered for the third time. It was a most unusual experience – to brace oneself for the end, and, after less than half an hour, to discover not only that one was alive, but that the enemy who had come to bring about that end had himself disappeared.

*   *   *

'What do we do now, Sig?'

Sigurd sat down. 'We wait.'

Finn pointed back to the town. 'Why pull us back?'

'Because we were not making much impression.'

'Is that what he said?'

'Those were the orders, and that was the reason.'

'How do you know?'

'I went and asked. You saw me.'

'Give us a chance,' said Finn. 'We have made only one attempt. How many towns fall at the first onset?'

'Whitby did. And the others – right up to the Tyne.'

'So what? Are we afraid of a bit of trouble?'

Sigurd looked at him. 'Are you going back there to say – to his face – that you think he gives up easily? I should like to be there.'

Finn did not wish to concede the point. 'Do you fancy the idea?'

'No,' said Sigurd. 'I do not. I want some credit for a success just as much as you do. I am going to be his son-in-law, remember? That is why I jumped at the chance to put this town in the bag. But we have not done it. So I have to accept orders. I have to be a dutiful son-in-law and do as I am told.'

'Thor and thunder, Sig. Why send us in if he is going to pull us out at the first sign of a setback?'

'Casualties. He does not want too many casualties.'

'*Casualties!*' exploded Finn. 'What casualties? Tore got scalded shoulders and Hakon has an arrow in his arse.'

'And Ket's broken arm.'

'All right – a broken arm. He fell off a damn ladder. Hardly murderous losses.' Finn flung out an arm towards the fleet at anchor. 'We have thousands of men out there.'

'And he wants them all in one piece – for York. It could be a long job. We have very little siege equipment. And there is the small matter of the English army.'

'Then why attack this place?'

'It was a trial,' said Sigurd. 'All the other places surrendered with hardly a murmur. This was something of a surprise.'

'So what? We could polish it off in a matter of hours.'

'Yes,' said Sigurd. 'And maybe lose valuable men in the process. He does not want losses and he does not want delay. He needs the manpower and he needs the time.'

'So what is mastermind going to do?' said Finn.

Sigurd waved towards the cliff-like hill behind the town. 'Look up there.'

Everyone squinted at the distant figures labouring up the side of it.

'What are they dragging? What are they doing?'

'Wait and see,' said Sigurd.

It did not take very long.

It was simple wood that everyone was dragging. Huge piles were built up on the side of the crest overlooking the town. They were set alight. Figures could be seen running round them like so many boys round a midsummer bonfire.

'Great God!' said Finn, as the realisation dawned.

Burning brands were snatched from the main blazes and hurled down onto the roofs of the town. The thatch caught alight almost at once. As with most towns, particularly those crowded against the shore, the buildings were close together. The flames spread with awesome speed.

Sigurd nudged Finn's elbow. 'See? Mastermind has indeed thought of something. That is the key to Scarborough – fire. Not Ket's arm and Hakon's arse. Now we can walk in. Come on. Before the valuable bits burn too.'

'The walls are still there,' said Magnus.

'But there will be nobody on them,' said Sigurd. 'They will be too busy trying to save their houses. All we have to do is break the gate.'

They did get a surprise, though, when they reached it. As they approached, wary and prepared for another shower of missiles, they saw the ponderous double gates begin to move, slowly, as if only one man were trying to open them by himself.

By the time they reached the opening, a scruffy, fat little man had emerged. He was puffing and sweating, and was clearly in a great state of agitation. The spots on his face seemed to shine. He grabbed the first man to arrive.

'See? I am unarmed. I have opened the gate for you. Who is your leader?'

They were staggered to be addressed in Swedish. They understood; most of them had a working knowledge of it. They passed him on to Sigurd.

'I am a poor man, sir,' said Gunnar. 'A poor man. It is all the reeve's fault. We tried to tell him. We are all loyal to Earl Tostig. Is the Earl with you? If I could only speak with him . . .'

Sigurd looked down on him with disgust. 'Old man, make yourself scarce. My master does not take kindly to traitors. My advice is: do not let him find you. Now – stand aside.'

Magnus hated it. He hated every part of it.

He saw terror and panic. He saw envy and selfishness. He saw disputes and quarrels. Bewilderment and despair. Defeat and surrender. Blood and death.

He saw worse on his own side – greed, wanton destruction, pillage and of course lust. What made it worse still was that some of the offenders were from Sigurd's own men – men he had suffered with, been lonely with, trained with, travelled with, even been seasick with.

They had lost their boredom. Here was a place that had given them a fight. Worse, a town from which they had been withdrawn because their first onset had failed. To add to their shame, they were now inside the town because of the simple ruse of their commander, as if they could not be trusted to try again by themselves. To thrust these unwelcome thoughts to the back of their minds, they ran riot.

Magnus recoiled in disgust. If it had been a simple captured town, taken after a respectable siege, or surrendered after a decent interval, by agreement between the rival commanders, he might have been tempted to join in the pillage, if only to pay himself for all the discomfort and danger they had suffered. But not this way.

Worst of all was the fire. He looked in the faces of those who rushed past him and saw the faces of his own family and household. He heard a beam fall, and looked up instinctively, expecting to see it crashing from his own roof in his own hall.

When he heard someone screaming, he froze. It was Sigrid. There could be no doubt. It was not *like* Sigrid; it did not *remind* him of Sigrid. It *was* Sigrid.

Every other feature of what was going on around him vanished instantly from his consciousness. The sole purpose of his entire existence was suddenly concentrated into one thing; find the voice.

It screamed again, and he knew at least which side it was coming from. One building was set slightly back from the street. There was an archway, or the flame-flecked skeleton of it. So it was a wealthy house. The man who had lived here was important.

He hesitated in front of the arch. Before he risked his life, he had to be sure; he might not get a second chance.

The voice came again. He did not speak any English, but entreaty and desperation spoke all languages. As he braced himself to run under the lintel, another figure dashed past him. He got a blurred impression of a slight young man, with the faintest of beards. Certainly not Norwegian. Surprised and just a little shamed at his lack of decision, he followed.

The young man moved as if he knew the house. Magnus stayed close behind him. Wisps of burning straw floated all round them. A door jamb collapsed as they went past. Smoke filled their eyes and roaring filled their ears. Only the voice guided them.

There were two young women, not one. The one who had been screaming seemed to recognise the man with the beard. She had clearly been attempting to drag the second woman, who lay prone on the ground. This second figure bore no marks of burning, but had almost certainly been overcome by the smoke.

The young man attempted to lift her, but she was too well covered for his modest muscles.

'Here.'

Magnus pushed him aside and picked her up in his arms. The other girl lifted her head to look directly at him. She said a couple of words.

It was a face he would long remember – covered with grime, shining with sweat, tense with fear, but a lovely face. Ridiculously, he wanted, in the middle of it all, to put out a hand and smooth her cheek.

Instead, he said, with total lack of logic or sense, 'Are you all right?'

The girl sensed his question, and nodded. Then she said something that clearly referred to her unconscious companion.

Magnus continued to gaze in wonder. This was a noble girl indeed. She was clearly still able-bodied, and had stayed behind in this awful danger to try to rescue somebody else.

Coming out of his brief trance, Magnus looked at the other man for guidance. The man made for the back of the house, as if he knew exactly what he was doing. Magnus followed. The Saxon took the first girl by the hand. Magnus momentarily wished that he were not carrying the other one.

Out in an alleyway, the Saxon man, once again, knew where to go, and made off into a network of other narrow passages, where the flames seemed slightly less threatening. Again, Magnus followed.

This went on until they were on the very edge of the town. The Saxon stopped, and indicated a bench beside a horse trough. Magnus laid the girl on it. Rather to his relief, the Saxon bent over her, and tried to revive her. Magnus felt free to turn back to the first girl.

Once again, for want of anything else, he said, 'Are you all right?'

She nodded, and said something that, again, probably meant 'Thank you.'

Silence fell between them. Despite the awful noises around them, that silence was palpable. The unconscious girl stayed still. The other three exchanged glances, and remained completely at a loss.

At last Magnus made signs to indicate that he had to go. They nodded their understanding. The man made it clear that he would look after both of the others. Surprisingly, he had a few words of Norwegian.

Magnus made helpless gestures to the effect that he could do no more. He urged them to get out of the town as soon as possible. He had seen what was happening. The fair girl said 'Thank you' again.

Leofwine and Gyrth came in and sat down without any formality.

'Well?' said Harold. 'Are the Bedford men in?'

Gyrth nodded. 'Not as many as we had hoped.'

'Or as we were promised,' added Leofwine.

'As usual,' said Harold. 'If anyone ever sent as many as he had promised, I should suspect treachery.'

The brothers laughed. Harold waved a message.

'I have heard from Bernard.'

'And?'

'Scarborough has gone. Burned to ashes, apparently.'

Gyrth looked at Leofwine, and back to Harold.

'So it is York now?'

Harold tapped the message. 'It appears not. Bernard says he has gone to sea again – down the coast of Holdernesse.'

'So, if he wants York, he must come up the Ouse?' said Leofwine.

'Looks like it.'

'Will they be ready?'

'The northern host? I sincerely hope so. Bernard has stories of pretty large numbers – on both sides.'

'Surely even Morcar can now work out what they are going to do.'

'I hope that too.'

Gyrth reached for a loaf and broke off a lump on the edge of the table.

'Nothing from the Bastard, I suppose?'

'No. No change in the wind.'

Leofwine poured himself a drink. 'Well, there is one thing: as things are—'

'– or as they seem to be.'

'– or as they seem to be – we seem to have made the right decision.'

'Going north. I agree. With any luck, we should catch him on one foot.'

People moved about as if they were ghosts. Even when they passed each other, they did not speak. Some stooped to turn over some piles of charred debris, in the vain hope of salvaging something. Others merely stirred the ashes with their shoes. One or two stunned families were digging graves. A few pots and pans had survived intact. Everything of value had been

taken. The enemy had not used much energy in the killing –
they soon became bored with that – but they had used a great
deal of energy, and ingenuity, in sniffing out the valuables.

Vendel could hardly recognise his own house. After three
days, some parts of it were still too hot to touch. Lead pipes had
melted, and slumped at crazy angles.

Vendel searched wherever he could, hardly daring to contemplate what he might find. He had not seen his father since the first
attack. Every time he pushed open a blackened door or peered
past an empty threshold, he steeled himself to meet a blackened,
stiffened effigy of a human being. But there was nothing.

At the back of the house, he shovelled away yet more ashes,
and uncovered the trapdoor. Miraculously, it was intact. Perhaps
it had escaped the attention of the looters because so much
debris had fallen onto it.

In anticipation of this moment, he had procured a lamp. He
now lit it. He had also brought with him an iron lever. Setting
aside the lamp, he cleared the ashes and prised up the trapdoor.
Not many houses had cellars. It was one of his father's preten-
tious ways of letting the town know that his house was better
than nearly everybody else's.

Vendel lay down, shone the lamp, looked, got up again, and
shut the flaps.

Gunnar was intelligent, too, and shrewd. He had known that,
if he were to bury his treasure, the obvious place to bury it was
in the household cellar. By the same token, therefore, it was the
obvious place for a looter to look. So Gunnar had had another
one made, at the other end of the house. He had even had the
trapdoor made of old timber, and had gone to the extent of arti-
ficially ageing it, with dirt and the scars of a knife – to make the
ransackers think it was very old. Something brand new would
have given the game away at once. As it had happened, the ruins
and ashes had done the job even better than he could have
imagined.

Vendel turned and made for the second trap. He cleared debris for the second time. Taking the lamp, he carefully descended the crude, improvised steps. His eyes watered and his lungs complained. The actual home of the treasure was in yet another hole, on the far side, behind some wooden chests and rotting bales (something else to put off the scavengers).

The lid was up. Beside the lid lay his father. Beside the body lay an open box, full of the profits of thirty years of successful business. His father had no wound on him. No burn marks, either. It must have been the smoke that had killed him. Perhaps the debris falling from the roof beams had flung the trapdoor shut, and had proved too heavy for him to lift.

He had crawled to a corner, where perhaps the smoke was less dense, and there he had opened his treasure. For one last look? Or just to make sure it was all there?

Vendel would never know. However, his father, still speaking in death, had told him what he, Vendel, had always known. Each fist was bunched tightly round a clutch of gold and silver coins.

Chapter Nine

'God – you look terrible,' said Gyrth. 'Can you ride?'

Harold grimaced. 'It is a case of having to. I have wasted one day on the privy as it is. I can not afford another. The horse must take its chance.'

Gyrth shrugged. 'You are the King.'

Harold managed a grin with an effort. 'Never fear, brother. If I fall off and have to be put to bed, you will have to take on Hardrada yourself.'

Gyrth looked at Leofwine and looked back at Harold. 'What does Edith say?'

'Edith understands.'

'You have a treasure there, Harold. Edith always understands.'

'She does indeed. Shall we be on our way?'

As they passed under the town gates of Hertford, Harold reflected that the Great March had not begun very auspiciously. The London contingents were coming in late. Some of the City guildsmen had not been as forthcoming with their financial support as their promises had suggested. He shook his head. No matter how severe the crisis, it always took a monumental effort to separate town and city businessmen from their money. Their pockets were so deep that no king could get his hand down to the coins.

The horse commissioners had not found as many beasts as

they had hoped. For some mysterious reason, horses had suddenly become very rare in Middlesex and Essex. Half of those they had located seemed to have only three good legs apiece.

The weather had not helped. True, there was no southerly wind, so the Bastard was still immobilised. But it was still blustery and gusty, with a wayward but vigorous sun, and little cloud. Between them they made you hot when you marched, and cold when you stopped to rest.

And now this. Harold had had stomach upsets before. Everybody did. It was part of life, especially on campaign. But this was in a different class. More annoying, he had caught it in London of all places. He had struggled for a while, but the nausea and the weakness had done for him in the end. He fell off his horse and had to be carried to a bed. For a few hours, he was so bad that it crossed his mind to wonder whether it would carry him off to his Maker without any need of the attentions of Hardrada.

Luckily, Edith appeared from nowhere and sent the potion-pushers packing.

'He needs only two things.'

'What are they, lady?'

'Peace, and me.'

She was right, but it took time, and all that time Harold fretted. Edith would have none of it.

'If Hardrada sees you like this, he will laugh. Do you want to arrive at the battlefield on a litter?'

'But I must get there. Time is vital.'

'Then you will just have to march faster when you are better. Besides, I know you. You are waiting for news from Waltham.'

Which was true: he was. Brother Albert was no Father Bernard, but he was competent. Unfortunately, he had little to report. The best he could manage was the news that the

Bastard had concentrated nearly all his fleet at St Valéry on the Somme.

Well, that was something. They did at least know where somebody was. They knew, too, that that somebody could not move till the wind moved round to the south, or at the very least southeast. One worry less.

For the time being. Sooner or later the wind would change. And, in the meantime, Harold had to march two hundred miles, take Hardrada by surprise, and throw his Vikings into the North Sea. And get back south again.

So he would have to leave Brother Albert and Waltham. It was north, north, north. He was in a most un-Harold-like mood, and only Edith had the handling of him. He knew she was right, that he was too ill to function. For Edith it was a simple case of holding him close to her as long as she could.

When the worst signs of the flux had abated, she knew that *he* was right. He would have to go.

She enjoyed the familiar firmness of his body as he held her for a while.

'Kiss the children for me. We shall meet again, and soon.'

'This side of Heaven, I trust,' said Edith. 'God go with you, my love.'

Harold felt warm at the thought, as he set his face north on the old Roman road.

Edith could always be relied on not to make a fuss. Unlike his mother, the Lady Gytha. She had arrived at his headquarters totally unannounced. It was a mercy she had left his saintly sister behind . . .

For a while, there was a distinct danger that she and Edith would almost come to blows over the right to look after him. But for once Gytha had seen sense.

'Then just give me ten minutes of your valuable time.'

Harold glanced at Edith, who nodded and left the room. Harold pushed himself up into a sitting position.

'Now, Mother. What on earth is it that brings you here at a time like this?'

Gytha sat by his bed and folded her hands – not a good sign. Before she had been speaking two minutes, it had become clear that it was not concern for Harold that had brought her, but concern for Tostig.

'Just talk to him.'

'The time for talking is past,' said Harold.

'Of course it is, if you always say the same thing.'

'What do you suggest? That we talk about the weather?'

'No.' Rings were twiddled. 'Make him a new offer.'

When Harold heard what it was, he found it difficult to keep his temper.

'Mother, he is a traitor. He is a criminal. He was banished for being a bad earl. And you want me to ask him to come back and say all is forgiven?'

'He is your brother.'

'And what do I say to Morcar? That we want his earldom back to give to his enemy?'

Gytha waved a hand in impatience. 'Morcar is a boy. You said so yourself. Harold, all Tostig wants is justice – his earldom. Give him that, and he will be satisfied.'

Harold thought for a moment of Tostig's intrigues with almost every monarch, count and duke in northern Christendom; of his temper and his lurid threats; of his raids and his wastings; of his alliance with a man who was coming to try to wrest the crown.

He thought of Morcar, who would of course be sweetly reasonable and leave York like a lamb. He thought of Hardrada, who would say, 'Oh, what a shame!' and go home.

'Mother, Tostig will never be satisfied.'

Gytha stopped moving her ring and leaned forward.

'Please, Harold, just one more chance. Give him the chance . . .'

Leofwine came alongside now. 'Well? How are you?'

Harold nodded. 'I shall manage. What are the reports from Bedford and Huntingdon?'

Queen Ellisif had lost count of how many times she had stood on this quayside. This was the spot where Harald had left her. She could still see him waving his huge arm to tell the boat's crew to pull away to his great longship. Every piece of metal on it was burnished fit to dazzle. Every piece of canvas almost shone with newness. The wind had not yet taken the great sail to its fullest bloom, but the mighty black raven was clearly visible. The wind rippling the canvas made it look as if the beast were moving, almost flying. Anxious to be on its way.

Ellisif went through the scene yet again. Over the years, she had witnessed such spectacles many times. Was this one any different? Well, it was bigger, that was sure. Her husband had never before taken the leadership of such a host. But then he had never before been on such a quest. It was enough to bemuse any man.

Even Harald? Ellisif for once was not sure. Her famous second sight – or, as she would have it, her insight – did not come up with a clear answer.

Was he really bewitched by the sheer enormity of it? Or was he going to surprise them, as he so often had, by showing once again that he knew exactly what he was doing? Had he really calculated the odds carefully? Or was he being driven by the thought that this could be the last great adventure? After all, he was fifty.

Ellisif found herself looking back rather than forward. It had been a good twenty-odd years. More than that, if you took into consideration the length of time that her father had made them wait before he gave her away.

It had been far from a model marriage. As a Russian, and as the outsider, and as the woman, she had had to adapt much more than her husband. But Harald, for all his formidable personality, was fair-minded. Perhaps because he was such an individualist himself, he respected individuality, and was prepared to tolerate it in her. It did not make for easy relations sometimes, and their disagreements were loud and famous. But the mutual respect was there.

It had come out, too, in daughter Maria. As she grew to womanhood, it had meant not two liberated spirits in the royal household, but three. It was a lively ménage.

Then there had been the difficulty of Harald's second 'marriage', and his two sons by that union. Ellisif had had to adapt to that, too. But she understood that a Viking king needed sons, and Harald had brought them up to become good Viking monarchs. Even now Magnus had been left as regent in Norway in case anything untoward befell, and young Olaf was with his father on their way to the Great Adventure of England. Ellisif found herself being proud of them.

She was proud, too, of the fact that it was she, not her rival wife, whom Harald had brought with him. If he were to become King of England, it was she who would be crowned Queen. That was something worth swallowing a bit of pride for.

The more frequently she visited that quayside, the clearer it all became, and the more she appreciated her husband's sharpness of vision. He really did seem to have it all worked out – either way.

When Maria slipped a hand in the crook of her arm, she did not jump. It was almost as if she had been expecting it. Indeed, Harald had observed more than once that Maria was growing second sight like her mother. Servants certainly whispered among themselves that mother and daughter often seemed to know what each other was thinking.

Maria laughed gently. 'The girl on the dock thinking about her man?'

Ellisif smiled. 'Something like that.'

'All right for you; you have only one man to worry about. I have two – now.'

'Do you mind?' said Ellisif.

Maria shook her head. 'I would not have it any other way.'

'Nor I.'

They stood and gazed in silence for a while. Then a sudden thought struck the Queen. She turned to her daughter.

'Are you all right, by the way?'

Maria nodded vigorously. 'Never felt better.'

The Prior laid down his pen and put his fingers to his mouth. 'I am not so sure about that, daughter.'

Coelwen leaned forward. 'Please, Father. I shall go mad with this waiting if it goes on much longer. I must *do* something.'

The Prior looked directly at her. 'What do you have in mind?'

Coelwen stood up straight again. 'I can work.'

'You mean food?'

'Yes.'

The Prior shook his head. 'This is a holy house. For men. It would be unthinkable to have women in the refectory.'

'You have them in the kitchens,' said Coelwen.

'Yes – scullery maids. You are the daughter of a reeve. It would be most unseemly. You do not know what you are offering to do. It is not God's way; we must all know our place.'

Coelwen had an answer. 'God placed me in my uncle's kitchen when I was sent away from Scarborough. And I ran it – quite well, actually. Nobody complained about that.' (Well, only her aunt, and not very much.)

The Prior shook his head again. 'Menial work. You are not a menial.'

Coelwen met him head on. 'I am not talking about cutting bread or serving it. I am talking about *baking* it. And I know you have lost three good men from the kitchens to the fyrd. You need a baker.'

The Prior looked as if he were about to weaken. This girl was right. She was very determined too. And as a shepherd of souls he had some idea of what she was going through.

As if she were reading his thoughts, Coelwen added one more touch. 'Did not the Blessed St Benedict tell us that to work is to pray? *Laborare est orare*?'

The Prior stared. 'Where did you learn that?'

Coelwen smiled. 'Vendel. And *he* learned it from *you*.'

So Coelwen got her work, and Thora crept in at her apron tails.

It was not a total relief. Her thoughts were still a burden to her, but at least she now had other worries to compete with her concern about her father.

She had scarcely seen him since the moment when he had sent her to the house with firm instructions to lie low. The last of him was a glimpse over her shoulder – giving orders to the parties of water carriers after the alarm had been raised . . .

For an agonising time she had obeyed, held indoors by the noises outside – the rushing and shouting. When the flames began, she told herself that the streets were still more dangerous and that her father's advice was still sound. Certainly the noises were worse. By the time she had realised that there was greater danger inside, it was too late to get out.

Thora panicked and rushed blindly, only to be overcome by smoke. Coelwen had struggled to drag her back from the worst of it, and used her ample lungs to scream for help.

That was when the young Viking arrived. Vendel too . . .

She barely had the time to thank the soldier, and she had no idea if he understood what she said. All she remembered later was that he was rather good-looking.

It was the memory of Vendel that now took over, just as Vendel did himself. In hindsight she found herself marvelling at his coolness and resource. Somehow he looked older than she had ever remembered him. Perhaps it was the beard that Thora seemed to like so much. It was indeed growing thicker and longer.

At any rate it was Vendel who took control. It was Vendel who had found a wagon on the outskirts of the town. It was Vendel who knew where to hide until the Vikings had, mysteriously, departed. It was Vendel who made the decision to go back to the monastery.

The Prior, of course, was pleased to see him, but suitably sobered by his news.

'You must of course stay here. It is the only place. We must wait and pray.'

That did not satisfy Vendel.

'We are grateful, Father Prior. But I can not stay long . . .'

When he came to say goodbye Coelwen scarcely knew what to say.

'How do you thank somebody for saving your life?'

'And mine,' said Thora.

'I did what I had to do,' said Vendel. 'And I could not have done it without that Viking.'

'But you knew what to do when he had gone,' said Coelwen. 'So you helped to save our lives twice over.'

Vendel inclined his head by way of acknowledgement.

'Why are you going now? And *where* are you going?' said Coelwen.

'Scarborough.'

'What!'

'We both want news. I shall try to find your father.'

Coelwen suddenly felt tenderness to this unusual young man. It got the better of her. She almost simpered.

'You are doing this for me?'

Vendel brought her to her senses. 'Not entirely. There is my father, too.'

Coelwen pulled herself together. Of course. It was only to be expected. She found herself saying, 'Anything else?'

'Yes.'

'Oh?' There was no simper now.

Vendel began to put some food into a satchel. 'Scarborough will be in ruins. It will need rebuilding. Somebody will have to rebuild it. There is an opportunity waiting to be taken.'

Coelwen felt yet another change of mood.

So Vendel was a son of his father after all . . .

Coelwen dug her fingers into the dough. Nevertheless, Vendel had said he would come back with news. She did not know now what to make of him, but at least she knew he was more reliable than his father. He would be back.

And what, she wondered, had happened to that young Viking?

Bernard of Lorraine stalked through the streets of York on his way to the chancery offices. He did not quite know why, but he found it difficult to control a feeling of distaste, almost disgust.

It was at times like this that he saw his fellow man at his worst. One could almost smell the fear. Houses were being boarded up. Groups of worried people hastened out of alleyways and across squares, their faces set with a fixity of purpose that allowed for no niceties of everyday courtesy. Furtive clusters of shifty men stood at corners, gazing over shoulders, as if they were waiting for something to take advantage of. Wealthier citizens were loading carts and wagons, and harrying servants, grooms, valets, maids, scullions, ox-boys – anybody within swearing distance.

Rumours of Tyne and Tees and Cleveland were spreading as much panic as the very fires in those unhappy places. There was not a scrap of nerve or determination or resource to be seen. Scarborough was in ashes, but at least the reeve there had shown some spirit, had set an example, had demonstrated that there was an alternative to despair, flight or surrender.

Perhaps it was not all their fault. There was no sign of either of the northern earls. Obviously, you could not house an army in the city itself, but there seemed to be no sign at all of their presence. At times like this, people felt entitled to have at least a sight of their earl and master. They felt abandoned.

Bernard entered the chancery building, noting that there were only about half as many employees about as usual. He climbed the stairs to his office. Conrad rose when he came in. Bernard waved him to his chair.

Conrad pointed to Bernard's table. 'I have everything ready, Father.'

Parchment, pens, ink, knives, wax – everything was there. One of Conrad's great virtues, Bernard had noticed, was that he thought ahead. He did not simply wait to be given orders. On a day like this, with the latest couriers in from the coast, there would be a lot to say to the King, and Conrad had used his initiative to make himself useful. Bernard understood why the King thought so highly of him.

'Would you like some refreshment, Father?'

Good for the boy; he had thought of that, too. 'A cup of wine now. And perhaps something hot in an hour or so.'

Conrad was already on his way.

Bernard sat down, pulled a fresh sheet towards him, selected a pen (they were in perfect condition) and sat still for a moment.

If he were honest, the situation was dangerous, but it was not catastrophic. All those citizens who were sweating out there were missing the point. They had been so smitten with the horror of Hardrada's actions that they had given no time to pondering his purposes.

The King of Norway, who was an expert in these matters, was doing what all invaders did when they arrived to steal another country. They set out to create terror. Terror sapped morale. Weakened morale sapped strength. Lesser strength led to early defeat, at lower cost. It was sound business. It was creating your own odds. Bernard knew exactly what Hardrada was up to, and he had only had to look in the streets as he came to the office to see how well the man's methods were working.

But burning coastal towns and wasting the hinterland was one thing. Destroying the capital of an earldom was quite another. Hardrada had Tostig with him, and Tostig was an ex-Earl of Northumbria who wanted to get his earldom back, preferably in one piece. Certainly with his capital in one piece. Even from Hardrada's own point of view, it made sense to leave York untouched. If Hardrada wanted to exploit the differences between Northumbria and Wessex, between north and south, it would be bad policy to burn the very basis of the support he hoped to get against Wessex. Whether he coveted the whole kingdom or only half of it, he needed the goodwill of the Scandinavian part of it.

Hardrada, for all his terrifying reputation, was a shrewd campaigner, and fully understood the importance of staying close to the overall strategic objective. No calls of pride, jealousy, hate or anything else would get in the way of that. And it was to be hoped that Tostig, for all his spleen and spite, would not be so stupid as to allow such emotions to spill over.

Bernard dipped the pen:

Sunday, 17th September,
in the year of Our Lord one thousand and sixty-six

Majesty,
*   The wasting of the Norwegians has continued – from*
Scarborough, down the coast, and through Holdernesse. So

*he is not coming to York across country. Our observers
have noted the invasion fleet turning into the Humber. By
the time you receive this, my guess is that they will be
moored somewhere in the Ouse. He will get as close to York
as he can by boat, while at the same time leaving his fleet
close enough to the sea for speedy withdrawal in the event
of any disaster. It will call for fine judgement.*

The earls Edwin and Morcar—

Bernard poised his pen for a moment and looked at what
he had just written. Everybody always said 'Edwin and
Morcar'; they never said 'Morcar and Edwin'. And it was
Morcar who was Earl of Northumbria; it was Morcar who
commanded the army of the north. Odd. Was it a reflection
of Morcar's youth? But, then, Edwin was only two or three
years older. Was it that people thought that Edwin had a
longer head on his shoulders? Whichever way you looked at
it, it was still – well – odd.

Bernard applied his pen again.

'The earls Edwin and Morcar have assembled a worthy host,
and have encamped outside the city. The army is in good spirits,
especially after the success against Tostig –' even Bernard found
himself nearly putting 'Earl Tostig' from force of habit – 'on the
Lindsey coast.'

He made no mention of the situation in York, or of the news
he had heard of the councils of Edwin, Morcar, and their sister
the Queen. Similarly, Bernard, ever the traditionalist, found it
difficult to write 'Queen Gwen'.

He restricted himself to the military situation, and left the
King to read between the lines. What would Morcar do? What
was his attitude? What was the atmosphere in York? Were there
enough men in the northern host? When would the battle
come? Where?

Bernard sanded the letter and shook it.

Just then Conrad came back. He was followed, somewhat apologetically, by Wilfrid and Oswy.

Bernard looked up. 'What are you doing here?'

The two housecarls stood before him like two chastened choirboys. They looked at each other.

Bernard sensed that there was something on their conscience, and decided that it would be good for them to have a knuckle or two rapped.

He lowered his fearsome eyebrows. 'Well, come on. I do not have all day.'

At last Wilfrid took half a step forward.

'We are from the King's household, Father.'

'I can see that,' snapped Bernard. He had no intention of making it easy for them. 'I repeat, what are you doing here?'

Conrad, who was setting out Father Bernard's refreshment, allowed himself a furtive smile.

Wilfrid made a sort of feeble circling movement with his right hand.

'Well, you see, Father, it was rather unfortunate. Oswy's horse went lame.'

'Were you not doing training with the fyrd?'

Father Bernard seemed extremely well informed.

'Yes, Father. In several places.'

'Some of them quite near your home property. Is that right?'

After his initial shock at this further proof of the canon's omniscience, Wilfrid swallowed, and nodded firmly.

'Exactly, Father. And, having discharged our duties, and having a little time on our hands before having to join the main army, we thought . . . that is . . .'

'You slid off to make a fuss round your property in Grimsby.'

Oswy put in a word. 'Just outside, actually, Father. Great Coates and Little Coates.'

Bernard smiled drily. 'I doubt if a mile or two makes much difference to the general offence of being absent without leave.'

'Only one of us at first, Father.'

'Yes, you see, Father, everything was so quiet. You sort of get used to nothing happening, and you get to feeling that nothing is *going* to happen.'

Bernard nodded. 'I see. And the King was not there. So you took it upon yourselves.'

Wilfrid swallowed. 'We came, Father, as soon as we heard the news. We came here as fast as our horses would allow. As I said, Father, Oswy's went lame. Mine cast a shoe.'

Bernard folded his brow into a parody of pained sympathy. 'What a shame.'

'We thought York was the best place. For all we knew, His Majesty might be here already. But here we are, Father. And ready to serve.'

'Yes, indeed, Father. Just give us a commission. Anything.'

Bernard screwed up his eyes. 'As a matter of interest, are your properties intact?'

Slightly puzzled, Wilfrid replied warily. 'Yes, Father. It seems that the enemy has turned up the Humber. We are safe.'

'I am glad to hear it,' said Bernard.

Wilfrid and Oswy beamed, thinking that they were out of the danger area.

Bernard sat back.

'Well, rest awhile. You can ease your consciences and your bodies at one and the same time.' He indicated what he had been writing. 'It so happens that I have been writing to the King.'

Wilfrid pounced. 'Then let us take it to him, Father.'

Oswy was all eagerness. 'Yes, Father. We shall ride like the wind.'

Conrad poured some wine, still finding it difficult to stop smiling.

Bernard pushed the letter towards Conrad. 'Sealing and binding,' he said. 'As soon as you can.'

Conrad left, this time with a straight face. Bernard turned to Wilfrid and Oswy.

'Well, I have some more news for you. You will *not* take this letter.'

The two housecarls exclaimed in one breath. 'But Father!'

'You will not take it, because I want you to take the next one.'

They looked puzzled. 'The next one, Father?'

Bernard began to put away the inks and pens.

'What I am sending now is news of the wastings, of the approach. The King can guess a lot of it.'

Wilfrid frowned. 'Father?'

Bernard placed his hands palm down on the table and leaned back, savouring the moment.

'Because, my wayward housecarls, Hardrada will be outside the gates of York in a couple of days, and the Earls Edwin and Morcar will come out to meet him. And the King can not guess what the outcome of that will be. He will have to be told. He will have to be told quickly. He is on his way here from London, as you know. And you will have to find him.

'If you wish to ride on a mission to put yourselves in the King's good books, then I have just the thing for you. So you have two days to get your precious horses back into perfect condition.'

He gave them a final twitch of the eyebrows. The eyes bored holes.

'Do I hear any more excuses?'

'No, Father. No, no. We are at your service.'

'Day or night,' added Oswy.

'I am sorry about your father,' said Edric.

Vendel made a face and gave the slightest of shrugs. Was the boy more stricken by shame than he was by grief? It was difficult to say. He had given a most coherent account of Gunnar's fate.

Edric did not pursue the matter. He was grateful to Vendel for bringing the news he did. It was clear that his daughter owed her survival to his clear thinking and resource. The young Viking had carried off the dramatic rescue, but it was Vendel who had made the rest of the escape possible.

'I am in your debt for what you did for Coelwen.'

Vendel made another, even smaller, grimace.

It was curious. The slight figure, the poor physique, the lank hair – they were all the same. There were no dramatic gestures, no striking cadences in the voice. It all looked as unobtrusive as before, when he had stood silent while Gunnar had made his tactless pronouncements. Yet it was undeniable: Vendel was more impressive now. Edric took notice of him. And it was not just the beard, and it was not just because of what Vendel had done for Coelwen.

It was Vendel who resumed the conversation. 'What will you do now?'

Edric cast a hand about him. 'As you can see, I have the gate-house, but not much else.'

'So you will stay?'

Edric shook his head. 'No. There is no town – well, nothing to speak of. Hardly any people, either. It will be days, maybe weeks, before many venture back. Right now I have other business.'

'Coelwen.'

'Yes. But not so urgent now. Thanks to you, I know where she is, and I know she is safe. So long as I did not know, I felt I should stay here, to find out. But, now that I know, I can turn to other business.'

Vendel looked puzzled. Edric motioned to him to sit down.

'I tried to serve my King by staying here – when many saw fit to – to go away.'

335

He did not elaborate. Vendel ignored the implication. His father was gone. Gone, too, it seemed, from his mind, almost as if he wanted to put his father away somewhere.

'I can not serve my King here any more,' continued Edric. 'Well, not for a while. But I can serve him elsewhere.'

'York.'

'Yes. Sooner or later Hardrada will come to York or Earl Morcar will march out of York to face him. I wish to be there, and I have only a short time to get there.'

'To strike a blow.'

'If you like.'

Vendel nodded to show he understood. 'Will you go to see Coelwen first?'

Not the over-familiar 'Col', as his father had done.

Edric shook his head. 'I do not have the time. The battle can come soon. It will take me two days to get there. I am not even sure yet that I can find a horse. I can not go to see her.'

Edric paused and looked at Vendel.

'But you could.' He paused again. 'Would you do me this last favour? Tell her I am well?'

Vendel stood up, bowed formally, and put his hand across his chest.

'Consider it done, Edric.' He had never addressed him like that before.

Edric opened his mouth to say something, but Vendel went on. 'Perhaps, when this is all over, we can work together to build a new town. Maybe even build a relationship better than my father's.'

Vendel lowered his head a little. 'My father – my father was not good at relationships.'

Edric knew how much that admission must have cost him. He put out his hand, and Vendel took it firmly.

'And this time,' said Edric, smiling, 'tell her that she has to stay there.'

*　　*　　*

'All shipshape, Sig?'

Sigurd flopped down beside Ketil Splitnose. 'Oh, shut up.'

'It was only a joke, Sig,' said Ivar.

Sigurd swore, and reached out for a piece of meat on a spit.

'Do not talk to me of ships any more – do you understand?'

Ivar and Ketil exchanged glances, then looked round at the others. They were answered by grimaces and shrugs. This was not like Sigurd. He was the one who, normally, lifted others out of bad humour.

In the journey south from Orkney, Sigurd had coaxed, chivvied, encouraged, made jokes, and generally made the trip as bearable as any sea voyage down a chilly, windswept coast could be. There had been some excitement at the early prospect of burning and looting, of some action. Maybe even profit, though there was not much room on board to store one's pickings from a burning house.

So they had entered, and left, the mouths of the Forth, the Tyne and the Tees, and caused general havoc around Cleveland. But the excitement soon wore off. There was next to no resistance, so there was little chance of feeling the satisfaction of a successful encounter. They felt they were throwing blows at an enemy who was not there. Where was the pride in making civilians run away?

Scarborough had at last shown some spirit, and, just when things were beginning to look interesting, Hardrada had called off the assault, and sent some of them puffing up hillsides to light bonfires.

All the time, Sigurd had kept their spirits up with black jokes, lurid imprecations, and the usual bawdy barrack-room humour.

'Just wait till we get to York, lads. Now there is a city for you. That will tickle your fancies.'

Nobody had ever been to York, and neither had Sigurd, and the words were meaningless, but it was a joke, and it sounded good, and they laughed.

They continued to laugh when Hardrada turned the fleet into the great estuary, which apparently was called 'Oomber', according to the few prisoners who were careless enough to get caught. Sigurd's jokes carried them up the River Ooze, or something like that.

They anchored near a village called Riccall. The know-alls said it was only a stone's throw from York itself. So they unloaded the ships with a will, and made them stable and secure, and set up camps, and foraged for firewood and did the usual things needed for sheltering and feeding several thousand men.

The talk was big that night about some real action, and some proper loot. Many crews had managed, miraculously, to preserve some drink, and there were the usual slurred verses and braggart speeches round the fires on the shingle.

The bad heads in the morning had to cope with the bad news. They were not to be allowed to march on York. Well, not all of them. A significant proportion of the army was to stay behind to guard the ships.

This was typical Hardrada. He was always appearing to fall short of his legend. He was not dashing at all; he was forever being careful, prudent, wary, taking precautions so as to have a way out if things turned nasty.

Sigurd swore. 'This is our reward for doing a good job.'

He waved at the regular lines of longships drawn up, made stable, held fast, almost ghostly in the absence of disarray.

Magnus once again found himself admiring Sigurd's ability. He was one of those rare people who, no matter what they had been charged to do, no matter how little they knew about it, no matter how much they disliked it, always managed to make an efficient job of it.

Hardly surprising that Ket had made the joke about being 'shipshape'.

Hardly surprising, either, that Sigurd had reacted as he did. Not surprising to Magnus at any rate. Because Sigurd took him into his confidence so often, he, Magnus, knew how much this adventure meant to him. The rest of the company – Ketil and Ivar and Tore and the rest – enjoyed the jokes, admired the leadership, responded to the demands. Only Magnus saw the burning ambition underneath.

Sigurd was able – very able – and knew it. He wanted so badly to have the chance to demonstrate it. The more so now that he had won the heart of the Princess Maria. He had to prove it not only to the world, but to Maria. And to her father. For all that he was a few years younger than Sigurd, Magnus could see that it was a sign of lingering immaturity.

Confronted suddenly with this latest order from the King, he had reacted almost like a boy who had been denied a promised treat.

'Caretaker! Housekeeper! What does he think we are?'

'Does it not occur to you,' said Magnus, 'that what you have been charged with is in fact the most important job of all? You are the anchor. You are the insurance. If you fail, the whole enterprise is doomed.'

Sigurd would not be comforted.

'Who does he think we are?'

'He has left his son with you. He has left Thorfinn's son, too.'

Sigurd stared. 'Olaf? Paul? What chance have I got? They outrank me.'

'Rubbish,' said Magnus. 'Hardrada knows perfectly well that they are too young for proper command. If anything – God forbid – should happen, it is you who will take charge.'

Sigurd spat. 'Nothing will happen; that is the trouble. Hardrada will march to York. He will defeat Morcar if he has an army. And, when Harold arrives from London, he will defeat him, too. He will take York.' He stabbed himself in the chest with his finger. 'And we shall not be there.'

Magnus fell silent. Was it possible that just a little more of the Hardrada charm was wearing away? Yet Sigurd had had more chance than all of them to observe this great man. The great man's own wife, Queen Ellisif, had reminded him time and again that with Hardrada test came before trust. This was a good test too; it was combined with a compliment. It meant that he was giving him a worry that he did not dare to give to any other junior. Not even his own son.

In short, was Sigurd failing to appreciate the great lesson that the King was so often dinning into them: always keep in sight the overall strategic objective?

Magnus leaned back against the hull of a ship and shut his eyes. While it was so quiet, he had time to contemplate a face. A handsome face. Not a tortured face. The memory of Sigrid was beginning, at last, to lose its dimension of horror. This new face was company now, not a ghost, not a demon. It warmed; it did not chill. And it had said 'thank you'. At least that was what he thought it had said.

Gwen paused at the threshold and looked round.

'Where is Morcar?'

'Gone,' said Edwin.

Gwen came forward, giving her gloves to a maid. 'Already? And you are not with him?'

'I shall be with him, Gwen, never fear. But there are many things to see to before I leave York.'

'Things he has overlooked.'

'Something like that.'

The Queen arranged her gown carefully and sat down. A curt nod dismissed the girl.

'So he can not wait, eh?'

Earl Edwin of Mercia made a rueful face. 'I am afraid not. You did too good a job on him.'

Gwen nodded. 'It is as we feared, then. He is too anxious to get to grips.'

Edwin nodded back. 'I shall do what I can. There are a hundred things we can arrange. It is simply a question of whether we have enough time to arrange them.'

Gwen sighed. 'I take it we must engage?'

'We have no choice. Our scouts tell us he has landed at Riccall.'

'How far away is that?'

'Barely nine miles. Once he starts, he can be here in three hours.'

'But he has not started.'

'Not yet. Not even Hardrada can disembark an army and get it on the move in the twinkling of an eye.'

'You are sure he is coming here?'

Edwin looked surprised. 'Where else would he go? Why else did he come right up the Ouse to Riccall? York is the prize. York is the lever he wants to put under England and prise Harold out.'

'Morcar understands this?'

Edwin smiled. 'Yes, I think he understands.'

Gwen sighed. 'Bleak, is it not?'

'Not that bad, Gwen. We have good troops. They are well fed and prepared. They have been waiting for this test.'

Gwen pounced. 'And you ought to be commanding, Edwin.'

Edwin shook his head. 'Morcar is the Earl of Northumbria, not I. It is his earldom. And our brother is brave, if nothing else.'

Gwen looked glum. Edwin patted her on the shoulder. 'It is not that bad, sister. I shall be there. We shall each command half the army. We have the best position available. They have to approach us between a river and a marsh. We have a suitably narrow front. We can not be outflanked. They have to come to us. And they have to get here. All we have to do is wait just outside York.'

Gwen made a face. 'Yes – all.'

Edwin managed a smile. 'Whether you like it or not, it is what we have. There is no other choice. He is the invader. It is our country. He is the sinner. And Tostig is the traitor. We have God on our side.'

Gwen came as near to a grunt as a lady could allow herself. 'Then I hope God will know where His duty lies.'

> *21st September, in the year of Our Lord,*
> *one thousand and sixty-six*

Majesty,

It is my sad duty to tell you that York has fallen.

I write this in secret, because the city fathers have formally surrendered their city. Even now, the agents of Hardrada patrol the streets, seeking out the hostages who have been named by your brother Tostig [he did not feel the temptation this time to call him 'Earl Tostig'] to which the city fathers have agreed.

It was particularly easy for the enemy to seize the most important citizens because Tostig, naturally, knew exactly who they were, and, in many cases, where they lived. There will be more to be taken tomorrow, and arrangements have been made to hand them over at an agreed spot outside the city precincts. This will take place on Monday, the 25th September.

I understand that Hardrada has given hostages himself, as a pledge, presumably, that he would not put the city to the fire, as he has done everywhere else ever since landing.

As he wrote these lines, Bernard allowed himself a smug smile, as if to say, 'What did I tell you? York is safe. *He* wants it, too.' It had not stopped the panic, but it had eased it. One could at least now pass the streets without tripping over hastily loaded wagons at every corner. He dipped his pen again.

You must not blame the Earls Edwin and Morcar for this disaster. They fought valiantly, if, in Morcar's case, a little too eagerly. They are young, and did not have Your Majesty's experience. From what I can gather, Morcar charged early, and made inroads in the right wing of the enemy army. But Hardrada was able to hold Edwin on his left, and gradually turn Morcar's flank. Once he had done that, Morcar's line began to fold in on itself, and was pinned against the marsh on that side. Edwin was unable to help, engaged as he was on the river side of the field.

Casualties were heavy on both sides, but it was the enemy who held the field at the end of the day. They boasted that Earl Morcar had been killed, but I am pleased to report that this is not so.

He and Earl Edwin are, as I write, struggling to re-form the survivors, but they are scattered over a wide area on both sides of the field, and they will have to re-group to the north of the city, because Hardrada now controls the southern approaches.

It is for this reason, among others, that the city fathers decided that surrender was the only option. Further resistance would have provoked the very disaster they feared above all others, and they had no idea how far away you were – or are.

If it is of any help in your coming to a decision, the enemy appear to be under the impression that the reason for Morcar's resistance was his conviction that you were in the south, over a hundred miles away at the very least, maybe even in London.

343

When Bernard showed this despatch to Conrad, the boy's eyes lit up as he read the last paragraph.

'Then—'

'Exactly,' said Bernard.

'Then why do you not put it in the despatch?' said Conrad.

'Because I have the highest regard for the King's military instincts,' said Bernard. 'He will be perfectly capable of reading between the lines. And, if he does not work it out, you can tell him.'

Conrad stared. 'What do you mean?'

'Because you will be carrying this message,' said Bernard. 'You once told me you knew how to ride. Now is your chance to prove it. I suspect the King will be approaching Lincolnshire by this time. At any rate he will be on the old Roman road above Huntingdon, maybe even nearer. You will find him and give him this, in time for him to reach here before Hardrada even suspects he has left London.'

A flush of excitement came to Conrad's cheeks. He turned to go. Bernard held up a hand.

'Not quite that fast. This message has to be sealed and bound. And made waterproof. We must also make two more copies.'

'Copies?'

Bernard fixed a gimlet eye. 'Young man, you do not suppose we are going to let you ride all over the north by yourself, do you? If something happens to you, your escorts will each have a copy.' He smiled to himself. 'Not that they will understand a word of it. But they will keep you out of trouble.'

'Who are they?' asked Conrad.

Bernard smiled again. 'Two of the King's housecarls – Wilfrid and Oswy. I am sure you know them by now.'

'Are they ready?' asked Conrad, all bustle and eagerness again.

'I doubt it,' said Bernard. 'They do not even know yet. Perhaps you would enjoy the pleasure of telling them.'

Conrad made for the door a second time. Again Bernard called him back.

Eye and eyebrow focussed together. Conrad almost felt the heat.

'I am sure I do not have to emphasise the importance of what I am commissioning you to do.'

Conrad drew himself up proudly. 'No, Father, you do not.'

'Good. I shall give you the necessary commissions to commandeer any horses and food you need. Come back when you are dressed for the road and I shall have them ready.'

Conrad nodded. 'Father.'

'Ride, then. Ride as if your life depended upon it. Indeed, all our lives may depend upon it.'

'Any complaints now, Alfred?'

Alfred grunted, and eased out his legs. 'Well, at least we are going in the right direction.'

'How do you know? Can you read a map?'

Alfred glared. 'No. But I know about the sun.'

'You mean that it is hot?' Owen and Llew pretended to exchange admiring glances. 'Bright lad, our Alfred. He has worked out that it has been a hot day. Tell us some more, boyo.'

Alfred did not rise this time; he was getting used to the teasing. 'You know what I mean. All right. Prove me wrong.'

Llew shook his head. 'No, lad. There is no arguing with you. Now – tell us where the next stop is.'

Alfred leaped to show off his knowledge. 'Lincoln.'

Owen and Llew clapped in appreciation. 'Well done. You will be shaking hands with Hardrada before you know it. Eh, lads?' He looked around the group at the fire.

Alfred took the bait. 'You mean Hardrada is in Lincoln?'

'No. But he is not far off. It is in the air that he is in the Humber.'

Alfred frowned. 'Humber?'

'The river mouth that leads to York.'

'So he will take York?'

'Not if Earl Morcar can stop him. And Earl Edwin.'

'Will they do it?'

Owen shook his head. 'I gather news, boyo, not prophecies. It depends on a lot of things.'

'Such as?' said Alfred.

'Well,' said Owen. 'Such as numbers. Who has the bigger army?'

'Who has?'

'No idea. Then there is the question of the ground. Is it good for fighting? Whom does it favour?'

'Well, *whom* does it favour?'

'I do not know. And who has the stronger spirit?'

'Who does?'

'I do not know. And where does the goddess of luck bestow her favours?'

'Luck?'

'Oh, yes. Even the best generals agree that one needs to be lucky.'

Alfred spread his hands. 'So nobody knows anything, and it is all up to luck?'

Owen jumped in as if he had been waiting for this. 'That is about right, Alfred.'

There was a general chuckle.

A fyrdman patted Alfred on the shoulder. 'Not even the King knows much more than we do. He simply has to be a good guesser.'

'And a lucky one,' said somebody else.

'And let us hope he has his wits about him on the day. That he has had a good sleep the night before.'

Owen jumped in again. 'A funny thing you should say that, lads. Because I think we might have a slight advantage there. They say Hardrada has bad dreams the night before a battle.'

Alfred sneered. 'Get on. How do you know that?'

Owen looked knowing. 'Oh, you hear things. They are in the air.'

'Such as?'

Owen leaned forward eagerly. 'All about trolls and demons and a slavering witch who rides on the back of a wolf. And this wolf had a dead warrior in its jaws.'

Alfred fell to listening in spite of himself. 'God!'

'And then,' said Owen, sensing a captive, 'when the wolf had devoured the blood-soaked corpse, the witch dropped another body into its jaws. And another. And another.'

Alfred's jaw fell open.

'And then,' said Llew, 'there came a flock of eagles and ravens, and one of them perched atop the masthead of every ship in his fleet.'

'Just like the great raven on his battle banner,' said Owen. 'Remember? The Landwaster.'

Alfred snapped himself out of the spell. 'Get away. You make it up as you go along.'

Owen sat back. 'I hope you say that, Alfred, when you meet him. Eight feet tall if he is an inch. An axe that no other man can lift, never mind swing. And over him and all round him, swirling in the wind, five ells of the great white banner with the black raven and the bloody claws – the Landwaster.'

A fyrdman bent towards Alfred. 'When you see that, lad – and you will, pretty soon – you will wish you were here listening to Owen's stories.'

Wilfrid never forgot that ride.

Before they had gone a mile he realised that Conrad was twice the horseman that he and Oswy were. That was the first surprise.

The second was when they found that it was *Conrad* who was encouraging *them*, not the other way round. They had taken one look at his soft, pink cheeks, slender figure, and, of course, the tonsure, and had jumped to the obvious conclusion.

By noon, he was not only encouraging them; he was chivvying them. More than once Wilfrid exchanged flushed faces with his cousin. They had no choice but to obey. They were on the King's commission. After the scalding castigation by Father Bernard, they could do nothing else. Whatever Conrad said or did, they had to accept and make the best of it. But it was clear on that ride that a natural leader was emerging before their eyes.

When they stopped to exchange horses, he paced restlessly, while Wilfrid and Oswy flopped on benches and wolfed some food. When an officious local sergeant or pompous clerk showed signs of lack of co-operation or plain bumbledom, they marvelled at Conrad's flow of language, at his absolute command of the situation, at his blistering authority. Commissions were waved in the air. Dire threats were uttered. Sheer energy swept all obstacles away. As Wilfrid said many times afterwards to anybody who would listen, 'He would have brushed aside an earl.'

When they finally reached Lincoln, there were similar attempted delays. It was the same as before. Sentries, sergeants, officers, senior clerks, chaplains – all wilted before the storm of urgency and the total confidence. Within minutes of the first challenge at the gates of Lincoln, Conrad was in the King's presence.

Harold sent Wilfrid and Oswy to get some food and rest, and told Conrad to sit down.

A clerk came forward and held out his hand for Bernard's despatch. Conrad, all sweat and dust, hesitated. Harold sensed the situation at once. He motioned the clerk to retire to the end of the hall, and turned back to Conrad. For a moment they looked at each other.

Then Harold smiled. 'I daresay, after all the trouble you have taken to bring it, you would like the pleasure of reading it to me.'

Coelwen stared at her father.

'But Vendel told me you were going to York.'

'True. I was.'

Coelwen pulled her father by the hand, till they were both sitting down. Her chest was still heaving with excitement and relief – and shock. Each sat for a while, each simply savouring the sight of the other. The Prior, who had brought Edric to the kitchen, slid quietly away. They deserved this moment. If things went badly, they might not get another.

At last Coelwen spoke. 'Vendel told me everything.'

Edric smiled. 'I find myself thinking more of that young man each time I meet him.'

Thora, who was watching from a discreet distance, thought so too. The beard was looking more fetching every time she saw it.

'So you decided not to go,' said Coelwen.

Edric continued gazing at his daughter. 'You know perfectly well why.'

Coelwen kissed his hands. Then a thought struck her. She looked up sharply. 'Will you go now?'

Edric shook his head. 'Not yet.'

'Not yet?'

'It is in the air that the battle has already taken place.'

'So you will stay here?'

Edric hesitated. Coelwen pounced.

'Surely you can do nothing now. Victory or defeat, there is nothing you can do now.'

Edric let go of his daughter's hands and sat back. 'Well, that is not so sure.'

Pain began to return to Coelwen's face. 'What do you mean?'

'It has been either a victory or a defeat,' said Edric. 'If it has been a victory, then I must return and begin to rebuild Scarborough.'

'And I shall come with you,' said Coelwen firmly.

'But, if it has been a defeat – the King will come sooner or later to put that right.'

Coelwen groaned. 'Oh, no—'

'So there will be a second battle – somewhere – sometime soon.'

'But you do not have to go. You are a reeve. You are not in the fyrd. You are over age.'

'That is not the point,' said Edric.

'You did not fight the first battle. You came to see me. I am still here. Do I not matter?'

Edric smiled. 'Of course you matter. That is why I came. If I had gone straight to York and fought that first battle and something had happened to you, I should never have forgiven myself. But I know now that you are all right. You are safe here. And you have Vendel.'

'Vendel.' Coelwen found herself shrugging. Then wondering. Surely her father was not beginning to think what she feared he was thinking. How could she explain? It was stupid, impossible. She had had one glimpse of a handsome face, topped by a mane of wild blond hair, chainmail and muscles, sweat and dirt. Not much to go on. And how could she begin to explain to her father? And he was one of the men who had burned her father's town. She would never see him again.

Now it looked as if, having had her father by some miracle restored to her, she was about to lose him again. In a mist she realised that her father was talking.

'Col, listen. When it was a case of my duty, I put Scarborough first. That was why I sent you away, because I knew that, if you were there, I could not have done my duty. You came back, and I

350

loved you for it. When the attack came, I did what I could to protect you, while, once again, I did my duty. Luckily for both of us, Vendel rescued you – he and some young Viking he spoke of.

'When he came to me and told me you were here, I knew I had to come and see you. I had no town to protect any more. All I had – or thought I had – was the chance to play the young warrior. But I found that love was stronger than adventure. I am glad I did.'

Coelwen's eyes glowed. Her father swept on, in case she interrupted.

'Now I have seen you. And I know that you are safe. I have no power to make you any safer. I have done all that a father can. Perhaps you will allow me now to indulge an ageing man's desire to play the young warrior just once more, and serve my King in the best place of all – at his side.'

As always, when her father talked like that, Coelwen knew she had no answer.

Edric leaned forward, kissed her on the forehead, and tweaked her nose.

Harold heard Brother Eustace before he came in.

'Please. Please God – your arm. I can not put one foot before the other.'

The door opened, and Eustace made his dramatic entrance, each elbow supported by a puffing housecarl. His legs were splayed, almost as if he still had a horse between them. His face was grey with fatigue. Both the chins and the bags under the eyes looked as if they had been stuffed by a poultry chef. They sagged and wobbled. His brow shone with sweat.

Harold inclined his head towards a chair, and the housecarls eased him down on to it.

'Careful, now, for the love of God.' He pulled the most terrible faces. 'So tender. So sore.'

He barely acknowledged the presence of the King. Harold leaned his elbows on the table, and cupped his hands under his chin. He watched while the housecarls assembled Eustace into as near one piece as was humanly possible at the time. Then he nodded for them to dismiss. They bowed and withdrew.

Harold himself poured a drink, and held it out to Eustace. With the other hand, he beckoned for the message.

Eustace, still puffing with difficulty, extracted it from the folds of his habit.

'I can tell you its contents, Majesty, if you wish. You can confirm them afterwards when your clerk reads it to you.'

A servant placed a plate within arm's length. Without waiting for permission, Eustace reached out and took some pieces. He ate and drank almost simultaneously. Harold waited patiently, a faint smile well evident. He passed the message to the clerk, motioning to him to wait.

At last Eustace felt up to the task. 'Majesty – Majesty – as I hope for eternal salvation – a ride unparalleled – unmatched – in the annals—'

Harold decided that enough was enough. He put up a hand. Eustace paused.

'Where was Bernard when he wrote this?' He indicated the despatch.

'Still in York, Majesty. But for how long I could not say. He is in hiding.'

'Very well. What is his news?'

'York has fallen, Majesty.'

'I know that. What has happened since?'

'Hostages have been taken.'

'I know that, too.'

'But there will be more. The first hostages were taken from the city. The second group will be taken from the county. And the King of Norway will offer hostages of his own. One hundred and fifty from each side.'

Harold began to take notice. This was the real news. So Hardrada was also offering hostages. It did not look therefore as if York itself was in any danger. Possibly Tostig's influence. Or even perhaps the other way round; if Tostig was under one of his red clouds, it would take Hardrada to stop him unleashing his spite on his own city.

'When will they be exchanged?'

'On Monday, Majesty, the twenty-fifth of September.'

Harold glanced at Gyrth and Leofwine to the side of him.

'Two days,' said Gyrth.

'Where?' said Harold to Eustace.

'A bridge. Over the River Derwent. At Stamford.'

Harold threw a question at Gyrth with his eyes.

'About nine or ten miles east of York. There is a good road.'

'Why not stay in York?' said Leofwine.

'Supplies, I imagine,' said Harold. 'He needs to feed his army. And they can bring supplies up the river.'

Harold looked at Eustace again. 'Did they give any sign of military preparations?'

Eustace shook his head. 'No, Majesty. Indeed, they are celebrating already. Father Bernard reports that there are very few scouts out, on either side of the city. He has heard rumours that games are planned after the hostages have been handed over.'

Eustace sat, still puffing and blowing, till Harold dismissed him. When he had staggered out, with more pitiful groans, Harold turned to his brothers.

'Are you thinking what I am thinking?'

Leofwine grinned. 'He has no idea we are here.'

Gyrth smacked a palm on the table. 'We have done it.'

Harold nodded with great decision. 'Complete surprise.'

'All we have to do is get to Tadcaster by tomorrow night.'

'From here, only about twenty-five miles. And a good road all the way.'

Leofwine grinned again. 'Tadcaster to York by mid-morning. The enemy by mid-afternoon.'

Gyrth smacked the table again. 'And we have him. We shall give him something to have games about.'

Harold poured three drinks and passed them round.

'Tadcaster it is, then, brothers, by tomorrow night. And on Monday –' all three touched cups '– the bridge at Stamford.'

Chapter Ten

'God Almighty!'

'If you moan about your precious feet once more, Alfred, we shall throw you in the next river.'

'Well, they hurt.'

'Of course they do; we have done nearly twenty-five miles. But at least we are going somewhere definite at last.'

'How do you know?' said Alfred. 'They have deceived us before.'

'Use your eyes, Alfred. Use your common sense. Look at the King. Look at the earls, the housecarls. Have you seen them with an expression like that on their faces before?'

'We have the whole army with us, boyo,' said Owen. 'They do not bugger themselves about, just marching to and fro. Oh, no – we are going somewhere all right.'

'Where?'

'York is my guess,' said Owen.

'Stands to reason,' said Llew. 'Hardrada has invaded. He has won a victory. Of course he will go to York. It is the capital.'

'It is Tostig's old capital,' said Alfred, who relished any chance to show off his knowledge.

'All the more reason why they should go there.'

'You mean a siege?'

'Could be.'

Alfred pondered this for another quarter of a mile.

'But there has been a battle. Everyone says. And the northern earls have been beaten. It is even said that York has surrendered.'

'True, O wise one,' said Llew. 'So it is not Hardrada who besieges Edwin and Morcar; it will be us who besiege Hardrada.'

Alfred whistled. 'Have any of you been in a siege before?'

'Always a first time.'

'So you have no idea, either,' said Alfred.

A fyrdman sighed wearily. 'How many times do we have to tell you, Alfred? When the war actually starts – battle or siege – nobody knows what is going to happen. It is always what you do not expect. You will find out soon enough.'

'And then you will wish you had not,' said somebody else.

'How long do we have to wait, then?'

'Not long, son. Tadcaster tonight. Hardrada tomorrow.'

'How do you know?'

'Saints alive, Alfred. Do you not hear anything that is in the air? It is all round you.'

Alfred opened his mouth to ask another question, but the fyrdman headed him off.

'Tell us a story, Owen, for God's sake. It will take his mind off his feet. Anything to get us there. It can not be far now.'

Before Alfred could argue, Owen launched himself into his next performance.

'Did you ever hear about the mad Vikings?'

Alfred fell for it. 'Mad Vikings?'

'Oh, yes,' said Owen. 'They used to say that if a man saw a ship full of Vikings coming for him, he could count the remainder of his life in hours. But, if he saw a mad Viking coming for him, his life would be a matter of minutes.'

'Why? If he is a lunatic?'

'I do not mean soft in the head,' said Owen. 'I mean crazed, wild, like a raving bear. They catch some kind of fever. Some men blame poison, which inflames the brain. A mushroom, it is

356

said. They go fighting mad; they care not what happens to them. They howl and they roar. They bite their shields. They have the strength of ten. They can fight on much longer than ordinary men. They are so possessed that they strike anything in their path, regardless of whether he is friend or foe.'

Llew timed his entry perfectly. 'They go berserk. That is what they are called – "berserks". They are possessed – by the gods. No ordinary weapon can injure them. They can not be wounded by fire or sword. "Berserks".'

'Bareserks?' said Alfred warily.

Owen nodded emphatically. 'You have it, son. They say "berserk" means "bare shirt". In other words, they have thrown off their mail and fight without protection. "Berserk". God save you if one of them comes after you.'

It certainly drove all thought of his feet out of Alfred's head for the rest of the day.

Morcar spoke with bowed head. 'My lord – I do not know what to say.'

There was no bravado now no vaunting about his sending Tostig off from Lindsey in craven flight. No attempt to put a bold shine on what had happened at Fulford. No arrogant tilt of the head. No tug at the little beard. There was no other way to view it except as a total defeat.

As the news filtered in from all sides, it had become clear that, though the Viking losses had been heavy, English losses had been much heavier. Earl Edwin's right wing had been pushed back, and driven against the River Ouse. There they had sold their lives dearly, drowned, or slipped away to York with their tails down. Morcar's left flank, after an initial successful drive, had been caught up in a maelstrom of action, in which it had been almost impossible to give commands. With virtually no battle experience, let alone command experience, Morcar had had to watch the battle slipping inexorably out of his hands barely an hour after it had started.

Hardrada, thanks to his great presence of mind, huge experience, and unconquerable confidence, had been able to outflank Morcar's half of the army. He then drove it back on itself, and pushed it into a position similar to that of Edwin on the other side of the field. Instead of a river, Morcar's men drowned in a great ditch, and, beyond it, in a huge marsh. Survivors were reporting that the pursuing enemy were walking dry-shod on the backs of the bodies.

'You did what you could,' said Harold. 'Nobody will blame you for what has happened.'

Gyrth and Leofwine looked at each other. They could think of no other man who, in such circumstances, would have offered such a generous verdict.

'How is Edwin?' asked Harold.

Morcar lifted his head. 'Well enough. But he needs time to heal. He can not take the field at present. He sends his excuses, but—'

Harold waved it away. 'I understand.'

'Do we have any men from your host still fit for action?'

Morcar showed the pain once more. 'A few hundred perhaps.' He waved his hands ineffectually.

There was a pause. Morcar summoned up a great effort. 'If I can be of service, my lord.'

Harold looked at him. The boy was completely demoralised. He had been thrust into a situation that had turned out to be quite beyond his strength, spirit and experience. He was washed out. No use to any campaign, certainly not in any active capacity. Harold partly blamed himself.

But this young earl had to be given some role. He could not be pushed aside completely. It would destroy him. His pride and his honour were shaken enough. If Harold ignored him now, they would be in tatters.

'How many horses have you left?'

Morcar looked surprised at the turn of conversation, but answered readily enough.

'Several hundred. In York. Our housecarls dismounted before marching out to Fulford, and left them in stables in the city.'

Harold clapped his hands. 'Good. Many of our horses are near exhaustion. Now – what I want you to do is get them out to my camp here in time for our start at dawn tomorrow. I want as many housecarls mounted as possible. Can you do it?'

Morcar looked puzzled. Harold explained. 'It means working all night while my men rest. And nobody will work unless they have authority driving them. I need your rank as earl to get them moving and to keep them at it. I repeat, can you do it?'

Morcar drew himself up. 'If I have to whip every man personally, you will have your horses.'

'Good. I will give you two of my best housecarls, Wilfrid and Oswy, to help you with the allocations. Have no fear for their willingness.' He smiled. 'They are in disgrace, and will do whatever you ask. Oh – and a young cleric called Conrad. Wilfrid will tell you how to get hold of him. We have discovered that he has shown great gifts at getting action out of reluctant servants. Conrad. Do not forget.'

Gyrth and Leofwine exchanged glances again. Their brother had, with one stroke, helped to restore a young earl's broken spirits, arranged for a vital component of the army to be delivered, and had done it without adding to the tiredness of his own men. He had given two of his misbehaving housecarls the chance to redeem themselves, and his young secretary a splendid opportunity to distinguish himself. And Morcar was leaving with a spring in his step. It was little short of genius.

Harold shouted after him. 'Send Father Bernard to me.'

*   *   *

'Feel better now?' said Llew.

'Much better. Professionals at last.'

Owen waved a hand at the regiment of archers who were marching all around them.

'Proper soldiers.'

They marched in silence for a while. Then Llew suddenly said, 'By the beard of the Great Druid, it is glad I am to see the back of them.'

Owen looked at him. 'The fyrd?'

Llew spat. 'Amateurs.'

'We were grateful for their company at the time.'

'That was then. This is a different time. This is a real time.'

'How far do you think?' said Alfred.

'About seven or eight miles. Not much.'

'Where are we going?'

'To a place called Stamford.'

'Stamford?'

'Yes. It means stones over a ford.'

Alfred tossed his head. 'I know what it means.'

'There is a bridge there, too. Did you know that?'

Alfred frowned. 'Why build a bridge if there is already a ford?'

'It is still quite deep, especially at certain times of the year. And the river there is tidal. Years ago they put great stones across the stream. But since then they have built a wooden bridge on the stones.'

'You seem to know a lot.'

'I come from round here.'

'Then why were you not in the northern host?'

The man looked grim. 'I was. I fought at Fulford.'

Alfred was impressed. 'Was it bad?'

'It was terrible.'

Alfred came to march closer. 'What happened?'

'It was terrible,' repeated the man.

'But—'

'Leave it, Alfred,' said a fyrdman.

Alfred took another look at the man's face, and understood. He tried another tactic.

'Why are we going to Stamford?'

'Because that is where they promised to deliver the hostages.'

'To Hardrada?'

'To the whole damned army.'

Alfred began to look alarmed. 'But is there not the danger that we shall bump into them on the march?'

'They are coming up from their camp, where they have left their ships. They are coming from the south. We are approaching from the west.'

'Ah.' Alfred was not quite sure he understood, but did not like to show it.

'And they have no idea the King is here,' said the fyrdman.

'Ah,' said Alfred again.

The Fulford survivor allowed himself his first sign of animation, in the shape of a grim smile.

'We shall have a chance to get some of our own back. I lost friends at Fulford.'

He turned to Alfred as they marched. 'They think they are going to get some hostages. Instead they are going to get us.'

'What do the scouts say?' said Harold.

'Nothing,' said Gyrth. 'They have seen nothing. Not so much as a whiff of an enemy patrol.'

'Hardrada must be very sure of himself,' said Leofwine.

'Unlike him,' said Gyrth. 'All the reports I have heard about him say he is a very cautious man. I would wager he has left a sizeable guard on his ships.'

'I agree,' said Harold. 'I have sent patrols south to try to locate them. With strict orders not to get involved.'

'Just to find out.'

'Exactly. All of which,' said Harold, 'seems to indicate that he is convinced that the campaign is over. He thinks he has won, and this morning he is looking forward to cleaning up the spoils.'

Harold rode in silence for a while.

So far, so good. They had achieved the main object of the forced march – total surprise. The men had had a good rest at Tadcaster. Indeed, every camp on the march had provided ample food and shelter. Just as he had planned all those weeks ago.

Advance planning was a lonely business. You look ahead as clearly as you can, and you provide for as many eventualities as possible. But there is never any certainty that your plans and schemes and stratagems are going to meet the events that you expect to arise, for the very simple reason that it is often a completely different set of events that actually does arise. And for every plan that you put together, there are always advisers – often respected advisers – to tell you that the plan needs changing, or even that it is a poor plan in the first place. You have to observe, analyse, construct, proceed, and follow your own judgement and instincts – alone.

Well, the strategy of planning a long march north, and having camps and supplies ready, had proved to be the right one, and Harold felt appropriately vindicated. When a king had the double worry of two likely invasions, at opposite ends of the country, any boost to the confidence was extremely welcome.

And now – in only a few hours – he was about to come face to face with a monarch, a general, a warrior, whose reputation resounded across Christendom from the Baltic to the Black Sea. There was hardly a country – from Frisia and Denmark to Sicily, Bulgaria and the Holy Land – that he had not fought in.

Many of his enemies were so remote and outlandish that one could barely pronounce their names, much less identify clearly where they came from.

Harold smiled ironically. Earlier in the year he had rebuked his brothers for being unduly influenced merely by a man's reputation. And now here he was, jogging along towards a battle with such a man, and forced to admit that a mere reputation was giving him food for thought.

This would not do. He glanced guiltily at Gyrth and Leofwine beside him, but they had not noticed anything amiss in his expression. Thank God for that. In any case, his job was to put confidence into other people, regardless of whether he felt it himself. He knew from experience that such a procedure was indeed possible.

Now – practicalities. Bernard had done his sums and read his reports, and had told him that, in all probability, he outnumbered Hardrada. He had taken into account the Norwegian losses at Fulford, and the dribble of casualties in their progress down the east coast. It was more than likely that Hardrada had left an appreciable portion of his army to guard the ships. Any general worth his command would have done the same.

True, Edwin and Morcar had suffered heavy casualties at Fulford, and had been able to supply only a few hundred able-bodied survivors whose confidence had not been smashed to pieces. But that was the northern host. Harold's southern army was fresh, and had not fought a major battle. Hardrada's army was tired, and it had.

Morcar had risen to the challenge Harold had set him, and the horses had arrived in time for a dawn start on the road to York. It had taken a while to get them fairly distributed among the housecarls, but the job had been done in the end. Wilfrid and Oswy had performed prodigies of labour, persuasion and discretion, each of them with a weather eye open to catch fleeting signs of the King's returning approval.

The real surprise, of course, was young Conrad. Wilfrid and Oswy had been full of his energy, drive and resource on the great ride down from York.

'Such authority, sir. Just like a young duke.'

'It was as if he was used to it. Had done it all his life.'

'I tell you, sir, he made *us* jump more than once.'

'And ride. You should see him ride.'

Harold eased his back. It was looking as if he might be about to lose a perfectly good secretary . . .

Sigurd stumped along the beach at Riccall. Scores of longships were drawn up, the fastidious symmetry of their lines clear evidence of skeleton crews who had far too much time on their hands. Hulls were too clean; ropes were coiled too neatly; sails were reefed too regularly.

Men were lounging, yawning, sleeping. Some were repairing nets, stitching canvas, splicing rope; others were carving pieces of oak, incising small shafts of bone, polishing favoured pebbles. Ketil was smoothing the handle of his favourite hand-axe. Ivar was busy with his whetstone and knife. Tore, Finn and Haldor were absorbed in a game of knucklebones, in which no word was spoken.

Sentries had ceased pacing, scarcely bothered to scan the surrounding countryside. Spines were too often propped against trunks of trees, weapons laid aside. It was only too easy to accept the warm morning sun. The wind had dropped, as if it did not dare to disturb the peace and stillness.

Sigurd grunted in disgust and turned to Magnus at his side.

'Just look at it. Compared with this, winter in our huts was a storm of excitement.'

'We are here,' said Magnus. 'That was what you wanted. That was what we wanted, too. An adventure in England.'

'An adventure in England, yes. But not this.' He gestured towards the scene.

'It has barely started,' said Magnus.

'It is nearly all over,' said Sigurd. 'The English host has been scattered.'

'*Half* over,' corrected Magnus.

'You heard the news,' said Sigurd. 'York has surrendered.'

'York, yes. But not the south. They will come soon. They have to. They have no choice.'

'Yes. And, while all that is happening, we sit here on our arses and do nothing, once again.'

Magnus inclined his head in speculation. 'Suppose Harold springs a surprise and attacks us first.'

'What?'

'I would not put it past him. Think about it. He is coming up from the south. He has to pass us before he reaches Hardrada.'

'Why bother with us? We are not the threat; Hardrada is.'

'He is a clever general, Sig, or so I have heard. He conquered Wales, and you tell me of anybody else who has ever done that. If he came for us now, with his full force, we should stand no chance. It would put Hardrada in a very difficult position. Harold could then attack our main army whenever he felt like it, knowing we have nothing behind us but the North Sea.'

Magnus laughed. 'That would get this lot off their arses all right.'

Sigurd scoffed. 'He is miles away.'

'How do you know?'

'Hardrada said so. You heard what he said this morning. He is up there.' He waved towards the north-east. 'He is up there receiving hostages right now. He has the initiative. He can turn and face Harold of Wessex at his leisure.'

Sigurd reached the end of the beach where the last ships were moored, turned about, and began to stump back again.

'Look at them. Did you ever see a third of an army and a whole fleet so fast asleep?'

Magnus smiled in agreement. 'Lars would be in his heaven.'

'I wonder what he is doing now,' said Sigurd. 'Poor old Lars.'

Magnus decided to keep his mouth shut. Whatever Lars was doing right now, it was not in Norway, that was for sure.

Maria watched her mother.

'Do you think about him all the time?'

Queen Ellisif gazed into the low flames. 'Mostly. Nothing else much to think about, is there? Under the circumstances.'

Maria put down her drink, leaned forward, clasped her hands and rested her elbows on her knees.

'We are not much company for Jarl Thorfinn, are we? Distinguished guests, and all that.'

'On the contrary,' said Ellisif. 'He has sent his son with them, so he suffers too. He understands. We understand each other.'

'So we sit and wait?'

'Everybody who has anybody sits and waits at some time or other. When I had you, your father sat and waited.' She turned to her daughter. 'I hope one day Sigurd will have to sit and wait for you.'

Maria sighed. 'It is no fun, is it – waiting?'

'It is terrible,' said Ellisif. 'That is the price you pay. If you want the greatest blessings, you pay the greatest prices. Risk, strain, worry. It is called living.'

There was a silence for a while. Then Maria said, 'Do you really get it?'

Ellisif turned to her. 'Get what?'

'Second sight. Can you really see into the future?'

Ellisif laughed. 'You have known me all your life. Have you ever heard me make a forecast that came true?'

'No,' said Maria. 'But we have never been in a situation like this before. I have never been betrothed before. We have never shared loved ones separated from us like this before. To that extent I do not know you. I can not know you – not completely. So – I ask you again – do you get second sight?'

366

Ellisif looked at her. 'Would it be any comfort if I did?'

'If you did, would you tell me?'

'I doubt it.'

Maria sat back. 'Not much point in asking, then, is there?'

'For your own good.'

'I knew you would say that. Parents always do.'

'Parents are right.'

Maria smiled. 'And daughters are wrong. Yes, I know. But what do you *think*?'

Ellisif smiled too. 'I *think* that your father will have a great adventure, that he will have a wonderful time, that he will be talked about all over Christendom.'

Maria caught the spirit. 'He will lift his great eyebrow and frown fiercely with the other –' Maria put on a parody of her father's expression '– and he will wave his great banner.'

'He will preside at a great feast, and he will declaim some of his ghastly poetry, and everybody will get enormously drunk.'

They laughed together, then fell silent, and gazed once more into the fire.

Then Ellisif said, 'I tell you this, though, Maria: whatever he does, it will not be small, and it will not be uninteresting. Your father never creeps up on you; he bowls you over. I would not, for the world, have missed a minute of it.'

Suddenly, Ellisif shivered.

Maria noticed at once. She got up. 'I shall go and get your great wrap.'

Ellisif looked up. 'Send a servant.'

'No,' said Maria. 'Not this time. I want to put it round your shoulders myself.'

When she had gone, Ellisif let out a great sigh.

For some reason that she did not understand, she found herself thinking about King Harold, and about his woman that everybody talked about. Edith, they said her name was.

She had a daughter, and a son. Maybe two or three. Was she sitting in front of a fire in a hall somewhere – like herself – waiting?

Second sight or no second sight, one thing was sure: one of them was going to pay the greatest price.

'Quickly, sir, come and see.'

Wilfrid and Oswy reined in beside the King and beckoned ahead of them.

With barely a glance to see if Gyrth and Leofwine were following, Harold spurred forwards till he breasted a slight rise. Suddenly the whole valley of the River Derwent opened out before him.

The ground sloped gently down to the river, and to the wooden bridge on its stone piles. On the far side it rose rather more sharply.

'My God, Harold – we have them.' Leofwine could barely sit in the saddle for excitement.

Harold was forced to agree. It was more than he had dared to hope.

'Look at them,' said Gyrth. 'They had no idea. The slope behind us did it. We have only just come into their view.'

'Look at them running,' said Leofwine.

'I would wager they thought we were the hostages from York.'

Harold glanced over his right shoulder at the bright, late-morning sun. 'You would think we would have been given away by the sun glinting on our helmets and spear-points.'

'My guess is they could not believe it. Harold, we have done more than spring a surprise; we have started a panic. Look at them.'

It was an attacking general's dream. In the land right before them, parties of the enemy were engaged in stripping the land-scape of supplies. Barns were being ransacked. Trees were being stripped of fruit. Cattle and sheep were being rounded up and driven towards the river. In the warm sun, nobody seemed to be wearing mail. Few helmets were in evidence. There were no sentries to be seen.

At the river itself, a token force of provost units were organising the crossing of the bridge. It could almost have been the prelude to a market day in a town beyond the river.

All three brothers lifted their amazed eyes to the higher land beyond the bridge. They saw more signs of urgency. It was as if the enemy had just woken up and found their house on fire. Men were running to and fro all over the place. They could just catch the stress in the bawled orders. For a while it all looked totally patternless.

As if by family instinct, all three brothers realised the paramount importance of speed.

'Get down there,' said Harold. 'Catch them against the river.'

Gyrth prepared to turn his horse. 'What sort of formation do you want?'

'To hell with formation,' said Harold. 'If we do not move fast, we shall lose the chance. They are helpless.'

'Where do we leave the horses?' said Leofwine. Like every housecarl he had become so used to fighting on foot that he failed to see that habit and proud tradition had congealed into instinct. It did not occur to him to fight in any other way.

But it occurred to Harold.

'Ride, ride! Get down there. Catch them before they reach the bridge. Round them up. The fyrd will follow. I shall see to that.'

'Come, brother,' said Gyrth. 'It is work for swords today, not axes.'

As they galloped off, Harold turned and gave the orders to the housecarls in charge of the various fyrd detachments.

'Get down as fast as your legs will carry you. Never mind the formation.'

'What about the enemy over there, sir?'

Harold glanced across the river beyond the bridge. It was still more like a colony of upset ants than an army.

'Do not fear them. They are far too taken up with preparing their own position. These poor devils down here are dead as far as they are concerned. The longer they spend dying the better those up there will like it. So get down and polish them off and we can get on to the real fighting.'

Gyrth and Leofwine collected as many mounted housecarls as they could, split them into two and rode down upon either flank of the dismayed enemy. Caught in the open, totally unprepared, they gaped, dropped ropes, baskets, bales and cattle goads, and rushed about frantically to collect weapons, and, if they had been prudent, helmets.

By the time they had begun to look like soldiers, they could see that the English housecarls had ridden behind them to cut them off from the bridge. Surging down the slope were hundreds of roaring Saxon fyrdmen, armed with everything from swords, spears and axes to billhooks, clubs and scythes.

'How are your feet now, Alfred?' panted a fyrdman beside him.

Alfred's eyes were staring. His heart was threatening to choke him. He had never felt such terror in his life. He had just enough breath to gasp, 'Jesus help us.'

'I only hope he does,' said his companion, as he lifted his sword and brought it down on a shoulder bare of any chainmail . . .

On the left wing, Gyrth had deployed the regiment of archers.

'Get as close as you can. You will have the fyrd beside you, and the housecarls will be at the back of these bastards, to stop them running away. All you have to do is shoot them down – and take care that you do not shoot any of us at the back.'

As they scrambled into their allotted position, Llew managed to gasp a comment. 'Not proper archery, boyo, is it? Not really. By the druid, bloody target practice.'

Owen got out his bowstring and fitted it. 'Archery is shooting. That is what we have been looking for all this time. What occurs to me is that we stop thinking and just shoot.'

A housecarl came by. 'Let go as soon as you are ready. And remember what Earl Gyrth said: be careful of our lads at the back. Aim low.'

Llew was right. It was not satisfactory work. It was too easy. The enemy, once they realised that their position was hopeless, turned and simply stood. They had realised that the only contribution they could make to the battle was to provide time for their comrades on the other side of the river to organise themselves. So all they could do was to take as long as possible dying.

The fyrd bludgeoned from the front. The housecarls hacked from the rear. Gradually the groups of surrounded enemy became smaller. Wherever a gap opened up in the fighting, or whenever the two ranks of combatants stood back for a moment to ease their arms, Llew and Owen had a free view and a still target. What made it even easier was that, as the enemy fell or edged back, it was a simple matter to retrieve spent arrows.

Slowly, very slowly, the fighting edged towards the bridge. When it got there, the provost party became involved. Incredibly, groups of Vikings even came back across the bridge to try to support them.

One of them was a large man with a huge axe.

'Get out of the way, you poxy little Welsh ferrets. You have had your fun.'

Wilfrid bundled aside a group of archers with the shoulder of his horse.

Owen and Llew and their partners stumbled out of the way. Llew raised a fist. 'Yes, I know. We soften them up, and you wade in when it is easy and carve them up and get all the glory.'

'Seen it a hundred times,' shouted Owen.

Oswy waved an arm towards the bridge. 'Look there, you stupid sheep muckers. It is close-quarter stuff now. You will not have room to pull back a single string.'

'We can still do it from a distance,' said Owen, aggrieved.

'Yes,' said Oswy, 'and shoot half our lads in the back. Very likely, with your aim.'

'You will have your chance when we cross the river,' said Wilfrid. 'Look at that shield wall they are building.'

'Fat chance,' said Oswy, glancing in that direction. 'Someone will have to move that bastard with the axe.'

'Fancy your chances?' he added, turning to the archers. 'No, I thought not. Quite happy to let us do that bit of dirty work, eh?'

'Believe it when I see it,' said Llew, his normal good humour thoroughly evaporated.

'Then stand by,' said Oswy. 'Coming, Wilfrid?'

Wilfrid and his cousin pushed their way to the front of the line of housecarls, which penned the last of the Vikings against the river and the bridge.

It was total chaos. To the right and left of the bridge the two sides swung and hacked at each other as long as their arms provided strength. By now, for every Viking there were two or three English. It was going to be only a matter of time. But it was going to be a very untidy time.

Men stumbled over bodies and tussocks of wet grass. Men who only half an hour before had been contented cattle rustlers now cursed and swore, threw away sticks and staves and snatched weapons from dying hands on the ground. Livestock of every size and variety ran terrified everywhere. Vikings, driven right back to the bank, turned and jumped in, finding the water much deeper than they had believed. For the first time some of them found that not wearing mail had suddenly become an advantage. Those who had been blessing their good luck in wearing it now cursed a wayward deity for changing their luck.

Others, more adventurous, tried to scramble along the bridge by clutching at individual timbers. A few delighted English archers were picking them off.

At the mouth of the bridge itself, the huge Norwegian continued to swing a tireless axe. Because the passage was so narrow, only one Englishman at a time could come at him. The more limb-lopped bodies that were strewn in his path, the more difficult it became to get at him.

Oswy paused in the second rank and sized up the situation.

'Poor technique, would you not say?' he said to Wilfrid. 'I have seen better from a drunken cadet.'

'Well, which one of us takes him?' said Wilfrid.

'My idea,' said Oswy. 'Here – hold these.' He handed over the reins of his horse. Wilfrid clapped him on the shoulder.

'Off you go, then. Maybe I shall learn a thing or two.'

Oswy elbowed his way through the front rank, and placed himself with unmistakable deliberation in front of the Viking champion. Their eyes met. Sensing the moment, the men on either side of Oswy fell back a pace. The Viking kicked a body aside, and blatantly wiped blood off his blade. He licked his lips and flung a challenge with his stare.

For a man who had been fighting alone for over half an hour he was in amazing condition. True, there had been a lull between each contest and death, but the number of bodies around him testified to his prodigious strength and stamina.

Luck, too, thought Oswy, as he sized him up. As he had observed to Wilfrid, the man's technique was lacking. Crude. No subtlety. No variety. He relied on sheer muscle.

Well, we should see about that. Taking his two-handed grip, Oswy stepped forward.

Reaching the timbers of the bridge, he placed his front foot in position, and slipped on a patch of blood.

The Viking, moving very fast for a big man, hit him before he had reached the floor of the bridge. One blow was all that was necessary. Oswy's helmet flew off, but it was obvious from the state of his skull that he would not rise again.

There was a roar from the Viking side, and the victor raised his arms in triumph. The English fell back a pace further.

Eyes turned to Wilfrid. After a few seconds of dismay, Wilfrid handed the reins of both horses to a fyrdman. To everyone's surprise he began to move to the left and rear, shouting over his shoulder, 'Keep him occupied. But be careful.'

'Oh, we shall do that all right,' said somebody. 'What are you going to do?'

'You will see soon enough. You? Come with me.' He commandeered a young spearman. 'Bring another spear as well. And some rope. Hurry.'

'It is taking shape,' said Gyrth.

Harold took his hand away from where he had been shielding his eyes. 'Yes. A shield wall.'

'Would you have expected anything else?'

'With Hardrada, I never dare *expect* anything,' said Harold. 'But, yes, he has done the most likely thing, under the circumstances. But see? He has still given it a twist of his own.'

Across the river, at the top of the rising ground, the Norwegian king was indeed drawing up his men in the traditional form – the kite-shaped shields locked to make an unbroken barrier. There were circular shields too; the tactic was not as regularly carried out as it might have been. So there was already an appearance of rush and improvisation.

Unusually, there were no ends, no wings in the normal way. The extremities bent back on the rest of the seething crowd of hurrying men, so that the defensive line became almost circular, or at least a rough oval. There was no way it could be outflanked.

Harold made a noise of appreciation. 'Clever. Quick thinking. You have to hand it to him.'

Leofwine rode up from the rear, where he had been marshalling more troops.

'Do you think he will be ready by the time we attack?'

'A very good chance, I should think. We have only just cleared the bridge.'

'Wilfrid?'

'Yes. He found a fisherman's hollowed-out log or swill tub or something. Paddled it under the bridge, tied two spears together, and got him up through the timbers.'

Leofwine winced. 'Christ!'

'Yes. Right up through the groin, poor devil. At any rate, we are over. Time for the next move.'

'Attack?' said Leofwine.

'Not quite,' said Harold. 'My next move may—'

'Great God!' said Gyrth suddenly. 'Do you see that?'

A huge man, in a bright-blue tunic, appeared in front of the Viking shield wall. He appeared to be directing operations. He rode a magnificent black horse and wore a helmet of such bright metal that, even at that distance, it sparkled in the sun. As all three brothers concentrated their eyes on this dramatic sight, the horse seemed to stumble. The rider was thrown to the ground.

He was up on his feet in an instant, remounted in another, and continued with what he was doing.

Leofwine turned to Harold. 'Do you suppose . . .?'

Harold nodded, unconcerned. 'Could be. Big enough.'

'What does it mean?' said Leofwine. 'An omen?'

'Absolutely nothing at all,' said Harold. 'All we can hope for is that it impresses his men. It does not impress me. A man falls off his horse. We have all done it. Sheer bad luck. The best we can hope for is that it is the beginning of a run of bad luck – for him.'

Leofwine was not totally convinced. 'He is said to be very lucky.'

'Well, he was not then, was he? So stop worrying and listen to me. I want to talk to him.'

Both brothers stared. 'What?'

'And Tostig.'

Gyrth pointed up the hill. 'But you have them. We outnumber them. They are still in confusion. Look at them. God knows why, but half of them are without mail or helmets.'

'I know why,' said Harold. 'They were not expecting us.'

'My whole point,' said Gyrth. 'All the odds are in our favour. We have them at our mercy. And you want to *talk*?'

'"Mercy" is the word,' said Harold. 'Do you want to slaughter them all just because it is easy?'

'They want our country, and are prepared to kill us to get it.'

Harold shook his head. 'No, brother. I ask you, which is the more important – that we kill them all – and kill hundreds of our own men at the same time – or that they go away and leave us in peace, and nobody dies?'

'They will not accept,' said Gyrth.

'At least,' said Harold, 'we give them the chance.'

Gyrth looked at Leofwine, and back at Harold.

'It is Mother. Admit it.'

Harold stayed silent. Leofwine looked puzzled.

'It is Mother,' repeated Gyrth. 'Or, rather, it is Tostig.' He looked again at Leofwine. 'We must not harm our precious Tostig.'

Harold spoke at last. 'Gyrth, I will not have a brother's blood on my hands if I can possibly avoid it. And, if you were in my position, neither would you. Would you like to face Mother with such news? Because that is what I may have to do.'

'So you are going to talk?'

'I have already arranged it. If you look up there –' Harold pointed up the hill '– you will see my heralds coming back from the shield wall. I expect an answer to my offer.'

'Offer?' exploded Gyrth. 'You *offered* them something? Why?'

'Because I hope they might accept. You must make the offer worth having.'

Leofwine patted a restive horse. 'What did you offer?'

Harold looked pensively at both of them, as if he knew what their reaction was going to be.

'I offered Tostig his earldom back.'

'What?'

'And up to one-third of England to rule over.'

Gyrth was dumbfounded. 'After all this?' He pointed up the hill again.

'Better peace than war.'

Leofwine found his tongue. 'And you expect him to accept?'

Harold nodded to the approaching horsemen. 'We shall soon know.'

The delegation reined in.

'Well?' said Harold.

The spokesman slid off his mail coif and took a deep breath. 'You realise, sir, that I speak with your brother Tostig's voice and not my own.'

Harold made an impatient gesture. 'Get on with it.'

The man cleared his throat. 'Your brother, sir, said that your offer did not come well from a man who had offered him nothing but hatred and contempt last winter when he banished him. If he had been more reasonable then, many a man's life would have since been saved.'

Harold leaned forward in the saddle.

'*What was his answer?*'

'He replied, sir, with a question. He said, "King Harald of Norway has been my friend and ally, and has taken many risks on my behalf. What will you give him for his trouble?"'

Harold laughed harshly. 'That is easy. Tell him he can have seven feet of English ground. Or, if he is too tall for that, whatever else he needs to accommodate him.'

The man turned to carry out the King's order. Harold stopped him. 'What did he say to my offer?'

'He rejected it out of hand, sir. He said that he and his ally had come too far to stop now. Honour would not allow them to do otherwise. It was all or nothing – victory or death.'

Harold nodded. 'So be it.' He waved an order to his spokesman. 'Tell them my answer to Hardrada.'

As the horses galloped off, Gyrth said, 'I hope news of this generous offer of yours does not get to Morcar.'

'Who is going to tell him – now?' said Harold.

Gyrth turned to Leofwine. 'What did I tell you? Waste of time.'

'I did not do it to waste time,' said Harold. 'I did it to save my conscience.'

'Where is your horse?' said Sigurd.

The messenger paused, sweat pouring down his face. 'Collapsed. Did the other two get through?'

'Obviously,' said Sigurd. 'We are here. We got the message. Go on to the ships and get some food and rest.'

The man nodded, and made off, still running, as if he still had a message to deliver.

Sigurd turned to Finn and the others. 'That is a dutiful man,' he said. 'No horse, and still bringing the news.'

'Bad news,' said Finn.

'Any news is better than none,' said Sigurd. 'Now we have something to do.'

He raised his head and looked around him. Everyone had taken the opportunity, when Sigurd had met the messenger, to stop and rest. Sigurd now bellowed his orders.

'Keep formation. In hundreds. Change first and second ranks. But keep the tallest in the front; we want the longest possible stride for all to keep. Five minutes only. Then we go again.

'And keep your mail.'

'We are boiling in it,' said Tore, whose shoulders still complained about the scalding water from the walls of Scarborough.

'Better than bleeding without it when you get there. And keep formation. When we do get there, we shall have to attack straight away, and we must have shape and purpose. If we go in all over the place, they will blow us away like autumn leaves in a gale. We strike with shape and we strike with force. Shape! Force! Do you hear?'

'Do you think they are listening?' said Magnus.

'I doubt it,' said Sigurd. 'But what else can I do except tell them? I am trying to shorten the odds, that is all. How many times have I told you? It is all about the odds.'

'Do we have much chance?'

'My guess,' said Sigurd, 'is that we are Hardrada's only chance. If he had been winning, he would not have sent for us.'

'And if he had been losing, it might well be all over by the time we get there.'

'It might well,' agreed Sigurd.

'So what do we have in our favour?'

Sigurd took a huge breath. 'Surprise, I should say. The English will not be expecting us. Just as Hardrada was not expecting the English this morning.'

'So we might tip the scales,' said Magnus.

'We might. We might just.'

Magnus offered an ironic smile. 'Long odds.'

Sigurd smiled back to acknowledge the thrust. 'Indeed. But I have just done what I can to shorten them. If you have any better ideas, now is the time to tell me.'

Magnus put up both hands by way of surrender.

'Good,' said Sigurd. 'Then let us be on our way.'

He raised his voice again. 'Up, lads. Nothing like a good strong run in the autumn sun. Does wonders for the body. And the appetite. Think how many English you will eat when you get there.'

Half an hour later, the remaining messenger tumbled to the ground beside a ghost fleet. In his search for food, he found half-stitched sails, abandoned carvings, and a handful of knucklebones scattered across a whitened deck.

'Fire as your bows bear. Go for the gaps. The gaps. No wastage. Make every one tell.'

The archer sergeants strode up and down behind the lines of the regiment, bawling over the din.

To Harold and his brothers, near the foot of the slope, the battle was one shapeless monster of noise. To give commands over it was impossible. All they could do was send in the house-carls to back up the fyrd contingents, and keep some groups of fyrdmen in reserve – if they could be restrained. Sometimes the housecarls led; sometimes they were spaced among the fyrdmen, to stiffen their resolve. Many a survivor afterwards testified that it was a tremendous boost to the confidence to have at one's side a member of this elite brotherhood, to sense the awesome swing of the great axe, to roar as it found flesh, to revel in the damage and confusion it caused, to see the terror and dismay on enemy faces.

Several housecarls stayed mounted, as long as their horses could sustain the exertion. Which was not for long, for any army attacking up a hill has to work that much harder. While they were mounted, their greater height gave them the advantage of clearer and further sight, which in turn improved their judgement, and their ease of decision as to where precisely to strike next. They were also a more fearsome enemy.

Nevertheless, some grew tired of this unfamiliar manner of fighting. The traditional way was on foot, with the axe. Bending from the saddle, with the sword, did not come easily to them. Norman knights had been doing it almost from birth, but it was not the Saxon way.

Perhaps for that reason, the early attacks did not make much impression on the enemy shield wall. Each time the Saxons retreated, as much from exhaustion as from failure, a few Vikings burst out from the wall and rushed forward. They were soon cut down. That was where the mounted housecarls did enjoy themselves; it was almost as easy as pig-sticking.

The less enjoyable work was rounding up the fyrdmen who broke away from the attack when their arms began to fall impotent to their sides. But there was nothing wrong with their legs, and the housecarls were soon yelling themselves hoarse to get the infantry back into some semblance of order for the next advance.

Nevertheless, everyone, from the King right down to the smallest Welsh archer and dimmest apprentice fyrdman, could see that the battle was going only one way. The English outnumbered the enemy. The Viking host was static, beleaguered, totally, it seemed, without initiative. It was going to be only a matter of time. A long time, perhaps, but time was the only matter worth considering.

Alfred leaned on his sword. There was no blood on it yet, but he did know what it felt like to swing it, and to swing it at an enemy. He was past nerves now, past fear, past tiredness, past disillusion, almost past even thinking. His breath was one continuous rasp. But he could see what everyone else could see.

'God in Heaven – we are going to win.'

A fyrdman beside him held up his own sword and fingered the edge. 'Then pray to God in Heaven that you will still be here to witness it.'

Owen and Llew could see, very early on, that there were gaps where the smaller, round shields left spaces because they simply did not have the height to provide cover. When somebody did strike a target, it took time for the shield wall to repair itself. Inevitably, there were some foolish soldiers, as there are in any army, who poked their heads over the top to get a better view. So the targets were there, and now and then they struck one.

'This is more like it, boyo,' said Llew.

'Keep a few for later on, remember,' said Owen.

Llew waved a hand up towards the top of the slope. 'We shall be up there within the hour. Then we can get half of them back.'

'I would not be so sure of that,' said Owen.

Lower down the slope, a similar conversation was taking place.

'We are making an impression,' said Leofwine. 'I swear that wall is not as big as it was when we started.' He looked at Harold. 'It is only a matter of time.'

Harold made a grimace of doubt. 'We are winning, but it is too slow. We shall still lose men.'

'If we are winning, then Hardrada is losing,' said Leofwine. 'That is good enough for me.'

'You forget one thing,' said Harold.

'Oh?'

Harold pointed. 'That is Hardrada up there.'

'So? His position is hopeless. He can do nothing.'

'He did not get his reputation by doing nothing.'

'Who was it said that we should not be upset by a reputation?'

'I am not,' said Harold. 'What is important is what he did to *get* that reputation.'

'Does it matter?'

'Yes, it does. We have hemmed him in, and we keep on battering at his shield wall until it gets too small or collapses. If he is going to snatch anything out of this, he must regain the initiative.'

'How can he do that?' said Leofwine.

'I wish I knew,' said Harold with feeling. 'I am not Hardrada.' He looked at both of them.

'But rest assured, brothers. He will do something.'

'How much longer do you think?' said Magnus.

'Half an hour, an hour. Who knows?'

Sigurd's face was awash with sweat. All around them faces were puce with exertion, grey with fatigue, white with nausea. Empty water flasks were tipped up, examined, and tossed aside with fury. Despite dire warnings and desperate exhortations, some chainmail was being removed. Tore had long since thrown his hauberk away. Hakon was limping from his punctured buttock. Ketil's broken arm, for all the tightness of his sling, jarred him with every step.

'It is impossible, Sig,' said Tore. 'Do you want us to get there or not?'

'Which do you need?' said Haldor. 'Our mail or our muscles? We can not take both.'

Sigurd did not have the breath, the patience, or the time to argue. Haldor was right; the important thing was to get the men there. It was not hauberks that won battles; it was swords and good sword arms. At least nobody was throwing away any weapons.

Magnus was not so sure about the mail. What was the point of arriving, swords and all, if they had no means of protection? He looked around at the bent shoulders, the heaving chests, the desperate stretching, as if by some magic they were going to reach up beyond the heat of the day that lay like a blanket over everybody and find blessed fresh air above it.

None of these men had it in him, by the look of them, to go berserk, and charge into the thickest of the enemy, without thought of personal safety. He knew them all; they were far too human for that.

Sigurd read his thoughts. 'Do not worry; they will do their best. They will justify my confidence in them. They are good lads. And we have one great gift, remember. Surprise,' he added, before Magnus could open his mouth.

'And think for a minute,' went on Sigurd. 'We are considering only ourselves. What about the English? Perhaps they are on their last legs, too. Perhaps our onset will just be enough to tip them off their balance. All the chainmail in the world will not make any difference; it will be the timing – and the odds.'

Magnus felt a surge of admiration for this man. In the depths of their exhaustion and the consequent collapse of confidence, he was thinking of victory. He really thought it was possible.

Before Magnus could think of anything else to say by way of disagreement, Sigurd took a deep breath and looked about him again. Somehow he managed to make a glow of expectation show through the sweat.

'Do you realise that we could make all the difference? We could win the battle for him.'

'A long chance.'

Sigurd looked sharply at him. 'But a chance – you must agree with that. And then, and then – just think. He has already promised me his daughter. If I give him a victory by way of return, he will be able to deny me nothing.'

Magnus stared. This man's bounce and confidence were without limit. Was there no end to his imagination and assurance?

'Anything else?' said Magnus with heavy irony.

'Plenty,' said Sigurd. 'He is going to need people to run England for him. He can not be in two places at once.'

Magnus contrived to manage a sort of breathless laugh. 'So it will be "Jarl Sigurd", eh?'

'Why not?' said Sigurd, dusting his hands as if about to start a big job. 'We have had "Jarl Thorfinn" in Orkney. Why not "Jarl Sigurd" in England?'

'Oh, come now,' said Magnus, still following his joke. '"Jarl Sigurd" *of* England.'

Sigurd grinned. 'Something like that. Yes – I will settle for that. So let us be about our business, eh?'

As they all ran on, the ground was left littered with empty water flasks, hauberks – and helmets.

Maria woke up. For a moment she could not work out where she was. But she felt so comfortable that she almost felt tempted to let herself slide back into sleep again.

Then she felt the familiar fur in her hands. Her mother's favourite wrap. Maria smiled as she remembered. How many times had she felt total peace and security as her mother had wrapped her in it when she was small? Whatever dangers lurked outside, the minute she had felt the thick fur, she felt safe.

Remembrance of the fur at once brought back remembrance of her mother. It was to get the wrap that Maria had come into the room. Now she was shaken into full wakefulness.

What was she doing on the bed? She shrugged. Must have fallen asleep. Easy enough. The warm sun streamed through the window. Such heat on an autumn day was rare. People from her country were not used to it. Small wonder that she had felt drowsy. Especially after the full meal they had taken shortly before. Jarl Thorfinn's hospitality was not rich or rare, but it was ample.

As she gathered up the wrap, she wondered idly why her mother had not come up to get it and to find out why she had been so long. Patience was not among the first of her virtues. She smiled. The Queen had a good appetite. Perhaps she had felt drowsy too.

* * *

'What now, sir?'

Wilfrid and the other senior housecarls waited expectantly round the King.

Harold did not look at them. He was looking intently at the next advance he had ordered. 'We wait.' Then he remembered something.

He now turned to Wilfrid. 'I am sorry about Oswy.'

Wilfrid nodded. 'Sir.' Harold nodded back, and returned to watching the line.

The two lines clashed as they had done many times before. Just as before, a formless braying sound surged down the slope towards them. Just as before, Harold had to wait till the outcome made itself clear, either in a fissure in the shield wall or in a retreat by the attackers. Further control at this point was impossible.

He glanced across to the left, where the archer regiment waited expectantly. They could not fire while an attack was in progress. On the right, Alfred stood, tense, with the fyrdmen that Harold had designated as the tactical reserve. Alfred had no idea what a tactical reserve was. All he knew was that he had to wait. After all the rage and panic of the earlier advances, he found the waiting nearly intolerable. At the same time, he dreaded the order to go forward again. He wanted with all his being to be there, in the midst of it, and at the same time he wished with every fibre of his body not to be there.

Suddenly he caught sight of something very near the front of the Norwegian line. Something told him that he had seen it before, but for some reason he had not noticed it. Perhaps because he had been attending to the business of staying alive. He had had dreams like this – when you saw something properly for the first time, but you knew in your dream that you had seen it before.

It swayed, and doubled in size. It billowed out like a newly laundered sheet being dried in the breeze. Great God and angels! It was the banner, the black raven with the dripping claws. It was the Landwaster. Alfred swallowed and crossed himself.

A bigger surprise followed. A mighty space opened up in the enemy shield wall. This was no accident, no result of negligence or injuries, no minute crack that might appear in the most solid fortification. This was deliberate. It was not a mistake of defence; it was an expedient of attack. Men came pouring through as if released by the breaking of some giant dam.

'What did I tell you?' said Harold. 'I said he would do something.'

Gyrth and Leofwine gazed in consternation. Gyrth pulled himself together first.

'What now, brother?'

Harold was ready for him. 'Get the reserve fyrd in formation at the foot of the slope. Let them use up some energy getting to us. Move the archers round further to the left, so that they fire on their flank. But tell them to continue firing as well at the rest of the wall up there. We must keep their heads down.'

Gyrth made off. Harold turned to his other brother, who had just managed to pull up his jaw.

'Lef, collect as many housecarls as you can, and put them out on the right, in a compact body. When they pause, hit the bastards with everything, all at the same time.'

'What about the front?'

Harold set his jaw. 'They have the worst job of all – just to hold them. That is all I want them to do – hold.'

That was what they did – just. But it cost many their lives. It looked as if the battle was going to degenerate into a thousand scrappy little contests all over the slope between the bridge and the remains of the shield wall.

Suddenly, it seemed as if the whole field let out a gasp.

Men continued to pour out of the hole in the shield wall, but it was not the flood of humanity that made men pause in near-disbelief. It was the thing in the middle of it. It hovered above, like some human siege-tower. As men continued to gaze transfixed, it moved to the front, carving a way like the bow of some huge ship in still water. The sunlight flashed from its head.

The archer regiment, on the point of following orders to move to the left, paused, hypnotised.

'Christ and holy Ffestiniog!' said Owen, crossing himself.

Even though no man in the English army had seen him before, no man in the English army needed to be told that they were face to face with Harald Sigurdsson, King of Norway, the mightiest warrior in all the north – or anywhere else for that matter. In that moment of revelation, in the heat and the fever of battle, not even Odin himself could have made a greater impact.

What made it even more horrific was the fact that he was all wrong. He had no elite bodyguard around him. True, he wore a helmet, from which the sun reflected dazzling stabs of light. But he wore no armour. The famous hauberk Emma – mail right down to his knees – was nowhere to be seen. He carried no shield. No spear.

All he had was an enormous sword, which he swung with an awesome two-handed grip. His mouth was wide open, but the terrible noise took away what he was shouting. Nevertheless, men swore afterwards that they could hear what it was. Others, equally convinced, said they could see the gleams in his eyes.

They were the lucky ones. Those who found themselves directly in his path did not get the chance to form any impression at all. They went down like corn before the sickle.

Alfred, with his fyrd companions, scores of yards away in the reserve, went hot and cold almost at the same time. He muttered one word: 'Berserk.'

'Poor bastards,' said somebody.

Towards the left, Owen tugged at Llew's sleeve. 'Come on, Llew. For Christ's sake, come on.'

Most of the archer regiment had carried out their orders and shifted leftwards. Llew stood still, unable, it seemed, to move. Suddenly he drew an arrow from his quiver and began to fit it.

Owen tugged at him again. 'Llew – for the love of God!'

Llew shook off his hand. 'Just one shot. Time for just one shot. We shall never get another chance like this. Look at him.'

Owen almost wept in frustration. 'It is a chance in a million. Llew!'

By the time he had said this, Llew was on his own. Every other archer had moved, including Owen.

They watched – open-mouthed, helpless, bewitched – as Llew took aim and fired.

It took Hardrada directly in the throat. For an instant he stood, rigid. His arms dropped. The sword tumbled in front of him. Blood gushed from his mouth. Then, still rigid, like some lofty pine under the shipwright's axe, he toppled and fell.

Queen Ellisif woke up. She was relieved. She had been dreaming. As so often with everybody after dreams, she struggled to recall what they were, but soon gave up. All she remembered was that they had been unpleasant dreams, so unpleasant that she felt grateful that she could not recall them.

Then she remembered. Maria. What they had talked about . . .

Why had she slept? From experience, she guessed that it had been to escape. Just as one often yawns before attempting a nerve-racking problem, so one often sleeps to escape unwelcome thoughts.

She sighed. It seemed to have worked. She felt much better. Then she remembered. Maria had gone to fetch her wrap. She looked around.

Odd. She should have come back by this time. Perhaps she had come back, found her mother sleeping, and gone away again.

Just as she was accepting the explanation, the door opened and Maria returned.

'Sorry, Mother. I fell asleep.'

'I guessed.'

Maria laughed. 'I would wager you did, too. All that heavy food of Thorfinn's.'

She came up behind her and began to place the bearskin round her mother's shoulders.

Ellisif did not turn. She sat still, the better to enjoy the contact with her daughter. She could feel the hands under the fur. She knew Maria was enjoying it, too. For both of them, it was an aesthetic as well as a physical pleasure – the thought as well as the deed – as a cat likes having its back stroked.

Suddenly the movement stopped.

Ellisif waited for a moment. The movement did not begin again. There was a slight rustle behind her. She turned, questioningly. 'Maria?'

Then she saw.

'Maria!'

Alfred blinked. The terrible Landwaster had disappeared, too. For a moment Alfred wondered whether he had imagined what he had just seen.

For the second time a sudden, dread hush fell momentarily on the whole battlefield. Men on both sides reacted as if God had suddenly said, 'Halt!'

After a brief incredulous paralysis, the Norwegians around the dead king fell victim to instinct. They began to scramble back towards the shield wall. The English in front of them looked backwards towards their commanders, as if awaiting confirmation that they had done their work.

A small party of mounted English made its way up the slope, and stopped near the spot where the great king had died. The English, housecarl and fyrd alike, fell back before them. Perhaps this was the confirmation they had been looking for.

No Norwegian touched a missile. The remaining murmur of wonderment faded into total, if expectant, silence.

One last voice still issued orders behind the enemy shield wall. Beckoning Gyrth and Leofwine to follow, Harold rode a few paces further forward.

'Tostig!'

Both sides froze. The voice behind the shield wall stopped.

Harold shouted again. 'Tostig!'

'Yes?'

Harold looked at his brothers, then turned back to face the shield wall, now closed again.

'I offer you your lives. Just go.'

There was a pause, while Tostig obviously translated to his remaining staff and nearby warriors staring down over their shields. Not that it needed much translation. A low growl rumbled along the Viking line. From nowhere the Landwaster rose again and fluttered gently, as if the black raven were surveying the field for its next victim.

'Harold?'

No mistaking Tostig's voice.

'Yes?'

'Go to hell.'

'What was that?'

'What?'

Ivar cocked his head again. 'That.'

'I hear nothing,' said Finn.

'That is just the point. The noise has stopped.'

All around them men lifted their sagging heads, listened, and looked at each other. They felt near the end of their powers.

That simple act, during their rest period, was almost too much for them. Ketil clutched his bad arm, his face grey with pain.

'What does it mean, Sig?'

'One of two things,' said Sigurd.

For some time now, the murmur, the distant braying storm, had grown steadily. Every man knew that they were getting close. Or thought they were. But the battlefield refused to come into view. It was like the ascent of an obstinate hill; every time one could have sworn that the summit was just over the rise, one breasted it only to see yet another slope that looked steeper than the last. It was heartbreaking.

'Well?' said Magnus. He was one of the few now left with mail in place. He carried his helmet on a strap bouncing on his back.

'You know as well as I,' said Sigurd. He looked haggard. The breezy confidence, the almost lazy assurance, had gone.

'Which do you think?' said Magnus.

'What does it matter?' said Sigurd. 'We still have to get there.'

'Why?' said Finn.

Sigurd rounded on him. 'Because we must share. We share the spoils or we share their fate. If we stay here, we share our shame with nobody. On your feet, damn you!'

He turned to Magnus and said out of the corner of his mouth, 'We must get them there before they throw away even their swords.'

Owen scrambled to a halt in front of Harold. Through his sweat he glowed with pride and satisfaction.

'Well, sir, what is it we do now, our sergeant wants to know?'

Harold smiled grimly. 'Was it you, then?'

'No, sir. But it was my friend Llew. I said to him, I said, "Llew, it is now or never. Have a go," I said. I said—'

'Yes, yes, I follow your general idea,' said Harold.

'Do you want us to get Tostig as well, sir?'

It was the wrong thing to say. Harold did not react. Instead he looked up the slope again. Owen blushed through his sweat, and suddenly wanted to be somewhere else.

Gyrth pointed. 'Look at that.'

A second breach had occurred in the shield wall, over on the enemy's right. It was once again clearly deliberate. Smaller numbers this time, but just as determined. And just as oblivious to the risks they were running. It was clear to everybody on the field that it was only a matter of minutes before they would be surrounded and wiped out.

Only this time they did not come straight down the slope, but swung off to their right. They bore down like avenging angels on the regiment of archers.

'Holy Mary!' said Leofwine, crossing himself. 'Revenge. That is all they want.'

'That is all they are going to get,' said someone.

There was nothing they could do but watch. It took a moment before the archers fully realised their danger, and by that time it was too late. Unable to let off more than a feeble flurry of badly aimed shafts, they went down beneath a forest of swords and axes.

Within minutes the Vikings themselves were surrounded, and they too soon disappeared under the tide of English.

Owen gazed aghast.

Llew had been so proud. 'The best shot of my life,' he had said.

Owen went to the rear of the English line and unstrung his bow.

A delighted fyrdman clapped him on the shoulder. 'One of your lot got him, then.'

Owen put his bowstring carefully away.

'An incredible shot,' said the fyrdman. 'How did he do it?'

Owen blinked and grimaced.

'You will not hear it from me. I shall never tell another story.'

*　　*　　*

Magnus was not in the first groups to arrive. He was one of the minority who had refused to cast off their mail. Hakon and Ketil were among the laggards at the rear.

He heard the shouts up ahead of him. They were gathering along the slight ridge that clearly looked across the battlefield. Instinctively he began to slow down, partly because one always did at the end of such a huge effort, partly because he expected a delay while proper assault groups were organised. Sigurd had given orders to the column commanders before they had started.

'When you get there, wait. Look. Think. Use your sense. If the battle is not yet won, we must make the biggest possible impact. We shall not do that by charging in blindly in twos and threes.'

Before he arrived up on the ridge, Magnus could see that Sigurd had been wasting his breath. Exertion had half-blinded them with sweat. The elation at having completed such a prodigious run could not be controlled. The excitement of actually seeing the battlefield laid out before them overrode considerations of prudence, judgement and timing. Fresh strength came from nowhere.

There was the shield wall, now clearly shrinking before their eyes. English housecarls were riding round the outer circles of the conflict, spying out the weaker places in the wall, and ordering fresh assaults. Because these assaults did not come in unison, it meant that the line of shields, and their owners, did not get any general respite between separate attacks when the whole English line retired. There were parts of the English that were engaged all the time somewhere or other. The effect on Viking morale was crippling – a shrinking line, mounting casualties, constant onslaughts from the growingly confident English, who sensed victory more sharply with every swing of axe or sword. It was becoming too much.

Sigurd's men took in all this with a single glance. These were their countrymen being ground down; they had come all this way to help; if they did not help very soon, there would be no shield wall to stiffen. More than once they saw the Landwaster sway, as if the bearer had been struck and another had struggled to recover it. They could not stay still; they might be too late. The shame of that would be unbearable.

Yet more men began to throw off the mail coats that they had nobly worn for the whole run.

'To hell with discipline,' they shouted when Magnus protested to them. 'If we continue to wear these things, we shall have no strength to lift a sword. What is the use of discipline if our arms are weak?'

And off they went, in dozens and half-dozens, roaring battle cries. As Magnus stood and watched in bafflement and despair, more many-limbed creatures of humanity – staring, yelling, possessed – careered past him.

He turned to look for Sigurd, and was horrified to see him hastening up, obviously bent on doing the same as his men.

Magnus put out a hand to grab. 'Sig! Wait! What are you doing?'

'What we have come to do,' said Sigurd. But he did stop for a moment, if only to stab a finger in the direction of the battle.

'Have you not heard it? The King is down. The word is everywhere.'

It was true; Magnus had heard too. The arrow in the King's throat had sped across the whole field like a flat pebble cast across still water.

'Then we are going to lose,' said Magnus.

'Tostig is still there. Look.' Magnus had not heard it, but that too was in the air.

The Landwaster still swung defiantly.

But, as they looked, it suddenly sagged, sank and disappeared from view. The shouts of Viking defiance seemed to get fainter.

Sigurd fastened the thong of his sword hilt round his wrist. Magnus tried to shake his arm.

'Sig. Think! Look at you. Where is your mail?'

'I need strength for what I want.'

'What about the odds you always talk about?'

'That was when I was talking. I was being clever. Then. Now I am fighting. Fighting is not about being clever. To the midden with the odds.'

Magnus tried again. 'There is nothing for you over there – not now. Hardrada is gone. England is gone. The dream has gone.'

Sigurd turned to him, and, for the first time, gave him his full attention.

'But not the honour. Hardrada promised me his daughter. How do I face Maria and the Queen if I abandon the cause when there is the slightest chance of—'

'Of glory?' said Magnus. 'It is a false god.'

Sigurd's face was a picture. Covered with sweat, dust, and richly red, but curiously still and at peace.

'I do not have to live with the gods, Magnus. I have to live with myself. Hardrada has shown us the way to a life and a glory offered to very few men. If I do not follow him, life will not be worth living.'

'There is nothing for you there.'

'There is now.'

He turned away, lifted his sword, but turned back for one more remark.

'Somebody has to pick up the Landwaster again. For all our sakes and for the sake of Norway. It is my destiny; I made it for myself. It is not yours. I shall not think the worse of you for staying.'

He rushed towards the battle. Magnus recognised many of his lads round him – Ivar, Haldor, the sceptical Finn, who so often found an objection to his plans. Sleepy Lars, and Tore, who had forgotten his sore shoulders. Behind them limped Hakon, still cursing his buttock, which had begun to bleed again. Ketil Splitnose, who had lost his precious axe on the ladder at Scarborough, now grasped a sword, leaving his bad arm to swing loose at his side. Most of them were unprotected, too. Some did not even have helmets.

Magnus cursed himself for his common sense.

The shield wall shrank further. As Sigurd's company rushed across the intervening space, an English detachment moved up from the English right to intercept them. From their deliberate movements, it was a tactic clearly planned some time before. It took the attackers in their flank.

Some went down to the English fyrd; others fell before mounted housecarls. A few reached the shield wall and were welcomed inside. Magnus saw the Landwaster raised on high once again.

The English ring of iron closed even more tightly. The Landwaster toppled yet again and fell. This time it did not rise again.

That was the moment. The Viking army – what was left of it – broke and scattered.

Edric plodded back to the English camp between the bridge and York.

He had not done much, but he did not feel dissatisfied. He had stood in a line with English fyrdmen; he had joined in an attack; and he had struck a blow or two. True, the enemy had been far too disorganised to produce a coherent resistance. They were only half-armoured, some even had no helmets. They seemed exhausted. A few could barely swing their weapons.

It had not been much of a contest. The younger of them had derived some grim satisfaction, and had laid into the enemy with a will. One young fyrdman had nearly severed a Viking's arm with his sword – quite a good sword, too. Then he had fallen out of the attack, collapsed onto his knees and vomited. Luckily for him, the fight had soon left him behind.

Indeed, it had soon become more of a pursuit than a stand-up contest. The fatigue of face-to-face combat was bad enough. Edric knew that his stiff muscles would not sustain a pursuit, maybe miles of it. That battle had been won; the enemy, the remnants of them, were in full flight.

He had fought for his country and his king. Edric felt justified.

Shortly after that, he felt tired and he felt hungry. Hence his decision to turn round and seek the main camp. Surely there would be some food to be had. The King was a good organiser, and should have provided something.

Conrad reined in with a flurry. Harold looked up from where he was sitting on a stone.

'Well?'

'There are only a few prisoners, sir. There is hardly anyone alive left inside the shield wall. As you can see, the field is almost empty.'

It was true. There were plenty of bodies, but very few standing, hardly any engaged in combat. Away up the slope to the east one could still see the signs of the pursuit. Small groups of men were scattered in every direction, mostly chasing other groups that were fading from sight. The light was beginning to weaken. At long last the sun was showing some mercy.

Harold stretched and eased his shoulders. His groom waited expectantly with a fresh horse. Conrad fidgeted in the saddle.

'What are your orders, sir?'

Harold looked at him again. All this riding and message-bearing, and today on the very edge of battle. The boy was having the time of his life.

Harold did not often wish he was half his age, but this time he did. Conrad was positively glowing with the excitement of riding, of being trusted and important, of living at the heart of drama, of being young and so able to take advantage of his physical powers. Right now Harold felt old; his complaint was catching up with him again. He was blowing hot and cold, his stomach hurt, and he ached all over. There was no question of his being able to command the pursuit.

'Orders? Here they are. You are to ride like the wind to the Earls Gyrth and Leofwine. The enemy are running east at the moment, because we came from the west. All they can think of is getting away from the battlefield. But sooner or later they will turn south, towards their ships.'

'So we cut them off,' said Conrad eagerly. 'And polish them off.'

Harold smiled. 'Where are all your vows now, Conrad?'

Conrad blushed. Harold laughed outright.

'Never fear, son. We can still give full play to your Christian charity and allow full scope for a good, old-fashioned military chase. We do not want them dead and cluttering up the countryside. Look at that shield wall. Is that not enough killing for you?'

'So what do we do, sir?'

'We chase them onto their ships and see them off,' said Harold. 'My guess is that they will not be eager to come back.'

Conrad prepared to turn his horse. Harold put out a hand.

'Make it clear to the earls my brothers: we offer quarter. We let them go if they promise never to return. Is that clear? I want no more piles of dead littering the fields of Northumbria.'

'Sir.'

'And come back to me as soon as you can. I may have other work for you.'

When he had gone, Harold beckoned to a servant and ordered some water. Food just then did not seem a very good idea.

As he sipped and wiped his lips, he felt that he wanted only two things at that moment. York was one, because it meant normality and security. The other was a bed. But, before that, he would have to arrange for news to be carried. Bernard would have to be told, and he in turn would have to send the news wherever it was needed. Contact would have to be made with Edwin and Morcar. And the Lady Gytha would have to be told about Tostig. Come to think of it, so would Tostig's wife Judith. How on earth was that to be achieved? Where was she? With him in England? Waiting in Orkney? Or still in Flanders with the children?

Harold sighed . . .

They had found the body soon enough. It was near the Landwaster. Piecing together what they had been able to gather from stunned survivors, they reasoned that it was Tostig who had seized the fallen standard when Hardrada's man had dropped it. It was Tostig who had taken command, and who had inspired the last defence before he was cut down. Or, rather, not quite the last defence. When Tostig fell, men spoke of a young warrior who had appeared from nowhere and who raised it again. He and his men had fought, they said, like demons. Almost like berserks. Cared nothing for their own safety. Hardly any of them were wearing mail; some had no helmets. They had died like heroes, and very expensively.

Normally it would have been very difficult to identify one man in all that slaughter, but Harold had told them to look for a man with a large wart between his shoulder blades. They found him sure enough. Harold knew that his mother would never be satisfied that her precious Tostig was dead till he was identified beyond any argument, and by a family member.

It was a terrible moment. Harold had tears pouring down his cheeks . . .

Now he picked up his riding gloves. God alone knew what would happen when his mother was finally told. And God protect the man who would have to bear the news.

He beckoned to his groom. 'Now, son. Get me on this horse.'

In the growing darkness, all the longships looked the same.

Groups of desperate fugitives simply made for the first refuge hull, clambered aboard and threw together what defence they could find. Those still with weapons turned on the beach and formed a human wall in front. There were very few shields that had survived the retreat.

Luckily for them, the pursuers were just as disorganised. Their only advantage, naturally, was the elation of victory. They too arrived in irregular and undisciplined bunches, with no plan and no policy beyond killing every Viking who came into sight. But some of them got careless; they forgot the old adage that a wounded boar or a boar at bay is a dangerous boar. A blow from a twilight axe gave them little time to reflect on their mistake.

Magnus fought on the shingle till his sword was knocked out of his hand. He leaped on board the ship behind him, just in time to avoid a huge swing from a housecarl's axe. It buried itself in the gunwale. Magnus and the housecarl found themselves tugging at the same handle, in opposite directions.

Magnus felt he was losing, when suddenly a huge pole swung past his ear and the housecarl dropped out of sight. Magnus turned to thank his rescuer.

'Lars!'

'Seems I arrived just in time.'

'Thor and thunder, man – where did you come from?'

'The battlefield, just like you.'

'We never saw you.'

'Of course not,' said Lars. 'I took care of that.'

'So you were not with the boys?'

'No.'

'Why not?'

'I left the ships late, after they had gone. I arrived late, too.'

Magnus stared. 'You surely were not asleep.'

'Only a nap. But I did not hear the messengers, you see. I was under some rocks away from the boats.'

Lars paused to shove his pole in another Saxon's face.

'Anyway, a good thing I was late, or I would be dead, and maybe so would you.'

They could not talk for some minutes after that. Then the attacks fell away. Everything became mysteriously quiet.

Somebody somewhere lit a fire. Somebody somewhere fired arrows on board the ships. Somehow, somewhere, a few long-ships began to spout flashes of flame.

Magnus, who had flopped onto the deck beside some piles of canvas and ropes, became aware of a terrible smell. Suddenly everything came back – the sting, the choking, the panic, the roaring, Sigrid's screaming.

He lost all reason. Scrambling to his feet, he rushed to the side of the ship, vaulted over onto the shingle and began running without aim or purpose. Simply to get away.

Lars called after him, but he barely noticed it. A Saxon fyrd-man, surprised by the sudden rush of a single enemy, was bowled over, and managed only one swing of his sword as Magnus passed. He fancied that he caught him on the back of a leg.

Edric gaped. 'What are you doing here?'

Vendel tied off the reins to a nearby post. 'Being late, it seems.'

Somehow, Edric could not imagine Vendel hurrying to the place of action in order to display his fighting prowess. But, once again, this young man surprised him.

Vendel pointed to the sword and scabbard that he had fastened to the horse. 'I do not think I would have achieved much, but at least I made the effort.' He shrugged sadly. 'Once again, it seems that intentions were not enough. My punctuality also has been sadly lacking.'

A scholarly turn of phrase, thought Edric. Probably the fruit of his time with the brothers.

Nevertheless, Edric found himself warming to him. He was clearly aware of his physical limitations, but the spirit was there.

'What made you late?' said Edric.

Vendel looked a little reluctant. 'I made a detour to the house again, to see if Coelwen and Thora were still safe.'

Edric extended a hand to a place beside the fire. 'Then I am in your debt yet again.'

Vendel saw to the horse before he came to settle down.

'The least I could do.'

'But they are safe,' said Edric.

'Oh, yes. And I have the Prior's assurance that he and the brothers will continue to care for them.'

He allowed himself a small chuckle. 'You will be pleased to know that your daughter has been busy.'

'What?'

'Baking,' said Vendel. 'Baking, if you please.'

It was Edric's turn to smile. 'My daughter can not stand idleness.'

'From what I could see,' said Vendel, 'she is organising half the kitchen.'

The more this conversation went on, the more Edric found himself regarding Vendel as an equal. His next remark showed that he coupled the two of them together in his mind.

'Well, we have each done his best to strike a blow – however feeble.'

Vendel sensed the new comradeship. All his life he had seen how people treated his father, and therefore, by implication, himself, as outsiders. It was difficult to put it into words, but he suddenly felt much more English.

Was it his decisiveness in making his father return to Scarborough? He remembered being surprised at himself while it was actually happening. Was it the death of his father? Was it the attack on Scarborough? Was it his efforts to save Coelwen? Once again, he had found himself doing things that he would never have conceived possible a short time before. True, the help of that huge Viking had been decisive, but he knew his own contribution had been important, too.

Edric broke into his thoughts. 'What shall we do, then?'

Vendel again noticed the 'we'. They had both shared the pride of being men of England, however briefly and however ineffectually. Now they were merely two men of Scarborough, marooned in the debris of war, in a sea of strangers. Without further words between them, they both felt that their place was now in their home.

Scarborough was a ruin, but it was at least not a charnel house. It would be rebuilt. And they were the two men best placed to rebuild it.

'In the morning, then,' said Vendel. 'Do you have a horse?'

'No,' said Edric.

'Leave that to me,' said Vendel. He patted a pocket. 'There should be plenty all over the field, and, if there are not, I know where they can be bought.'

As they settled for the night, Edric said, 'Have you given thought to the means of building the town again?'

'No,' said Vendel.

'The pursuit followed them all the way back to the ships.'

'I would have guessed that.'

'Now,' said Edric, 'think of the slaughter today. How many ships will they need to go back to Norway?'

'None, if Harold has killed them all.'

Edric shook his head. 'The word is that the King will offer quarter. Even so, think of all the ships that will *not* be needed for the return.'

'So?'

'Think of all that timber. Seasoned timber. Waiting to be used.'

'What if it is? I am not a shipwright.'

'No. But you are a timber merchant, like your father. Think of all the supplies he gave me for the defence of the town.'

Vendel sat up. 'You mean we . . .?'

Edric shrugged. 'Why not? They are all lying there, going begging. If we do not do it, someone else will. I get a new town; you get a new business. What do you think?'

'Have you eaten?' said Harold.

'Barely a bite, sir,' said Conrad.

Harold waved him to a table. 'Sit. And eat. But talk. I want to know everything.'

Conrad looked hesitant. 'Will you be sitting, sir?'

'I doubt it,' said Harold. 'I have no idea what I shall do. That partly depends on what you tell me. But I am telling you, sit down, eat and drink. And have no qualms about sitting in my presence, and you do not have your mother here to warn you about talking with your mouth full.'

'Sir.'

'Now,' said Harold, 'what happened?'

'It was a triumph, sir,' said Conrad, flushing at the very thought. 'They tried to make some kind of a stand at the ships, but everything was disorganised. Our men were not much better. Some of the ships were set on fire.' He reached out for some more bread, and broke it on the edge of the table. 'But we outnumbered them, oooh, three to one, I should say, if not more. At last Earl Gyrth made himself heard and gradually the fighting stopped. He and the Earl Leofwine offered the terms you said.'

'Did they accept?'

'At once, sir. I think it was too much for the young jarls.'

'Which ones?'

'Paul of Orkney, Thorfinn's son, and Olaf, Hardrada's boy. I think they were overwhelmed by what had happened. It would have taken another Hardrada to make anything else out of a situation like that.'

'So they went?'

'Like lambs, sir.' Conrad gulped some beer. 'All of them.' Then he remembered something. 'And what about this, sir? In the King's ship they found a huge ingot of gold. Solid gold. It took twelve men to unload and carry it ashore.'

Harold whistled. 'Hardrada's gold. At last. So it was true.' He chuckled. 'All those paving stones from Miklegaard. I would wager that he left twice as much behind in Norway. No matter. Any gold is welcome.' He chuckled again. 'It will pay for the campaign. Neat.'

'And nobody can steal it, either, sir. Much too heavy.'

Harold grinned smugly.

Conrad was not finished. He paused and looked over the rim of his cup. 'And do you know how many ships it took?'

Harold could see that Conrad was enjoying this almost as much as the engagement itself.

'To take them back? Go on.'

'Twenty-four, sir. *Twenty-four*. And to bring them it had taken three hundred.'

Conrad sat back for a moment, beaming with so much satisfaction that it seemed as if he had arranged the whole thing himself.

Harold poured himself a drink, and topped up Conrad's cup. 'Then let us drink a toast to victory, eh?'

'Sir.' Conrad took another eager swig.

Still fidgeting with the excitement of it all, Conrad could hardly sit still. 'What now, sir?'

'I have more orders for you.'

Conrad wilted just a little. He had been in the saddle for hours, and, for all Harold knew, had himself been engaged in physical combat at the ships. The change in him from habit to hauberk was almost complete. Indeed, he was now wearing a hauberk, though Harold did not dare ask how he had come by it.

But the boy was exhausted, there was no doubt about that.

'Now listen,' said Harold. 'As soon as I have given you these orders, you will go to rest, for as many hours as you want. If you think you have done some riding today, just wait till you hear what I want you to do the day after tomorrow.'

Conrad was not sure whether to look excited or dismayed. He sat silent, not knowing what to expect.

'First,' said Harold, 'you go to see Father Bernard. You know where his offices are near the minster. He is drafting despatches to the senior members of the York Witan. That is the first of your errands. Secondly, he must contact the Earls Edwin and Morcar, if he has not already done so, and they are to bring all their remaining troops into York, here. Father Bernard is also making arrangements for the burial of Earl Tostig.' (Harold carefully awarded his dead brother his former title.) 'Father Bernard will also arrange to send the news to Earl Tostig's wife, the Lady Judith. She may be in England; she may be in Flanders. That is for him to seek out. Tell him he has the authority to draft as many messages as it needs, employ as many messengers as it needs and use as many of my seals as is necessary, too.'

'Sir.' Conrad was listening with lowered brow.

'Then,' said Harold, 'you will tell Father Bernard to draft a message with the news to the Lady Gytha and the Queen Edith, my sister.' Harold paused and looked Conrad in the eye. 'You will also take news to my lady Edith. Do you understand?'

Conrad blushed slightly, but kept his face straight. 'Sir.'

'You will have as escort my housecarl Wilfrid.'

Conrad had a memory of a red-faced, slightly overweight, puffing warrior at his side over many miles.

'Not Oswy as well, sir?'

'No,' said Harold. 'Oswy gave his life at the bridge.'

'I am sorry, sir.' Conrad meant it. Over all those many miles, the three of them had built a bond.

'Have you got all that?'

'Sir.'

Harold looked doubtfully at him. 'Just to make sure, I shall send Brother Eustace with you.'

Conrad looked astonished. 'Brother Eustace, sir?'

'Yes, I know,' said Harold. 'It will be something of a shock for him, but two memories are better than one. And most of your energy will be taken up with smoothing the journey. Wilfrid will provide the protection. Eustace will provide the diplomacy. Have no fear; you will make a splendid team. You will learn a lot about diplomacy, and Eustace will learn a lot about riding.'

It was Conrad's turn to look doubtful. 'Have you told him, sir?'

Harold smiled. 'No. That is your next job, before you collapse completely. Send him to me. You will probably find him in the kitchens.'

Conrad wilted. Harold clapped his hands.

'Now be off with you. Eat some more and sleep a lot. You have a whole day, till the morning after tomorrow.' Conrad bowed, and turned to go.

'Oh, and send Wilfrid to me,' said Harold. 'He will not be far. He knows I want him for special work.'

Sooner than he had expected, Wilfrid came in.

'Sir?'

'Have a talk with young Conrad before he falls into bed. I want you for special escort duty.'

Wilfrid looked dismayed. 'What, now, sir?'

Harold looked sardonic. 'I knew you were going to say that.'

'Well, we are so near, sir.'

Harold nodded. 'I understand. And I remember the properties. Near Grimsby. Great Coates and Little Coates, is it not?'

Wilfrid smiled in spite of himself. This king knew everything. Then he looked serious.

'I have some news to bring to Oswy's household, sir.'

'Yes, I know. And I am sorry. So you will do that tomorrow. But I want you back here by nightfall. I have a kingdom to run, and you are part of it. Leave as soon as you like.'

As Wilfrid hurried to the door, Harold called after him. 'And no over-staying your leave this time. I want your word you will be back.'

'You have it, sir.'

'Good,' said Harold. 'If you are not, believe me, I shall revoke your housecarl's commission.'

When Wilfrid had gone, Harold sat sipping his beer for a while. Then he rose, and, still holding his cup, walked to the main door. He acknowledged the salute of the duty housecarl, and went out into the courtyard.

He looked up at the sky. It was still unseasonably warm. He could feel the accumulated heat of the day.

For a moment he was completely alone. He smiled thoughtfully. That was how it had been right through the campaign. No commander has company, not when he is commanding. He stands or falls by his own decisions, for right or wrong. Solitary decisions. The whole country stands or falls by his solitary decisions.

Well – it was beginning to look as if his decisions had been the right ones. He took another draught from his cup. It was over. And already everything had slowed down. Some fire had gone. Odd.

He looked up again. There was a suspicion that the wind was changing. Was it swinging round to the south? Possibly. Tomorrow would tell.

He tossed away the dregs of his beer. Well, at least a southerly wind would help to shoo the remnants of his enemies all the way back to Norway.

Magnus had given himself up for dead when Lars appeared.

'Seems I arrived just in time once again.'

Magnus could barely move. The fyrdman's sword had cut the hamstring. He had lost a lot of blood. He was chilled to the bone after a night in the open with no cover.

'How on earth did you find me?'

'Easy. We followed the trail.'

'What trail?'

'Blood.'

'You said "we",' said Magnus.

'They are coming,' said Lars.

Right on cue, Ivar and Ketil appeared from some undergrowth. Ivar, festooned in crude bandages, could barely see. Ketil had the sling round his bad arm once again.

Magnus stared. 'How did you escape?'

'We were lucky; we went down first. Everybody trod all over us,' said Ivar. He pointed to his bandaged head.

'We lay low till it was all over, and waited till it was dark. Then we crept away. But we missed the boats. Much too slow.'

'What happened to the others?' asked Magnus, though he knew in advance what they were going to say.

'All gone. Sig was the last. And Finn. They held up the Landwaster almost to the end. But it was no use.'

Magnus lay silent while Lars tried to bind his leg with a torn-off shirt.

'We can not stay here,' he said at last.

'Where, then?'

'South is out of the question. They are scouring the whole country right down to the estuary.'

'West is no good; that leads back to York.'

'Then it is north or east,' said Magnus.

'The direction may be right,' said Ivar, 'but we need food and rest and shelter, or we shall all go.'

'We need a crutch for you first,' said Ketil.

All they had was Ketil's sword and Ivar's knife. Ketil had one good arm, Ivar could barely see, and Magnus could not stand. Only Lars was in one piece.

But they did it. They had company, and their own people. They had purpose. Spirits began to rise.

'What a silly bastard you were to throw away that axe of yours,' said Ivar.

'I should have cut your balls off with it when I had the chance,' said Ketil.

Somehow they levered Magnus to his feet, fashioned some kind of padding at the top of the crutch, and shoved it under his arm. Ketil tightened his sling yet again, and Ivar peered through the drapery of his bandages.

'Follow me, then, lads,' said Lars. 'At the double. Hup! Hup! Something will turn up.'

Something did. From behind them. And it caught them out on an open track. Running was out of the question. All they had between them was Ivar's knife and Ket's sword.

'Well, this is it, then, boys,' said Lars. 'What a shame, after all that.'

'Fancy going to sleep now, Lars?' said Ivar, as the couple approached.

Magnus squinted. 'They are not soldiers. Look. No mail.'

'One of them is grey,' said Ivar. 'Probably one of their fyrd, I think they call it.'

'The other one looks a weed,' said Ketil. 'Maybe we do have a chance after all.'

Magnus laughed mirthlessly. 'It will be some contest.'

They straddled the path as the two Englishmen came closer. Suddenly Magnus stiffened.

He remembered the lank hair and the skimpy beard. Vendel recognised him at the same instant. He and Edric came to a halt in front of the bloodstained quartet. After what they had been through during the day, not one of them moved a hand towards a weapon.

Vendel spoke first. 'Scarborough.'

'Yes,' said Magnus . . .

The Prior had prepared himself for possible wounded men, but it had not crossed his mind that they might be enemy wounded. He did not like it, but he followed his vows.

Vendel did the explaining – the battle, the end, the pursuit, the meeting on the road to Scarborough. Putting Magnus and Ketil on their horses. He pointed at Magnus.

'He saved Coelwen when Scarborough burned,' he said.

'We both owe him,' said Edric. 'We shall pay for their care.'

The Infirmarian had Ketil and Magnus carried away, and the Guest-Master led Ivar and Lars to the kitchen. Vendel turned to Edric.

'I wonder if she will recognise him.'

Edric, who knew the story, said, 'I wonder what she will say.'

Vendel wondered what Thora would say.

'Well, when do we go home?' said Alfred.

There was a silence, as glances flew from one fyrdman to another. Alfred tried to chase them with his eyes. It took several flights before he caught one.

'Why not? What do we have to do now?'

More glances, and grins this time, too. 'More marching, Alfred, I should not wonder.'

Alfred flung his sword on the ground. 'I do not believe it.'

'We have only won a battle,' said one of his friends. 'We have not won the war.'

Alfred stared. 'But surely the Bastard will not come now? After what we have done with Hardrada?'

'Oh, it was us, was it, Alfred? I thought the King and his housecarls had something to do with it.' Chuckles now followed the glances.

Alfred blustered. 'But it is October now. Men do not go campaigning in the winter. Not our winter, anyway.'

'We can only hope you are right, Alfred.'

Alfred hesitated. 'He would not come *now* – would he?'

'You never know with war.'

Alfred blustered again, in a different way. 'Well, if he does, we can see *him* off as well.'

'Just one small problem, Alfred.'

Alfred fell for it as usual. 'What is that?'

'We have to get to him. The small matter of two hundred miles.'

Alfred gaped. 'What?'

'Maybe more. How are your feet these days, Alfred?'

'Built any good beacons recently, Alfred?'

'Dug any good privy pits this week, Alfred?'

'Never mind, Alfred. Perhaps the Bastard has heard how we beat Hardrada, and he will not dare.'

'That sword of yours, Alfred. Deadly.'

Harold sat down, as the hall rang with cheers and violent applause. He smiled at Gyrth and Leofwine on either side of him.

Gwen shook his arm. 'Well spoken, husband. You hit all the right nails smack on the head.' She smiled mischievously. 'I notice you did not mention the gold, though.'

'Well, would you?' said Harold. 'Have no fear, my Queen. It is safe with Aldred in the minster. It would take a brave man, willing to risk the pain of hellfire, to rob the Archbishop of York in his own cathedral.'

Gwen nodded. 'And a strong one, I hear. Did it not take fifty men to lift it?'

'The number grows with each telling. And they can tell it as often as they like.'

'Well done, Harold. It was all well done.'

Harold smiled at her. 'Thank you. You know I value your approval.' He wondered whether his Edith would say the same.

'One thing I particularly appreciated,' said Gwen. 'That was your tribute to Morcar, and Edwin. But it is Morcar who feels it more keenly. After all, he was in command.'

'Morcar did his best,' said Harold. 'And it was I who put him there in the first place. The responsibility is as much mine as his.'

Gwen squeezed his arm again. 'If it ends well, it is all well.'

'I only hope it does,' said Harold feelingly.

He wondered what his mother would say. No matter what he might have told Bernard to write in his despatch, it would not be right. Whatever the outcome of the battle might have been, the Lady Gytha would have been mourning the death of a son, maybe two or three.

He tossed his head. And sister Edith would be praying and weeping . . .

Leofwine leaned across the table, his eyes aglow. 'We have shattered the world. We have produced the greatest military surprise of the century.'

Harold acknowledged the compliment. 'Well, at least Malcolm will not try anything, I grant you that. The cat has at last jumped much too far for him to do anything about it.'

'You wait and see,' said Gyrth. 'The Bastard will think twice too – *now*. After that long summer in camp, doing nothing but wait, his army must be on the verge of mutiny. After what we have just done, they will be shaking in their shoes. With the weather he has been having, he dare not try. It is too late, much too late.'

'The wind is turning,' said Harold.

'Pah!' said Leofwine. 'Gyrth is right. William has missed his chance. War is about timing. He has missed it. Believe me, brother, you have heard the last of the Bastard and his precious little Matilda.'

'Well, when do you think you can walk?' said Lars.

'No idea,' said Magnus. 'That medicine monk – whatever they call him – does nothing but shake his head and pull his chin.'

Lars glanced at Ivar and Ketil. They nodded to each other. Ivar could at last see them clearly. Ketil felt much more comfortable now that the Infirmarian had set his arm.

'No matter,' said Lars. 'We shall wait. If they will have us.'

'Oh, they will do that. Edric has paid them well in advance.'

'Ah.'

'What do you mean "We shall wait"?' said Magnus. 'What for?'

Lars looked blank. 'Why, for you to be ready to go home.'

Magnus avoided looking them in the eye.

'I am not sure about that.'

All three laughed.

'That baker girl,' said Ketil. 'He is mad about the baker girl.'

Magnus shook his head. 'I have a debt.'

'She has a debt. You saved her life,' said Ketil.

'And she saved yours,' said Lars. 'She and that hooded bandager. You are equal.'

Magnus shook his head again. 'It is not as simple as that.'

Ivar laughed. 'I bet.'

'Anyway, how are you going to get back to Norway? Three of the enemy at large in a foreign country.'

'Foreign country? They are all half Scandinavian round here. We shall manage. Perhaps that Vendel man will get us onto a boat, when things have settled down.'

Magnus lifted his shoulders and let them fall again.

'So it will be just me?'

Ketil grinned. 'Looks like it.'

Lars laughed. 'After all that – three hundred ships and two mighty battles. How will it feel, Magnus, to be the very last Viking left in England?'

Acknowledgements

As I am given to understand, there is a saying in the trade to the effect that anybody can write a first novel; it's writing a second one that is the real test.

Well, here we are – novel Number Two. It is for you, the reader, to decide how closely I have come up to scratch – or how far I have fallen below it.

But, above or below, I still have not done it all by myself.

For a start, there are all those hundreds, probably thousands, of pupils I mentioned in the Dedication. If you liken the (unwitting) contribution of each of them to a grain of sand, the pile they have put together, over the years, amounts to a pretty fair dollop of what you could call, in a word, 'experience'. I like to think I have learnt a thing or two about putting it across, and they taught me that. Not always without pain and grief, because pupils make few allowances. Nevertheless, they may teach you hard, but they teach you good.

As before, my agent, Jim Gill, of United Agents, has maintained his support and encouragement. It was his canny management that secured me a most welcome two-novel contract in the first place. I thank him also for thinking I was worth two novels. I hope I have lived up to his expectations.

My editor, Clare Hey, has given her laser attention to the text of this second book, as she did to that of the first one. I am pleased to say, though, that she needed to offer only about

417

one-third of the 'suggestions' that she found it necessary to make for *The Last Conquest*. She even accepted some of *my* 'suggestions' for the cover text. So – my goodness me – I must be learning. Still, very generous of her. She has been both open-minded and fair-minded, tolerant too of what some others might have dismissed as mere pedantry.

Finally, and as always, Yvonne Reed – friend, colleague, listener, fearless commentator, eagle-eyed scrutineer, and steadfast interested party – has read every syllable and offered her corrections, comments, and verdicts.

I am well served by all three.

Berwick Coates